About th

Synithia Williams has loved romance novels since reading her first one at the age of thirteen. It was only natural that she would one day write her own romance. When she isn't writing, Synithia works on water quality issues in the Midlands of South Carolina while taking care of her supportive husband and two sons. You can learn more about Synithia by visiting her website, synithiawilliams.com

Stacy Connelly dreamed of publishing books since she was a kid writing about a girl and her horse. Eventually, boys made it onto the page as she discovered a love of romance and the promise of happily-ever-after. In 2008, that dream came true when she sold *All She Wants for Christmas* to Mills & Boon. When she is not lost in the land of make-believe, Stacy lives in Arizona with her two spoiled dogs.

Award-winning author **Zuri Day** snuck her first Mills & Boon romance from her older sister's collection and was hooked from page one. Knights in shining armour and happily-ever-afters spurred a lifelong love of reading. Zuri now creates these stories as a full-time author. Splitting her time between the stunning Caribbean islands and southern California, and always busy writing her next novel, Zuri still loves to connect with readers via zuriday.com

Once Upon a Time

Once Upon a Time:
A Perfect Fit

SYNITHIA WILLIAMS

STACY CONNELLY

ZURI DAY

MILLS & BOON

First Published in Great Britain 2023
by Mills & Boon, an imprint of HarperCollins*Publishers* Ltd,
1 London Bridge Street, London, SE1 9GF

www.harpercollins.co.uk

HarperCollins*Publishers*
Macken House, 39/40 Mayor Street Upper,
Dublin 1, D01 C9W8, Ireland

Once Upon a Time: A Perfect Fit © 2023 Harlequin Enterprises ULC.

A New York Kind of Love © 2016 Synithia Williams
Small-Town Cinderella © 2014 Stacy Cornell
Silken Embrace © 2015 Zuri Day

ISBN: 978-0-263-31978-1

A NEW YORK KIND
OF LOVE

SYNITHIA WILLIAMS

For my aunt, Annie Mae 'Duke.'
I miss you.

Chapter 1

"Congratulations, Faith Logan. You're the lucky winner of a weekend in New York with Irvin Freeman!"

Faith jerked her cell phone away from her face, frowning at the unfamiliar number on the screen. This had to be a joke. Her eyes darted to the two other nurses sitting around the nurses' station. Neither appeared to be concealing a smile. There were no covert glances her way to see if they'd duped her with some elaborate prank. She looked up and down the hall, but as usual for a Wednesday in Laurel County, South Carolina, the labor-and-delivery ward of the hospital wasn't very busy. Only one mother who'd had a baby earlier that day was walking down the hall. Dorothy, the older nurse, even stood and left the station to check on the mother, instead of sticking around to hear if Faith fell for the joke.

She put the phone back to her ear. "Excuse me?"

"You heard correctly," said the overly bright voice

on the other end. "You won the grand prize in the contest held by Starting Over, Irvin Freeman's foundation to raise alcohol awareness. Out of the thousands of entries accompanying donations to the foundation, your name was drawn. You are the lucky woman chosen to spend a fabulous, all-expenses-paid weekend in New York City with Irvin Freeman. Your prize includes a makeover, and you will be Irvin's date for the premiere of his new movie, *Running from Murder*!"

The woman's voice rose with each word until she sounded like a speaker on the stage at a "gee, life is great" high school prom.

"Is this a joke? I'm at work, and I really don't have time for jokes."

There was a pause before the voice continued in its prom-queen tone. "This is no joke, Ms. Logan. Don't you remember entering online?"

Faith frowned and tried to remember entering a contest. All her money went to her parents' medical bills and household expenses. She didn't have extra money to donate to the foundation or extra time to enter a contest.

Except for that one time...

She spun around to glare at the nurse closest to her. Marie, her best friend since she'd moved home two years ago and the person who'd helped her land the job at Laurel County Hospital, flipped through a magazine. Faith nudged Marie with her foot. When Marie looked up, she nailed her with a "this is your fault" look. She'd known it was a bad idea when Marie urged her to enter. At the time it had seemed like a good idea to contribute a few dollars to a worthy cause. Never in a gazillion years had she expected her name to be chosen.

Marie held out her hands. "What's wrong?"

Instead of answering Marie, Faith responded to the

woman on the phone. "Yeah, I remember entering that contest. I just didn't expect to win. What weekend is that? I don't even know if I can go to New York."

Marie's dark eyes widened, and she jumped from the chair to bounce on the balls of her feet next to Faith. Even without her Tweety Bird scrubs, Marie would look like a woman far younger than her thirty-three years. Her pixie cut and always-smiling features in a dark brown heart-shaped face made her instantly likable.

"Can't go?" The voice lost some of its peppiness. "Ms. Logan, this is the opportunity of a lifetime. You will be the envy of all women. A five-star hotel near Times Square..."

Faith tuned out as the caller went through all of the reasons—some of them valid—why she should go. Excitement tickled her insides, and she felt the urge to bounce around like Marie. But the cold, hard reality of her life tamped it down. Reality had smacked her in the face when she'd given up her fantastic job, lost what she'd thought was the guy she'd one day marry and moved from Houston back home to take care of her parents.

She wasn't bitter—that particular emotion was a drain on energy she couldn't afford to waste. She'd give it all up again if she had to. But going out of town right now was out of the question. Her mind raced with all the reasons this wouldn't work: Who would watch her parents while she was gone? What if it was a weekend she was scheduled to work? All of her leave was used up from taking her mama to doctors' appointments. What would she wear? Her "new" clothes were two years old and were the complete opposite of stylish or trendy. Unless scrub chic suddenly became the fashion rage.

Then there was the biggest reason not to go. Irvin Freeman: dark eyes, mahogany skin and a swagger that would put Shaft to shame, topped off with a British accent. The man oozed sex with every breath he took, and he probably expected the winner of this thing to fall into a gooey puddle of estrogen at his feet.

"I appreciate the offer." Faith cut in on the prom queen's stream of reasons why she should be falling over herself to get to New York. "But I'm not sure—"

Marie snatched the phone out of Faith's hand. "Hello, this is Marie, Faith's, um, personal assistant. We'll do some maneuvering with her schedule and make sure she's there."

Faith tried to grab the phone back, but Marie skipped away to the other side of the nurses' station. "What weekend is it, again?" Marie nodded at whatever the caller said and flipped to the calendar with the work schedule. "Perfect! She's available for that weekend. You have her email address from the entry form, correct? Just send the details and copy me, and I'll get her to the airport on time."

Marie rattled off her email address and said a few more words. When she hung up the phone, she squealed as if she'd won the prize herself. The screech got the attention of the other nurse and the mother walking down the hall.

"You are the luckiest woman alive!" Marie rushed over and gave Faith a hug, surrounding her with exuberance and the smell of her strawberry body spray.

"That depends on your definition of *lucky*. Marie, I can't go."

Marie leaned back and gave her a hand wave that said "Whatever." "Oh, yes, you can. And you will. Even if I have to knock you out and drive you to New York myself. Girl, you just won a date with Irvin Freeman. How are you not excited about this?"

Dorothy and the mother walking in the hall quickly

caught on and chanted their agreement. Faith visualized a weekend listening to Irvin brag about how great it was to be him. Sure, he always appeared down-to-earth and approachable in television interviews, but a man who had half the women in the world drooling over him couldn't be that centered. All his apparent humbleness probably hid a mountain of arrogance.

"My parents," Faith said, not wanting to get into what would surely be a debate with Marie if she dissed her friend's favorite actor. "Who's going to help them?"

"They'll be okay for one weekend. I'll look in on them personally every day you're gone."

"Do I work that weekend?" Faith crossed the station and picked up the schedule book.

"No, you're off."

Faith dropped the book and crossed her arms. "If I'm off, you're working. You won't be able to check on them."

Dorothy came over to stand before Faith, looking just like the surrogate grandmother she was to every baby born on the floor. "Your mom is doing so much better than she was when you first came home. If you prepare meals before you leave, she can heat them up for herself and your dad. Don't forget, you're not in a large city anymore. Your friends and neighbors are happy to help out."

Dorothy was right, but Faith had done everything for her parents on her own. It was her way of making up for not being there when the bottom fell out of their lives. She wasn't used to accepting help from neighbors. Besides, doing so would only increase her regret. The thought tightened the knot of guilt that had made its home in her gut since she got the call that her mama was unconscious in the hospital after suffering a stroke.

"I don't want to be a burden," she said.

"Burden, shmurden," Marie said. "You won't be. You

going on this trip will be the highlight of the year for half of Laurel County. The newspaper will probably do a write-up about you before and after. Do you know how many people will be happy to say they helped out while you went away for an all-expenses-paid weekend with a Hollywood movie star?"

Faith did chuckle at that, because it was true. Nothing this exciting had happened since Tamara Blake from Laurel High School won Ms. Laurel County and was first runner-up in the Ms. Patriot pageant back in 2001. People still bragged about their part in her win, from selling her a pair of earrings to bringing over fried chicken the night the family had a watch party.

"I get that," Faith said, "but I just don't feel right asking other people to look after my parents. And this thing is just a few weekends away. I don't have anything to wear to something like that."

"You get a thousand dollars of spending money. Buy what you need while you're there."

"A thousand dollars in New York is probably like five dollars here. It won't go far," Faith said.

"If it'll buy you a sexy dress that'll make it impossible for Irvin Freeman to keep his eyes off you, that's far enough."

Faith couldn't help but visualize the eyes referred to on a recent list as "most likely to send a woman into cardiac arrest." The guy did have a way of looking at his leading ladies with such heat you could practically hear the sizzle on-screen. To think he would turn them on her was laughable. Yet her heart did do a disloyal skip against her ribs.

"The man dates models and Oscar winners," Faith said. "Even if I were naked, he wouldn't be interested."

"Every man is interested in a naked woman," Dorothy said, laughing. Marie nodded. The idea of being naked in front of Irvin only increased Faith's body heat.

Nope. Stop. Don't go there.

Even if she were to travel to New York—which she really doubted she could—she wouldn't be sleeping with Irvin Freeman. She loved the guy's movies and thought he was a great actor, but in his charming TV interviews, there were always questions about his love life. He was constantly linked with his frequent costar Selena Jones and photographed with a string of other actresses and models between his on-screen hookups with Selena. Faith would be setting herself up to look like America's biggest fool if she went to the city with even the slightest intention of landing in bed with him. He'd laugh at her attempts, or worse, take her up on it, and she'd be the latest groupie with her name attached to his. Something she'd never live down here in Laurel County. She couldn't afford that, not with all the work she'd done to keep the Logan name free of scandal over the past two years.

A more chilling thought crept across her mind. Going on this weekend trip would put her in the spotlight even if she wasn't attached to Irvin for more than a few days. People might want to know more about her. Which could lead to questions about her family—and her twin. She wanted to go on pretending her twin had magically disappeared into thin air.

"I won't be naked with Irvin Freeman. I won't be anything, because I'm not going. They can pick another name. I have too much to do here."

"Stop it," Marie said. "You don't have too much to do, and you aren't a horrible daughter if you take one weekend to enjoy yourself. It's been two years. Go and have a great time. Your parents would agree with me."

"I know they will, because I'm going to call them now and tell them the good news," Dorothy said, picking up the phone.

"Dorothy, no. Don't bother them," Faith said. Her mama had been urging her to do something fun for the past month. If she got wind of this, she'd knock Faith out and lend Marie her wheelchair to roll Faith to the airport.

"Too late. It's ringing. Get ready to pack your bags, girlie, because you're going," Dorothy said. "Hey, Virginia, guess what? Your daughter just won the trip of a lifetime."

Marie did a little dance. Dorothy grinned and gave her a thumbs-up. Faith's palms sweated. This was not a good thing. Fate had a way of hitting her in the gut when she least expected it. And once again, it was ready to give her a sucker punch.

Chapter 2

"Well, she could have sounded a bit more enthusiastic."

Irvin looked up from the script he was reading. Kitty Brown, the head of his publicity team, stood staring at her cell phone. He'd barely heard her over the various conversations of the members of his *entourage*. A word that made him cringe inwardly—and at times outwardly—whenever he said it. The entourage was Kitty's idea; he would be perfectly fine without the lot of them. It was days like this he missed the anonymity that came with being a poor kid from the dodgy end of London. Now, thanks to Kitty, all his appearances were preplanned and scheduled for potential photo ops.

"What's wrong, Kitty? She didn't scream until her voice gave out before breaking down in tears?" He was only partly teasing. He still couldn't get over the dramatics some women went through when they met him.

"What screaming? The woman didn't scream, sigh, cry or show the least bit of gratitude that her name was selected."

Kitty crossed his crowded living room, the night sky and twinkling lights of the New York skyline visible behind her through the wall of windows in his flat. Her jet-black hair had one bright red streak in the front, which stood out against her sienna skin and the all-black suit she wore.

"Hopefully, she'll be more excited once it sinks in what she's won. I can't have the winner of your first charity contest frowning in every picture."

"How do you know she'll be frowning?" Irvin asked, glancing at his watch. It had been ten hours since the entourage had arrived to prepare for his appearance on *The Tonight Show* that afternoon and decided to stick around afterward. He was ready for all of them to leave and give him a moment of peace.

"I can hear frowns," Kitty said, waving her hand. "This woman was frowning."

"I don't care if she smiles or not," Irvin said. "I did this to raise money for the foundation. The money we raised will do a hell of a lot more than having the winner smile in your photographs."

"True, but I expected more. I didn't make you the country's most desired man only to get some lackluster response."

"I'd prefer a lackluster response every now and then."

"Don't tease," Kitty said. "You'd be bored without all this." She held out her arms to encompass the ten other people milling around the flat, each one either talking on the phone or making connections via social media. All in an effort to keep his name in front of people and build his image.

Some days—days like today, actually—he wanted to tell the lot of them to sod off. But he couldn't deny that being Hollywood's biggest celebrity had its perks, the best one being the money. Money brought safety and security. Two things he'd gone without for most of his childhood. And the money kept rolling in with every action film or dramatic role he churned out. Telling Kitty to bugger off wasn't worth losing the security blanket his celebrity afforded.

He must be tired, or he wouldn't be so annoyed with his normal routine. The New York premiere and contest weekend would be the end of a whirlwind of promotions and premieres for the film.

"Bored, maybe," he said, "but I wouldn't regret a slight decrease in all of the attention that comes with being a celebrity."

"No one likes a hermit, Irvin. You're approachable, which makes America love you all the more. Stuck-up celebrities aren't bankable."

He'd argue that some celebrities who shied away from the limelight were, but his mobile phone chimed. His heart rate revved up like the sports car he'd driven in his last film, as it had done every time the phone rang since the day he'd sent his screenplay to Kevin Lipinski a week ago. Kevin was one of the most sought-after and successful producers out there. Every film he touched turned to box-office gold, and if he liked Irvin's screenplay and agreed to produce the film, he might be Irvin's ticket out of the camera's glare and right behind it. Irvin wanted to direct.

The mobile's chime indicated a new email, which sent anticipation and dread flowing through his bloodstream. There were only two answers he could get.

Kevin would either love it or hate it. Both answers scared him.

He pressed the email icon on the phone and held his breath. Then released it in a sigh of disappointment. The new message was a party invitation. He unsuccessfully tried to tamp down his frustration. How long did it take to look at a script?

Kitty rambled on in the background about plans for the premiere. A member of the entourage let out a loud laugh at whatever the person on the phone with him had said. And another flipped the channels on his sixty-inch television with the volume turned up to high. It was information and annoyance overload. Irvin was done.

"Now that you've informed the lucky winner, we can call it a day," he said, cutting off Kitty's speech. He held up the script he'd been trying to read ever since they got back. "I've got to get through this." Another action movie. Not bad, really, but he knew the drill. The formula for his success didn't change much: he'd save a beautiful young woman, run through traffic in a big city with no shirt and haul around a big gun.

"No, we can't call it a day," Kitty said in a rush. "We need to go over the itinerary. Every moment of the premiere weekend has to be planned perfectly."

"Something that you can do without my direct input. Just tell me where to go and when to be there. The only thing I care about is when we present the check to the head of the foundation. Make sure there is plenty of time before and afterward for me to talk with him and the staff. I want to know if there is anything they need me to do to help the cause."

Alcohol awareness wasn't the sexiest issue for a celebrity to pick up. Kitty thought he should be kissing kids in third-world countries or building playgrounds for at-risk youth, where the photo ops were. He did contribute some to those causes, but preventing and stopping alcohol abuse were his passions. He'd witnessed the damages of alcohol abuse firsthand.

"Now I'd like my flat back," he said, looking at the people buzzing around. He used his normal charming tone of voice, but there was no mistaking the underlying steel beneath.

Kitty huffed but didn't argue. She was good at reading when he was tired of the show.

"Fine, but at least go over the itinerary before the end of the week." She grabbed her bag and pulled out a thick folder, which she handed over to him. "It took a while, but I managed to dig up a picture of the winner."

He flipped open the folder to find the photo. A woman with thick, dark hair and clear reddish-brown skin, wearing a conservative navy suit, stared back. Her lips were curved in a cool smile that didn't reach her eyes. Kitty should have known better than to expect this woman to scream. She didn't look the type. He frowned and studied her professional demeanor; he wouldn't have expected her even to enter the contest.

"Where did you get this picture?"

"She used to be the chief nursing officer at East Houston Regional Medical Center. It was her employee ID photo."

"She's no longer there?"

"No, left two years ago. Something about an illness in the family. I couldn't dig up a more current picture. Can you believe she doesn't have a profile anywhere?" Kitty said it as if the idea of going without an online presence was akin to going without electricity.

"Some people prefer their privacy." He looked away

from the picture to eye Kitty. "If she's not online, how did you dig this up?"

"I can't have you going out with a person with a rap sheet, Irvin, really. Before we called and confirmed her as the winner, I did some digging."

He glanced at the pinned-together woman in the picture. He doubted she would appreciate the probe into her life before being confirmed as the winner. He smirked. Well, she'd better get used to it. She'd be a pseudo celebrity while spending the weekend with him. Still, he felt a pang of regret for the digging, no matter how necessary it might have been.

"If you've got enough information to know she's not a criminal, no more researching into her past."

"For now," she said. She turned to the group. "Okay, people, let's get out of Irvin's way."

The lot of them packed up their phones, tablets and other gadgets. With waves, well wishes and another reminder from Kitty to review the itinerary, they were gone. He relished the silence for a few minutes. It seemed like a hundred years since he'd had an entire day of silence. He couldn't imagine a day in the future when he would.

"Full mouths shouldn't complain," he could hear his mother saying. It had been her way of telling him to shut up whenever he tried to say something about the beating she would take for stealing money from his dad just to put food on the table.

He pushed the uncomfortable memories aside. His mouth was full. If the lack of quiet or personal time was a side effect, then he wouldn't complain. His mother had endured far worse. She might not be around to enjoy the perks of his celebrity anymore, but childhood lessons died hard.

He flipped through the script and found the standard love scene. It had a full back shot. Kitty would love that. If she had her way, her number one client would go shirtless in every scene and have at least one back shot in every movie. It made her job of promoting him so much easier.

He tossed down the script in disgust. *Full mouth. Full mouth. Don't complain.*

Still, he checked his phone and silently hoped for a call from Kevin about his script.

There was a knock on the door. If it was Kitty returning to tell him another thing for the premiere weekend, he would lose his mind.

He checked the peephole, relaxed and opened the door with a smile. "What on earth are you doing here?"

Dante Wilson, the R & B star with a fan base as big as Irvin's, grinned from the other side. "I've got time before my concert tour and decided to come early for your promotional weekend."

Irvin shook his head and stepped back so his friend could walk in. "Why do you need to be here for my weekend?"

"Kitty thought it would be good to show off your high-profile connections as you become the highlight of this woman's life," Dante said. "Her words, not mine. Jacobe is coming up from Florida."

"Brilliant. I haven't seen Jacobe in weeks," Irvin said.

Jacobe Jenkins was the starting center for the Jacksonville Gators. The twenty-eight-year-old had been drafted at the end of his freshman year of college, let the easy money and women go to his head and started his professional basketball career as a wild party boy. Irvin and Dante had met him about a year ago at a party and become mentors for the young man. He still partied, but he wasn't getting into any foolish trouble anymore.

"But you didn't have to come early."

"It wasn't just for you. I met this model who's doing a show here this week."

That made more sense to Irvin. "Can I get you a drink?"

"You know you can." Dante shut the door behind him. "You drinking?"

Irvin shook his head. "I've had my one for the day."

"Kitty didn't push you to have two?"

Irvin laughed. "Kitty always tempts me to have two. But two leads to three and…"

He went to the bar to fix a whiskey for Dante and a cola for himself.

Dante crossed the living area to stare out over the skyline. The living definition of a pretty boy, he looked younger than his thirty-two years in designer jeans, white shirt and tie with a gray vest. Whereas Irvin was growing weary with the celebrity life, it was all Dante knew. He was the son of music legends, had grown up in front of the camera and enjoyed the fame that came with being a star.

"You should sell me this apartment," Dante said when Irvin came over and handed him his drink.

"You shouldn't get your hopes up," Irvin said and took a sip of the cola.

"One day I'll convince you."

"I doubt it."

Dante chuckled and lifted the glass. "Are you going to bring her here?"

"Who?"

"The winner of the contest." Dante gave him a sly

look. "Are you going to show her all that New York has to offer?"

"You know I don't bring women back here. It's the one place where I can escape, when Kitty's not around, at least." They both chuckled at that. "Besides, I doubt I'll get a half hour alone with the woman. Kitty will have every appearance scheduled and I'll just show up, do my charming smile, sign an autograph and then come back here to blessed silence."

"Pity."

"Not at all. This isn't a sleazy way to shag some woman. I can go for a ride without going through this much trouble. It's to raise money for the foundation."

"I'm just saying it wouldn't hurt to have a little fun out of it. Obviously if she entered, she's interested in you."

"I'm not taking advantage of a fan just to get my kicks. Besides, I have more important things to worry about than showing her a good time."

As if summoned, his phone chimed again. He rushed across the room to where he'd left it on the bar. Disappointment stooped his shoulders as he read the email from Kitty, reminding him to check the itinerary. With a swear, he dropped the phone back onto the bar.

"What's got you so worked up?" Dante asked.

"I'm waiting on a response about my screenplay."

"You finally sent it off. Good for you. You know it'll get picked up."

"I don't want it picked up because of who I am. I want it picked up because it's a good story."

"Who cares why it's picked up as long as it is? You worked on it for over a year. Push your weight around in Hollywood and get it made."

"That's not the way."

"It is the way. What's the point of all this fame if we don't put it to good use?" Dante spread his arms to encompass the spacious area.

"I'll wait and hear before I make a decision about pushing my weight around."

"Who did you send it to?"

"Kevin Lipinski."

Dante cringed. "He's the toughest producer out there. And he hates screenplays from superstars. Are you trying to kill your writing career before it starts?"

"If he says yes, then I'll know it's good. If he says no…he'll at least give me a reason why he doesn't like it."

"And tear you to pieces in the meantime. There's nothing that guy likes better than to put celebrities with inflated egos in their place."

Which was exactly why Irvin had sent it to him. If he had any chance of getting behind the camera, this was the test. If Kevin liked his script, Irvin planned to barter and plead to direct it. He'd earned his money and his fame, repaid his mother the debt he owed before she passed away, and now he was ready to move behind the camera. He loved Hollywood, loved the satisfaction of bringing a story to life and the pride when it was done well. But he could experience all those things without being the half-naked guy on-screen. It was his one shot to keep the security he had now without many of the headaches.

"I don't have an inflated ego to burst," Irvin said.

"You say that now, but wait until his comments come back."

Irvin drank his cola to swallow the sinking feeling that Dante might be right.

Chapter 3

"I don't have to go," Faith said, twisting a pair of underwear in her hands.

Virginia Logan rolled her wheelchair across the threshold into Faith's room. She shot Faith the same "are you crazy" look she'd given her when Faith was a girl and asked to stay out past her curfew. Except now the left side of her scowl drooped a little. It was still a vast improvement from the complete loss of motion and feeling Virginia had had on that side right after the stroke.

"Have you lost your mind, child?" Virginia asked in the softly slurred voice that still held a lot of her old spunk. "You deserve this vacation and a dozen more like it."

Faith tossed the underwear in the bag. "I don't deserve anything. I should stay. I could have filled in for one of the nurses who needed off this weekend. I'm so close to paying off the credit card, it seems foolish to lose twenty-four hours of overtime to hang out with an actor and party."

"There's nothing wrong with enjoying yourself when the opportunity arises." Her mama wheeled closer and reached out her hand. Faith took it and squeezed. "You gave up a lot moving back here from Houston to take care of me and your dad. As much as I hate that you had to sacrifice so much, I'm also grateful."

"It was nothing. Especially after what Love did to you two."

Virginia sighed and let go of Faith's hand. "It's time for you to stop feeling guilty over what your sister did."

"I know, Mama, but we're twins. I should have sensed that she was capable of taking advantage of you."

Virginia laughed and patted Faith's arm. "This is real life, not some sci-fi movie. Just because you're her twin doesn't mean you can read her mind. There was no way any of us would have sensed that Love would get caught up in drugs or steal our money and skip town while I was in the hospital."

"But shouldn't I have realized that something was wrong with her? Heard it in her voice, or had some clue that she could be so heartless?"

"Your sister isn't heartless, Faith. She's sick. Thank the good Lord she finally agreed to go to rehab."

Faith turned away from her mama. She walked over to the closet and calmly took down a few sundresses for the trip. She wanted to scream at her mama's insistence on trying to find the good in Love. Despite years of dealing with Love's fight against addiction, when she'd wiped out their parents' savings the day after her mama suffered a stroke, Faith considered that the end of her relationship with her sister. Her parents had worked hard to build up their nest egg for retirement. Her mama had worked as a schoolteacher and principal for twenty years. Her dad had been a superintendent at a delivery company for years until he was flung from his delivery truck four years ago in an accident and broke his back in three places. Thankfully he could walk, but the injury prevented him from working. Her mama had taken care of him before her stroke.

Faith couldn't forgive Love for stealing from their parents. Who were already struggling after her dad's injury. From what her mama said, Love had got away with all of their savings. Savings that would have gone a long way toward helping pay the ongoing medical bills and retrofit the house to accommodate her disabled parents. All things she'd depleted her savings to pay for and worked hard to continue to pay for.

"Love isn't sick, Mama. She's a junkie," she said, not bothering to hide the contempt in her voice. She walked back to her suitcase and tossed the dresses inside.

Virginia took out the dresses and started folding each of them. "Don't hate your sister."

"After what she did, it's hard not to."

"Family is family, and she'll always be your sister. I know it's hard for you to understand how she let drugs take over her life, but she wants to get better." Virginia placed the folded dresses in the suitcase. Then she gave Faith a direct stare. "And when she's out, we'll do what we can to help her. Right?"

Faith looked away to zip her bag. That was a promise she couldn't make. This wasn't Love's first stint in rehab. She'd believed her sister once before, and less than a year later, her sister had betrayed their parents.

"If you're not going to talk me out of going, then I guess I'd better go catch that plane," Faith said instead.

Virginia sighed but didn't push.

Faith took her overnight bag from the bed. "I've made dinners for every night and they're in the freezer," she said.

Virginia shook her head and chuckled. "I know, Faith."

"And Marie said she'll check in on both of you every day. I'll keep my cell phone with me the entire time. If anything happens—"

"Nothing is going to happen, and there isn't much you can do from New York anyway," Virginia said.

"You're right. I should stay."

"Child, come on and quit fussing. Everything will be fine." Virginia turned her wheelchair around and left the room.

Faith followed her mama to the front of the house. It had taken most of the past two years to retrofit the house with wider doorways, bathroom handrails and other changes to make life easier for her parents. After Love's grand theft, Faith had offered to move her parents to Houston, where she had the salary to take better care of them, but they'd refused. They'd both lived in Laurel County all their lives and didn't want to move. If they insisted on staying, then Faith insisted on making sure their house was worth staying in.

At the front of the house, they went out into morning air, already warm and humid for early June. Marie sat on a white porch rocker, talking with Faith's dad. Jimmy Logan and Marie were both laughing, probably at a joke that Marie had made. Her friend was always good at making her parents laugh.

"Well, I guess I'm set," Faith said.

The smile on Marie's face fell. "You're going wearing that?"

Faith ran a hand across the sleeveless lavender top

and jean shorts. "What's wrong with my outfit?" Faith asked. "I'm going to be on a plane all morning."

"And when you get off, you're meeting *Irvin Freeman*. I knew I should have come over and picked out your outfit."

Jimmy placed his hands on the walker in front of him and stood. "She looks beautiful just as she is." He shuffled over to her. "You have a good time up there. Don't worry a bit, and take dozens of pictures for me and your mom, okay?"

She smiled and leaned over to give him a hug. "I will, Daddy."

"Let's get you to the airport," Marie said.

"Did I tell you where the spare key is?" she asked Marie. "And don't forget that I called in my daddy's prescription and it'll be ready later today. I left the money—"

"On the kitchen table," Marie cut in, rolling her eyes. "I know. You've told me and your parents a dozen times. Just go and have fun and quit worrying about things here."

"But I just want to make sure—"

Marie took her arm and pulled her toward the steps. "We got it. Wave goodbye to your parents."

Faith couldn't wave because she had to grab her bag as Marie dragged her by her other arm down the porch. Her parents waved and grinned as if they enjoyed watching Marie pull her away.

"Call me if you need something," she said to them.

"You just have a great time, child," her mama called back.

Her parents looked so happy for her, she thought as Marie drove off. She'd have to try to enjoy herself for their sake, at least. Truthfully, a small part of her was excited about going to New York and not having to worry about how much an item cost or how much the meal was before ordering it. She missed that part of her old life, but she didn't reflect on it too often. She'd done what she had to do, and there was no need to relive memories of a past that wasn't coming back.

As they pulled away, she couldn't help but take in the wheelchair ramp that needed replacing and the patch on the porch roof that leaked during hard storms. There was still so much to do, so much to fix. Since Love had robbed them blind, fate had kicked in to make sure everything that could go wrong did, including the house. She should stay at home, tending to those items, not travel to New York to party. No telling what bad luck fate had in store for her for going on this trip.

Hours later, Faith rolled her overnight bag off the plane, into LaGuardia Airport. She moved with the crowd toward the exit, anticipation and nervousness making her hands slick on the handle. She'd traveled around the South and West a lot, but she'd never been to New York. Even though she hated leaving her parents, this trip was giving her the opportunity to see the city, something she wouldn't have ever done on her own.

On the plane ride, she'd convinced herself to find the silver lining in winning the contest. Since she'd got the call that her mama had had a stroke and arrived to find out that her sister had stolen all of their money, she didn't put a lot of trust in luck.

But she refused to become one of those angry, bitter women who couldn't appreciate things. Since her family had practically pushed her out the door to come, she would make an effort to enjoy herself and the city. She even admitted that it might be slightly cool to meet

Irvin Freeman. However, she doubted the star wanted to spend the entire weekend playing tour guide. She could definitely suppress any eye rolls or sarcastic remarks if he did turn out to be a stuck-up snob during the few limited interactions she was likely to have with him.

She hoped.

She found her way to the pickup area of the airport. The instructions she'd been given said a car would be waiting for her. She only hoped she could find it in all of the activity.

A cameraman, a photographer and a guy holding a large sign with her name on it were the first people she saw. No problem recognizing her ride.

A woman with a bright red streak in her black hair stood next to the sign guy. She was dressed in a black suit that hugged her body so closely it had to have been custom-made for her. She fired off directions to the men. She must be the one in charge.

"Hi, I'm Faith Logan," Faith said, walking over to the group that was getting the attention of everyone in the departure area. "I guess you're my ride."

The woman in the suit stopped talking and spun to face her. The smile on her face flickered for a second, about the same amount of time it took to do a quick inventory of Faith's hair and outfit, before she got her features back in order. Faith wasn't sure what that was about, but this woman probably made her living sizing people up in one look.

"Faith Logan, welcome and congratulations! I'm Kitty Brown, Irvin's publicist and your host for this weekend," she said in the cheerful voice Faith recognized from the phone call.

The photographer lifted his camera and pointed it in Faith's direction. Kitty shook her head and motioned with a finger for him to lower it. "Not now. We'll get a shot of her meeting Irvin instead of coming off the plane." She turned to Faith with another big smile. "And we'll get you just right for the introduction."

"I really don't need anything extra just to meet him," Faith said, not liking the implication that she was somehow not ready to see the guy. Granted, she had hoped to put on a little makeup—lip gloss and some mascara—and even change into one of her dresses. But the way Kitty came across, it was as if Faith hadn't spent the past few hours on a plane with an hour layover thanks to engine problems.

"Nothing extra," Kitty said, "but we can…freshen you up a bit. We don't have a lot of time. Your plane was delayed, you know." Kitty said it as if Faith had some part in that. "So instead of the elaborate wardrobe, hair and makeup session we planned, we can go with a few changes for the photo shoot. We'll save the major make-over for before the club tonight."

"If the photo shoot is me meeting him for the first time, why do I need to change clothes?"

Kitty stopped in the middle of turning to the rest of the crew to raise her eyebrow at Faith. "Well, we can't shoot you in that outfit."

Faith bet that eyebrow and disdainful tone made people quake, but she had worked for one of the meanest hospital administrators in Houston. She'd been raised in the South, where an older woman could throw shade so fast and easy you wouldn't realize she'd called you a bitch until two weeks later. Kitty didn't intimidate her.

"What's wrong with my outfit? Look, I'm willing to go with the flow, but I will not be insulted. Not my clothes, hair or anything else. If you wanted a starlet type, you probably could have picked one, but you didn't. You chose me. So you're getting me."

The corner of Kitty's mouth rose in a cynical smile. "A random-number generator chose you, not me. But I know how to make do with what I'm given. The offer wasn't given as an insult—it's part of the weekend. Makeover and photo shoot with Irvin. Don't you remember that in the itinerary?"

"I haven't read the itinerary," she admitted.

Something very close to relief came across Kitty's face. "No wonder you aren't very enthusiastic. Just wait until you hear about all the fun I have in store for you. Prepare to be pleasantly surprised."

Kitty slid her arm through Faith's, as if they were old friends, and headed for the door. With a wave of her hand she indicated that the rest of the crew should follow, before diving headfirst into a speech on how lucky Faith was.

Faith tried to summon up the small amount of enthusiasm she'd felt on the plane, but Kitty barely gave her a chance to think, much less absorb it all. Plus, the woman wouldn't take a breather so Faith could call her parents and let them know she'd arrived. It was unlikely that anything catastrophic had happened since that morning, but she would have felt better checking in. However, as Kitty kept up the chatter out to the limo and on the ride to the city, Faith gave up hope of calling until they reached their destination. She couldn't help wondering if Kitty's constant chatter was her punishment for going on this trip.

Chapter 4

Irvin flipped through the pages of the latest *Men's Health* magazine as he lounged on a sofa in the Manhattan studio of photographer Rafael Sims. Kitty was late, which was very unusual for her, but he wasn't in a rush. The photo shoot with him and the winner should take about an hour, and his only afternoon plans were to not check his emails every six minutes. He wasn't doing too well with that. Rafael had helped distract him for a few minutes with idle conversation until the photographer had got a call. Irvin glanced at his watch; five minutes had passed since he'd last looked. Which meant he might as well check his phone again.

He put down the magazine and picked up his mobile. As expected, there were no emails from Kevin Lipinski. He would have been better served leaving his mobile at home. He tossed it back onto the glass table in front of him and picked up the magazine.

"Is there anything I can get you while you wait?" Rafael's young assistant came over and asked. Her smile indicated she offered a lot more than water or juice. She'd checked on him every five minutes since he'd arrived. He knew, because it was how often he'd checked his mobile.

He gave her a smile but shook his head. "No, thank you, Tina. I'm fine."

"I don't mean to be a bother. I just know that I hate waiting. Sometimes it helps to have a distraction," she said, emphasizing the last word.

Inwardly he groaned. If he wasn't *the* Irvin Freeman and was just a plain bloke walking down the street, would she even give him a passing glance? He doubted it. When he was growing up, his looks were considered average at best. Amazing how swagger, money and fame had taken him from regular guy to sex symbol.

He held up the magazine. "I have a distraction," he said, not letting the smile drop from his face. He might get annoyed with the groupies, but he was never rude. Full mouths couldn't complain, after all.

"Oh, well, if you need anything, just call me."

She turned to walk away, and he did watch her stride across the room. She was beautiful—he'd give her that. Nice bum, small waist and tan skin. When he'd first started in the business, he would have accepted her offer. Back when being desired by a multitude of women was new, not annoying.

Tina glanced at him over her shoulder and caught him watching. The light in her eye nearly made him cringe for real. Now he'd have to convince her that he might have looked, but he had no intention of touching.

The moment was interrupted when Kitty and the rest of the group burst into the room with a wave of conversation and laughter. Though he'd known they were coming, the arrival of Kitty and the entourage came with the anxious feeling he had back when he'd started out in some small off-Broadway play. Every move he made while they were around would be watched, scrutinized and reported on some social-media site if deemed interesting enough to boost his celebrity status.

He scanned the group for the winner. Kitty had texted him that she still didn't seem very excited, so he expected to find the cool smile and reserved expression from her employee photo. His scan came to an immediate halt when it landed on the smiling cutie talking to one of the cameramen.

In his mind he let out an appreciative whistle. This was not the reserved woman from the picture, not with that smile. It was what he noticed first. She had the brightest, most beautiful smile he'd ever seen on a woman. Then there were her legs: long, shapely and enticing in the short denim shorts. The lavender shirt showed off toned arms and looked good against the red undertones in her skin. Her dark, thick hair was pulled back into a ponytail.

Coming from the UK, he'd never understood the girl-next-door thing that American men went for, at least not until this moment. This woman made him think of barbecues, bike riding and picnics. All that down-home stuff Hollywood portrayed in their good ole American films.

He slowly stood and grinned. The weekend wasn't going to be as bad as he had originally thought. He'd still stick with the "look but don't touch" approach, but at least this woman was nice to look at.

She stopped talking and turned his way. The smile on her face froze, then became stiff around the edges.

She took a deep breath and just watched him for what felt like hours, but was probably just a few seconds. He waited for the excitement, frantic fanning, shriek of joy and tears. He was usually good for a tear or two.

They never came. Instead, she calmly walked over and held out her hand. "It's nice to meet you, Irvin."

That accent... Hers was a slow, husky drawl that wrapped around him and made him want to hear it whisper his name. He normally didn't care much for Southern accents, but he could listen to hers all night.

He took her hand in his. "The pleasure is all mine."

She swallowed and gave a short nod before pulling her hand back. She rubbed it across her shorts then stuck both hands in her back pockets. "I appreciate you saying that. I'm sure this is kind of an imposition on you."

"I wouldn't have offered if it were. I'm always excited to find new ways to raise money for alcohol awareness."

She nodded, but the look on her face said she didn't quite believe him. "I guess it's time for my total transformation."

At that moment, Rafael came out of his office. To see him on the street, no one would guess that Rafael was a famous photographer. His curly hair, thick square glasses and unassuming white shirt and gray khakis didn't set him apart from any other guy in his midthirties.

"Is this our winner?" Rafael asked in a loud, excited voice. He took both of Faith's hands in his and held them out. "We don't have much work to do with you. Look at those legs and that smile. You've got the cutest face, my dear."

From the way she glanced around, Irvin wondered if she was uncomfortable with the praise.

"That's very sweet coming from a man who photographs women far more glamorous than me."

"Glamour is a mirage. A mirage that I create," Rafael said, placing one of his hands on his chest. "The lens can make the meanest person look like a saint when it's in the right hands, and my dear, I've got the right hands."

Faith smiled, and Irvin was blown away by how cute she was. "The right hands and a way with words."

Rafael laughed, then snapped his fingers for Tina to come over. "If you think I'm good with words, wait until you see these pictures. Now on to hair and makeup."

"Not too much makeup," Irvin said.

Faith and Rafael looked at him with varying degrees of surprise. Though Rafael's look was tinged with a bit of curiosity. Irvin was not a makeup expert, but he had a feeling too much would only take away from her charm.

"Irvin has spoken," Rafael said. "Not too much makeup." Rafael and Tina ushered Faith to the dressing room.

"What do you think?" Kitty asked as Faith and Rafael disappeared.

"I like," he said.

"Good. She's a bit reserved. I still can't get a read on her, but I'll figure out what makes her tick."

He knew what that meant. He pointed at Kitty. "No more digging. She's here and she seems normal."

"Normal is a mirage," Kitty said, waving her hands in an imitation of Rafael that made Irvin laugh.

Several minutes later, Faith was back with her hair out of the ponytail and framing her face in a sleek bob that gently curled below her chin. They'd replaced the sleeveless lavender T-shirt with a sparkling yellow tank top and followed his instruction to not put too much makeup on her. Only enough to enhance her rounded cheeks, brown eyes and full lips.

"I'll start with pictures of you. Then we'll move on to both of you," Rafael said. He led Faith over to the gray backdrop where they'd pose for the shoot.

"What am I supposed to do?" Faith asked.

"Be your sweet Southern self, my dear," Rafael said with a wave of his hand. "Where are you from, again?"

"South Carolina. Laurel County."

"Hmm, I've been to North Carolina. Had a shoot in Charlotte once." Rafael started snapping pictures.

Faith gave him a tight smile. "That's not very close to where I'm from."

"Either way, relax, my dear. Just be yourself."

She glanced around at the background with barely concealed panic.

Irvin hurried over to her side. "Why don't we start with both of us?" He took her hand. Her palm was slick. She was more nervous than she let on.

Her eyes widened and she tried to jerk her hand away. He held on more tightly and pulled her closer to his side. "Relax."

Her hand flexed in his, and she cut her eyes toward Rafael snapping away. "Easier said than done. You weren't hustled from a plane to a photo shoot without a chance to breathe."

"Are you nervous?"

"Just a bit."

He gave her his lady-killer smile. "Don't be. I don't bite."

A frown came across her features before she lifted her chin. "That's good to know, but it's not why I'm nervous. I know I just have a few scheduled appearances with you, which is how I prefer it."

She slid her hand away and wiped it on the leg of her shorts. How she preferred it? He hadn't had a woman say she preferred spending minimal time with him since he'd left London. He started to ask why when it hit him. He'd had women try to play the reverse-psychology thing on him before. Pretend disinterest in hopes of gaining his attention. Several years ago he'd done a film in which the leading lady's character used that dishonest tactic to win over the heart of the politician he'd played. Ever since, women tried it with him constantly. Thinking she would do that was surprisingly disappointing.

"So let me guess. You entered the contest to spend a weekend with me, but are hoping to limit our time together. Not secretly hoping that something would happen between us."

Her incredulous look was almost believable. "You've got to be kidding. Do you really think I'd want to add my name to the list of forgettable women you sleep with?"

Rafael snapped faster. "Closer, my dears. You're happy about this weekend."

Irvin wrapped an arm around her shoulders and pulled her against his side. She smelled good, a light flowery fragrance. And her body fit nicely with his. A fact he wished he wasn't so acutely aware of.

"Are you accusing me," he said through his fake smile for the camera, "of planning to seduce the winner of this contest?"

She was stiff beside him, but she relaxed and pasted on her own smile when Rafael ordered her to look happy. "Honestly, the thought never crossed my mind that you'd try to seduce me. Though I doubt you'd turn down sex if I offered."

He turned to face her, almost entertained by her attempt to throw the offer out there in a backhanded way. "Oh, really. Please tell me why you think I'd take you to bed."

She hesitated, and he could tell she was wondering whether or not to say more. When determination filled her gaze he grinned. She was playing this all the way.

"You're used to women throwing themselves at you," she said. "You're linked to a different woman faster than I can change underwear, and this month *Essence* magazine's readers voted you the man women most want to sleep with. I highly doubt you turn down many offers for sex."

"Are you calling me promiscuous?"

"All I'm saying is that you don't lack for women lining up to warm your bed, and I didn't come up here to be your next electric blanket." Her voice rose on her last words. She sounded almost sincere. He struggled with wishing she was and wishing she wasn't. He no longer slept with groupies, but he had to admit, this particular one went from cute to sexy when she pretended to be angry.

It took a second for him to realize silence filled the room. They both turned to find Kitty nearly fuming, Rafael laughing and the rest of his entourage wearing expressions of disbelief.

"That's a wrap," Rafael said, balancing his camera on his shoulder.

Faith stepped away from Irvin. She looked from one end of the room to the other. "I've got to make a call. Is there a place where I can go for privacy?"

Rafael pointed to his office. "Right in that room."

"Thank you." She hurried to the office and pushed the door closed.

Kitty rushed to Irvin's side. "I told you she didn't

want to be here. I knew I should have handpicked the winner instead of using a random selection. She should be happy—"

"If you're going to say she should be happy to sleep with me this weekend, then save it. All that was a ploy. I've had women try to pull this on me before. She's probably in there right now telling her girlfriend that she's brilliant and has me fooled."

He crossed the room to Rafael's office. The door hadn't closed all the way, and he felt no remorse about eavesdropping on her conversation. He would pay money that she was in there calling someone to say the plan was working. That she was on her way to convincing him she wasn't just another fan out to land Irvin Freeman in bed.

He needed to hear it to take his mind off how incredibly sexy she'd been as she'd dressed him down. How her eyes sparked, and that accent of hers grew thicker. In that moment he imagined his name swirling out of her mouth in that drawl, and he needed to snap out of it.

He leaned close to the door, ready to hear her gloating or strategizing her next move.

"The man is exactly what I thought—another spoiled, rich playboy who thinks women are here only to please him. I told you I should have stayed home, Mama. This weekend is going to be terrible."

Her angry rant immediately proved him wrong. And for Irvin Freeman that was a first.

Chapter 5

"What are you talking about?" Virginia asked.

"I'm here and already it's a hassle. Irvin isn't the nice guy he comes across as in those interviews. He thinks I'm here to seduce him."

"Well, maybe you should."

"Mama, please don't say ridiculous things."

"Okay, that was a bit much, but it won't hurt to just let your hair down and have a little fun. You can do that without being around him."

Faith sighed and pushed the hair away from her face. Now that the shoot was over, she was pretty sure Kitty had said she was going to the hotel. She could get away from Irvin immediately.

"You're right. He'll go his way and I can walk around and explore the city a little bit before going to the party tonight."

"Can you say the word *party* without sounding like you're going to the gallows?"

Faith laughed. "Fine. I can't wait to go to the party with the arrogant actor who thinks I'm here to trick him into bed," she said with false charm and cheer.

"Goodbye, Faith," her mama said, chuckling.

"You and Daddy can call me whenever you need to. And be sure to warm up one of those meals I froze for dinner tonight. And if I forgot something on the grocery list, just call Marie and she'll get it for you. And—"

"Seriously, Faith, goodbye. Don't worry. Your daddy and I will be fine."

Faith was being overprotective, but it had been her role for the past two years. One she took so seriously she sometimes forgot they were the parents. She took a deep breath and reminded herself that her mama was a thousand times better now than she'd been when Faith had first come home, and her daddy had been living with his disability for years.

"Okay, Mama, I'll call you later."

She ended the call, then tapped the phone on her chin. Now what? She wasn't ready to face Irvin. Admittedly, she was very disappointed that he fit the entitled-guy mold. As her excitement had budded on the plane, she'd hoped he would be somewhat normal. If only Marie could have taken off work and come with her. She could relax if she had her friend along.

With a sigh, she turned and opened the door—only to jump back when she nearly walked right into Irvin. Her heart went from a tango to a standstill. The man was fine: square jaw covered by a precisely cut beard, wide, flat nose and piercing dark eyes that made her secretly swoon whenever he gave whatever lucky leading lady was starring opposite him a sexy stare.

Why, oh, why were good looks bestowed on men who didn't deserve them?

He wasn't handsome in the traditional sense. He made up for not having the classical good looks with a swagger that couldn't be ignored. It oozed from every part of him: the way he walked, talked, dressed. He was classy and dangerous, gentleman and bad boy, nice and naughty all wrapped in masculine appeal.

And he thought she wanted to get him in bed.

Well, it's not like it would be a hardship.

She gave herself a mental shake. No need thinking that. She would not be another fan tossing her panties at Irvin Freeman. No matter how seductive he looked.

"Were you listening in?"

"I was," he said in that wonderful British accent that melted women's underwear like butter on a hot skillet.

Her insides quivered. Literally quivered as if she were the virgin heroine in some medieval fairy tale. And though her virginity was long gone, something about the raw sexual energy he wore like a second skin made her believe all her previous sexual encounters were fumbling attempts at the real thing.

She crossed her arms and nailed him with the stare that used to make slacking nurses cower. "Care to tell me why?"

"I actually came over expecting to hear you gloat or come up with a new plan to flirt with me." He held up his hands when her eyes narrowed. "But I was wrong, and I apologize. How about we give it another go?" He shot her that smile. The one that tugged up the corners of his full lips just enough to tempt a woman to forget the rules and follow him to the nearest bedroom.

She held her ground and stared him down. "Why

don't we simply agree to get through the weekend with minimal contact?"

"I can't agree to that," he said.

"Why not?"

"Because I offended you, and I want to make up for it. You must understand that I meant no disrespect to you. I'm bombarded by women, as you so readily pointed out, but I don't take up every offer."

He moved closer to lean against the door frame, and his gray T-shirt stretched over made for grabbing broad shoulders. His jeans were scuffed up just enough to make them look intentionally worn. A casual outfit that seemed sexy only because the clothes were on his perfect body.

"I understand, and accept your apology. Still, you don't have to make up for it. I know this weekend is an obligation for you."

"It might have started that way, but my outlook is definitely changing."

His inviting gaze swept across her body. It was a quick and thorough examination. The kind of look a man gave when he wanted a woman to know he was interested. A look with all kinds of naughty promises. A look that tightened her nipples and sent an unexpected jolt between her legs.

"That's nice of you to say."

"I wouldn't say it if I didn't mean it. Let me make it up to you."

"It's really not necessary. Your people flew me up here. We're doing the party tonight and the premiere tomorrow. We just had an unfortunate misunderstanding, and everything will be smooth from here on out."

"Have you been to New York before?"

The abrupt change in topic threw her for a loop. "No. It's my first time."

"Then let me show you around."

Inside she squealed at the thought of getting a personal tour of the city from Irvin, but his apology and sex appeal were already making her forget that she wasn't here for a Hollywood hookup.

"I'm tired. I just want to go back to the hotel and relax. But thank you, Irvin."

He watched her for several seconds, then pushed away from the door. Before she could blink, he'd taken her hand in his. "Until tonight, then." He brushed his lips across the back of her hand.

She fought very hard not to sigh and tremble in tandem with the shivers inside her belly. "I'll see you at the party."

He let go of her hand, then motioned for her to precede him. She breathed in the traces of his cologne, clean, crisp and completely delicious, as she swept past him. When she approached, the rest of the crew tried hard to pretend they weren't paying attention, though she was confident they were doing nothing but. Kitty went into a flurry of instructions to her staff. In seconds they had their fingers flying across their phones. One even snapped a picture with his phone before typing something.

A sinking feeling went through her gut. Everything Irvin did ended up on some gossip site. Their little interaction was probably already posted somewhere. Another reason to limit her time with him. She didn't need people probing into her past and discovering what her sister had done. Her family's dirty laundry wasn't for public display.

And neither was she.

She was so ready to get to the hotel, away from the prying eyes of his staff. And from Irvin's hot glance and inviting looks.

Chapter 6

"There—all done."

The makeup artist stepped away from Faith. Kitty and several other people in the makeover squad Kitty had summoned to Faith's room swarmed closer to get a look. If it weren't for the fun of having a full make-over, Faith would have been annoyed by the way they studied her like a specimen under a microscope. But everyone on the team had been so nice and enthusiastic that she couldn't help but get drawn in.

"Perfect," Kitty said, clasping her hands in front of her. "She's a knockout. She'll look fantastic on Irvin's arm tonight."

Of course Kitty would be worried about how good of an arm piece she'd make for Irvin. But even that couldn't suppress Faith's eager smile. For the past four hours, she'd been pampered like she'd never been before. A full body massage, facial, hairstyling, makeup and even exfoliating. She blushed to think about how every single hair deemed unnecessary had been removed by the team. Through covert peeks in the mirror, she'd glimpsed some of her transformation, but now she could barely suppress her excitement to see the final results.

"Can I look in the mirror now?" She turned to do just that, but Kitty grabbed her arms.

"Not until you put on the dress."

There was a collective gasp by the team, who whispered, "The dress!"

Grinning, Faith got up from the chair and ignored the temptation to take a look at herself in the mirror. She shouldn't enjoy this so much. If she was back home, she'd think how superficial and shallow all of this really was. Right now, though, she decided to allow herself to enjoy this fantasy weekend. Besides, it was hard not to get excited over a designer dress tailored just for her. The team had taken her measurements at the start of the makeover, and the dress had arrived a few minutes ago.

She was having so much fun that she couldn't even rustle up any annoyance whenever Kitty remarked about how surprisingly easy it was to turn her into a knockout. A comment to which she'd responded in her heaviest Southern drawl, "Good thing I got my teeth fixed a couple years back." The team laughed at her joke. Kitty only looked relieved.

Within minutes she was in the dress. They did a final gloss of her hair and makeup, and then she was in front of the mirror with an embellished "Voilà" from Kitty.

Faith's jaw dropped. The woman in the mirror wasn't Faith Logan, shift nurse and parent caretaker. The person looking back at her was the perfect arm candy for a Hollywood superstar.

The dress was long-sleeved, but there was no chance

she'd get too warm. Made of sheer material enhanced with silver stones strategically placed over her more personal areas, it clung to every curve and stopped in a wisp of material at the tops of her thighs. Full curls framed her face, and her makeup... Good gracious, her makeup was flawless. Her face shone with just the right highlights and shadows. She looked like a celebrity. In fact, she almost felt like one, surrounded by the team oohing and aahing over her appearance.

"So, what do you think?" Kitty asked with what sounded like uncertainty in her voice.

"I'm stunning," Faith whispered.

Kitty clapped and congratulated the team. "Finally, a response from you I can take."

Faith continued to stare at the stranger in the mirror... a stranger she kind of liked. If only Marie could see her now. Once again she wished her friend could have got off work to be here. She'd have to take a picture and send it to Marie and her parents. They wanted her to have fun, and this makeover was fun.

There was a knock at the door, and the excitement and buzz of conversation from the team elevated.

"That must be Irvin," Kitty said.

Faith's heart pounded like their feet on the floor of the hotel room. She broke out in a sweat. Dang it, she couldn't sweat. Not in this barely there outfit and perfect makeup. She fanned herself to cool off, but Kitty was already ushering her out of the bedroom and into the living area of the hotel suite.

Don't sweat. Don't sweat. Don't sweat, she chanted internally, as if that would stop her.

Kitty positioned her and the rest of the crew for Irvin's entrance. Vaguely she wondered if the man ever entered a room without Kitty arranging everyone on the other side of the door.

When Kitty swept the door open and he entered, Faith forgot to think, to breathe, as his sexy, dark eyes zeroed in on her. He wore a white shirt, black-and-white-striped vest and dark pants, but on him the simple clothes covered him in sex appeal. She'd heard the expression "sex on a stick" before. Standing before her, this man brought that expression to life. And she was going out clubbing with him tonight.

Don't be a fangirl. He already thinks you're only here to seduce him. Despite her warning, she couldn't help but think it would be pretty darn nice to seduce someone that good-looking.

She gave herself another mental shake. *Get it together.*

But her command fell flat when his dark gaze ran over her from head to toe, once, twice and a third time. Her body temperature soared to near nuclear levels with each sweep. He focused in on the gemstones barely covering her breasts, and her nipples immediately beaded. A slow smile spread across his full lips as he raised his gaze to hers. The look he gave her made her think about what it might be like to be his date for real. For the promise in his eye to be there not for the cameras capturing the moment, but because he was going to live up to the promise later that night.

"You look beautiful," he said, crossing the room to stand before her.

Heaven help her, she'd nearly forgotten about that voice. Desire soaked her panties. She tried to remember the annoyance she'd felt with him earlier that day. Something ridiculously hard to do with him eyeing her like that.

"Thank you," she said. She was relieved that her voice didn't waver. "I thought you'd just meet us at the club."

"A gentleman always picks up his lady at the door."

"Well, I'm not your lady. Not really. We both know this is a promotional thing." She said it to remind herself more than him.

"Promotional thing or not, I'm already enjoying myself."

He ran a hand down her arm. The flimsy material of the dress did little to block the sizzling heat of his touch. "Nice dress."

She hated herself for trembling, but it was hard to suppress. Their gazes met, and she could have sworn she saw desire in his. She blinked and glanced around at the room full of people. He was an actor, she told herself; it was his job to make women feel beautiful. This wasn't attraction and it wasn't real.

"Kitty picked it out."

"I can tell. It's not quite you."

She frowned and stepped away from his touch. Here she was thinking she was all done up to look like his perfect match for the night, and he said the dress wasn't her? True, she wouldn't have picked it out, but she looked damn good in it.

"How do you know what is or isn't me?"

"Because you don't need all of this—" his hands motioned from the top to the bottom of her dress "—to make yourself desirable. Yes, the end result is breathtaking, but your loveliness is much more subtle."

Heat flared across her skin. *Don't sweat!* Had he really called her lovely? Yes, but it didn't mean anything, she told herself, despite her fluttering heart.

"You're joking with me." She lifted her chin and stepped back.

He moved toward her, and she forgot about the crowd of people in the room watching their interaction. Awareness sizzled across her nerve endings at the subtle hint of his cologne. It was some designer fragrance she wouldn't know the name of, but it was all male. "There are a lot of things that dress makes me think about doing, but joking with you isn't one of them."

Heaven help her, he was flirting. She needed to put a stop to it before she forgot that, like the clothes and makeup, this was an illusion. He was just another high-profile guy used to getting what he wanted. From the look in his eye, he wanted her. For now. He'd quickly forget all about her come Monday morning.

She cleared her throat before she spoke. "Look, I meant what I said at the photo shoot earlier. I won a date with you through some random drawing, but I'm not here for anything more than that."

The corner of his mouth quirked up, adding a sexy tilt to his full lips. "You keep saying that, but as the winner of the prize, you could rightly demand that I do everything you request of me to make your time memorable."

"I didn't plan to request sex."

"*Didn't* implies past tense. Does that mean you've changed your mind?"

Her eyes widened. "Yes. I mean, no. I mean, I wasn't… I'm not thinking that you'd want to…that we'd…"

Heat spread across her cheeks. She held up a hand and was ready to go off on him when he chuckled.

"Relax—I'm only teasing," he said with humor in his eyes. "We're going to have a great time tonight."

Kitty hurried over. "And we're going to be late if we don't leave now."

Still thrown off by what had just happened with Irvin, Faith tried to change the subject. "What will we be late for?"

"I sent out Irvin's arrival and departure times to ensure the best photographers are there," Kitty replied.

She'd wondered earlier whether Kitty planned every move Irvin made. Now Faith had her answer. Again, the thought was disheartening. She enjoyed the new clothes, the makeover and celebrity treatment, but she could never live this life.

"Off to the limo," Kitty said. "I can update both of you on what to expect when we arrive."

"That won't be necessary," Irvin said. "It'll just be Faith and me. You and the rest of the group can follow in another car."

Everyone in the room froze. So did Faith's heart, which she was sure had decided to lodge itself in her throat. Irvin held out his arm for her to take. "I'd like to get to know my date better."

Irvin walked behind Faith to the limo and wrestled with the need to haul her against his body and explore the soft skin revealed by that flimsy material she called a dress. He couldn't keep his eyes off her thighs, the hint of a flat stomach revealed between the crystals, or the fullness of her lips tinted red and glossed against her pretty brown skin. As they slid into the back of the limo, and her dress rode up her thighs when she crossed the seat, his cock stirred in his pants. It was going to be a long night if he had to pretend he wasn't interested in doing exactly what she'd accused him of earlier in the day.

"I think Kitty is going to pop a vein," Faith said once they were settled.

He glanced back at his publicist and the pinched expression on her face before the limo door closed. "Kitty likes to be in control of everything."

"And you don't have a problem with that?"

"Her efforts, no matter how pushy, are part of the reason my career continues to be so successful."

He reached for the champagne chilling in a bucket of ice and raised an eyebrow. "Would you like a glass?"

"I guess it would be ridiculous to turn down champagne in the back of a limo with a movie star."

"Only slightly ridiculous."

She glanced at the bottle before her lips curved into a smile. "It's been so long since I've had good champagne."

"Then you'll definitely have a glass."

As he opened the bottle, she reached for her small beaded handbag and pulled out her mobile phone. He expected her to take a picture of the inside of the limo or snap a selfie with him. Instead, she made a call, then frowned.

"Problem?" he asked her.

"Yeah—my parents aren't answering their phone. It's close to midnight. There's no reason for them not to answer."

The worry in her voice pricked his concern and surprised him. Once again he'd expected her to act like any other groupie and she'd done the opposite. He couldn't remember ever going on a date with a woman who was more concerned about calling her parents than having a drink with him.

"Maybe they're asleep," he said.

"No, my parents are night owls. They watch the eleven o'clock news, then stay up for *The Tonight Show*. They should be sitting in the living room now."

"Maybe they went out. It is Friday night."

She shook her head. "No, they don't go anywhere. My mama's in a wheelchair and my dad is hurt. I take care of them and go out for them. There's no reason for them to be out."

"Is there another number to call?"

She was already dialing before he got the words out. A voice came through the other end, and her shoulders sagged with relief. "Marie, what's going on? I called home, and Mama and Daddy didn't answer."

She paused as the frown on her face deepened. "The movies? What?"

There was a bottle of sparkling cider chilling next to the champagne. He opened the champagne and poured a glass for her. Then he opened the cider and poured it into a glass for himself. He sipped his drink and watched her as she had her conversation. It was interesting that it never occurred to her that her parents might want to go to a movie. She'd said she was their caretaker. Having spent the majority of his youth looking out for his mother, he could relate. He'd worried so much about taking care of his mother and trying to save his father from himself, it had taken a tragedy for him to realize he wasn't living.

She probably deserved this weekend away more than most of the women who'd entered the contest.

Her call ended, but she continued to stare at the phone as if she were waiting for a different outcome.

"I take it you found your parents," he said as he handed her the glass filled with champagne.

She took it without really looking at him. "They went to a movie. They wanted to see the new action one with all of those stars who were popular in the '80s."

"What's wrong with that?"

"They never go to the movies." She sipped from the glass. He got the impression that she did it absently. Her mind was clearly occupied with the news of her parents' outing.

"They never go, or they never tell you they want to go?"

She spun to face him, giving him an annoyed look that only increased her sex appeal. The makeup, dress, hair were all outstanding, made her a knockout. But he'd liked her better when he'd first seen her. When she had reminded him of a life away from the limelight and argued with him at the photo shoot. The look she shot him now brought some of that woman back.

"What's that supposed to mean?"

"Obviously your parents wanted to see a movie. Which leads me to believe either your parents had an epiphany and decided it was time to break their ban on going to the movies, or maybe the more obvious choice is they decided to wait for their caretaker to leave before doing so."

She sputtered as if searching for the right words to toss back at him. "They weren't waiting for me to leave."

"So they begged for you to stay?"

Her mouth opened, then snapped shut. She took another sip of the champagne, then smiled. "My mama practically pushed me out the door. I guess I keep them from doing a lot. I just worry about them. And things have been tight." She bit her lip and looked away.

He got the impression that she regretted letting that slip out. "Tight how?"

"Not tight, really. Things have been harder because of my parents' health. I've been their caretaker."

"Is that why you're no longer the chief nursing officer in Houston?"

"How did you know that?" Before he could answer, she held up a hand. "Let me guess. Kitty."

They both laughed. "Yes. She did a check on you before calling to let you know you won."

Something flittered in her eyes before she looked away and picked at the crystals on her dress. "Not surprising. She couldn't have some crazy person winning."

"Her words, not mine."

"Did she say anything else?"

"No, I told her to stop looking into your past. You're only here for a weekend. It wouldn't be right to probe into your background like that."

She looked back at him, relief and happiness clear in her wide eyes. "Thank you for being considerate of my privacy."

He shrugged as if it weren't a big deal, but he liked it when she looked at him like that. "No problem at all."

She gave him a smile that made his heart speed up in his chest. He was definitely attracted to Faith. But it wasn't a good idea to start up anything with a woman who was around for only a weekend. Come Monday, he'd never see her again, and he shouldn't invest too much in this spark he felt. Still, he found himself asking, "So things have been tight since you moved back home to take care of them?"

She nodded and sat back on the seat. She ran a finger across the top of the champagne glass. "It's been a difficult transition. My parents were very independent, and a series of accidents have made it so that they can't be."

He slid closer to her on the seat. "Are they resentful of needing the help?"

"No, they were hesitant at first and tried to downplay the amount of help they needed, but overall they're appreciative. They think I spend too much time worrying about them and not enough time worrying about myself."

How many times had his mother pushed him to get out and live his own life instead of sticking around trying to make up for his father's shortcomings? Though he didn't regret ultimately leaving London and making a success of himself, he understood the guilt that came when you took time for yourself after giving so much to others.

"How long have you been looking after them?"

"Two years."

"Is this your first vacation since going home?"

She nodded. "It is. I still can't believe that I won. I only signed up because my friend insisted and because the proceeds benefited alcohol awareness. I saw so many patients come into the hospital who were suffering from alcohol abuse. Still, I never expected to win the contest."

"So the possibility of a date with me had nothing to do with you entering?"

She sipped her champagne and gave him a shy look from the corner of her eye. "I will admit the fantasy of it all did have some appeal."

He raised his brows and chuckled. "Some appeal. Wow."

"Oh, come on. What do you want me to say?" she asked with a laugh. "That I stayed up every night praying that I'd be chosen?"

"Not quite that, but surely you were somewhat excited."

"See, that's the problem." She pointed a finger at him, but her brown eyes flashed with humor. "You're used to women throwing themselves at you. This weekend will be good for you."

"How so?"

"You need a few days with a woman who isn't trying to get something out of you. I'm more excited about seeing the city, going to a movie premiere and trying on clothes I wouldn't be caught dead in back home than in seducing the movie star."

He placed his arm on the back of her chair, making sure to let his hand brush across her shoulders, and moved closer to her. Her eyes widened and her full lips parted with a quick breath before she looked away and finished the rest of the champagne in her glass. She might talk a big game, but Faith was attracted to him, as well.

"That's the third time you've said that. Who are you trying to convince?"

"You. I know what you're up to, sliding close to me and giving me the sexy-voice-and-eyes routine."

"You think my voice is sexy?" he asked, lowering his voice an octave.

She shook her head and laughed. "Don't go all Barry White on me."

"I'd like to go all Irvin Freeman on you," he said in his regular voice. Though he tried to keep the tone light, some of his seriousness came through.

Her smile faltered, and he saw by the warming of her eyes and the catch of her breath that she'd heard it.

"Is that what you do with your leading ladies?"

Her soft, sweet drawl slid in beneath his skin and heated his insides. It had got thicker with her question. How thick would it get if he were deep inside her?

"What I do with my leading ladies is acting. I'm not acting right now. What I'm thinking and feeling is all real."

She shifted in her seat. "I don't believe you."

"Then believe this."

He lowered his head and pressed his lips against hers, with enough firmness to let her know he was serious, but lightly enough for her to pull away if she didn't want the kiss. Her body shook, and her lips parted with a gasp. He wasn't a man to pass up an opportunity, and he took the chance to deepen the kiss.

He'd never believed in electricity or sparks igniting when a man kissed a woman, but something he'd never felt before happened as he kissed her. His skin tingled, the blood rushed through his veins, and his senses heightened to everything around them. The sweet scent of her perfume, the softness of her lips, the way she tasted of champagne—all seemed amplified. And like a man who'd got a taste of something he really liked, he dived in for more.

He put his own glass down—on the tray, he hoped—and brought his hands up to feel the softness of her hair. She made a sexy whimpering noise before her own hands came up to clutch his arms. It was on after that.

He shouldn't kiss her as if they'd been lovers for years, but damn if the woman didn't kiss well. He let his hands run across her shoulders and down her sides, which were free of the crystals and allowed the heat of her skin to sear his palms. He stopped at her hips. If he went farther, he'd find it hard to stop.

She pressed closer to him. One of her hands moved from his arm to his shoulder; the other came up to clutch the back of his head. He forgot trying to slow down then. He pressed forward, hesitantly at first, and when there was no resistance, he laid her back on the seat, his body blanketing hers. He lifted her left leg and settled between her thighs. The heat that greeted him there hardened him even more.

He trailed kisses down her neck as his hand slid up her thigh until it gripped her hip so he could pull her closer. Her body twisted beneath him; soft moans and whimpers came from her lips, each one heightening his desire.

His fingers brushed the waistband of her thong. In the back of his head he acknowledged that this was getting out of hand. That he needed to stop and get things back under control. Until her hips shifted and she moaned his name. He hooked his finger in the waistband and was ready to pull it down when her hands shoved against his chest.

"We've stopped," she said and pushed him again.

He rose, and she scrambled from beneath him to the other side of the seat. "What am I doing?" she asked beneath her breath. Her hands tried to straighten her hair and she rubbed her lips, but there was no hiding what had almost happened. She had the look of a thoroughly kissed woman.

And he wanted to pull her back in his arms and finish what they'd started.

"Faith—"

"Not now. No talking about this right now."

He reached for her, but she jerked away. The car door opened and the interior lit up with the flash of dozens of camera lights. Kitty popped her head inside. She looked from one of them to the other, raised an eyebrow and gave him a smirk that said she had a pretty good idea what had happened.

"Showtime," Kitty said. "Smile for the cameras."

He turned to Faith, who met his gaze, then immediately looked away. He took her hand and gave it a reassuring squeeze. He wanted her to look at him. He wanted more time to figure out what had just happened between them. But she pulled away and hurried out of the limo. He got out beside her and waved at the awaiting crowd, putting on his practiced smile for the paparazzi.

Chapter 7

Faith entered the club on shaky legs. If it hadn't been for the flashing cameras outside and the constant attention of the people in the club, she was sure her weak knees would have caused her to hit the floor. No need to fall on her face and be the woman who'd lost all of her pride. She was already the woman who'd quickly become a liar when Irvin kissed her.

Smile. Walk in a straight line. Don't sweat.

She repeated her mantra to keep her mind off what had happened. Irvin Freeman had kissed her. She'd made out with him in the back of a limo as if they were teenagers on prom night. And instead of being embarrassed for doing it, she kind of hated they'd been interrupted. Which was the dumbest thing she'd ever felt. He must think she was full of crap. One minute spouting off about not wanting him, then practically letting him have sex with her two minutes later. She knew she shouldn't have come to New York.

She lifted a hand to smooth her hair, even though Kitty had given her a quick fix before they'd entered. Between the mussed hair, wobbly legs, rumpled dress and swollen lips, it wouldn't take a rocket scientist to figure out that Irvin Freeman had already had a little fun with his prize winner.

Heat crept up her cheeks. What was she doing? Playing this game she didn't know how to handle. He'd forget all about her, and she'd return home as just the latest in the line of women who'd slept with him.

Beside her, Irvin bent over until his lips brushed the outer shell of her ear. "If you keep looking guilty, people will know that I kissed you."

She jumped and stepped away. "I don't look guilty."

"You keep checking your hair, pulling your dress and touching your lips. All the signs of a woman caught kissing."

Her hand froze in the middle of smoothing her hair. She dropped it and lifted her chin. "Point taken. How am I supposed to look?"

"Let's go for enjoying yourself."

The thing was, she wasn't sure if she could enjoy herself with all the thoughts about kissing Irvin going through her head.

"Okay, what do you want to do first?" The heated look he gave her was a sign he wasn't thinking about hitting up the bar. "I mean, who would you like to talk with first?"

"Let's get to our table. Then look around to see who else is here tonight."

The club was dazzling. Black and white tiles covering the floor, oak ceilings, leather sofas around marble tables, gold and black walls. The place was packed, and as she looked around, she had to bite her lip to stop herself from gawking at all the celebrities there. It wasn't long before they were at a table close enough to the bar to be seen but far enough away to avoid the crowd around it.

She sat next to Irvin, and the rest of his entourage surrounded the two of them. The group spoke with him but didn't really get too close.

"Are these all your friends?" she asked.

He'd leaned in to hear her question over the music. After having been covered by his body a few minutes earlier, the nearness of him sent heat skittering across her skin and wetness pooling between her legs.

"I know all of their names and the members of their families, and I spend most of my nights out with them, but no, they aren't my friends," he said. Again he spoke close to her ear, and his warm breath sent tingles through her body.

"Do you have any friends?"

His eyebrows rose, and immediately she felt bad for asking. It wasn't her business if he had friends. "Sorry, prying is one of my not-so-lovable traits." She turned away to look at the people in the club.

"I have a few friends," he said. "But for a celebrity of my stature, it looks better to travel with more than two people around you."

She spun back to him and frowned. "Are you really that conceited?"

"Kitty's words, not mine."

"You use her words a lot. Don't you ever get tired of living by your publicist's philosophy? What would Irvin prefer?"

He didn't answer. He just stared at her for several seconds. His silence made her uncomfortable. Prying and insulting him were the perfect ways to make sure he didn't kiss her again. Too bad that hadn't been part of her plan.

They were interrupted by the arrival of a group of people.

"Irvin, I thought that was you," a woman said.

They both looked up. A huge, warm grin came across Irvin's handsome face. "Selena." He stood and the two embraced.

Selena Jones was beautiful in movies but dazzling in person. Tall, thin, with the grace of a ballerina, the Brazilian actress was most men's fantasy. And the woman reportedly linked to Irvin.

"This is Faith Logan, the lucky winner of a weekend in New York with me," Irvin said after he and Selena broke apart.

"It's nice to meet you, Faith," Selena said, a genuine smile on her perfect face. "May we join you?"

"Of course." Faith slid over in the booth. What was she supposed to say? *I just kissed your boyfriend, so it might be kind of awkward*?

Irvin slid in next to Faith, with Selena on his other side. Faith prepared herself for an evening of watching the two lovebirds completely ignore her. Instead, Selena drew her into conversation, and the rest of the group at their table brought up the next film Irvin and Selena were going to start shooting in Canada the following week. Selena didn't seem possessive of Irvin or unfriendly toward Faith, and before long, Faith forgot about feeling awkward and began to enjoy herself.

The entire experience was like a dream. Rappers, models, actors, singers and reality stars all came by the table to speak. Some she loved, others she hated, but after having a conversation with a hip-hop mogul and his superstar wife, she was thoroughly starstruck.

She could even forget for a few minutes that she'd easily fallen under Irvin's spell in the limo when her favorite television star asked her if she wanted to dance.

After shaking her body on the dance floor, she was introduced to an R & B singer she'd idolized since her teenage years. She knew she'd be embarrassed later for nearly crying when she met her and going on about how she'd related to her albums since her first one came out when Faith was fourteen. But thankfully, the singer accepted Faith's fangirl moment with aplomb and even laughed when Faith joked about trying to dye her hair platinum blond to be like her.

She stopped short of asking if she could take a picture with the woman, but was grateful when someone else suggested it.

After snapping the picture, Faith didn't care how much of a Kool-Aid smile she had on her face as she walked to the bar and ordered a bottled water.

"You're so lucky," a woman said next to her.

Faith turned to the woman, who was tall and curvy with long, dark hair highlighted blond. Faith recognized her as one of the women who'd been hovering around Irvin's table in hopes of taking a picture with him.

The woman grinned, revealing even white teeth. "You won the weekend with Irvin. I entered one hundred times and didn't win."

Faith's jaw dropped. "A hundred times?"

"Yeah, but I'm a big fan." The woman lowered her eyes and flicked her long hair over her shoulder. "Anyway, I just wanted to say congratulations. Enjoy your weekend."

"Yeah, thanks," Faith said. The woman gave her a tight smile, then walked away. Faith shook her head. *One hundred times?* She'd known Irvin had a big fan base, but to enter the contest that much... Faith couldn't imagine living with so many people obsessed with her life.

Irvin strolled over with two guys. She recognized one as the singer Dante Wilson and the other as a professional basketball player. She didn't follow basketball and didn't know his name, but he was hot right now and in every commercial out there. Dante was dressed casually in jeans and a screen-printed T-shirt, while the basketball player wore dark pants, a white shirt and a gray blazer.

Irvin gave her a smile that nearly melted her like hot candle wax. It seemed like the kind of smile a guy wore when he spotted his woman. Happy, bright, promising that even better things were sure to come. He was such a good actor, because it couldn't be genuine, but his smile made her wonder what the weekend would be like if it were.

"You haven't asked for a picture with me, yet you seem to float in the air when you take a picture with every other celebrity," he said with mock hurt.

"What can I say? Tonight's been amazing."

He turned to the guys. "Faith, I'd like you to meet Dante Wilson and Jacobe Jenkins. Gentlemen, let me introduce you to Faith Logan. She is the beautiful woman you both were asking about earlier, and she also had the misfortune to have her name selected as my date for the weekend."

The guys chuckled before directing their attention to her. Their appreciative looks threw her off. She couldn't believe she had three handsome, rich and single men all focused on her. Nor could she believe the two newcomers had asked about her. And if they had, what on earth had Irvin said about her?

"Very nice to meet you, Faith," Dante said. "You're the lucky winner. You must be very excited that your name was selected."

"It was a surprise," she said. "I only entered to support the foundation. I really didn't expect to win."

"But it isn't too much of a hardship," Jacobe said with a grin.

"I wouldn't be so sure," Irvin cut in. "On the way over, she was telling me her only reason for entering was to support the cause. I'm fairly sure she would be just as excited if I were completely cut from this entire weekend."

"Oh, really?" Dante asked. "Not many women say that. Maybe you're just what he needs."

"That's doubtful," she said. "I'll leave on Sunday, and this will just be another packed promotional weekend for him."

Jacobe smirked. "You've already made a big impression on my man. I think he'll remember this weekend."

The comment froze her insides. She quickly got an idea of what Irvin might have said to them about her. They must know about the kiss and how quickly she'd contradicted herself. She gripped her bag, embarrassment and anger coursing through her body. Why she should have expected him to keep what had happened to himself, she didn't know. There was nothing special between them. She was just another groupie for him to have a little fun with. Of course he would tell his friends what had happened.

"Are you having a good time?" Dante asked.

"Actually, I think I need some air. A few minutes away from all this would be nice. Is there anywhere to go that isn't as crowded?"

"You can go on the roof. There's seating up there, but

only a few of us have access, so it's not as crowded," Irvin said. "I can take you."

She didn't want to go somewhere less crowded with him, but she had little choice. "That'll work. Then you can come back down to the party. I'd like to be alone."

He frowned, and his friends exchanged looks. "Excuse us," Irvin said. He took her elbow and led her away from them. She immediately pulled out of his grip. She felt his gaze on her, but she didn't meet it. She'd made a mistake falling for his charm earlier. She was not going to do it again.

Faith followed Irvin to the office of the club owner. He was a tall, handsome man with golden-brown skin and the smoothness that came with spending his time catering to the rich and famous.

"I'd like to go to the roof, Calvin," Irvin said. "My date needs some air."

Calvin raised a brow and gave Faith a brief once-over. "Well, this is a first. Follow me."

The statement seemed odd, but she didn't have time to consider it. She just wanted to get out of the heat and the crowd and then dismiss Irvin back to Selena and his friends. Maybe they'd all have a good laugh about the country girl who easily fell for his lines.

Calvin took them through a door in his office that led to a staircase. He smiled at Faith, a kind and genuine smile, and she couldn't help but return it. "Enjoy the view."

Irvin placed a hand on her back and directed her to the stairs. She tried not to focus on how good his hand felt through the skimpy material of her dress by reminding herself that he'd bragged about kissing her to his friends.

She failed miserably.

They walked out onto the roof, and Faith gasped. "It's beautiful," she said. White lights were strung around the roof, and small lanterns cast a soft glow on the cushioned chairs. The music from the club played softly in the background, allowing the few people there to have intimate conversations. The shining lights of the New York skyline added to the view.

"I'm surprised everyone isn't up here," she said, following Irvin to one of the vacant cushioned seating areas, but they didn't sit.

"Calvin only grants a few people access. It's where I come when I need a break from the crowd and whatnot."

"Why only a select few?"

"Because it's for those who really want to escape the attention. Not for people who just want to say they have access to another exclusive area of a club."

She glanced around at the skyline. The breeze blew her hair in her face, and she tucked it behind her ear. "You must not use it often." When she glanced back at him, he wore a confused look. "The 'this is a first' comment from Calvin."

"He didn't mean me. He meant I brought you. It's rare to bring someone who doesn't have access with you. Too easy for a person to brag about being part of the so-called 'in crowd.'"

"How do you know I won't brag?"

"For some reason, I trust you won't. It doesn't seem your style."

The softly spoken words, the night air and the twinkling lights were all sucking her back into his spell. She turned away before she found herself in his arms again.

"You can go back to the club now," she told him. "I'd rather be alone."

"I'd rather stay and find out why you're suddenly acting so cold." He made a motion to a server she hadn't noticed standing off in the shadows. When the guy came over, Irvin ordered a bottle of champagne.

"I'm not being cold," she said after the server walked away. "And if I were, it's not like you don't deserve it."

"Because I kissed you?" He sat down.

She crossed her arms. "That and because it's obvious that you let the rest of your celebrity group know about it. Did you have a good laugh about it, or did you make bets on how soon you'd score?"

The server returned with the champagne. He uncorked it and poured two glasses before melting back into the shadows. All the while, Irvin clenched his jaw, and she could have sworn there was frustration in his eyes.

"I didn't tell them about what happened in the back of the limo," he finally said, reaching for his glass and sipping while looking away from her to the beautiful view.

"Really? Then what was the comment about you not forgetting this weekend?"

"I told them both to back off when they asked about the sexy woman on the dance floor." He looked at her and said it as casually as he'd ordered the champagne. "I didn't like that, and I made it known."

"I'm not yours," she said. Her breathless voice gave away the whirlwind inside her that his words had stirred up.

"Maybe not." He took a sip of the champagne but watched her the entire time, his dark eyes seductive in the low light. "But after that kiss, I find myself wishing you were."

The breeze might as well have come from a hair dryer;

it did nothing to cool her off. Her heart pounded like the bass of the music. Unable to trust her knees, she slowly sat on the edge of the seat and reached for her own glass.

"You're teasing me again," she said. "And I don't like it." It was one of the biggest lies she'd ever told. She liked what he'd said way too much.

"I'm not teasing you. I believe in fate, destiny, whatever you want to call it. It's the reason you're here this weekend instead of some mindless groupie."

"I don't believe in fate. If it's real, fate is good at kneeing you in the stomach and laughing at your pain. The only thing that brought us together was a random drawing."

"A random drawing doesn't explain this attraction... or that kiss."

Why, oh, why did that man have to say *kiss* like that? Silky smooth and soft enough to make her immediately remember how good his lips had felt on hers.

She didn't answer, couldn't answer. She couldn't explain the attraction. Sure, he was a sexy-as-hell movie star, and most women in America would have taken PMS for life for one night with him. But she'd never been drawn to a man just by his looks. If she'd come here and Irvin had turned out to be the jerk she'd first taken him for, he might as well have been Freddy Krueger. But he hadn't. He'd been nice, kind of funny and able to laugh at his own celebrity. He'd apologized for his assumption and had been nothing but charming and honest since then.

But she couldn't fall for it. She'd thought she'd found a total package before, and he'd turned out to be runner-up for asshole of the year. So what if there was a spark of attraction? Come Monday, Irvin would be off to Canada with his on-again, off-again, beautiful costar.

"Unless…" His words broke into her thoughts. "…you kissed me because of who I am. Unless it isn't attraction on your end, and you are just another woman waiting to go home and tell everyone you almost made love with Irvin Freeman in the back of a limo."

"That isn't why I kissed you," she said quickly. "I wouldn't do that."

"Then why?" He slid closer. The man knew how to penetrate a woman's defenses. She couldn't keep her guard up when he was so close to her. "Did you kiss Irvin the star, or did you kiss me because you feel this thing as much as I do?"

Her insides quivered. Desire blossomed between her legs, and she held her champagne flute with shaky hands.

"I feel it." When he moved closer, she slid away. She faced him and shook her head. "But I don't trust it. This isn't meant to be more than a weekend of fun. I don't want to be that girl you slept with on a promotional weekend, and I really don't want to walk into something that might hurt me in the long run. I don't know your true dating history—just what's printed in the tabloids—but I can guarantee a weekend fling wouldn't change your life as much as it would mine. I can't handle that."

His dark eyes searched hers. Then his gaze moved away to follow every feature of her face. He finally smiled and brushed the back of his hand across her cheek. "I understand. So, we'll have fun and get to know each other over the weekend."

"Without the kissing."

"I'll try, but I make no promises." The smile he gave her made her want to sigh and melt into his chest.

He leaned back in the chair. "Tell me about your life before your mum got sick. Do you miss it?"

"Sometimes. I loved my job in Houston. It was challenging and was taking me on the fast track to success. But honestly, it wasn't until I came home and started working as a shift nurse that I realized how much I missed working with patients."

"I take it from your surprise about the movies that you don't go out much. Did you before?"

"In Houston I did. Fund-raisers, galas, luncheons. Every weekend there was some reason to get dressed up and hit the town." She glanced down at the crystals on her dress sparkling in the low light. "Though you were right about one thing. I wouldn't have gone out in this dress."

"Was there a guy? Is there a guy?"

"There was a guy." She frowned. "We split after I came home."

"The distance?"

"No, the sleeping with the woman who took my old position. She fit his image more."

"Was he a celebrity?"

"No, worse—a man with political ambitions," she said with an eye roll. "He was the county treasurer, and as chief nursing officer, I had a lot of connections with our legislative delegation. He dated, then married the state senator's daughter who took the job after me. Now Corey is state treasurer."

She swallowed her champagne to push back the bitterness she felt. She hadn't missed Corey as much as she'd expected when she returned home. A part of her accepted that their relationship was coming to an end. She just hadn't expected him to jump in bed with another woman the same week she said she wasn't coming back.

"Then he's a prat."

"A what?"

"Idiot."

She nodded. "Well, prat or not, he's history," she said. "Now it's a quiet life for me."

He nodded, a serious expression covering his handsome face. "Must be nice. I'm always running from one place to the next, always in front of a camera. Sometimes I miss the anonymity I had before I was famous."

"That's a lie and you know it."

His eyebrows drew together. Maybe she'd overstepped her bounds by saying it, but that prying part of her was popping out again.

"Why would you say that?" he asked.

"I watch enough television to know some celebrities get more media attention than others. And the ones who get the most cater to the cameras and paparazzi. Kitty and your entourage prove you're a caterer."

"It keeps my career relevant."

"It keeps you in the public eye."

"That doesn't mean I couldn't be happy with a simple life. Maybe on a farm with a wife, kids and a dog?"

She actually laughed out loud. "Now you're confusing yourself with the guy you played in that movie last year. I can't see you as the farmer type at all."

He didn't seem to take offense at her laughter, and he actually chuckled. "You're right about the farm. But I do get tired of the constant pressure. I'm trying to break into directing. Start my life behind the camera instead of in front of it."

"Would you be happy with that?"

"Yes," he said without hesitation. "I needed to reinvent myself, and I have. Now I want to get back a bit of the Irvin I was before. I wouldn't be a farmer, but I could see myself in some secluded house in the country. No longer having to make club appearances and being known for how many shirtless scenes I have in a movie."

"You had to predict the fame that would result from being an actor," she said.

"The thing is, I didn't expect to become such a success. I came over to America and needed a job, any job. A mate suggested I make easy money being an extra in this play. I liked it, so I tried for a few parts and got them, surprisingly. Then I met Kitty, and before I knew it, my career took off."

"You can always walk away from it for a while and pursue directing."

"It's not that easy. I'm supposed to be in Canada next week to start filming another movie."

"Then walk away after that."

His eyes narrowed in on her before he turned away and put down his champagne glass. He'd taken a few sips but didn't drink it all. She hadn't said anything, but she noticed that he'd drunk cider in the back of the limo. She wanted to ask why but decided not to. Getting to know him too personally wasn't part of the agenda.

"Let's get out of here," he said.

She thought of going back into the crowded club. Sure, she'd had fun mingling with the stars, but right now she enjoyed the quiet. And her conversation with Irvin.

"I guess we should get back to Kitty," she said.

"No, I mean let's get out of here altogether. Just the two of us."

Faith hesitated. She didn't trust how comfortable things felt between them. Being alone with him made it easy to forget that. "I'm not sure."

"Would you rather leave with Kitty?"

She cringed and shook her head. "No."

"Then trust me."

He held out his hand. She met his gaze as her mind seemed to jump back and forth from her preconceptions about him to the man he really was. "Is that possible, to leave without her?"

"I don't just dream of walking away from the spotlight. I've found ways to avoid it."

"How?"

"New York is a massive city. Anyone can become a face in the crowd."

She was in New York with a handsome movie star who wanted to show her a good time. Hadn't she promised herself she'd enjoy this weekend? Pushing aside her worries, she put her hand in his.

The smile he gave her was dazzling in its intensity. "Come on, cutie. I'm going to show you how I walk away from it all."

Chapter 8

"We'd like to leave," Irvin said to Calvin.

The club owner stopped scrolling through his tablet and looked up at them from the seat behind his desk. He didn't speak for a few seconds, just looked between Irvin and Faith. Though his expression was blank, Irvin knew Calvin thought he was out of his mind. If he were Calvin, he'd think the same thing. The private exit out of the club was kept private for a reason. Letting Faith see it not only compromised other celebrities' ability to leave by avoiding the waiting crowds but also compromised Calvin's reputation of being able to offer that service to his most distinguished clients.

Irvin hoped his instincts were right about Faith. He believed she wouldn't run to the media and talk about everything that happened this weekend for a few extra dollars.

Calvin finally set the tablet on the desk and rose from his seat. "I'll show you out."

Faith gave Irvin a questioning look that he answered with a smile. Calvin led them to the other door in his office, which opened to an empty hallway. At the end of the hallway was a freight elevator.

"You know your way," Calvin said to Irvin. He turned to Faith. "I'm sure we'll meet again."

Faith gave him a doubtful look but held out her hand. "It was nice meeting you."

"Tell Kitty I'll call," Irvin said to Calvin.

"I'm afraid one day she's going to really hurt me for doing this." But Calvin's grin said he wasn't afraid at all.

The two men shook hands, and as Calvin went back into his office, Irvin placed his hand on the small of Faith's back and guided her down the hall to the elevator.

"Where do we go from here?" Faith asked.

"We take the lift down to the basement, which is connected to the building behind the club. From there, we go up another lift into that building and exit."

"Won't Selena miss you?"

Irvin laughed. Selena was probably busy doing her own exit. "No, she won't miss me."

Faith looked down the hall toward Calvin's office door and back at the elevator, a frown on her cute face. "And no one knows celebrities sneak out this way?"

Irvin pressed the button to open the elevator door. Once inside, he inputted the code for the basement and turned to her with a grin. "So far we've been good. Paparazzi stalk the entrance and marked exit on the side of the club, but they don't tend to walk around the block to see who's coming out of this building."

The ride down was swift. They exited into the brightly lit basement and crossed through another door into the connecting building. From there they got on another lift and took it up to the first floor of the adjacent building.

"How do you keep people from seeing you leave from here?"

"Calvin owns this building. It has offices and event space he rents out on the top floor. If there was an event going on, he would've warned us. Otherwise, it's normally empty on the weekends."

He pulled off his jacket and passed it to her. "Still, you'd better put this on. No one will be able to ignore you in that dress."

She slid her arms into the sleeves, which went well past her wrists, and pulled it tight. Immediately he missed the enticing sight of her skin beneath the sheer material. Thankfully her sexy legs were still visible.

"No one will know who I am regardless of this dress. But how in the world can you stop people from noticing you? You're the most wanted man in America."

He stepped close to her. Close enough to smell her sweet perfume and see that her eyes were a lighter shade of brown than he'd originally thought. She tugged the jacket closer around her. She looked both nervous and expectant. He'd promised not to kiss her again, and he would keep that promise. For now.

He took a pair of shades out of the pocket of his jacket. When he stepped back, she quickly looked away. He wasn't sure if it was relief or disappointment she tried to hide. He then slid out the hat he'd tucked into the back of his pants and pulled it low over his eyes.

"Am I inconspicuous now?" he asked, holding out his arms.

She covered her mouth and laughed. "Hardly. I don't see how anyone wouldn't recognize you."

He took her hand and led her down the hall to the

front of the building. "Because no one is looking for me. Just wait and see."

"I take it you slip in and out of places unnoticed quite often."

"It drives Kitty crazy."

As expected, the adjacent lobby was empty except for one of Calvin's security guards at the front desk. He gave a slight wave to Irvin before pressing the button to unlock the front door. It was well after two in the morning, but so close to Times Square there were still plenty of people on the sidewalks. The honks of horns from the vehicles in the crowded streets punctuated the night.

He wrapped an arm around her shoulders and pulled her close to his side. They joined the crowd on the sidewalk. He expected her to pull away. Instead, she wrapped an arm around his waist and fell into step with him.

"I'm surprised you didn't tell Calvin he wouldn't be seeing you again."

She kept her head down as they walked. "I figured saying that would only increase his discomfort. It was pretty obvious he wasn't tickled by the idea of letting me use your secret exit. He must really trust your judgment."

"He was one of the first people I met when I moved to New York. He knows I wouldn't put him out like that if I wasn't sure what I was doing."

"I was thinking," she said. "He could charge whatever he wants for secret exits and secluded rooftop tables."

"Calvin opened his club as a place for adults to hang out without a bunch of young kids starting a fight every night. He didn't expect it to become the celebrity hangout it's turned into." His own regret crept into his voice. Calvin's club had risen in popularity at the same time Irvin's fame had.

"He can't dislike that completely. It's made him successful."

"True, but he's a private man who has cameramen hanging around his business constantly. He understands the need for an escape."

"I guess I can understand that."

She lifted her head and looked around, an eager smile on her lips. "Are we going to Times Square?"

Her excitement was infectious, but first he had to make sure no one had spotted them.

"Eventually. I haven't yet worked my magic to blend into the crowd."

She chuckled. "What's next? A fake mustache to go with the shades and hat?"

"Something more subtle," he said. Then he slowed. "We're here."

"This building?"

"No, this corner."

Irvin walked over to a man sitting on a bucket at the side of the building. He had a patched-together easel in front of him and used charcoal to sketch the surrounding buildings and street corner.

"How's it going, Carl?" Irvin said to the man.

Carl stopped sketching and grinned, revealing a crooked-toothed smile. His brown suit sported a few worn spots, and in the dark Irvin couldn't tell if it was clean.

"My man Freeman. I was wondering if you were coming by tonight," Carl said, leaning his elbow onto his knee.

"You almost didn't get me," he said, taking one of the buckets next to Carl and flipping it upside down. "I had to go to a party."

Carl took a look at Faith beside him. "Skipping out on me for a hot date?"

"You could say that." He pulled Faith forward. "Faith Logan, this is Carl."

Faith smiled and reached out her hand. "Nice to meet you, Carl."

Carl grinned first at Faith then at Irvin. "She's pretty, and Southern, too. Where are you from, Faith?"

"South Carolina, the Upstate near Greenville."

Carl nodded and crinkled his brow. "I've been to Charlotte before."

Faith chuckled. "That's North Carolina, but that's okay."

"There's nothing like a Southern girl, Freeman. You better treat her good tonight."

Faith gave Irvin a quick glance. "He's done well so far."

Irvin's brows rose. "A compliment! I should have taken you away from that party hours ago."

"I don't mind giving them when they're deserved. Not just because they're expected," she said with a cute grin.

Carl leaned forward. "This is the first time Freeman has introduced me to one of his lady friends. It's a special occasion."

Faith gave Irvin another one of her shy glances. "Is it, now?"

"Mind if we sit with you for a while?" Irvin asked.

"Not at all, Freeman. I'll even draw your picture while you're here." Carl was already pulling down the canvas with the landscape and putting up a blank one that was propped against the building behind him.

Irvin looked from Carl to Faith. "Do you mind?"

Her mouth twisted into a half smile, and she shrugged. "Why not?"

Right then and there he realized he was right to trust her. Many women wouldn't enjoy sitting on a corner with his nearly homeless friend. She hadn't hesitated or batted an eye. He was liking her more and more each minute.

"Looks like you've got a client, Carl," Irvin said.

Carl rubbed his hands together. "Then have a seat and let me get started."

Irvin sat on the overturned bucket.

"Where's the lady gonna sit?" Carl asked with a grin.

Irvin took Faith's hand and pulled her down into his lap. "It can seat two."

Faith wiggled on his lap. "You think you're sly."

"I'm too direct to be sly. I just like the idea of you sitting on my lap."

Carl chucked. "My man Freeman."

"Did you go by the place today, Carl?" Irvin asked.

Carl shook his head and began sketching. "Not today."

"You know it's there waiting whenever you're ready," he said.

"I know, Freeman. One day I'll take you up on it."

"One day soon, I hope," Irvin said.

Faith gave him a questioning look, but he shook his head. With a nod she turned back to Carl. "How long have you been drawing, Carl?"

That was all it took to get his friend started. Before long, she had him telling stories about all of the interesting things he saw while sitting on corners around the city, drawing pictures. The more she conversed with Carl, the more Irvin believed fate had selected her to win his contest for a reason.

Whenever he left Calvin's club, he'd sit beside Carl and blend into the background. His friend normally camped out here on Friday nights, especially if he knew Irvin was going to be in the vicinity. People didn't pay much attention to two guys sitting on a corner drawing sketches of the city. He'd watched several cameramen walk right by, too busy looking for Irvin in the crowd to notice him right beneath their noses.

It was a welcome moment of quiet, but tonight Irvin couldn't enjoy it as all of Faith's soft curves in his lap drove him mad. Every time she shifted, his erection swelled. It brought back memories of how her body had cushioned his earlier in the limo and made him want to do a lot more than have her sit on his lap.

Faith shifted again, bringing her bum firmly against his erection. She froze, then tried to move away. He gripped her waist and pulled her back. He watched her pulse flutter at the base of her neck. She brought a hand to her chest and rubbed as if she were having a heart attack. He could relate. His heart pounded hard, too.

She kept talking while he watched her. The people passing by, the hum of the city—all became nothing. There was only Faith, her soft body and her sweet fragrance.

Suddenly she jumped from his lap. "Sorry, Carl, I'm getting a back cramp," she said, rubbing her lower back.

"I got a good start," Carl said. "I can finish this later and give it to Irvin the next time I see him. I think you're clear to take off, Freeman."

Reluctantly Irvin stood. "I did promise to show her Times Square," he said.

"You've never seen Times Square before?" Carl asked.

Faith shook her head and stuffed her hands into the

pockets of his jacket. "I have not. I've traveled throughout the Southeast, but this is my first trip to New York."

"Then he better show you a good time," Carl said.

Irvin wrapped his arm around her shoulders. She didn't stiffen or pull away, just relaxed into the embrace. He didn't think too hard about how much he liked it. "I'll make sure she does."

He pulled out his wallet and took out several bills. "For the portrait."

Carl shook his head. "You know you don't have to pay me."

"Still, I want you to have it." He held the money out, but when Carl hesitated, Irvin dropped the bills in Carl's art case. "I'll see you around, Carl."

"You two have a good time," Carl said with a wave.

Faith waved back as he led her away. "Have a good night, Carl."

"You too, beautiful," Carl called back.

As they walked in silence Irvin tried to make sense of what he was feeling. He'd experienced lust before. But this was different. He didn't just want the woman beside him. He wanted to get behind the walls she surrounded herself with. Even though she'd kissed him back, she'd wished she hadn't. She didn't deny that there was an attraction between them, but then she asked him to ignore it.

He was a man and a celebrity; he'd had his share of weekend flings. She was right—he easily moved on afterward. He never had an urge to keep up with the woman once the affair had run its course. Faith was wrong about one thing, though. He doubted he'd walk away from an affair with her without consequences. Faith wouldn't be so easy to dismiss from his thoughts.

"Do you always give him money?" Faith asked after several minutes.

"Not all the time. Sometimes I bring him food. It's nothing."

"Your nothing probably is a big something for him." They walked in silence for a few more minutes. "How did you end up hanging out with him?"

He shrugged. "It just kind of happened. One day I was trying to dodge a cameraman and saw Carl sitting there, drawing. I tossed my coat in the trash, slid on the hat I keep in my pocket, sat down next to him and asked for a portrait. He studied me for a while, then told me I needed to face him more so he could get a good angle. That put my back to the cameraman, who walked right by us." They paused to let traffic through, then crossed 34th Street. "Another day I left the club early but saw a few paparazzi on the corner. They don't know about the exit, so they didn't notice me. I walked a few blocks, and there was Carl again. Then I started noticing him around the city. If I could, I'd sit with him, and if I couldn't without attracting attention, I didn't. We started talking after a while, and here we are."

"Does he realize who you are?"

"I don't think he did at first. Then one day he said I resembled a guy in a picture he found and pulled out an issue of the *New York Post* with a picture of me."

"What did you say?"

"Just said it was interesting."

"And he hasn't ratted you out."

"No, he hasn't."

"Where's he from?"

"New Jersey. He lost his job, family and home because he's an alcoholic."

"Has he stopped drinking?"

"He struggles with it. It's why he's still homeless. I rented a place for him, but he only goes there when he's sober." Irvin took a deep breath and pulled her closer. "He hasn't been in weeks. I'm hoping one day he'll stay for good. But he's got to do it on his own, you know. I learned that watching my father."

"Your dad drinks?"

He shook his head, trying to shake out the regret of his past. "My father drank. He died ten years ago."

"I'm sorry. Is that why you try to help Carl, because you couldn't help your dad?"

He stopped and turned to stare at her. They were almost in the heart of Times Square, but he didn't notice the lights or the noise. Just her beautiful face and her softly seductive words punching right to the heart of something he never wanted to admit even to himself.

"Maybe, in a way. I know from experience you can't make someone struggling with addiction quit unless they want to."

"No, you can't." Her voice rang with regret. Then she shrugged. "But it's nice that you're trying to help him."

"What can I say? He lets me hide out with him, so it's the least I can do."

The smile she gave him was brighter than all the lights surrounding them. "I think you're all right, Irvin Freeman." She leaned up and kissed his cheek.

He ran his hands up her arms, wishing he could feel her skin instead of the jacket. "I think we better get moving before I show you how to really break that no-kissing promise we made earlier."

She didn't reply, yet her eyes said she wanted him, too. He lowered his head. Anticipation at tasting her lips again urged him on. A group of people bumped into her as they passed. She jerked forward, and he placed a steadying hand on her arm as the rest of the group of twentysomething kids rushed by. They wore T-shirts with Greek fraternity letters and chanted what must be their mantra. Faith rolled her eyes and grinned.

"Oh, to be young," she said.

He returned her smile, while inside he hated that the moment was broken. "Come on. Let's see the bright lights of the big city."

Chapter 9

It was after four when they finally left Times Square. Faith had to admit it was a sight to behold at least once in a lifetime. And once was about all she needed. Even this late, the Square was as bright as daylight and so crowded it hummed with an excitement that she felt in her bones. They'd managed to blend in with the crowd. Every time people gave him a double take and looked ready to ask if he was who they thought he was, he and Faith were able to blend into the crowd first.

They'd sat and watched the people, he'd bought her an outrageously good cupcake from a local bakery, she'd flirted with a police officer at the NYPD station beneath lit billboards higher than any building back home, and they'd even given tips to the street performance artists. Though why you had to pay to take a picture with some-one who invited you to take one, she still didn't quite understand.

"You know that's a racket," Faith said. They were walking down Broadway, back toward her hotel. The crowd and excitement from earlier were fading away as the night turned into morning.

"What is?" He had his arm around her shoulders. During the walk, she'd snaked her arm around his waist.

She didn't know when it had happened, but somewhere between the rooftop and her cupcake, she'd lost her apprehension about opening herself to him. His sense of humor, the way he didn't make a big deal out of his celebrity, his kindness. Her plans to not get close chipped away like cheap nail polish.

"The people in Halloween costumes or body paint asking for tips to take their pictures," she said.

"I don't belittle anyone's hustle," he said.

"I get that, but the one guy who just painted his face silver and could barely walk wanted me to give him five dollars for a dance. No, sir."

Irvin's smooth laugh filtered through the early-morning air. "I'll agree with you on that. But that lady did deserve a tip."

She slapped his stomach with the palm of her hand. "You would say that." She thought about the woman who was naked except for pink-and-blue body paint, a G-string and a showgirl headdress. Faith couldn't imagine doing that, but had to admit it took guts to put it all out there for the whole world to see. "Maybe she did deserve something," she agreed with a laugh.

"Did you enjoy yourself?"

"I did. Seeing Times Square on television doesn't do it justice."

"So you'll be back?"

She shook her head. "Not for a while. It was fun, but way too crowded for me."

"You can come to New York and not go to Times Square."

Making a return trip was the problem. It would take a lot of time and funds she couldn't spare to plan a vacation for her and her parents here. "Who knows when I'll make it back to New York?"

He stopped and turned her to face him. "Maybe you'll have a reason to come back quickly."

Was he hinting that *he* would be that reason? The idea touched her heart and set off an intense pang of longing. They'd had a wonderful night. Admittedly, there was a spark between them. Maybe if they were in the same social circle, or it was remotely feasible that a movie star would fall for a small-town nurse, they could actually become a couple.

Standing there with her hands in his and still wearing her designer dress, she could almost pretend that this could work.

"Maybe I will."

His eyebrow quirked, desire flared in his eyes, and the corner of his lips rose in the smile that melted female hearts from New York to New Delhi.

He lowered his head, brushed the tip of her nose with his, and her breath caught. She wanted him to kiss her. Screw it—she wanted him to do a lot more than kiss her. The way she was feeling, she wondered if she should take this fantasy as far as it could go.

Dark eyes stared into hers. He tilted his head and leaned in close. His lips barely brushed hers when a loud clang startled them both. They jumped apart and turned to the noise. Faith's heart pounded, not from the noise but from the broken anticipation of kissing Irvin again.

A couple who looked to be in their late fifties were bent over trying to pick up hundreds of tiny sheets of paper. A metal bowl, which must have held the papers, spun in fast circles before it finally stopped.

The few people still on the street with them hurried past without helping. Faith frowned and rushed over.

"Can I help you?"

The couple exchanged a look before eyeing her warily, but that didn't stop Faith from bending down and picking up the various scraps of paper.

"Thank you so much," the woman finally said. She had kindly blue eyes, and her salt-and-pepper hair was pulled away from her face by a headband. She wore a long-sleeve white shirt and slim-fitting blue jeans.

"It's no problem at all. If I were at home, everyone who saw this would have stopped to help."

"Where are you from?" the man asked. He was trying to get the pieces that had fallen into a puddle in the gutter.

"South Carolina."

"Ah, I should have known," the woman said, smiling. "The accent. I have a cousin who lives in Atlanta. Have you been there?"

Faith laughed and shook her head. Apparently South Carolina didn't exist to people in New York. "Yes, but it's about three hours from where I stay."

By then Irvin had come over and got the last pieces of paper and the metal bowl. They placed the handful of dirty papers into the bowl then handed it to the lady.

"Now they're ruined," the woman said with a sigh.

"It'll be okay. We'll rework them as we go," the guy said, though the tone of his voice didn't support his reassuring words.

"What were they?" Irvin asked.

The woman pointed to a shop next to them. "This is our flower shop. And these—" she held up the bowl

"—were the greeting cards for our orders today. Our girl who normally writes them quit suddenly, and we spent the night putting them together." She looked at the guy and sighed. "All of that work."

"Can't you rewrite them as they go out?" Faith asked. She had no clue about how a flower shop operated, but she assumed it shouldn't be too hard to scribble a few lines before attaching them to a bouquet.

The guy straightened his shoulders. "Of course not. We are Belles Fleurs. We create beautiful bouquets, and they're accompanied by a card with handwritten calligraphy. We can't just write them quickly."

"I've ordered flowers from you before," Irvin said. "Your cards are your signature."

The man grinned, apparently mollified by Irvin's recognition. "Then you know the effort that goes into each bouquet."

"I do. And I know your cards. Calligraphy, when done correctly, is beautiful. I learned it myself several years ago."

Faith turned to him with wide eyes. "Seriously?"

"Yes."

Faith put a hand on her chest. "I used to practice calligraphy until it was perfect. When I was a teenager I used to dream about sending a handwritten love letter like a heroine in one of those Victorian novels. Or receiving one from some dashing hero." She shrugged and chuckled. "Now I use the art to write out my yearly Christmas cards."

A moment passed between them. Another area of common ground and similarity. She saw in his eyes that he was falling deeper into this, too. Or at least, she hoped that was what she saw. She'd hate to be in this on her own.

"Then you realize we have a lot of work to do before we open," the woman said. "Thank you again for helping us."

"Wait a second," Faith said as the woman began to turn away. "We can help."

"I beg your pardon?" Irvin said.

"Excuse me?" the woman said simultaneously.

"We both know how to write in calligraphy, and you need to rewrite all of those cards. We can help."

The woman and man exchanged another look and eyed them from head to toe.

"It's obviously been a late night for you two," the woman said. "We appreciate the offer but—"

"I'm not tired," Faith blurted out. "Irvin, are you tired?"

His eyes lit up and he grinned. "Not at all."

They both turned to the couple with a smile. The woman slowly returned it before shrugging and glancing at the guy. "Xavier, what do you think?"

"I need to see their writing first, but any help would keep our orders on time today," he said with a wave of the hand.

Faith clasped her hands together. "Then let's get to it."

"These are excellent!" Xavier exclaimed two hours and two espressos later.

Faith shook out her hands and smiled. "It was kind of fun to write all the different notes."

"There are a lot of people in love out there," Irvin said. He too stretched out his fingers.

Xavier grinned. "That is one of the reasons I enjoy owning this shop. Every day I get to help a couple express their love for each other." He looked at Irvin. "And to thank you for your help, your next bouquet for your girlfriend is on me."

Irvin gave Faith a smile that would melt ovaries. She jumped down from her stool in the front of the flower shop. The next girl he bought flowers for wouldn't be her.

"I couldn't take them for free," Irvin said. "Not after learning exactly how much work you all put into these bouquets."

Faith pulled out her cell phone and checked the time. "Wow, it's past six thirty." She looked at Irvin. "Kitty's supposed to be at my hotel room at seven."

They'd stayed out all night. She couldn't remember the last time she'd stayed up all night and it wasn't work related. College, maybe. But she'd never had this much fun, and it had everything to do with him.

"The itinerary can wait," Irvin said, standing. "You need to get some rest."

"What about you?"

"I'm used to being on set for long hours. This was nothing."

He muffled a yawn as he said it, and they both laughed. Now that the excitement of helping out Xavier and his wife, Diane, was waning, she was starting to feel the fatigue set in. The caffeine in the espressos had nothing on a body not used to staying up partying.

Diane came from out back, where the truck had just arrived with the latest batch of flowers for the day. "All done?" she asked. "You've got to let us buy you both dinner or do something else to say thank you."

"Yes," Xavier quickly agreed. "We would still be working right now without your help. And look at how beautiful you both write. I may ask you both to come back again."

Something close to disappointment flashed across Irvin's face. The same emotion blossomed in Faith's chest.

"Tonight was a onetime deal for me," she said with a forced smile. "I go back to South Carolina tomorrow. But if I'm ever back in New York, I'll definitely come by again." She walked over to Diane and held out her arms. "I'm from the South, and we do hugs."

Diane grinned and hugged her. Then Xavier did the same.

Irvin shook Xavier's hand. "I'll ask around about people with calligraphy skills to help you fill that position."

Faith never would have expected him to agree to assist in the first place, but offering to help them find a replacement was even more than he needed to do. Heaven help her, in less than twenty-four hours he was making her fall for him.

"That's too much," Diane said. "You have to let us give you something. Xavier, do something."

Irvin walked over and placed his hand on the small of Faith's back. It sent a rush of pleasure across her skin. She could get used to him touching her. "What's your favorite flower?"

"Nothing fancy or exotic. Roses are my favorite."

He turned to Xavier. "You wouldn't have a dozen for my date, would you?"

Faith waved her hands. "That's not necessary."

Xavier patted her arm. "Never stop a man from giving you flowers." He hurried across the room to a refrigerator filled with flowers and came back with a beautiful bouquet of red roses. "This isn't enough to pay you back for what you've done."

"It seems like adequate payment to me." Irvin raised a brow at Faith. "For you."

"Perfect." She couldn't say any more.

They made their way to the front of the store, but Diane stopped them at the door. "Before you go I just… wanted to ask. I mean…you look just like him. Are you…Irvin Freeman? The movie star?"

Irvin gave his showstopping smile. "Guilty as charged."

Diane squealed and squeezed her husband's arm. That started another round of thank-yous and questions about what they could do to repay him and Faith. All of which Irvin gracefully declined.

"You are full of surprises," Faith said as they walked the last few blocks to her hotel. The sun was up, and the streets were slowly filling again with early risers. "I got carried away when I offered to help them. You could have said no."

"I thought it was sweet that you were so quick to jump in. Do you always do that?"

She thought about the way she volunteered for the assignments no one else wanted and how back in Houston she was the one to dive in and organize the fundraisers at the hospital. Then how she easily gave up her life there to come home and help out her parents.

"Yeah, I guess I do."

"And who helps you, Faith?"

She shrugged. "I don't need any help."

"Everyone needs help now and then."

"I manage," she said. A glance at his face told her he was about to argue. The truth was, there'd been several times she'd wished she'd had help. Wished that her sister hadn't stolen money from their parents or that there was someone who could help her care for them.

She loved them dearly, but some nights it just seemed so overwhelming.

"We're here," she said as they approached the hotel.

They stopped at the door, where Irvin took her free hand and pulled her around to face him.

He grazed the finger of his other hand across her cheek and down her neck. The featherlight touch sent out a warning that she was nearing dangerous territory. He was going to kiss her. And she wanted him to.

"I had a good time tonight," she said.

He pulled her closer. "So did I."

"I appreciate your effort to make things fun. I know this probably wasn't your ideal Friday night."

"It's going to be hard for future Friday nights to live up to this. I've discovered that my date has a big, caring heart." His eyes lowered to her lips. When they flicked back to her eyes, they simmered with desire. "And even though we keep getting interrupted, and I promised not to, I'm going to kiss you."

"Maybe I should go inside and make it easy for you to keep your promise."

He rubbed the sensitive skin of her wrist. The other hand brushed the side of her neck. Her brain turned to scrambled eggs.

"Walk away and I'm likely to follow you and drag you into my arms."

It felt like slow motion as he slid his arm around her waist. His fingers pressed into the soft skin of her back while his erection pushed against her stomach. Desire infused her bloodstream, heating her body, while her breaths became shallow, as if she were coming down with something. Not surprising. The need in his eyes was contagious.

"I must be dreaming," she whispered.

"No, cutie, this is no dream." And then his wonderful lips gently kissed hers.

She sighed softly, then tentatively ran her tongue across his full lower lip. He groaned but didn't push forward. He tasted like the peppermint gum he'd chewed in the flower shop. His tall body was as solid as the city skyscrapers and as hot as the streets in summer. He completely enveloped her in his strong arms. Everything about the kiss—his firm lips, the brush of his beard on her face, the hard press of his body and slow glide of his tongue—was divine.

Her hand gripped the front of his shirt and tugged him forward. The roses were crushed by their embrace, their sweet fragrance surrounding them. Oh yeah, she was definitely getting into this. The tension in his body snapped, and he kissed her back with an urgency that made her core tremble. Long fingers sank into her hair, which had become frizzy sometime during the long night. His hands tightened, and he turned her head to deepen the kiss. The pull of his hands in her hair, combined with the pleasure of his mouth on hers, sent her body on a dizzying ride. Proof that something wonderful could get infinitely better.

Would he make love as well as he kissed? She could find out. She could actually succumb to this need and know what it was like to make love to him.

"Oh, no, not out here on the stoop. Anyone can snap a picture and splash it all over the internet before we get upstairs." Kitty's voice broke them apart. "And where have you been? For God's sake, we've got to be ready to leave in less than two hours."

They jerked apart. She tried to breathe as Kitty approached, talking nonstop about the stupidity of disappearing from the club and reappearing kissing in front of Faith's hotel. Embarrassed, and reminded that she was only here as a publicity stunt, Faith stepped away from Irvin. She couldn't look at him. Couldn't forget this wasn't real. It was time to get back to reality.

Chapter 10

Faith's blaring cell phone jarred her from sleep. It was at the highest volume, the setting she'd put it on last night in the club in order to hear it if her parents called. Now she wanted to slam the phone with a hammer and never get another call again.

After poking her head out from the mound of covers and groping around the nightstand, she finally grabbed her phone and answered it.

"Why do you sound as if you're asleep?" her mama asked.

"Because I was asleep." Faith rubbed her eyes and pushed herself up against the headboard. Kitty had thankfully agreed to cancel the morning plans so that Faith could be rested for the premiere that night.

"It's ten o'clock. You never sleep this late. You must have been up really late last night. Partying until the break of dawn with a handsome movie star."

"I wasn't partying until the break of dawn," Faith said through a yawn.

"Maybe you ended the night seeing the sights...or kissing in front of a fancy hotel."

Faith was suddenly wide-awake. She sat forward. "What are you talking about? How would you...?"

"Know that you spent all night roaming New York City with a movie star and ended it kissing in front of your hotel? Marie called me because a picture of the two of you was posted on the internet this morning."

"We thought we were away from the cameras," Faith said. Had they been followed the entire night?

"Honey, when it comes to celebrities, you're never away from the cameras. According to the article, someone at the hotel snapped the picture with a cell phone and sent it to the website. I doubt half the story is true."

"What does it say?"

"You two were spotted at the club, left early and turned up at your hotel first thing this morning. I must admit, I wouldn't have believed it if I hadn't seen the picture myself. Are you two a thing?"

"No, Mama, we're not a thing. I leave tomorrow, and he's going to Canada to shoot a film next week. We just got caught up in a moment."

"Men like that don't get caught up. They know what they're about." Virginia's voice brimmed with warning. "Now, I'm not telling you to not have any fun. I want you to enjoy yourself. Snatching a kiss or two from Irvin Freeman isn't a bad thing. Just remember that when all the glitz and glamour is over, you're coming back to real life. Don't get too caught up in all the fantasy."

Faith ran a hand across her face before sighing. "I know that. Believe me, I do."

A few seconds passed before her mom spoke again.

"You've had a hard time moving home from Houston and giving up everything."

"And I'd do it all again. I love you and Daddy. I wouldn't just sit by and let you two struggle after what Love did."

"But you haven't done a lot for yourself. You haven't dated anyone since you've been home."

"I haven't had time to date," she said.

"You need to start dating again. It'll be good for you to go out with some nice guys around here. Start having fun."

And not fall for an actor who'd be shooting love scenes with Selena Jones the second she left, Faith added silently.

"Sounds like you and Daddy are having fun," she said.

"We just figured since you were off having a good time, we'd take advantage and do the same."

"Take advantage? Mama, seriously, if you wanted to go to the movies, I would have taken you. You don't have to wait for me to leave town."

"Well, you're always so worried about the bills, then saving whatever's left to make up for what Love took. *You* don't even go to the movies."

"Okay, I get it. But that doesn't mean I want you and Daddy to feel like we can't enjoy ourselves. We'll start going to the movies, and we can even eat out every once in a while."

"And you'll go on a few dates, too?" Her mother's voice was hopeful, almost desperate.

Now guilt crept in to join the embarrassment she felt from earlier. Thanks to the internet, her mama was now worried about her. "Yes, I will find a nice guy to start dating."

They chatted for a few more minutes before getting off the phone. Faith still had several hours before Kitty was coming back to get her ready for the premiere. Irvin had convinced Kitty to abandon the plans for a tour of the city today so they could both get some rest. Apparently it would be a long night of partying after the premiere.

In a way, she hoped it was. Maybe being surrounded by people instead of spending time alone with Irvin would help her do exactly what her mama suggested. What she knew she needed to do. Not get wrapped up in the fantasy, and not believe that the attraction between them could turn into anything more.

She put her phone back on the nightstand and lay back on the bed. Her phone rang again just as she pulled the covers over her head.

She frowned at the unfamiliar number, though she recognized the New York area code. She'd bet anything it was Kitty. No doubt the woman couldn't really let everything on her itinerary go.

"Hello?" She didn't bother to hide her frustration.

But the voice that answered her was not Kitty's. "Get out of the bed, come downstairs and meet me."

Irvin's tone sent a quiver through her body. She jumped up in bed and looked around the room as if he'd magically appear.

"I thought we were resting," she said.

"That's what I told Kitty to get her off our backs. I'm going to give you a tour of the city and deliver you to her capable hands in time to prep you for the premiere."

"Why would you do that? Kitty already had it planned out."

"Kitty and the rest of the entourage I don't want. This way it'll be just you and me. Now hurry up. We've got about thirty minutes before someone who recognizes me reports back to her and she comes after us."

She flipped the covers back and hopped out of the bed. "I can't get cute in thirty minutes."

"You're cute already, and much cuter without all the makeup they put on you last night. Just throw on some shorts, because I love your legs, and get down here." His voice was filled with a contagious enthusiasm.

She laughed and hurried to the closet. "I'll be down in no time."

"It must be nice to order up a ferry for two people."

Faith turned from the side of the ferry, where she watched the Statue of Liberty, to look at Irvin standing beside her at the rail. The wind whipped her hair around her face, and she continued to try to smooth down the strands. Irvin turned to her, too, and gave her a grin that was both overconfident and sexy.

"We could have waited in line for tickets," he said.

"Oh, no, I'm not complaining. I just wouldn't even know where to start to get my own ferry."

"Call it one of the perks of celebrity. Besides, I wanted to show you as much of New York as I could before tonight."

"Are you nervous? About the premiere?"

He shook his head. "A little," he said, leaning his forearms against the railing. "But at this point there's little I can do about it. People will either love the movie or hate it."

"Does it bother you if they hate it?"

"It used to. Not anymore."

She sensed a story behind the reason. "What changed?"

He shrugged as if it were no big deal, but he didn't turn her way. "My mother was always proud of what

I'd become and how quickly I found success. When I lost her, I lost the only person whose opinion I really cared about."

Faith nodded, not knowing what to say. She'd never been any good at speaking the right words when someone talked about a deceased parent. She remembered how all the well wishes people had sent her way when her mama was sick provided only a small amount of comfort. Useless words didn't do much to ease the pain.

"When you put it like that, I guess I can understand," she said. "When my mama got sick, my dad had already been out of work for two years because of a back injury. Then my sister—" She stopped, not prepared to reveal that private shame. "My parents had some financial trouble," she said instead. His eyebrows rose at that information, but she pressed on. "So I came home to fix things. I don't know what you know about nursing, but I went from the top of the food chain to almost the bottom."

"Why'd you have to do that? With your background, you should've been a shoo-in for the top position in your small town."

She laughed as she reached out once again and tamed her hair. She really wished she'd gone for the ponytail today. "I'll let you in on a little secret about small county hospitals. When certain nurses get a top position, the only thing that gets them out of it is death. Despite my qualifications, there wasn't anything available for me. Everyone expected me to be bitter about the change in circumstance. And for a month or two, I was." She glanced at him and raised a brow. "Pay cuts aren't fun."

"What changed your mind?"

"My mama. It was soon after her stroke and she still couldn't do much for herself. I'd worked the night shift and come in to give her a bath. She took my hand and squeezed." Tears burned her eyes at the memory. She turned her face to the wind to dry them. "She said thank you. The look in her eye said it was for more than just the bath. Right then and there I knew that if I had to do it again, I would."

"You mentioned a sister. Where is she?" he asked in a solemn voice.

Faith gripped the rail. "In rehab."

"Who's paying for that?"

"I am," she said in a clipped tone.

She glanced at him out of the corner of her eye. He looked ready to speak, but instead turned away to look at the view, a frown on his face. Maybe he was weighing his options just like her. Wondering how much to get involved.

"We're almost there," he said. He pointed, and she followed the gesture to the dock. "Are you sure you don't mind skipping a visit to Ellis Island?"

She nodded. "I don't have a name to look for. I just want to see Lady Liberty."

Though he'd sneaked away from Kitty, his bodyguard still accompanied him. She was glad for that, because it wasn't long after they got off the ferry at Liberty Island that people began to recognize him. Though the crowd didn't swarm him, there were more than enough people who came up for pictures and autographs. Irvin was nice to everyone, smiled for the cameras and signed the scraps of paper they produced before quietly asking to be excused to enjoy the view.

Despite the constant interruptions, she enjoyed being there. They managed to take their own pictures with the Manhattan skyline in the background, and they continued to laugh and talk as they walked around the monument. She loved the way his hands moved when he talked. He was so expressive when he got onto a subject dear to him. This wasn't acting, and she loved seeing him that way.

"You're so good with your fans," she said once they were back on the ferry for their return trip.

"They're the reason I can give you a private ride to the Statue of Liberty," he said.

He reached over and took her hand, threading their fingers together. Her shortness of breath had nothing to do with the wind whipping around them. Slowly he pulled her to him, the warmth of his body and the seductive scent of his cologne invading her senses. She expected a kiss; instead, he pulled her back against his chest and wrapped an arm around her waist. They stood that way for the rest of the ride.

When they docked, he took her uptown to Central Park. The only thing she wanted to see was the Bethesda Fountain.

"It's in all the movies. I've got to see it," she said.

"Then we'll see it," he said with a laugh.

They sat at the fountain, eating hot dogs and sipping sodas. Every once in a while his bodyguard had to push back fans, but for the most part Irvin accepted their requests with a humble smile. Throughout it all, he told her about his fascination with New York.

"It always seemed like this fantastic place," he said, spreading his arms to take in the city. "Full of energy and life. I needed that. I'd had so much energy drained out of me before I left home."

The need to understand why was like a physical tug in her stomach. She didn't know much about his past. She was a fan, but she didn't belong to any fan club or read everything she could about his life. She knew that he'd grown up in London, that his life there had been rough before coming to America and getting a break-out role ten years ago.

Knowing more about him and his past would only pull her in more. But staying detached was growing harder with each second she spent with him. His humor, his attention and even the way he insisted his bodyguard keep her away from the attention of his fans all endeared him to her. So instead of asking why, she changed the subject.

"What's next on the tour?"

He glanced at his watch. "We don't have a lot of time, but I wanted to take you to the Top of the Rock. I've arranged for us to get private access, so that should speed up the process."

She looked at a group of women who were obviously debating coming over to ask if he was really Irvin Freeman. "If you're tired of being out and about, we can go back."

He only smiled and shrugged. "It comes with the territory. Besides, I don't often get the chance to give a beautiful woman a tour of the city, even if it's a modified tour."

With the constant New York traffic, it took a while for his driver to get them to Rockefeller Center, but thankfully the celebrity perks of private elevators got them through the rush and to the top in no time. She was blown away by the magnificent views, rendered speechless.

"We were there," she said, pointing to the Statue of Liberty in the distance. They went to the other side of the building, and she pointed to Central Park. "And there."

He'd not only got them a private elevator but also

somehow worked it out that tourist trips to the top were stopped while they were there. It was the first time all day they weren't accosted by starstruck fans, and she noticed the difference in him. The lines around his eyes disappeared, and his laugh came a little easier. Being recognized might come with the territory, but she doubted Irvin enjoyed the constant attention.

When they got on the elevator to leave she pulled out her cell phone to record the blue-and-purple lights in the clear elevator ceiling, which made her feel as if the elevator was going warp speed up and down the shaft.

"What are you doing?" Irvin asked.

"My mama would love to see this," she said, holding the phone above her head.

"Then bring her back and let her see it. I'd be happy to arrange another private ride."

His voice held an invitation that went further than just helping her mama go to the top of Rockefeller Center. Her heart beat faster than the speeding elevator.

"I'd have to see," she said. "You're so busy, you might not have time to set something up."

"I'd make time for you."

His dark eyes held hers captive. The promise she saw there made her mouth go dry. Could he really mean it? Would he really make time for her after this weekend was over?

The elevator stopped and the doors opened. As they prepared to get off, a guy moved to get on. She recognized him as Lincoln Harris, the anchor of the news show she watched every week with her parents.

Faith grabbed Irvin's shirt with one hand and pointed at Lincoln. "Oh my God, it's you!"

Lincoln's eyebrows rose, and he smiled behind his signature dark-framed glasses. "It's me."

"I love you! My mama is gonna flip when I tell her I saw you. We watch you every weekend." She turned to Irvin and grinned. "Can you believe it? It's Lincoln Harris." She spun back.

Lincoln looked at Irvin and held out a hand. "Good to see you, Irvin. Good luck with the premiere tonight."

"Thanks, Lincoln." He placed a hand on Faith's back. "This is Faith Logan. She's my date for the weekend."

"Lucky you," Lincoln told Irvin with a wink. He wasn't in one of the signature suits he wore behind the news desk. Instead, he wore a plain white T-shirt and dark jeans. The gray hair at his temples only added to his sophistication.

"It was nice meeting you, Faith," he said, holding out his hand.

"Same here, Lincoln." She took his hand and pumped it up and down, giving him a big grin as he got on the elevator and they exited.

"You're excited to meet every other celebrity but me," Irvin said with a laugh. "I'm starting to get offended."

"Oh, please. I was excited to meet you. But I watch Lincoln every week. He's part of our routine."

Irvin took her hand and pulled her into the crook of his arm. "I see that now I'm going to have to become a news anchor so I can enter your living room every week."

The gesture was so familiar, so comfortable, that she didn't hesitate to slip her arm around his waist as they started walking toward the exit.

"I guarantee the news ratings would go through the roof if you did that."

"Who cares about ratings?" he said. He leaned over to her ear. "I only care about making you scream my name the way you just did his."

A tremble raced through her body. "You don't need to be on the news to do that."

His sexy grin turned her insides to lava. "What do I need to do to make you scream my name?"

Kiss her. Run his hands over every inch of her body. Make love to her as if she were the most beautiful woman on the planet. That was all it would take. She'd scream his name, and probably lose her heart at the same time.

But she couldn't tell him that. Instead, she said, "Wouldn't you like to know?" Then she hurried toward the exit before she succumbed to the temptation in his eyes.

Chapter 11

The lights of cameras temporarily blinded Irvin as he exited the limo at the Ziegfeld Theater in Manhattan for the premiere. He smiled and gave a wave before turning back to the limo and reaching his hand out to Faith. When she smiled at him, something hitched in his chest. Again, Kitty and the team had done a fantastic job prepping her for the premiere. There would be only a handful of men who would be able to keep their eyes off her tonight in the black-and-silver dress that dipped low between her breasts and stopped midthigh.

Faith's warm brown eyes met his, and her lips curved up into a soft smile. He gave her hand a squeeze and wished he could climb right back into that limo with her and go someplace private. Movie premieres were necessary in his line of work, and usually he enjoyed them. But right now, he'd take another escape like the one they'd shared last night. Just him and Faith.

He couldn't remember the last time he'd had such an easy relationship with a woman.

"Are you ready?" he asked.

She got out of the car and froze when the cameras flashed in her face like minibursts of lightning, casting them both in blinding bright lights.

"Wow, this is crazy." Her voice was filled with awe. "Do you ever get used to this?"

"Not really." He pulled her close and wrapped his arm around her waist.

Her body stiffened, and she tried to pull away. "They'll think something is going on between us," she said past a stiff smile.

"Isn't there?" he replied, raising a brow.

"But… I mean…we aren't really together."

"Tonight, you're mine."

Her lips parted. Only the flashing lights kept him from kissing her the way he wanted to. It had been less than twelve hours since he'd kissed her in front of her hotel, but it felt like years.

"Okay," she said, though the look in her eyes was unsure.

Before he could reply, Kitty was already rushing them forward. They went through the motions of smiling for the cameras and interviewers, stopping every few feet on the red carpet. Faith tried to step back—Kitty even tried to help her get out of the way—but Irvin wouldn't let her. He meant what he said. She was his date tonight, and he didn't want her hidden in the background.

During the interviews, he introduced her as the lucky woman who'd won the weekend with him.

"So you're really going to hate going home tomorrow, aren't you?" the ultrathin female correspondent for an entertainment show asked Faith.

"It will be difficult after such a great weekend," she said with a good-natured smile.

"What about you, Irvin?" the correspondent asked. "You'll be on your way to Canada for filming next week. Are you excited about the project?"

He wasn't excited about it. It was another action role that would require him to be shirtless, holding a gun and kissing Selena. He'd made the decision to send his screenplay to the producer the second he signed the contract to play the part. Once again, anxiety trickled down his spine. He still hadn't heard from Kevin.

But he kept all those thoughts to himself and told the reporter what she and his fans wanted to hear.

"I'm very excited. I've worked with Selena Jones before, and she's brilliant."

"You two really turn up the heat whenever you're on set," the correspondent said.

He rubbed his chin to remind himself not to roll his eyes. "All I do is stand there. She brings enough heat on her own," he said. It was vague enough to play up their upcoming movie without confirming anything. It was how the Hollywood machine worked. You had to keep up the buzz for the movie. It was how you sold tickets.

"I bet she does," the reporter said with a wink to her cameraman.

When he heard members of the cast being called together for a photo, he stepped back. "If you'll excuse us…"

He pulled Faith close and walked toward the rest of the cast on the red carpet. Faith didn't relax into his side the way she had earlier. This time her shoulders were stiff, and the smile he'd come to enjoy was replaced by a slight frown.

"You all right?"

She glanced at him out of the corner of her eye and nodded. "I'm fine. Just not used to the cameras and interviews."

He could understand. After ten years, it was still overwhelming to him, though in Faith's case he had a feeling it was more than that. "I didn't think about that."

"If you don't mind, I think I'll stay out of any upcoming photos. People are here to see you, not me."

He stopped and turned to face her, taking her hand in his. "But I'm very glad that you're here."

Her smile returned, though it didn't quite light up her eyes. "Thank you."

Kitty and the photographers called his name. He gave her hand a squeeze, then leaned over to kiss her. She turned her head at the last second so that his lips brushed her cheek. She didn't look at him when he raised his head.

He took pictures with the rest of the cast. The romantic comedy was filled with the top African-American actors of the day, and during filming it had been more like a large family gathering on set instead of a job. So the smiles in the pictures and the laughter during the interviews were all real and easy. But he couldn't keep his eyes from straying to Faith, who now hung in the background with Kitty watching.

Dante arrived, accompanied by screams from the women in the crowd and another flurry of camera flashes. Irvin was in the middle of an interview with another entertainment show with his on-screen girlfriend when his friend strolled over to Faith. Within a few seconds he coaxed a laugh and smile out of Faith. Irvin frowned as he watched the two. He wasn't the jealous type. After all, in Hollywood there was no need to be jealous, because if your date found another guy interesting, there were always more women waiting in the wings. But now he felt an odd feeling rev up inside him as he watched Dante and Faith smile for a picture together on the red carpet. A voice inside him yelled "Back off."

"If you'll excuse me," Irvin said, ending the interview in the middle of a sentence.

He ignored the startled expressions of his costar and the interviewer to cross the short distance to Faith and Dante.

Kitty stopped him midstride. "What are you doing?"

"I'm going to get Faith away from Dante," he said and tried to brush past.

Kitty grabbed his arm. He spun to tell her to let go, but she held up a hand. "Be careful there. She isn't what she seems."

"What are you talking about?"

"Her family is swimming in debt, and I believe her sister is the reason. I know you like her, but be careful."

"I know about her financial issues."

Kitty let him go. "You're always a target, Irvin. Don't let her Southern charm and sweet smile fool you."

Irvin restlessly tugged on his jacket and he processed her words. Faith wouldn't open up about her financial issues, but did that mean she was trying to deceive him?

He nodded at Kitty, who seemed to relax when he acknowledged her warning. Slowly he crossed the red carpet to Faith and Dante.

"Dante, how's it going?" He looked from his friend to his arm around Faith's shoulders and back.

Dante's eyebrows rose, but he also quickly removed his arm from Faith's shoulders. "It's a great turnout, Irvin. This movie is going to be a hit." He didn't have to say anything, but from the understanding in Dante's eyes, Irvin knew he got the message. *Keep your hands to yourself.*

"That's what the critics say." He glanced at Faith. "Are you ready to go inside?"

She nodded. "Is it time already?"

"Yes. We've done all the interviews and got enough pictures."

"But the real fun," Dante said, "will be the after-party I'm throwing at the Standard hotel."

She grinned at Dante. "You're throwing the after-party?"

"I throw the best parties." Dante looked at Irvin. "I'll see you both after the show."

"Are you having fun?" Irvin asked Faith.

"I am." He could see that her excitement from earlier was back. He hated that Kitty's words now made him question the reason. "Your life is so busy. A premiere today, then off to shoot another film in a few more days. When do you leave?"

"Monday."

"The day after I go home." The brightness of her smile dimmed. "Tomorrow will go by so quickly. I should tell you now that I had a great time."

"So did I."

Their eyes met. The end of their weekend together was coming soon. Could he really be feeling this connection to her, or would it go away once they separated? Was it all a ruse on her part, or was she genuinely the woman he was falling for? The one who helped people, hadn't asked him for anything and hesitated whenever they seemed to get close? He'd spent years studying people, learning their expressions to imitate them. He watched her and didn't see deception. Kitty might have told the truth about Faith's family, but he didn't believe

Faith planned to ask him to do anything about her financial situation.

Why did he have to let her go? Why couldn't they stay in touch? Why couldn't he date her? He knew plenty of celebrities who dated people from outside the industry. But she'd have to put up with the spotlight. Would she want to for him? The question unbalanced him. He'd never had to worry about a woman choosing not to be with him, and right now he was really worried that she would.

They went into the theater and were seated up front with the rest of the cast. As the movie played, he could tell it was a hit. He normally spent time watching his performance and critiquing what he could have done better. This time he found himself watching Faith's reactions. Celebrating when she laughed, and feeling completely satisfied when she gasped appreciatively at his shirtless shower scene. The same happened with the love scenes. As he watched her, his body heated quickly to its flash point. He imagined kissing Faith, holding her naked against him, filling her, bringing her to climax. He saw her chest rise and fall rapidly with her short breaths as she stared at the love scene playing out on-screen. Her tongue continued to dart out over her bottom lip. Then she twisted in her seat and looked his way. Her eyes widened when they caught hold of his.

He didn't care about the theater being crowded. Or about the stories already floating around of him kissing her outside of her hotel, or being unsure if she was willing to see where this would go. He had to kiss her.

He leaned over and brushed her lips with his. He felt her body tremble as her soft sigh caressed his face. Her eyes closed, and her lids sparkled in the dark lights of the theater. The gentle kiss wasn't enough. He'd just gone in for a real kiss when Kitty cleared her throat beside him and kicked his foot.

He glared at his publicist, who only gave him an innocent look. He got the message. There was no need to cause a stir at the premiere. But he didn't like it. He turned back to Faith and whispered, "Later."

He watched the battle in her eyes before she looked back at the screen. She was still afraid to trust what was happening between them. He trusted it. Before the night was over, he planned to make sure it would last longer than a weekend.

The movie was great, and the after-party was definitely jumping. The hottest DJ mixing all the hits, a view of the bay and skyline that was out of this world, A-list celebrities everywhere, even a hot tub that had her wondering where people got bathing suits from. Yet Faith couldn't have a good time. She gave a good show of enjoying herself, smiling, taking pictures to show her parents and trying not to wince whenever someone brought up how hard it would be for her to go home at the end of the weekend.

Irvin wasn't making it any easier. He kept her by his side, almost as if they were a couple. He'd already thrown her off by saying tonight she was his. But could she really be his for one night and move on? She'd have to. So the bigger question was, did she really want to be his for the night?

Umm, yeah!

The thought sent her heart into a frenzy.

She lifted up onto her toes so she could speak into Irvin's ear over the music. "I'm going to get a drink."

He turned away from the group they were talking with, which included Dante and Jacobe Jenkins.

"I can get it for you," he told her.

There he went again. Treating her like a girlfriend and making it harder for her to resist sleeping with him before this weekend ended.

"No, thanks. I just need a second."

Concern flashed in his eyes, and she had to turn away quickly. *Tonight, you're mine.* His velvety voice ran through her head.

He stopped her from walking away by taking her hand in his. Slowly he brought it up and lightly brushed his lips across the backs of her knuckles. Desire darkened his eyes.

"Don't go too far," he said in a voice laced with heat.

Breathe. Now was the time to breathe. Her lips parted with a shaky breath as she gently pulled her hand away. She didn't need to look over her shoulder to know he watched her walk away.

She strolled out onto the open area of the rooftop club. The New York skyline framed the well-stocked bar. The woman who'd congratulated Faith at the club the night before stood at the end of the bar. She smiled and waved. Faith lifted a hand and wondered if the woman found her way into every party Irvin attended.

"I see the way he's looking at you." Kitty's voice came from behind her.

Forgetting the superfan, Faith asked the bartender for water. No need to further cloud her judgment with alcohol.

She faced Kitty. "I don't know what you're talking about."

"Still playing coy," Kitty said with a smile. "There's no need. Irvin is smitten with you, and I haven't seen him that way in all the years I've known him."

"He's not smitten." She slowly turned her head to peek over her shoulder. Irvin watched her and Kitty.

"He's definitely something for you."

The bartender handed her a bottle of water. She quickly twisted the cap off and took a gulp of the cool liquid.

"He can have any woman he wants," Faith said after she wet her mouth.

Kitty nodded. The lights from the party made the red streak in her hair appear to glow, and she looked fantastic in a sexy black dress. "He can, but he wants you. Normally, I try to keep away the groupies and gold diggers. I may whore him out to the media, but I don't believe in setting up women in his hotel room. But you're different."

"Are you saying you want to whore him out to me?" Faith said in a tight voice.

Kitty held up a hand and shook her head. "No. What I'm saying is that normally he picks the women he wants to sleep with covertly, but he's been very open with laying claim to you."

"He isn't laying claim."

"He stopped midinterview with *Entertainment Tonight* because you were talking to his friend, a known ladies' man. He's kept you by his side all night, sneaked away from me and the rest of the team twice to be alone with you and kissed your hand before you walked away. Face it. He's laying claim."

That reminder to breathe would have been useful now. Air struggled to find its way into her lungs. "I leave tomorrow."

"We'll see. Either way, if you're going to become the girlfriend of Irvin Freeman, I'll work on promoting you, as well. We'll play the good-daughter angle, move you and your family to New York and set you up in style."

"Whoa, wait a minute. I'm not moving to New York. And just because there's some kind of spark between me and Irvin doesn't mean I want to become caught up in this publicity parade. I like my privacy."

"Like it or not, you're about to lose it. You're going to be the most envied woman in America, and everyone is going to want to know what it was about you that won his heart."

If people dug into her past, they'd learn about her twin and the money she'd stolen from her family. Or worse, Love might skip out on rehab and try to take advantage of Faith's relationship with Irvin.

"I'm just a weekend fling. Come Monday, I'll be another woman who was linked to him briefly in a long list of women."

"Maybe, but I doubt it." Kitty's eyes narrowed, and she leaned in. "So if there is anything you're hiding that may hurt his career, you need to spill it. From where I'm standing, you're his newest fling, and I need to know everything and have a story prepared."

With that, Kitty turned in a flourish and left to go talk with someone else, leaving Faith in a daze. The blood rushing in her ears drowned out the music, and she felt as if she might faint. Her eyes searched the room for Irvin, and in no time their gazes collided.

His gaze dropped to her lips. He shifted his stance and tugged on the waistband of his pants, drawing her attention to his groin. Her overactive imagination took over, and she pictured him slowly hardening until he was completely rigid and ready.

Ready for her.

Heat simmered across her skin, making her feel as if

she were on fire. She jerked her eyes upward, expecting to find a smirk on his face after catching her staring at his crotch. Instead, he gave her a smoldering look. He spoke to the people around him before coming her way.

She'd be a fool to turn that down, right? Nobody would dig into her life if she was only a one-night stand. Besides, she didn't want the fame, or the apartment in New York like a kept woman. One night was all she wanted. All she'd allow herself.

He stopped in front of her, his shoulders stiff and his brows drawn together. "Did Kitty say something to upset you?"

"No. Actually, she said something very interesting."

His brow quirked, and the barest hint of a smile graced his lips. "I'd like to hear it."

"She said you've spent the night staking your claim on me. That you've never looked at a woman the way you're looking at me, and that I should move my family to New York and be with you."

Her heart fluttered in her chest as she waited for his response. He would laugh, right? Scoff at Kitty's outrageous claim and tell her not to quit her day job. Instead, the heat between them sizzled and popped as he took a step closer and his eyes became serious.

"Kitty talks too much," he said.

"She's crazy. I knew she was crazy."

"She's accurate, as usual. Faith, I don't understand it, and I can't say that this is forever, but right now, at this moment, all I know is that I want more time with you. I don't want this weekend to end."

One night. That's all. One night. The words ran through her head like a mantra. "We don't know each other. This stuff doesn't happen for real."

"Then let's get to know each other." He took her

hand in his. The breeze carried his cologne to her, and the scent heated her insides.

"I don't know if we should."

"If I weren't Irvin Freeman the movie star and I was just a guy you'd met, would you say no?"

She couldn't lie. "I wouldn't."

"Then forget about who I am and how we met. Just trust that fate brought us together for a reason."

Before she could answer him, the moment was interrupted when someone yelled and jumped into the hot tub. The crowd cheered, and the music increased in tempo.

He glanced around, then turned back to her. "Let's get out of here."

"Where are we going?"

"My place."

Two simple words that held the power to change everything. If she said yes, she knew what would happen. If she said no, she'd regret it forever...

She exhaled the breath she held and whispered her answer.

Chapter 12

It wouldn't be very charming of him to pounce on Faith. Yet trying not to pounce on her was proving difficult, if not damned impossible. He wanted to take things slow, not scare her by ripping that dress from her body and making love to her long and hard. The problem was, there was no eloquent way to express what was going through him right now.

His driver could barely contain his shock when Irvin gave the order to go to his place. The place he didn't bring women was the first place he wanted to bring Faith. He didn't want their first time to be in a hotel room.

He wanted to taste every part of her. Have her wetness on his tongue, feel the hardness of her nipples between his lips and run his hands across every soft inch of her skin. And he wanted to do it all in his bed, then wake up in the morning with her curled up next to him.

She stopped as soon as they entered his flat. "The view is beautiful." Faith's voice, quiet and husky, nearly made him groan. She crossed the living area to the windows overlooking the city.

He didn't turn on the lamp; instead, he watched her from the doorway. Her body was a sexy silhouette against the city lights. Mostly hidden by the shadows as she was, he could make out only glimpses of her. A tantalizing peek at her elbow, a brief view of her face.

He cleared his throat. "Not as beautiful as you."

"Me being here pretty much assures you're going to get lucky. You don't have to toss on the flattery." He couldn't see it, but he heard the smile in her voice.

"I don't want you to change your mind," he teased.

"You don't have to worry about that. I know what I'm getting into."

He crossed the room to stand beside her. "What are you getting into?"

"A one-night stand with a movie star."

In the dim light, he could see the rapid rise and fall of her chest. He brushed the hair away from her neck and leaned down to kiss the soft skin below her ear.

"I'm not a movie star tonight."

"I know we said that, but I have to keep reminding myself that you are." Her breathless voice fired his blood. She leaned closer to him.

"Why?"

"Otherwise, I might start to believe this can be more."

He met her eyes. "It is more." He tilted his head toward the door leading to the balcony. "Come, let me show you the view from there."

He held out his hand for her and led her to the wide terrace overlooking the Hudson River. A concrete-and-glass guardrail ran along the entire west end of the apartment. The wind had picked up, the precursor of a forecast storm for the next day. Faith shivered and wrapped her arms around herself. He pressed a button at the outdoor bar that turned on a gas fireplace.

She gasped when the flames flickered, and she walked over to the warmth. She held out her hands, then looked around the outdoor space. "I bet you have amazing parties here."

He strolled over to stand beside her at the fireplace. In the twinkling firelight he admired the smoothness of her skin.

"Sometimes," he replied, "but nothing like the party we just left. I only invite a handful of friends to my apartment."

"So the after-party won't follow us here."

"No."

"Good." She nodded, then met his eyes.

The smell of her perfume wafted around him like a cloud of silk. Their eyes met and electric heat sparked.

To hell with not pouncing on her. He took her elbow in his hand and pulled her to him. She lifted her chin, then raised herself on her toes. It was all the invitation he needed.

The kiss started soft, but he couldn't keep it tame for long. With one hand he cupped her face; the other wrapped around her waist to press her body fully against him. It took a second to realize her hands were all over him. Rubbing his head, gripping his arms, clenching the sides of his shirt. Her soft moans punctuated the silence, and something deep inside him celebrated. He craved her desire more than he could have imagined.

As much as he loved kissing her, that wasn't his ultimate goal. He lifted his head to take in how good she looked in the moonlight. His mouth watered. He gently ran his hands up her arms, then around back to her zipper. He waited a second, giving her time to say no. She didn't.

He slowly unzipped the dress and pushed the straps off her shoulders and down her arms. The dress fell in a whisper of material to her feet. His heart thundered and his body trembled at the sight of her breasts in a red silk bra. The thin material clung to the protruding tips of her breasts. He would never forget how beautiful she looked.

He ran his fingers along the edge, then dipped one finger below the silk to brush the soft skin on the side of her breast. She pulled her lower lip between her teeth as the back of his finger traced closer to her nipple. Her small hands gripped his waist, pulling him closer. He watched as the peaks hardened even more.

He leaned forward to brush his lips across her neck, breathing in the sweetness of her perfume and something far more addictive that belonged just to her. He reached behind her to unfasten her bra, but in his urgency he pulled too hard and tore the material.

"My apologies."

"Unnecessary."

He lowered his head to kiss the chocolate tips of her breasts before finally sucking one deep into his mouth. Her sigh and moan were his rewards.

He let the swollen nipple slip from between his lips, giving himself a second to admire the glistening tip before turning his attention on the other. He wanted more.

She was actually doing this. It wasn't a fantasy, and he wasn't a figment of her imagination. There was no need to pinch herself, because the wonderful feel of his lips on her body was definitely real and better than anything she could have possibly imagined.

Her breathing staggered as he hooked his fingers in the edge of her panties and tugged them down, his strong hands caressing every inch of her legs along the way. The heat from his palms seared straight through the taut muscles of her thighs, making her wet and wanting.

When he disposed of her panties, Irvin leaned forward to kiss her softly. But they were way beyond soft kisses now. If she was going to do this, then she was going to get as much as she could out of it. The memories would need to last a lifetime. She grabbed the back of his head and kissed him harder.

The movement elicited a deep groan from him. His hot lips left her mouth to travel down her neck to her exposed breasts. Her head fell back, but her eyes remained open. She wanted to remember everything about this moment. The sound of their ragged breathing against the muted background noises of the city. The black velvet of the sky above their heads. The scratch of his beard against the tender skin of her breasts. She lowered her gaze to the top of Irvin's head, then bit her lower lip as she watched him kiss and suckle her breasts.

His tongue circled one dark peak, and she nearly gasped from the exquisite pleasure. She watched shamelessly as he savored her. He caught her watching him, grinned and gently bit the sensitive nub. Nothing in her life had turned her on as much as the sight of her dark nipple between his even white teeth.

"Do that again," she urged.

He did, playing and nipping until both tips protruded, hard and swollen from his attention. She floated in a haze of pleasure when he ran a finger across her wet core and nearly made her knees buckle.

He looked up. Excitement brightened his eyes before they burned hot with desire. "You're bare." He ran his fingers across her smooth outer lips as if checking to be sure.

"I don't like hair down there."

He made a sound, half moan, half growl, then stood back in order to stare at the treasure between her legs. She watched him, her breathing shallow, as he gently massaged the sensitive flesh. Her eyes closed when he softly pushed two fingers deep inside her. She forced them open again.

She pulled him back in for another kiss, this one more earth-shattering than the last with his long fingers sliding in and out of her.

Her body trembled. The need for release sent her closer to the edge. She reined it in. Not like this. She had to come with him inside her.

"Now, please, now," she said through clenched teeth.

"Not yet." He slipped his fingers out and spread her desire over the smooth lips of her sex. He gently cupped her in his hand before once again easing two fingers inside.

"Oh my God, Irvin," she said on a moan. Her body bucked. Pleasure exploded and popped across her nerve endings. Her inner walls clenched around the fingers buried deep inside her. She watched the satisfaction on his face as she came, the male pride clear in his features.

It took several seconds before she could form a coherent thought. Irvin kept his hand between her legs, which didn't help her regain her composure.

"I didn't want to come yet," she finally said.

"I plan to make you come over and over."

She frowned and shook her head. "That's the problem," she said in a shaky voice. "I can't come more than once. I've tried."

A delicious gleam came into his eyes. "You've never been my lover before."

Chapter 13

His *lover*. The word danced around her brain as he kissed her again and lifted her into his arms. *Lover* implied long-term. More than a quick weekend fling. No matter how much his use of the word thrilled her, she wouldn't get any crazy ideas. When the sun rose tomorrow they'd do the last appearance, giving his foundation the money he'd raised by offering himself up as a date. Then she'd get on a plane and go home.

But that was tomorrow. They still had tonight.

He carried her farther down the terrace. How he made his way when he continued to kiss her, she didn't know. She lost herself in his kiss, surrendering to the pleasure that came from being exactly where she wanted to be right now. She ached to tell him all the feelings that he'd awakened in her, all the longing that she felt for this to be more than one night, but she couldn't say those things out loud. But she could let him know by the way she touched him.

He took her through a door that led to his bedroom. Gently he lowered her beside the bed. Once her feet touched the floor, her hands went everywhere. Across his jaw to the tight curls at the back of his head. Over wide shoulders to push away the jacket of his suit. Then back to massage the hard muscles of his chest.

She eased him backward until he fell onto the bed.

"Come and get me." His voice wrapped around her and heightened her need.

She straddled his hips and lowered her head to kiss him again while his long fingers caressed her thighs. His pants rubbed against her exposed clit. She gasped and jerked away. It was not fair for him still to have on so many clothes. A sinful grin spread across his face as his hands ran up her legs to grip her bare behind and pull her firmly against his cock.

"Is that what you want?" He lifted his hips again.

She moaned. "Yes."

"Are you going to come for me again?" His hands cupped her breasts.

"I'm damn sure gonna try."

"Good, because I damn sure want to make you come several times before the sun rises." He grasped her thighs and pinned her legs with a steady strength while slowly lifting and lowering his hips beneath her.

Her pleasure mounted with each movement. Her hands became unsteady, her breathing more labored. Her eyes flicked to his dark eyes intently studying her. He looked ready to devour her.

She felt suddenly self-conscious, and her hands shook. She wasn't a vixen. Why had she pushed him onto the bed and jumped on him as if she were used to taking control? This man had sex with the finest women in the world. Her attempts were probably laughable.

She fumbled with removing his tie and unbuttoning his shirt. It should have taken seconds but felt like forever. With a deep breath, she raised her gaze to his. The tenderness she saw there reached far into her heart and banished all of her nervousness. He took her cheek in his hand and lowered her head for a kiss. It was softer, slower than before.

"I could watch you undress me all night," he said against her lips.

"I thought I would take all night."

"Then I could do this all night," he said, raising his hips again to rub against her wet center.

She moaned and tugged at the waistband of his pants. It didn't take nearly as long to get them undone. She gasped with pleasure as he lifted up to push them past his waist.

The weight of his erection bounced against her wetness. She mirrored his hip rotation to enjoy the wonderful sensation of his thickness against her.

"You feel so good," he said against her lips. "So damn good."

He swiftly wrapped his arms around her and flipped her onto the bed. They became a tangle of arms and legs. Soft kisses, caresses and words she wouldn't remember as they explored each other's bodies. As if they both realized what was happening between them was special, they took their time. Her body turned into one large nerve, tingling and tight with the need to explode. Her heart fell deeper and deeper for him with each passing second.

No other experience she'd ever had compared with what he was doing to her. She doubted it could be better, until he slid his body down and settled between her legs.

Through a cloud of desire she rose up on her elbows and stared at the slow plunder of his fingers inside her body. He trailed his tongue from her neck all the way to her waist and below. She froze with anticipation and nervousness. Would he really? He licked his lips. Oh, God, yes, he would. He slowly ran his tongue across the erect nub at the center of her sex.

She watched him, her vision blurring as he loved her body. Her moans were matched by his. It was one thing to have him kiss her this way, another to know he enjoyed it as much as she. Her desire built inside her, rising higher and higher until she knew he was going to prove her a liar. She was going to climax again.

But she wanted all of him, inside her, when she did.

She gripped his shoulder and tried to pull him up. She saw the reluctance in his eyes as he lifted away from her body. He met her eyes, then froze, a look she didn't recognize on his features.

"I can't let you go."

The words shattered any hope she had of not falling in love with him. She would be his forever. Even if he was hers for only tonight. She shoved the bittersweet thought aside.

She spread her arms and he came to her. She barely registered that he pulled a condom from the nightstand and put it on. Or that somehow in their twisting and turning, the duvet had come off the bed and they were lying on a tangle of sheets. The only thing that registered in her mind was the intense pleasure of them becoming one.

She took in everything. The weight of his body pressed against her. The way his hands gripped her hips and ran up and down her sides and across her cheek. He touched and moved against her as if she were precious, fragile. When he wasn't kissing her, his eyes never left hers. It was more than sex. It was a connection that she would cherish long after the night was over and they both moved on.

As her climax built, his breathing changed. His eyes grew urgent. His thrusts came faster, deeper, until she couldn't hold back. She let herself go, and the orgasm crashed into her like a freight train. Her entire body shook with the force of it. She felt it everywhere: skin, hair, toes and lungs. Every part of her reacted to the beauty of her and Irvin.

He held her afterward. Not just a simple arm around her shoulders. No, he pulled her back against his chest, one arm around her waist so his hand could cup her breast, and squeezed her tight. She was actually spooning with Irvin Freeman. But it was more than that. He had erased any thoughts of him being the movie star and made her see only the guy she was falling in love with.

Tears threatened. It would all end in less than twenty-four hours.

"Are you awake?" he asked and kissed her shoulder.

She closed her eyes to stop the tears and nodded. "Isn't it the guy who falls asleep afterward?"

His chuckle vibrated across her skin. "That was like a shot of adrenaline."

"It was pretty powerful," she said with a smile.

"The sounds you make," he said in a deep, sexy voice. He kneaded her breast in his hand and pushed the hair away from her ear to gently kiss it. "A guy could get used to hearing that."

A girl could get used to having someone bring out those sounds. Who was she kidding? After only one time, she couldn't imagine making love like that with anyone else. He'd always be in her heart. She knew that now. Her sexual partners were few, which meant Irvin Freeman would be a part of her for the rest of her life.

And he'd move on and forget her. Her heart stung

with the thought. A dozen wasps in her chest couldn't have inflicted more pain. She wanted more, needed more to take with her.

"Tell me about your family," she said.

His movements on her breast stopped, and his body tightened next to her. She held her breath as she waited. There wasn't much about his family life in the media. All she knew was what he'd mentioned earlier in the day. Now, knowing she'd go home with only a night of sex to remember, she wanted to know. Wanted to see a part of him that few others would.

He tugged on her shoulder until she lay on her back. Leaning up on an elbow, he stared down at her.

"Only if you'll tell me what you're hiding."

"I'm not hiding anything." Her voice didn't conceal her panic.

"Something happened with your sister. Tell me about that."

She frowned, not wanting to air her family's dirty laundry. Even to Irvin. It had been so hard, so humiliating to have her twin do that to their parents. He didn't press, not verbally, anyway. But his eyes never left hers. She understood what he was doing. If she was going to probe, then so would he.

"After my mama got sick, Love—my sister—stole everything."

"What do you mean?"

"I mean everything. She cleaned out both of my parents' bank accounts. Took any valuable jewelry they had and a few antique pieces that had been in our family for years. It ruined any chances they had for a comfortable retirement—" she sighed and pressed her palm to her forehead "—or for paying the medical bills for Mama's recovery."

"Do you know why?"

Anger made Faith grip the sheet. "My sister is a drug addict. She started when we were in high school. She'd stolen from us before, but it was always small. A couple hundred bucks here or there. Then she'd disappear for a while or try to clean up, only to start over. This time she went too far. Mama was still in the hospital, barely twelve hours past her stroke, when Love took everything."

"It sounds like something bad happened."

"Something bad did happen."

"I mean to your sister. She had to have been desperate."

Faith didn't want to hear anything resembling sympathy for her sister. She scooted away and sat up on the bed. She pulled her knees up and rested her elbows on them. "I would never be desperate enough to take everything from our parents."

"Are you sure she wasn't in trouble?"

Faith sighed and stared out of the glass balcony doors at the twinkling skyline. It was well past midnight. Back home everything would be dark; here everything still shone brightly.

"If she were in that much trouble, she should have come to me. I wouldn't have liked it, but I would have helped her. Despite her years of addiction, I wanted her to get better. But her doing that to Mama and Daddy... That was my last straw."

Irvin moved to sit up beside her. "You still pay for her rehab."

"Mama begged me to." She took a deep breath. "And she's my twin. I can't stop hoping, just a little, that she'll get better."

"People in desperate situations don't realize that all they need to do is ask for help."

"Asking for help is easier than hurting people you love."

"Have you ever been desperate?"

The way he asked made her turn to him. He too looked out at the skyline, with a faraway look in his eye.

"Have you?" she asked.

"I've watched people in desperate situations try to handle it themselves."

"Your family?"

He nodded. "My parents. My father struggled with alcoholism. Most days he was tolerable. Drunk, but tolerable."

"And on other days?"

A frown stained his features. "On other days he was a monster. Violent, angry and uncontrollable. When I begged my mother to get help, she always refused. She preferred to hide it." He gave Faith a sad half smile. "My mother actually came from a good family. Her father was a top barrister, her mother a well-respected professor."

"I've heard that about you," Faith said.

"Because her family claimed me after I became famous. When my mother met and fell for my father, they disowned her. Said she was making a mistake." He gave a humorless laugh and tugged on the sheet. "Funny how right they were. Still, she wouldn't give them the satisfaction. She became an expert at hiding my dad's problem and our bruises. I became an expert at pretending to be a happy child whose father wasn't an alcoholic. I guess that's why acting came so naturally to me."

Faith flinched, hurting for him and an upbringing she couldn't fathom. Hesitantly she reached over to place her hand on his back. He took her other hand in his.

"What happened?"

"My father got smashed one night and drove home. He killed an entire family." He nodded when Faith gasped. "Can't hide four dead bodies. So, off he went to jail. I couldn't forgive him, but my mother decided to be there for him."

"What did you do?"

"I stopped trying to protect her. I left and came to the States. Until then, I'd turned down every opportunity to walk away. I would refuse to spend the night at friends' flats so I could take the blows meant for her when he became violent. I turned down several scholarships, all to protect my mother. It wasn't until he killed a family that I realized I couldn't save people from themselves. I could only save myself from them."

"How did your parents die?"

He turned to look at her. "My father got hold of some rubbing alcohol six months after being in jail and drank too much of it. He died not long after I moved away. I tried to get my mother to move over here, but she refused. So I sent her money. Got her a fancy flat when I made it big, and would visit at least twice a year. By then, her family was ready to take her back into their fold. She got sick a few years back. Meningitis. It took her quickly."

Faith didn't say anything. Instead, she leaned over and kissed his shoulder. He wrapped his arm around her and pressed a kiss to her temple. When he lifted his head, she tilted hers back to stare at him. He was so handsome. But before the weekend, he'd seemed like a dream. This outrageously fine, untouchable man that hovered in the fantasy world of Hollywood. Now he seemed real.

"Make love to me again," she whispered.

"As if I weren't already planning to do that." He

kissed her and eased her back into the pillows. Faith let the sadness of their revelations melt away as their bodies came together.

Chapter 14

"It was a pleasure to help raise funds for such a fantastic mission. I've always believed that the small actions people take toward a cause add up to tremendous results. And though it may seem as if the biggest winner here is Faith, we all know that the winners are the people who will benefit from the funds we raised."

Cameras flashed, and the large group standing behind the podium all clapped. They were in the lobby of the headquarters of Irvin's foundation, Starting Over. Irvin was giving his speech before he presented the check for the money raised by this campaign. Standing behind him, Faith couldn't stop herself from staring at him. The man was devastating in a dark brown suit and tan silk tie. She'd overheard the appreciative gasps of the women when he'd walked into the room and flashed that smile. Instead of being jealous, she'd felt a little cocky. They had connected last night, if only briefly. She had something with Irvin that no other woman did.

For now.

She blinked and pressed a hand to the side of her head to push the thought away. The future didn't matter. What mattered was this exact second in her life. The last few moments she had with him. She needed to drink it all in. In a few short hours she'd be back on a plane on her way home.

Kitty treated her as more than just the weekend prop. The publicist hadn't seemed surprised to find Faith at Irvin's apartment that morning. In fact, she'd brought Faith's outfit for the presentation, a cute sleeveless coral dress that flared into an A-line skirt above her knees. She still barked orders and referred to the itinerary, but now she insisted that someone get Faith some water because she looked thirsty. And ordered one of the members of her crew to go out for cupcakes when Faith made an offhand comment about wanting another like she'd had with Irvin the other night.

Faith guessed the change was Kitty's assumption that Faith was Irvin's new woman. Though the thought flattered her, it also made her uneasy. She didn't want people fetching her water or running out for cupcakes on Kitty's command. She wanted only Irvin. But Irvin came with all that, and she wasn't sure she was up for the constant scrutiny.

The applause died down and Irvin spoke again. "I always knew I had the best fans in the world. But half a million dollars for my foundation was more than I could imagine they would raise. If I'd known offering myself up as a prize would raise so much, I would have done it a lot sooner."

That got a laugh out of the crowd. "Especially if I'd known the winner would be so wonderful."

He nailed Faith with a hot stare that whipped up

memories of the night before. The weight of his body on top of her, his hands caressing her breasts. He licked his lips, and her face burned with the memory of the way he'd licked her so thoroughly. Her passion ignited with such strength, she was surprised the hairs on her arms didn't catch fire.

She struggled to take in a breath.

"Irvin," one of the reporters at the press conference called out, breaking the moment. "Since this was so successful, will you do this again?"

Time stood still as she waited on the answer. A yes meant she was easily replaceable. A no meant… Well, it didn't mean forever with him, but it also didn't mean he was eager to have another woman spend the weekend with him.

"No," he said. "I hope to find other ways to raise funds."

A few reporters turned her way, and she fought not to squirm. After several more questions, Irvin presented the check to the chairman of the board and shook hands with him, and they posed for pictures. Then she noticed Irvin's artist friend Carl was looking at her, too, and smiling. He looked completely different in a pair of faded jeans and a button-down red-and-blue-striped shirt.

"Freeman put me on the list," he said when she walked over to shake his hand. "He's the only one left who has any hope I'll shake this thing."

"I have hope, too," she said, even more touched by Irvin's assistance to the man after his confession about his own father the night before.

"I'm almost done with your drawing. I'll make sure Freeman gets it to you." Carl gave her a knowing grin. "I'm sure he'll be in touch."

Faith wished more than anything that were the case.

After the press conference, a small group waited in the boardroom until the media cleared out. The foundation's chairman came over. "I bet you've had an exciting weekend."

"I have," Faith said with a smile.

"It's going to be hard to go home after this, huh?"

Painful was more like it. Still, she kept the smile on her face and nodded. "I'll manage. Besides, I'm looking forward to getting back. My parents are sick, and I'm their caretaker."

The chairman patted her on the arm. "Good for you."

It was an odd statement, but before Faith could comment, someone clasped her shoulder.

"Are you ready?" Kitty asked. "We've got to leave in order to get to the airport on time."

Faith's heart rate sprang into rocket speed. Already? The weekend would end just that quickly.

"Is it time?" She hated that her voice wavered with the question.

"Past time, really. But it took longer to clear the room than expected. Say your goodbyes and we'll be going."

Kitty rushed over to one of the members of her team. Faith's world tilted on its axis. How could she possibly say goodbye adequately? Had she overreacted and read too much into the weekend than there really was? She hadn't asked Irvin the details of her departure today because she'd known it was their last day together and she didn't want to spoil it, but she'd hoped for something other than an order from Kitty to say her goodbyes.

And where was Irvin?

She looked across the room to where Kitty had walked and she found him. He hadn't come to her after the press conference had ended. When they'd come in here, he'd talked to other people on the board. Was it because he didn't want to be the one to push her onto the plane?

Well, she would make it easy for him.

She hurried out of the boardroom and down the end of the empty hall. She stood in front of the window and stared out at the city, gray and damp with a rainstorm. She didn't want this life, but the thought of leaving made her throat tighten.

"Faith." Irvin's concerned voice came from behind her. "You all right?"

"Yeah... I just needed a second before I said my goodbyes."

"It should be easy," he said. Her back was to him, but she heard the humor in his voice.

She clenched her fists and glared out the window at the dreary landscape. "I guess it would be easy for you. A guy with your history must not have any trouble saying goodbye the next day."

"A guy with my history." All humor left his tone. "What's that supposed to mean?"

"I'm sure you've had your share of weekend flings. I know that what we did here isn't special."

In the reflection in the window, she watched him come closer. He crossed his arms, but she couldn't make out the expression on his face. "Where is this coming from, Faith?"

"You date a lot of women."

"Dating a lot of women doesn't mean I sleep with a lot of women."

"Come on, Irvin."

"Gossips like to link my name to different women, but it doesn't mean that it's true." He took her elbow in his hand and spun her to face him.

The hurt and anger in his expression took her breath

away. "What they report is nothing more than rumors. Despite what most of the world believes, I'm not sleeping with a new woman every night."

Her neck and cheeks prickled with heat. She shifted her eyes away from his. "I'm sorry. I didn't..."

"Let me guess. You didn't mean it?" He let her go and took a step back. "I thought last night meant something."

"It did. It does. I didn't want to come to New York, and I really didn't want to be another easy groupie that fell for you. But you turned out to be funny, and nice, and so sweet and considerate. And something clicks when I'm with you. Something that makes me want more than I can say." She met his eyes and felt her feelings for him rise up in her heart. "Then you kissed me and made love to me. It was like a dream come true. More than anything I ever could have imagined, and it touched something that I really didn't want you to touch."

The tension left his body, replaced by a look that was both nervous and unsure, as he came to her.

"Faith, I enjoyed this weekend with you. I didn't expect us to end up like this. It just happened."

"I know. I'm sorry. It's just that...this weekend doesn't mean as much to you as it does me. Okay, you don't sleep with a lot of women. I'll give you that. But by tomorrow, I'll be nothing more than the woman you had sex with one weekend after she won a date with you in a raffle. And right now, I need to remind myself of that."

He brushed the back of his hand across her face. "You're determined to believe that this isn't really happening between us. If you keep it up, I'm going to be insulted. I'm not letting this end. This is just beginning."

Her hands fell to her sides. "But Kitty told me to say my goodbyes."

"Yes, to the people here at the foundation. Not to me. You wouldn't really think I'd let her brush you off like that." He frowned, then held up a hand. "Never mind. What you said earlier means you would think that."

She tried not to get her hopes up, not when they still had an insurmountable problem. "How could we possibly make it work? I can't just leave my parents behind and move to New York."

"I wouldn't expect you to." He came close and took her hands in his. "But just because you're going home doesn't mean we're through."

"I've done long distance before. It didn't end very well."

"I'm not some prat who'll break up with you for taking care of your family."

"It wasn't just my family," she said, trying not to lose herself in the warmth of his eyes and smile. Long distance with her ex was one thing, but long distance with a man like Irvin seemed downright impossible. "My ex needed someone to fit his image. You're the same. You're Irvin Freeman. You're supposed to be with someone like Selena, not a country nurse."

"Says who? The gossip columnists? I'm supposed to be with the person I choose to be with." He tugged her hands to bring her forward. "And I chose you."

The look, his cologne, the voice… It all drew her in. Made her believe and trust that it could work. Still… "I'm serious, Irvin. It's going to be hard. This weekend was great, but it won't be like this always."

"I'm serious, too, Faith. I'll come see you in South Carolina. On your weekends off, you can visit me. I'll even pay for your family to come with you or for a live-in nurse to help out so the burden isn't all on you."

"I can't let you do that." She turned away.

He placed a hand on her chin and gently turned her back to him. "I want to. I told you once that I believe in fate. It brought us together, and I'm not willing to let go of what we started here just because we don't live in the same state."

"You make it sound so easy," she said.

"It may not be easy, but it's worth it."

He smiled, and her heart did a squat jump in her chest. Her breathing hitched as he lowered his head to kiss her.

"Not now, you two." Kitty's voice broke in right before Irvin's lips touched Faith's. "The plane is waiting."

Disappointment like she'd never experienced in her life weighed on her chest. "You've got to tell her to stop interrupting our kisses," she said.

Irvin grinned. "I think she has internal radar that lets her know I'm about to put her behind schedule."

"The time to go came so soon," she whispered.

"Saying goodbye is always the hardest part," Irvin whispered. He stepped back and took her hand in his. "That's why I'm going to make our first one special."

The look on Faith's face when she realized he was flying her back on a private jet made him happier than any flattering review for one of his movies. Her grin was more impressive than the luxurious furnishings.

"You own a jet, too?" she said, spinning around and taking in their surroundings.

"Sorry to disappoint you, but no. I don't mind traveling commercially and would rather put my money in real estate. This is my friend Dante's plane."

"I guess that makes sense. It looks more like him than you."

He chuckled and glanced around at the dark wood with matching Italian leather furniture, a fully stocked bar and a sixty-inch television in the main cabin.

"What makes it look more like him than me?"

"You're not as flashy."

He sat on one of the leather seats and pulled her down on his lap. Her laughter and warm curves lit a fire in his body that only grew hotter when he kissed her.

Still, he wondered how they would make this relationship work. For all of his talk back at the foundation, he was concerned about what would happen when they parted. As for him, he was used to long-distance relationships. The last woman he'd dated was also an actor, and they frequently were in different cities, or countries, depending on their schedules. When he was with a woman exclusively, he was faithful. He didn't have time to invite drama into his life. So he wasn't worried about his needs. He was worried about how Faith would deal with it. It was one thing to trust him when they were together, another when they were apart and the media began circulating rumors about him. The last thing he wanted was for his celebrity status to make her doubt him.

So he planned to make sure that she knew exactly how much he wanted her before he left her and every time they got together.

The flight crew interrupted their kiss to ask them to put on seat belts for takeoff.

"This is the worst part," Faith said. She clutched the arms of the chair.

"It'll be over before you know it."

She frowned. "And I'll be home before we know it. It's only a two-hour flight." She glanced at him from her seat, which she'd regretfully had to move into for take-off. "How long will you stay? I know you're supposed to be in Canada tomorrow."

"I'd hoped to stay the night."

"As much as I would love that, my parents might think it's weird for me to bring you home. And I don't think they'd approve of you sleeping in my bed."

"Prudish?"

"Not exactly. But take away your movie-star status again and you're a man I met two days ago, and you're spending the night with me already."

He winced and grinned. "It does sound like we've rushed into it."

"It does."

"So I won't spend the night, but I will stay in town. And come see you before I go in the morning."

"And I can spend some time with you at your hotel tonight. Though it won't be as luxurious as you're used to."

"With you in the bed, it doesn't matter."

The plane sped up on the runway then, and her grip tightened on the chair. He placed his hand on hers. Several minutes later, the flight attendant came by and let them know they could remove their seat belts. He also brought chilled champagne with an assortment of fruits and cheeses.

Faith didn't take off her seat belt.

"You can remove that," Irvin said with a smile.

"I know, but it just makes me feel safer."

"You don't like flying, I gather."

"It's a necessary thing. I don't hate it, but it's not fun, either."

He raised a brow. "You could find fun ways to distract yourself."

"I've tried them all. Reading, listening to music, watching a movie. Nothing distracts me enough."

"You know if we plummet to the earth, wearing a seat belt won't keep you alive."

She cut her eyes at him. "You're not helping."

He uncorked the champagne and poured her a glass. She raised an eyebrow when he put the bottle back into the ice.

"You don't want any?"

He shrugged. "I only have one drink per day."

"Why?"

"To avoid becoming like my father. When I first came to New York, it was easy to party and drink until the sun rose. I stumbled in one night after doing just that, looked in the mirror and froze. I looked exactly like him. It scared the life out of me."

She put her glass down and placed her hand on his. "To do what he did meant he didn't have your goodness in his heart. I can't imagine you becoming like him."

Her confidence warmed him more than any stage light ever had. "I appreciate that, more than I can say."

"If you're not drinking then I'm not," she said.

"Which means you still need a distraction."

Her hair was pulled back into a neat chignon. Between the hair and the dress she'd worn to the press conference, she looked like the cool and collected woman in the picture Kitty had first shown him. He wanted the warm and mussed woman that moaned his name in that sexy Southern accent of hers.

He popped off his seat belt and stood over her. "I'm about to help." He unhooked her seat belt and pulled her from the chair.

The second her soft curves met his hard muscles,

need stirred in his groin to have her naked against him once again.

"How are you going to help?" Her voice became husky and her eyes softened.

"Follow me." He took her hand and led her through a door beside the television to a separate bedroom. It was decorated in the same dark colors, along with a king-size bed with a chocolate duvet.

"You want me to take a nap?" she asked with a teasing smile.

"I want you in that bed." He stood behind her and slowly unzipped the back of her dress. "But not for a nap."

"I don't know. Sleeping is usually how I distract myself while flying." She teased him, but he could hear the desire in her voice.

He pushed the dress off her shoulders, then stepped back just enough to take in all of her wonderful curves from the back. He felt himself grow harder as his gaze fell on the skimpy black panties and the cuff of her butt beneath the edges.

"I'm about to show you a new way to enjoy a flight." He put his hand on her waist and pulled her against him. He pressed his cock into her backside. "How about that?"

Her head fell back. He looked down her body at her wonderful breasts in the sexy bra and all that silky brown skin. He wanted to taste every inch of her.

He brought his hand up to cup her breast, using his finger to trace the hardened nipple through the lace. She moaned and rubbed against him.

"Is that my answer?" he said against her ear.

She nodded, and he nipped at the bottom of her ear-lobe. His other hand dived past the waistband of her panties to her desire-slickened sex. His knees trembled as he caressed the smooth skin with his fingers. She was already wet and swollen. Ready for him. He ran his fingers against her dewy treasure before sinking his middle finger inside. Her walls clenched around him, and he groaned.

"When you touch me like that," she panted, "it makes me want to do things."

He slipped his finger out and dived back in. "What things?"

She turned in his arms. The smile she gave him turned his penis into granite. He was crazy about this woman.

"Why don't I show you?" she asked.

She lowered to her knees, tugging on the waistband of his pants as she went down. Each pull ignited an urgency inside him until her warm hand clasped him in her grip. The first press of her lips against him nearly toppled him down. When her hot mouth closed around him, he thought he would explode right then. He gripped her head, then had to force himself to loosen his hold. But it was difficult when her tongue did things to him he would never forget. The memories of this encounter would keep him awake and hard every night they were separated.

He felt his climax coming and pulled her up before it could arrive. Lifting her into his arms, he hurried across the room and fell onto the bed with her. His mouth didn't break from hers the entire time. It took only a few seconds to remove his clothes, and he would owe her another pair of undergarments because he tore her panties in his urgency to get them off.

He lowered between her legs and returned her favor. He loved the taste of her. And her bare lower lips gave him unblocked access to every nook and crevice.

"Irvin, yes. Please. Don't stop" were the words she said over and over.

"I'm not stopping until we both can't walk," he said against her sweetness.

Lifting away from this feast, he got a condom from his pants pocket, put it on and sank deeply into her body. Her legs wrapped tightly around his waist. Her hips rose to meet his thrust for thrust. She twisted and he moved with her; she begged for more and he gave her more. He didn't know if it was turbulence or the emotions Faith awakened in him, but his body shook. And when he followed her over the edge, he realized that despite knowing her only a few days, he was quickly falling in love with Faith Logan.

Chapter 15

Faith wished she could stop herself from smiling like the Cheshire Cat in *Alice in Wonderland*, but her mouth refused to cooperate. As the plane landed and Irvin continued to rub his thumb gently back and forth across the back of her hand in his, she felt like Alice. She'd fallen into a wonderful parallel universe or something. If it weren't for the delicious ache between her legs, she wouldn't believe this was happening. That she'd not only made love on a private jet, but that she was falling in love.

She almost hated to admit that she was falling in love with him. Insecurities tried to creep in, but every time he smiled at her, and she remembered how things were when they were alone, she pushed her doubts away.

They got off the plane at the private airstrip. She'd been there several times as a child. The owner, Gary Baker, used to invite the community over during the summer for trips in his small one-engine plane around the county. An event that turned into a minifair with game booths, food vendors and even a live band. He'd stopped it several years ago after his wife passed away.

"Hi, Gary," Faith said when they got off the plane.

Gary's dark eyes twinkled in his wrinkled face, and he opened his arms wide to give her a hug.

"As soon as they told me you were flying in, I had to come down and say hello," Gary said.

"How did you know I was on the plane?"

Gary pulled back and eyed Irvin over her shoulder. "You're the only one in town who won a weekend with a movie star. They told me Irvin Freeman needed it, so I put two and two together."

Irvin walked up and held out his hand. "Thank you very much for allowing us to use your strip. It was quite the surprise to find out there was a private airstrip here. I didn't think we'd get closer than Greenville."

"Well, that's what you get for thinking," Gary said with a wide grin on his face.

"I guess you're right," Irvin said, returning Gary's grin.

"It may not be here for long," Gary said, looking around at the empty bay that once held his plane. "I'm thinking of selling. Might move closer to town. Kinda quiet and lonely out here all by myself."

Gary and his late wife had loved each other deeply. It had been obvious whenever the two were around. He was still his normal good-natured self, but his smile had definitely dimmed in the years since she passed.

"You can always come have dinner with me and my parents," Faith offered.

"I would," Gary said, "if you were ever off work."

He looked to Irvin. "I'm so glad she won that trip. This woman deserves to get out and have a good time."

"I hope to give her a lot of good times in the future," Irvin said, taking her hand in his again. She'd never realized how much she loved holding hands with a man until she'd met Irvin.

"I take that to mean you'll be around for a while," Gary said.

"As long as she'll have me."

Gary nodded. "Good deal."

After a few more minutes chatting with Gary, they loaded up the back of the car Irvin had reserved for them and made their way to her parents' house.

During the ride she answered his questions about the town. But her anxiety grew with each mile. Two years of not bringing a man home and she was arriving with one after only a few short days. And not just any man. A movie star. Her parents were going to think she was crazy, or stupid, or both. Mama had told her to have fun, not fall head over heels. And she definitely hadn't told her to bring him home and say she was about to turn their lives upside down by dating someone so famous.

"We're here, cutie," Irvin said.

Faith jumped at his voice. She hadn't realized they'd stopped. She swallowed hard and turned to Irvin. "They're really nice…normally."

"Normally? Should I expect this to be an abnormal visit?"

"What do you think?"

He smiled, that damn wonderful heart-melting smile of his, then leaned over and kissed her cheek. "Just the first round of scrutiny in our relationship."

"I'd rather face the paparazzi," she said.

When the driver opened the door, she saw her mama

and daddy sitting on the front porch. Their smiles brightened when she got out of the car. Those smiles drifted into looks of confusion when Irvin got out, but then, like good Southern folk, they quickly pasted on a welcoming grin. Only Faith recognized they weren't very sincere.

"Hey, Mama and Daddy," Faith said after she and Irvin crossed the lawn to the front porch.

"Faith, it's good to see you," her mama said, her Southern accent full of questions.

She hugged her daddy first, then bent down to hug her mama.

"And you brought a visitor." Her daddy held out his hand to Irvin. "Jimmy Logan."

"Irvin Freeman." Irvin shook her dad's outstretched hand.

"I didn't know the prize included a personal return home by Irvin Freeman," her mama said.

Irvin shook her hand next. His thousand-watt smile turned on full blast her mama's way. Virginia wasn't immune. She shifted in her chair and patted the bun at the back of her head.

"It didn't originally, but I wasn't ready to say goodbye," Irvin said. He took a step closer to Faith and wrapped her hand in his.

Virginia and Jimmy looked at their entwined hands, then at each other.

"Just why weren't you ready to say goodbye?" her dad asked.

"Faith and I got along very well in New York," Irvin said.

"How well?" Virginia asked. She leaned her elbow on the arm of the chair and nailed him with a sweet smile laced with a bit of caution that seemed to say *mess up if you want to.*

Irvin cleared his throat and threw Faith a glance. She'd tried to warn him.

"Well enough for me to recognize that I'd like to spend more time with her," he said.

Jimmy crossed his arms. "Time doing what?"

"Dating. We've decided to start dating," Irvin answered quickly.

"Aren't you dating that actress Selena Jones?" her mama fired off next.

"No, ma'am. Selena and I are just friends."

Again her parents exchanged looks. She didn't know if it was the *ma'am* or the sincerity in his voice, but they both nodded and turned genuine welcoming smiles in his direction.

"Well, why didn't you say so?" Virginia asked. "Come on in. I just made some sweet tea."

Virginia maneuvered her chair around with her husband's help, and they went inside. Irvin wiped his brow and gave Faith a grin.

"What did I say that won them over?"

She shook her head. "I don't know if it was your smile or that sexy accent of yours."

"I doubt either would work on your father," he said with a grin.

They followed her parents into the cool interior of the house. The front door opened directly into the living room. Irvin stopped and looked around. She bit her lip as she watched him. Their house was clean and homey, but nowhere near as fashionable or spotless as his New York condo.

"I love it," he said.

"Really?"

"Yes, it feels like a home," he said. "I haven't been

in a real home in…" He paused and a sad look crossed his features.

His childhood home wouldn't have felt like one, not the way he described it. He might never have been in one. He'd left London and come straight to America and the life he lived now.

"Then we'll be sure to make you feel at home," Virginia said from the end of the hall. "Come on down. I made biscuits this morning."

The wistful look left Irvin's face, replaced with his smile. "I thought biscuits were a breakfast food," he said, glancing at his watch. "It's well past noon."

"It's never a bad time of day for biscuits and molasses," her mama said. "Faith, haven't you told him anything?"

They laughed and followed Virginia down the hall.

"We're really going to a place called Hole in the Wall?" Irvin asked Faith.

They were back in the car, heading out for a night on the town her parents insisted they have. He'd known he was going to like Virginia Logan the second she'd quickly broken his melancholy in her living room. He'd known his upbringing wasn't the happiest and had thought he'd come to grips with that. But seeing the Logans' living room with hand-stitched quilts, family pictures on the walls and old trophies had done something to him. Despite the problems with Faith's sister, her pictures were still there. A testament to the fact that the family, at one time, had loved each other.

"Yes," Faith said. She leaned against his side, his arm around her shoulders. She'd insisted that they didn't need to dress up and was wearing jean shorts and a dark blue blouse. He didn't think he'd like anything better than the skimpy dress she'd worn to the club, but he loved this simple outfit. It was how she'd looked when he'd first seen her. Without all the glamour they'd thrown on her for the weekend. It enhanced her sexiness more than any other outfit he'd seen her in.

"It's named after the Mel Waiters song."

"I don't think I've ever heard that one."

She lifted her head and looked at him as if he'd spoken in tongues. "You haven't heard the song? It's a classic. Don't worry. It's guaranteed they'll play it. You've got to get up and do the two-step when it comes on."

"I don't know that dance, either," he said with a laugh.

"It's as easy as it sounds," she said, leaning her head back on his shoulder. "Are you sure you're okay with doing this? It's not like the fancy nightclubs you're used to in New York, but the people here are friendly. And if you don't want to be bothered with autographs and such, they'll leave you alone."

"That stuff doesn't bother me," he said as he kissed the top of her head. "Besides, your father said this is the best hangout in all of Laurel County."

"It's the only hangout," she said with a chuckle.

They arrived a few minutes later, and Irvin had to admit the place lived up to the name. It was a large wooden building with Hole in the Wall painted on the front. The dirt parking area was full of cars, and more lined the dirt road.

"Busy place," he said.

"You should see it on Saturday night," Faith said.

"Do you come here often?"

She shook her head. "No. When I'm off I try to spend time at home with Mama and Daddy. But my friend Marie comes a lot. Her truck's right over there." She pointed to a dark truck parked a few cars over. "I guess you'll get to meet all the important people in my life today."

The idea sent an unfamiliar warmth through his chest. He wanted to know the people important to her.

They entered the club, if you'd call it that. Wooden tables and chairs crowded the floor. Cigarette smoke hung in the air, along with the smell of frying food. People talked and laughed all over the place and congregated on a small dance area next to an old piano. The stereo and speakers on top of the piano were so big he was surprised the instrument could support the weight.

This was a far cry from the clubs Kitty dragged him out to.

"Faith!" A woman's yell cut through the noise and music. A woman with dark brown skin and short black hair jumped up from a nearby table and ran over. She grabbed Faith into a huge hug. "When did you get home?"

"Today," Faith said.

"What? Why didn't you call me? You know I want to hear all of the juicy details."

Faith laughed. "That's why I brought the details with me." She turned to Irvin. "Irvin, meet my best friend, Marie."

Marie's mouth dropped open. Then a sly smile spread across her full lips. "You brought him home," she said, slapping the side of Faith's arm. "What did you do up there, girl?"

"She completely bewitched me," Irvin said, pulling Faith to his side.

"Oh my word, that accent," Marie said, fanning herself.

"I'm more of a fan of her accent," Irvin said with a grin.

Faith nudged him with her elbow. "Stop. Everyone

in New York kept asking where I was from the second I opened my mouth. Like they've never heard a Southerner speak before. I must sound terrible."

"You sound wonderful," he said, kissing her cheek.

"I can't believe it," Marie said with a grin. "Hey, everyone, Faith is back, and she brought one hell of a souvenir."

That called up a round of well wishes, and several people came over to meet him and shake his hand. All of them told Faith they were glad she'd had a good time and that she deserved to get out more. She'd told him that her life since coming home was devoted to taking care of her parents, and now their words proved it. He didn't know how, or if she'd even want his help, but he was going to find a way to bring fun and relaxation back into her life.

True to Faith's word, after the crowd greeted him, they went back to doing their own things. One woman had even told him she thought his last movie could have been better, but she didn't blame him for the funky ending. He'd laughed. No one in New York dared tell him his movies weren't good, and he agreed the ending wasn't the best.

"Are you ready to have a good time?" Faith asked him.

"Are you ready to show me a good time?"

"Just you wait and see, city boy," she said, her sexy accent filling him with heat. "I took tomorrow off already, so I can stay out all night."

They found a table near the bar. Marie and her boyfriend joined them. He heard the song the place was named after, and he learned the two-step. The song talked about whiskey and chicken wings, so he took his one drink of the day to pay homage to the lyrics before switching to soda. By the end of the night, he'd fallen hard not only for Faith but also for the people who welcomed him, then left him alone. No flash, no pretense and no worries about cameras or who was there with whom. He liked it.

It was close to 2:00 a.m. when they waved goodbye to Marie as they left the Hole in the Wall and got into the car.

"Did you have fun?" Faith asked, her voice husky from the singing and yelling over the music.

"That was the most fun I've had in my entire life."

She chuckled and pushed his shoulder. "I don't believe you. You party with superstars every weekend."

"None of whom will take whiskey shots in between servings of lemon-pepper wings."

"They were salt-and-vinegar wings," she said with a silly smile.

"Really?"

"Yep, Marie had lemon pepper. I had salt and vinegar."

"And I ate out of every basket on the table. My nutritionist would have a heart attack."

"Eating wings like those every night will give you a heart attack," she said.

"Is that the nurse in you coming out?" He slid across the seat and leaned over her, pinning her with his arms. "Are you worried about my health now?"

Her eyes turned dreamy, and she wrapped her arms around his waist. "Maybe just a little. I don't want you to have a heart attack. I'd like to keep you around for a while."

"Oh, really? Because I'd like to stay around for a while." Her grin made his heart rate speed up. He stopped smiling to stare into her beautiful face. "I mean it, Faith. I want this to last."

"I feel like I'm in a fairy tale."

"They always have happy endings," he said.

"But they aren't real." The smile left her face. He saw the doubts starting to creep back into her eyes.

He leaned down and kissed her, pressing his body against hers until she gasped and moaned against his lips. "Does this feel real?" he asked.

"Yes." She grabbed his head and pulled it back down, and he proceeded to show her just how real this thing was between them.

Chapter 16

Faith's stomach growled as she waited for her candy bar to fall in the vending machine in the hospital's break room. She crossed her fingers and hoped the decrepit machine actually worked this time. Only to immediately curse and kick the thing when the bar got stuck.

Great. Now she was tired, frustrated, horny and hungry. She shook the machine as much as she could, but knew it was useless. A call to the security desk would get someone up here to unlock it and hand over the candy bar, but at the moment she wanted to hit something.

Twelve weeks. Three months. Ninety days. Not long in the structure of a lifetime, but it might as well have been the length of the Cretaceous period. No matter how she thought of it, seeing Irvin only sporadically during that time was torture.

Whom did she see often? The paparazzi. Every time

she thought they'd move on, she'd find out about another attempt to get information about her. Usually from "friends" she hadn't talked with since kindergarten. Or she'd leave the grocery store and someone would snap a picture.

She'd known dating Irvin would change her life, but she hadn't realized how much. Or how hard it would be to keep hoping they could make things work. She missed Irvin, but being his girlfriend was wearing her nerves down to frazzled bits.

"Faith, do you have a second?"

Faith turned away from the dangling candy bar and looked to the hospital's chief nursing officer. Lisa Williams had been nothing but nice and supportive of Faith since she'd returned, even when she'd told her it would be next to impossible for her to get a higher-ranking nursing job at the hospital despite her qualifications.

"Sure, Lisa. Let me call down to the security desk for someone to grab my candy bar and I'll come to your office."

Lisa glanced at her watch. "Come on and we'll ask Marie to call down for you."

"Sure."

She followed Lisa out of the break room. They stopped at the nurses' station, where Faith asked her friend to call about the candy bar. Marie shot a curious look between Faith and Lisa, which Faith returned with a "beats me" look of her own. Lisa made her rounds through the hospital and knew all of the nurses, but mostly it was the floor and shift managers who dealt directly with Faith and Marie. Faith was doing either really well or really badly for Lisa to come down and get her.

Or neither one, she reminded herself. In the three months since she'd returned home, random people around town had asked about her time in New York. How did it feel to be Irvin Freeman's girlfriend? What was it like to kiss him? She braced herself for Lisa's questions.

The constant presence of the paparazzi made denying her relationship with Irvin impossible. But she'd downplayed the extent of their relationship. In hindsight, that had been a good idea. They'd talked, texted and emailed a lot when he'd first left for Canada. He'd surprised her with a visit one weekend, and another time she'd driven to Atlanta to see him, but they'd had only a day before he had to get back to the set. As he got busier, the correspondence dwindled. Now she got a few sporadic texts and hadn't talked to him in over a week. If he hadn't arranged for her to come up to Canada for the weekend, she would have sworn she was one phone call away from a breakup.

"So what can I do for you?" Faith asked Lisa once they were settled in her office.

"I've wanted to talk to you since you got back from New York, but things have been hectic and I haven't had the chance."

As Faith suspected, a Q and A session on her and Irvin.

"Oh, really," she said.

"Yes. When you moved here two years ago, I hated that there wasn't a position I could offer you other than floor nurse. With your qualifications and background, you really should be sitting here instead of down on the third floor."

Faith was usually good at maintaining a poker face, but Lisa's comment surprised her so much, she was sure her face had a weird look going on.

"Umm…thanks." She wasn't quite certain of the proper response when the boss said you should have her position. She cleared her throat and schooled her features. "I was happy to get any work that would help me take care of my parents."

"Many people say things like that and don't mean them. I waited for you to complain, or be resentful for having to start at the bottom of the chain, but it never happened."

Faith shrugged. "No use in complaining about things I can't change. My parents needed me."

"Still, I want you to know that I've paid attention." Lisa shifted through the papers on her desk, picking up one. "I suppose you know that Gwendolyn put in her resignation earlier this week."

Faith frowned and slid forward in her seat. Gwendolyn was the nurse manager for the intensive-care unit. She'd been at the hospital for over twenty years and said the only things she loved more than working there were her grandchildren.

"No, I wasn't aware of that."

"Well, she did. Her daughter got a job in Colorado, and she and her husband are moving. Which means Gwendolyn's grandkids are going. She can't stand the idea of them being across the country and her daughter having to rely on strangers to look after the kids. So she's moving with them."

"Wow, that's good for her."

Lisa looked up from the paper and smiled at Faith. "And good for you, too. I want you to take her position. I know it's nothing as big as what you used to do, but it's the best I can do right now. You'll be only on the day shift, so no more overnighters, and of course I'll start you at the higher end of the pay scale considering your background."

Faith's head spun with the news. After two years of

struggling, her work was paying off. It wouldn't be close to her salary in Houston, but it was more than what she was earning now. It would allow some cushion in the family budget. No more scratching up what she could after physical therapy for her mama, doctor appointments for her dad and rehab for Love. Some of the home repairs she'd put off could be taken care of. And she'd even be able to fulfill her promise to her mama to go out more without feeling guilty.

Though she wouldn't be going out with the person she wanted.

"Are you sure?" she asked.

"I don't have a second thought. I'd also like you to represent the nurses at the hospital board meetings. I've done it for the past few years and tried to get Gwendolyn interested, but she didn't want to. It has to be a member of the managing staff. The person brings the perspective of the nursing staff to the board and hospital president. It'll be a good way to get your name in front of the higher-ups. After all, I'm planning to retire in a few years myself."

Faith bit the inside of her cheek to keep her jaw from dropping. This was unbelievable. "Of course. I'd be happy to help."

"Great." Lisa went into the details of transitioning her to the new position.

Several minutes later, Faith made her way back downstairs. Marie was reviewing a chart behind the nurses' station when Faith walked up.

"Your candy bar," Marie said, picking up the candy and waving it in Faith's direction.

"Thank you." She walked over as if in a dream and took the candy. "You won't believe what Lisa wanted."

"What, to ask you about New York?"

"I thought that was it, but no. Gwendolyn's leaving, and she's giving me her job."

Marie's brown eyes widened, and a huge grin split her face. "That's awesome, Faith!"

Faith hesitated. Marie had worked at the hospital longer than her and had complained to her about the way the hospital often moved who they wanted into certain positions instead of advertising them. That was exactly what was happening with Faith.

"Are you sure you're okay with this? It's another move they've made without posting the position."

"And finally they made a good choice. No one deserves this more than you. We've got to celebrate." Marie reached over and gave Faith a hug.

When Marie jumped up and down, Faith joined in. It was exactly what she'd wanted when she first moved home. Finally, things were looking up for her family.

Faith called her parents to tell them the great news and Marie went home with her to celebrate. When they got there, Virginia had a cake on the dining room table, and Jimmy held a bouquet of flowers.

"Where did all this come from?" Faith asked, eyeing the cake decorated with yellow flowers and Congratulations Faith in icing.

"We got it from the grocery store. You can't celebrate without cake," her dad said. He handed her the bouquet of roses and gave her a hug.

The smell of the roses instantly brought back memories of being in the flower shop with Irvin. She'd sent him a quick email about the promotion but hadn't heard back. The silence broke her heart. It was silly, she'd tried telling herself. People didn't really fall in love over a weekend. But her heartache felt pretty damn real.

"You didn't have to drive to the store," Faith said after she left her dad's embrace.

"Your dad can drive short distances," her mama said with a teasing glint in her eyes. "And you know something cool? Grocery stores have these smooth floors that allow me to move my chair around easily."

"You think you're funny," Faith said, putting the roses on the table to avoid their bittersweet fragrance. "You know what I mean. Daddy shouldn't be driving."

"Faith, dear, that weekend you went away did all of us some good," Virginia said. "You got a chance to realize that you're still young enough to have a little fun. And your dad and I realize that we've been too dependent on you since you came back."

"No, you haven't," Faith said.

Her mama rolled over and took Faith's hand in hers. "Yes, we have. We talked about it, and maybe it was the combined shock of my stroke and what Love did, but instead of learning to live with our circumstances, we let you take care of everything."

Her daddy took her other hand. "It's true, Faith. I managed to get around before your mom's stroke. It's time for you to stop spending so much of your time taking care of us and spend time taking care of yourself."

"This promotion will allow me to do both," Faith said.

Her parents both shook their heads. "But you promised me that you'd start going out, having fun and living again," Virginia said. "And now that you've got a promotion, I'm holding you to it. If you keep working yourself into the ground, we'll be forced to boot you out of the house until you start enjoying yourself again."

Marie wrapped her arm around Faith's shoulders. "Don't worry, Mr. and Mrs. Logan. I'll make sure she has fun. Besides, she's got a famous boyfriend now who'll plan more romantic vacations like the one she has coming up."

"That's right," Virginia said. "I really like Irvin. When is he gonna finish making that movie?"

Just like Faith, her parents had fallen hard for Irvin's charm in the short time they'd known him. Her mama even squealed a little bit when he referred to Faith as his girlfriend. Their only complaint about her new relationship was the media attention it drew. Jimmy had threatened to shoot one cameraman lurking in their front yard. A story that the entertainment news programs had loved.

"In a few weeks, I think," Faith said. "Hey, let's turn on some music. This is a celebration, right?"

She went to the television to turn it to one of the music stations. When she flipped it on, an entertainment show with a picture of Irvin filled the screen. Her body froze, and the air in her lungs seemed to dissipate. His hands on her body, the way he said fate brought them together, the way his eyes lit up with laughter, and the secrets they'd shared in bed—all of those memories flew across her mind. They crammed out everything except how much she missed him.

"Turn it up," Marie said. She hurried over and snatched the remote from Faith's hand.

"And things are definitely heating up on the set of the newest Irvin Freeman film," the reporter said. "Sources say that Irvin and his sexy costar Selena Jones are once again lighting things up on and off camera. The two reportedly had dinner together last night and are frequently spotted away from the set, including the overlook of Niagara Falls." As the voice-over continued, grainy photos flashed on the screen of Irvin and Selena sitting close and looking at the view, laughing on set and holding each other during what must be a love scene. "His quick romance with small-town nurse Faith Logan must be over," said the news reporter. "Because the Irvin-and-Selena chemistry is definitely sizzling."

Faith took the remote away from Marie and quickly changed the channel. Big-band music filled the silence. She didn't look away from the television screen but sensed their gazes on her.

"Faith, don't listen to that," Marie said, placing her hand on Faith's shoulder. "He wouldn't invite you up if that were true."

She shook off Marie's hand and tried for a smile. Hard to do when her throat wanted to close up from the pain. "That's what I keep telling myself."

Their relationship would always be like this. Rumors of him with other women when they were apart. How long before temptation on the road overruled feelings for a long-distance relationship? For her ex it had taken only a few weeks. She'd cared for her ex, a lot, but she hadn't fallen head over heels for him the way she had with Irvin. Now her insides burned and twisted as if wrapped in red-hot barbed wire. The pain ripped and tore at the optimism she'd had after New York.

The doorbell rang. Thank goodness for a distraction.

"I'll get that." She left their frozen silence, knowing they'd break out into hushed *poor Faith* whispers the second she walked away.

She wiped her eyes and took a deep breath when she got to the door. Whoever it was didn't deserve to have a crying fool answer. She twisted the knob and opened it.

The pain inside her froze over, then hardened into a ball of anger so fierce she literally saw red.

"What are you doing here?"

Love hiked up the duffel bag on her shoulder. The

face identical to Faith's was cool and impartial as it stared back. "I'm done with rehab. Mama said when I was done I could come home."

Chapter 17

Faith hated leaving her parents with Love out of rehab, but as Marie said, she could stay home and fight with her sister or go away for a romantic weekend with her sexy boyfriend. With the rumors of Irvin and Selena, Faith chose the weekend. Plus, she couldn't stomach seeing her parents gush over Love "graduating" from rehab and welcoming her home with open arms. As if she hadn't left them penniless. Good thing all family accounts were now controlled by Faith. Otherwise, Faith would definitely have given up this trip to see Irvin.

Kitty walked next to Faith as they entered the mock apartment where Irvin and Selena were shooting a scene from the movie. "They should be finishing up. It's just a standard love scene. I believe this is their tenth take. They've probably got it down by now."

"Tenth?" Faith asked.

Kitty shrugged. "I stopped counting at six or seven."

Faith tried to push back her wariness. He was an actor. This was his job. It didn't mean anything. But ten takes?

Kitty squeezed Faith's arms. "Don't believe the reports. There's nothing going on there. They're both in relationships now, so the chemistry is off. That's why there have been so many takes."

Straightening her shoulders, Faith nodded. Kitty gave her another squeeze then turned away. Faith appreciated Kitty's efforts to make her feel better, and she mustered up a spark of excitement about seeing Irvin work. That spark fizzled and died like wet fireworks as she watched Irvin wrap Selena in an embrace. Irvin wore a towel and Selena nothing but a lacy bra and panties.

Not real. Not real, she repeated over and over. There were cameras, lights, dozens of people watching, but it didn't stop the volatile concoction of anger and jealousy from forming a knot in her chest.

They repeated lines. The director called out instructions. The scene progressed from an embrace to lovemaking—fake lovemaking, but the thought of it still left an inerasable picture in her mind.

Finally, after Faith was sure she'd ground her teeth down to nubs, the director yelled, "Cut!" Irvin immediately turned to her, his broad, handsome smile splitting his face. Faith forced a smile of her own and waved.

He took a bottle of water one of the people on set handed him and crossed the room to her.

"You made it," he said.

"Just in time."

Irvin lowered his head to kiss her, and she averted her face. His lips brushed her cheeks.

"You've still got some of Selena's lipstick on your face." She pointed toward his lips.

Irvin wiped away the red smears. "Sorry, cutie. We can wait until I get cleaned up."

"No problem." Her voice was light and breezy. But inside a storm raged.

Not real. Not real. To make this work, she'd have to deal with this. And the paparazzi. Her stomach twisted.

"Do you have to film anything else tonight?"

"No, I'm done and can get away for the weekend." He slid his arm around her waist and pulled her against him.

The feel of his solid chest and the hypnotic cadence of his accent eased away some of her discomfort. Faith wrapped her arms around his neck.

"Where are we going?"

"It's going to be just the two of us this weekend. No Kitty, no entourage, no intrusions. How does that sound?"

"Absolutely wonderful."

"Good. Now give me a second to wrap up some things here and we'll continue with our plans." He rubbed his nose against hers then let her go and strolled over to the director.

The entire crew seemed to gravitate toward him. Even the director seemed to soak in Irvin's words as they discussed the scene they'd just shot. He seemed so right for this world. She wasn't sure if she ever would feel as comfortable in her own skin as he looked on set.

Selena walked over. She'd put on a white bathrobe over the underwear Irvin had torn off based on the director's instructions and twisted her long raven locks into a knot on the top of her head.

"Faith, I'm so glad you came. Irvin has driven everyone crazy with missing you." Selena leaned in and wrapped Faith in a big hug. "You guys have a great weekend, okay?"

When Selena pulled back, Faith nodded. "Umm… sure. Thanks, Selena."

Selena hesitated. "I know today was kind of rough on you. My fiancé was the same way when we first started dating. Remember, it's *just* acting." She pointed to the set. "What he says, does and feels about you is real."

The tightness in Faith's shoulders diminished. "I'm trying to remember that."

"It'll get easier with time. And I think you'll be around for a while. Seriously, all he does is talk about you."

Faith chuckled, and she felt herself giving the other woman a genuine smile. "Thank you, Selena."

Selena walked away, and Faith glanced across the room and caught Irvin's eye. His face lit up, and his grin warmed every inch of her body. Her breath escaped in a soft sigh. She loved him. Realistically they'd only end in heartbreak, but for now she'd hold on to her love and the way he looked at her. And maybe, just maybe, if they did end, the memories would get her through the pain.

Irvin squeezed Faith's hand as they walked in and out of shops along Queen Street in the small town of Niagara-on-the-Lake. Sweat trickled down his back, not from the bright sun filtering through the tree-lined street but from nerves. He hadn't figured out the best way to ask Faith and her family to move to New York.

He was falling in love with her. He had realized that one morning when he'd spoken to her after she'd finished a night shift at the hospital. The sound of her voice had instantly brightened his mood after a long day on set. Three months in and he was absolutely smitten. He wanted her to be waiting at his place whenever he finished a job. Not thousands of miles away.

He glanced over at Faith, who looked fantastic in

a bright green dress that brushed the tops of her feet. Green-and-gold flats and a thin gold bracelet were her only adornments. Not that she needed more.

New York would be good for her career and her family. More choices in doctors for her parents' care. Better options in the nursing field. Plus, they'd be together. He swallowed hard. If only he could convince her moving wasn't completely crazy.

"Are you having a good time?" he asked.

Her grin warmed him better than the sun. "I am. This town is beautiful."

"It's considered one of the most stunning small towns in Canada. I thought you would prefer coming here over the hustle and bustle of a larger city."

She slipped her arm through his and leaned into his side. "Look at you, learning my tastes."

"Isn't that what I'm supposed to do? Know what my lady likes and get it for her?"

"I think you're trying to spoil me."

"If you consider this little getaway an attempt at spoiling you, then, yes, I am."

She chuckled and pulled him closer. Irvin took solace in the small movement. The look in her eye after shooting his scenes with Selena told him Faith would have a hard time watching him work. He could only imagine the thoughts that went through her head. He'd made a point to reassure her rumors of him and Selena were false.

Maybe admitting the depth of his feelings would ease her fears further and make his offer for her and her family to move to New York more appealing.

Faith sighed and leaned her head against his shoulder. "If only every weekend could be like this."

Just the motivation he needed. "Every weekend could."

She shook her head. "I didn't tell you because I didn't want to spoil the weekend."

"Tell me what?" He led her to one of the wooden benches on the side of the street and sat.

"Love came home right before I left. She's done with rehab, apparently, and Mama said she could stay."

He took her hands in his. "Are you okay?"

"For the most part. I started to stay, but again, my parents practically pushed me out the door." She grinned and shrugged. "She no longer has access to their accounts. Everything is in my name, and all information is locked away with Marie. I needed to leave or else I would have said something I'd later regret. This is a terrible time for her to return. I just got promoted. Now there's another mouth to feed."

"You were promoted?"

Her tight frown turned into a smile. "Yes, to floor nurse. Didn't you get my email yesterday?"

"Sorry, it was a long day. I haven't checked any email."

Disappointment shadowed her eyes. "Oh."

He squeezed her hands. "That's fantastic, Faith." But he knew a promotion would be less incentive for her to move to New York.

"I should be happy, not freaking out because my twin is back."

"Faith, you aren't responsible for your sister's actions, and you can't walk around waiting for her to fail again. Be cautious. But if your parents were able to move on and forgive, maybe you should, too."

"How can I forgive what she did?"

"Because she was in a very dark place. People in dark places do terrible things. Keep your guard up, but if she really finished the program, support her while she's clean."

"And if she slips up?"

The worry in her eyes made him wish he could guarantee Love would never screw up again. But he knew that was out of both of their hands. He brushed his hand across her soft cheek. "Send her back to rehab, or get her out of the house if she refuses help."

Her brows drew together. "I don't like those options."

Irvin swallowed and scooted closer. Now was the time. "There is another option."

"What?"

"Move you and your parents to New York."

Faith laughed. "Yeah, right."

He tugged on her arm until she looked at him. He didn't smile. "I'm serious. You can come stay with me. I—"

"My parents wouldn't even consider moving. And I can't leave them alone with my sister."

"I talked with your mum. She wants you to be happy."

Faith snatched her hand away. "You asked my mama already?"

"I wanted her to know that I'm serious about us. And to give you a reason to ignore any ridiculous rumors about me and Selena or anyone else."

"How about not shooting a love scene with her ten times?"

"Those ten takes were because it's hard to fake desire for Selena when all I can think about is you."

She sputtered, her mouth opening and closing as she struggled to speak.

He kept going. "You know I'm not sleeping with Selena, so why don't you tell me what's so terrible about me wanting you to move to New York?"

"Nothing, but you can't go behind my back and make

plans without asking me. You can't run my life the way Kitty runs yours."

Her words hit so close to the truth, he fell silent. Then his mobile rang, preventing him from replying. Faith crossed her arms and looked away. He pulled the device from his pocket.

One glance at the screen and his jaw dropped. "It's Kevin Lipinski," Irvin said, surprised.

Faith's frown transformed into an eager smile. She motioned toward the phone. "Answer it."

He quickly accepted and brought the phone to his ear. "Irvin, this is Kevin Lipinski. Did I catch you at a bad time?" Kevin asked in a brisk, no-nonsense tone.

Irvin glanced at Faith's curious expression. "I've got a minute."

"Good, good. Listen, I got around to reading your screenplay last night, and I've got to say, I'm impressed."

Irvin slid forward on the bench, excitement pounding through his veins. "Oh, really." His ability to sound so casual should've earned him an instant Oscar.

"Yes, the story of the son observing his mother in denial of her husband's alcohol problem. The way the kid tried to protect her, but ultimately couldn't save either of them. It really touched something in me. Where did you dream this story up?"

"I didn't. It's my story," he said.

"I should have known. That much emotion and realism couldn't be made up. Look, I know you're in the middle of filming, but why don't you fly out to San Francisco so we can talk. You had mentioned wanting to direct."

"I do."

"I'll consider it."

Irvin found Kevin's not-flat-out-refusal encouraging. "Look, Kevin, I'm wrapping up the majority of my scenes this week. I can fly out to see you after that."

"Sounds good. Just call me when you're in town and we'll do lunch. I'm looking forward to working with you."

"Same here." He ended the call, then let out a joyous shriek. He turned to Faith. "He loved my script and wants to talk about making it into a movie. I'm going to San Francisco next week to discuss it."

"That's fantastic." She wrapped her arms around his neck. "I'm so happy for you."

He pulled back. "It sure took him long enough."

"Good things come to those who wait."

He met her eye. "I don't want to wait on us. Faith, please consider—"

She placed her hand gently over his mouth. "Let's talk about that later. You've just got great news. Let's celebrate." She leaned in and kissed him.

Her kiss combined with the euphoria pulsing in his veins to awaken his arousal instantly.

A voice broke the moment. "Excuse me. Are you Irvin Freeman?"

Irvin turned to a woman holding up a camera phone.

"I am," he said, trying to sound pleasant. Trying to remember fans paid for his lifestyle. But he could think only of his moment with Faith being broken and their previous unresolved conversation.

"Oh my God, I love your movies!" the woman squealed. "Can I get a picture?"

Irvin glanced at Faith, who nodded. Then he looked back at the woman. "Sure—one picture."

One picture turned into two, and two pictures led to a crowd forming. Thirty minutes later he and Faith were finally able to escape. They made their way to a bed-

and-breakfast located at one of the town's wineries. He'd reserved every room so that he and Faith could be alone.

"Faith, we need to talk about what I asked," he said once they were in their room.

Faith shook her head. "Not right now." She pushed the sleeves of her dress down her shoulders. She did a little shake, and the material softly slid to her feet. Irvin's mouth went dry at the sight of her in the skimpy bra and panties. "Now we're celebrating."

She strolled over to him and pulled him down for a kiss. Irvin lost himself in her embrace, but also felt another hurdle grow between him and Faith.

Chapter 18

Faith refused to let Irvin talk to her about moving to New York any further. For the rest of the weekend, whenever he brought up the subject, she found a way to change it. Or someone conveniently interrupted them to get an autograph or picture. Even during the short car ride back to Niagara Falls, she'd distracted him with questions about his life in London. She didn't want to move, and based on his phone call from Kevin Lipinski, he was about to get a lot busier. Meaning their relationship would become even harder to maintain.

"This was one of the best weekends of my life," Faith said as they entered the hotel where the cast and crew were staying during the movie shoot. "I'll never forget it."

"There will be plenty more weekends like this," Irvin said.

Faith smiled and nodded. "Sure."

She broke eye contact to stare across the lobby. There

wouldn't be more weekends like this. She would end things once she got back to South Carolina. This wasn't the life for her, not with the constant rumors and intrusive fans. Telling him they should move on would be hard, but her one consolation was that she'd get to keep her feelings under wraps. He'd never know she'd fallen deeply in love.

"Are you okay?" Irvin moved into her line of vision, concern etched on his handsome face.

"I'm great." She forced cheer into her tone that sounded almost legitimate.

He frowned and questioned her with his eyes.

Faith's cell phone rang. She quickly diverted her full attention to the device.

Kitty hurried over. "Irvin, you got a sec?"

Faith's parents' number flashed on her screen. "Go talk to Kitty while I take this." She walked away and answered the call before he could respond.

"Are you going to be back tomorrow?" Love's voice snapped through the phone.

Faith tensed, bracing herself for bad news. "Yes, first thing. Why?"

"Because I just chased away another cameraman who tried to snap pictures of Mama and Daddy in the backyard."

Faith put a hand on her hip and scowled. "What?"

"You heard me. Ever since you were spotted on your romantic weekend with that movie star, this guy has been showing up trying to snap pictures." Love's voice dripped with annoyance. "This is all your fault."

"Hold up. I know you're not trying to chastise me."

"Look, Faith, I'll admit from now until the end of time that I screwed up. Stealing from Mama and Daddy was my rock bottom. I finished rehab and I'm staying clean. In a few weeks I'm moving to Greenville with a woman I met in rehab. We got jobs and are starting over away from the people and places that have always led us to trouble."

Faith's mouth fell open. She quickly snapped it shut. "You're what?"

"Moving. Getting a job. Sending money back to Mama and Daddy to pay for my mistakes." Love sighed. "Look, I don't expect you to believe me or believe in me, but I'm trying, all right? It'll take a while, but I'm going to do better."

Confidence and resolve strengthened Love's voice. Faith hadn't heard that type of power in her sister's tone since they were little girls. And she had missed it.

"I believe you."

Several seconds passed before Love responded. "Thank you. But you've got to do something about the paparazzi. Mama and Daddy aren't going to say anything, but it's bothering them, too."

"It'll all be ending soon," Faith said.

Irvin walked over and placed a hand on her lower back. He mouthed the words *Everything okay?* and she nodded.

"Hey, I've got to go. Tell them not to worry. I'll take care of it." She ended the call and slipped the phone into her purse.

"What do you have to handle?"

"Just a cameraman hanging around the house. They keep popping up since you and I started dating."

He rubbed his forehead and groaned. "I'm so sorry." He dropped his hand. "How do you want to handle it?"

By leaving you. The thought made her heart hurt. "We'll figure something out."

Irvin wrapped an arm around her shoulders, and she slid hers around his waist.

"There's something I've wanted to tell you all weekend," Irvin said as they walked to the elevator.

"What's that?"

Irvin used his finger to tilt up her chin. His deep stare held complete adoration that she'd seen only from guys looking at the woman they loved. Her body thrummed with anticipation.

"Faith, I—"

"Ready for another long week, Irvin?" One of the costars of the film, action star Lathan Taylor, walked up.

Faith's shoulders slumped, and Irvin's mouth tightened before he faced the action star and shrugged.

"The harder we work, the better the end product," Irvin said.

Lathan stepped onto the elevator with Faith and Irvin and kept up a constant stream of conversation about the filming. Faith normally would have been excited to meet Lathan, but she could muster up only tight smiles and stiff nods whenever he cracked a joke.

Maybe it was wishful thinking, or she really didn't want to break things off with Irvin, but she'd hoped Irvin would say he loved her. Not that his confession would change their situation much. She still couldn't move to New York and be left behind whenever he traveled to whatever city in the world his next movie would be filmed in.

They all got off on the top floor, where most of the cast were staying, and parted ways with the actor.

"Now you can tell everyone you met Lathan Taylor," Irvin said. "I'm surprised you weren't more excited. You're always excited to meet celebrities...that aren't me."

She chuckled. "You're never going to let that go, are you?"

He pulled the key card for the room out of his back pocket and slid it into the door. "Not anytime soon."

Irvin opened the door and stepped back for Faith to go in first. Faith slipped her finger into the belt loops of his navy slacks. She walked backward into the room and tugged him along.

"I'll tell you now, it was very difficult to suppress my fangirl sigh when I first laid eyes on you."

One side of his mouth rose in a sexy half smile. "Was that before or after you decided to pretend as if you didn't want to win?"

"Before, and the second you told me to relax because you don't bite was the first time in my life I actually wanted to be bitten." She jerked on his belt loop until his body brushed hers.

Irvin's brows rose and his dark eyes lit up. Sliding one long arm around her waist, he pulled her into the seductive heat of his body. "I'd prefer to do a little nibbling." He kicked the door closed with his foot.

"*Nibbling* is such a silly word."

He lightly nipped at the side of her neck. Trembles scattered across her skin. "Does this feel silly?" His accent deepened with his desire.

Faith's eyes fluttered closed and she shook her head. His nibble was far from silly and had her ready to strip in the living area and beg for him to do exactly what he was doing to other parts of her body.

The sound of footsteps running from the bedroom made them both freeze.

"Welcome back, baby!" a woman's voice called.

Faith pushed Irvin's chest. He looked just as surprised as she did.

"Ooh, you brought company," the woman said.

Irvin looked over Faith's shoulders. His body stiffened and his eyes narrowed. Faith spun around. The superfan she'd seen twice during her trip to New York stood completely naked in the middle of the room.

Faith's eyes bulged so hard she feared she had strained the muscles.

Irvin pushed Faith behind him. "How did you get in my room? This floor is monitored."

"You said some other time." The pitch of the woman's whine was high enough to shatter glass.

Faith glared at the back of Irvin's head. "You told her what?"

He turned to Faith. "I tell lots of people that. I don't mean it."

The woman rushed over. "You meant it with me. I felt it. Just give me time. I'll show you things you've never seen before."

The woman's eyes darted from Faith to Irvin. Faith couldn't tell if she was crazy or just hyperexcited to be there.

"Faith, call security," Irvin said.

Faith edged away.

A bewildered smile covered the woman's face. "No! Irvin, I love you." She reached for Irvin.

He stepped back. "Faith, call!"

Faith hurried to the phone.

"No," the woman yelled.

Faith looked over her shoulder, and the woman barreled into Faith's side at the same time. They fell to the floor. *No, this fool didn't just knock me to the floor!*

Faith rolled over and tried to push her off without touching too much of the crazy fan's naked body. But the lady must have covered herself in baby oil or something because Faith's hands just slipped across her feverish skin.

"You're not calling security. Give me a chance."

Pain shot through Faith's scalp. *She just pulled my...* Another sharp pain. That was it. Faith used her elbows, legs, knees and fists to fight the woman off of her.

Irvin was there instantly to pull the slippery woman off. She fought them both with earnest.

"He's mine. I should have won that contest." She screamed when Irvin finally got her around the waist and pulled her off Faith. She kicked and reached for Faith again. "It would be me in this hotel if I would've won."

"Not bloody likely," Irvin grunted as another of the woman's kicks connected with his shin.

The door to the room burst open. Kitty and her entourage flooded the room. For once Faith welcomed the publicist's intrusion. In a matter of seconds Kitty had two guys grab the fan. Minutes later, security guards were dragging the woman, naked and screaming, from Irvin's room.

Faith escaped to the bedroom while security and Kitty grilled everyone to find out how the woman had got in Irvin's room. Irvin came into the bedroom and sat next to her on the king-size bed.

"Are you okay?"

She shook her head. "I was just in a wrestling match with a naked woman on the floor. No, I'm not okay."

"Faith," he sighed. "I didn't invite her here."

Faith rubbed her aching temples. Her mind replayed the last scene. Interrupted by visions of the cameramen hanging around her family, and media reports of Irvin and Selena.

"I believe you. Something is obviously wrong with her." She dropped her hands. "But I can't do this. The paparazzi, the constant interruptions, the crazy naked women in hotel rooms."

"Faith, don't." His voice hardened. "Not over this."

She jumped up from the bed and paced back and forth. "It's not just this. I'm not moving to New York."

Irvin stood and took her arm. His pleading eyes bored into hers. "Then don't. We can make this work."

"No, we can't." Her heart broke with each second that passed, and she lowered her gaze to the floor. "The past few months were like a dream come true."

His hand on her arm tightened. "Don't."

"And I'll always remember the time we spent together."

"That sounds like a bad line from a movie."

"I'm not good at breakups."

He cupped her face in his hands. "Then don't break things off."

Kitty popped her head through the doorway. "Irvin, the cops are here. They need a statement."

Irvin groaned. "They can wait."

Faith pulled out of his embrace. "There's no need. I'm leaving."

"Faith." Irvin reached for her, but she dodged his hand.

"Kitty," she said, "please move my flight up if possible."

Kitty's concerned gaze went from Irvin to Faith. "If it's what you really want."

Faith took a deep breath, still smelling the crazy woman's perfume. What if someone equally as crazy went after her parents?

"It is." She spoke the lie with a confidence she didn't feel.

"Faith, cutie, don't do this." Irvin's warm hand clasped

hers. He tried to pull her into his arms. She wanted to go into his embrace and forget everything.

"If you won't talk to the police, then I will." Faith pulled out of his reach and refused to meet his eyes. She rushed past Kitty, knowing that if she looked at Irvin, she'd never walk away.

Chapter 19

The flight attendant told Irvin they were about twenty minutes from landing, so he pulled out his mobile to make the call. He'd flown to San Francisco to meet with Kevin the day before, and the two had made plans to begin production early the following year. Kevin, straightforward as he was, wanted to start earlier, but Irvin refused. He'd worked constantly on his career even before he struck it big. He was taking a few months off. If he wanted to win Faith back, he'd have to.

Therefore, he expected this phone call not to go very well.

"Irvin, where are you?" Kitty wasted no time waiting for his reply. She took off like a race car on a speedway. "Since you're finished wrapping up your scenes in Canada, I've got some things lined up for you. *GQ* magazine wants you to do a spread for their November issue, so we'll have to line up the photo shoot in the next week or so. Also, they're looking for several celebrity guest spots on the sitcom *Dolls and Calls*. That show is hot right now, and everyone who's anyone is guest starring. One spot calls for a sexy male chef, and you'd be perfect for it. Auditions start tomorrow, but once you let them know you're interested, you'll be a shoo-in."

Irvin rubbed his temple as Kitty rattled on. Of course it wouldn't cross her mind that he might want to relax after twelve weeks of filming. Then again, he'd never rested before, so she was only doing her job.

"Kitty, I just left San Francisco, where I had a meeting with Kevin Lipinski. He liked my screenplay and wants me to direct. We're going to start production next year."

"That's great, Irvin," Kitty said with what he could tell was hesitant enthusiasm. "I'll be sure to work that into your latest round of promos. And word on the street is you're getting the part for that new superhero movie. Filming is set to begin in December."

"I'm not taking the part."

There was laughter on the other end of the phone. "You're funny, Irvin. Now—"

"I'm serious, Kitty. I've already turned it down. I'm going to take the rest of the year off."

"Why?"

It was Irvin's turn to laugh. Kitty always went at her job 110 percent. He didn't think she'd ever taken a vacation in the time they'd worked together. On the rare days he did rest, she was always out there promoting.

"Because I'm tired, and I want to take a break. I want to live my life for a while without the constant flash of cameras. If this works out with Kevin, then I'm going to go for other directing jobs. I'm ready to get behind the camera."

"Where are you now?" Kitty asked, her suspicion as clear as the sky he glimpsed out the aircraft window.

"On a plane."

"Where are you going?"

"I'm not telling you, because I don't want you sending word ahead that'll have dozens of paparazzi waiting." Dante had a private airstrip at his home in San Francisco, so Irvin had taken his friend's jet to avoid the cameras.

"I can guess," Kitty said. "You're going to South Carolina. I knew you wouldn't give up so easily. You've finally fallen in love."

He couldn't tell by her tone if she was surprised, happy, pissed or confused. "I have, and I missed her the second she left. I think she won that contest for a reason. I was already tired and looking for an excuse to slow down. The screenplay was one reason. Faith became the other."

"Am I fired?" Kitty was direct as usual, but for the first time Irvin heard uncertainty in Kitty's voice.

"No, Kitty, you're not fired. After everything you've done for me, I wouldn't sack you so casually. I'm moving behind the camera, but I'm sure I'll still need your services occasionally. Just consider this your opportunity to put your efforts into making the next handsome guy Hollywood's biggest star."

Kitty chuckled. "I couldn't be lucky enough to come across another talent as good as yours." She sighed into the phone. "I wish you well, Irvin."

That surprised him. "Thank you, Kitty."

"You're welcome. Not everyone is lucky enough to have love strike as hard as it did with you two. Honestly, this move to directing and away from the spotlight is probably the best way to make it work. Just don't forget to invite me to the wedding. I expect to be maid of honor or best man or something. It was my idea to do the contest," she said. He could hear the smile in her voice.

"When we get there, I promise not to forget."

They ended the call, and he settled back into the soft leather seat. When they got there. He'd never thought about getting married before. Amazing what a difference a few days could make.

Irvin landed at the same private airport he and Faith had flown into. He'd already arranged to have a car waiting for him there. As soon as he got out and breathed deeply of the fresh air, he knew he'd made the right decision. He'd spent only a day and a half with Faith in her hometown, but that time felt more like home than years living in New York.

"You've given my airstrip more action than it's seen in years," Gary said. He stood next to the car waiting for Irvin.

"I hope to give it more attention."

"That'll be good news to whoever buys it from me."

Irvin took a look at the strip and the surrounding landscape. Thick pine trees and none of the noise that had been the constant backdrop of his life. "Do you own the land around it?"

"Most of it."

"Maybe I'll buy it from you," Irvin said.

Gary's eyebrows rose. "Now, why would you do that?"

"I'm thinking about moving here. If Faith will have me."

"Hmm...after the television report about that crazy fan sneaking into your room, and Faith telling the few cameramen hanging around town that you two were done, most folks around here didn't think you'd be coming back."

"That's what they get for thinking," Irvin said, throwing back the line Gary had tossed out when he and Faith first flew into the strip.

Gary laughed and stuck out his hand. "If you're serious, then we can talk. I've got no reason to keep the strip, and I'd rather sell it to you and Faith than someone else. She deserves a lot of happiness."

Irvin took Gary's hand and shook it. "I plan to give her a lot of happiness."

He said his goodbyes to Gary and got in the car for the short ride to Faith's parents' house, thinking about the airstrip. Once again, fate had stepped in and shown him he was on the right track. There was enough acreage out there to build a house and properly secure it. He could update the airstrip and fly directly in and out with no problems, making it even easier for him or Faith to travel. By the time the driver pulled up to Faith's home, Irvin's mind was bounding with excitement.

The car pulled into the driveway, and he got out without waiting for the driver to open the door. His hands were full of the gifts he hoped would remind her why they belonged together. He could see Faith in the backyard hanging sheets on the clothesline. Music playing from somewhere in back must have prevented her from hearing the car, because she didn't turn around. He preferred to surprise her anyway.

He went through the gate in the picket fence surrounding the house and crept up to her. She bent over to pick up another sheet, humming to herself and completely oblivious to him. As she reached up to hang the sheet, he took her arm in his.

"Guess who," he said, spinning her around and kissing her.

Something wasn't right. He sensed it a second before she jerked back and kneed him in the balls. He doubled over as pain exploded through his groin. His gifts hit the ground.

"Who the hell are you?" he asked through gritted teeth.

He glanced up through watery eyes into a face that was similar to Faith's, but wasn't hers.

"I'd ask the same thing, but I've figured that out," the evil body double said.

"Love?" he said, slowly standing straight though the pain had barely subsided.

Love twirled her hand and bowed. "The one and only."

Thank God for that, he thought. "I thought you moved to Greenville."

"I did. Just here for the weekend." She propped a hand on her hip and cocked her head to the side. "I thought Faith broke up with you."

"She did. I'm here to win her back."

Footsteps came closer from the rear. "You are?"

He spun toward Faith, then grimaced at the aftershock of discomfort caused by the sudden move. "I am."

She was in the outfit he'd first seen her in back in New York—the lavender tank top and cutoff jean shorts that had driven him mad from the start. He'd known he'd missed her, but not until that second did he realize how *much* he'd missed her.

He took a step toward her, which was more of a limp. Concern knitted her brow, and she hurried forward. "I saw what happened. Sorry about that."

"So am I." He flung a glare over his shoulder at her twin.

"My bad," Love said. "I'm not good with strange men grabbing me suddenly."

"I see that," he said. He looked to Faith standing next to him. "Is there somewhere we can talk?"

"Come in the house."

"I'll finish up out here and give you two some privacy," Love said.

"Yes," Irvin said, his voice barely hiding his eagerness to get away. "Do that."

The twins shared a look. He had a sneaking feeling that they could communicate an entire conversation that way.

He picked up a bouquet of roses and a black folder. He gave the flowers to Faith. "They're from Belles Fleurs," he said. Faith's eyes widened before her lips curved in a sweet smile. "I wrote the card myself. Xavier and Diane thought it was very romantic." He took a step forward and winced at the residual pain.

Faith blinked and broke eye contact. She waved him toward the house. "Come on. Let's get you some ice," she said.

Faith's entire body shook from the shock of having Irvin show up. She'd assumed he'd accept things were over and move on. She hadn't prepared herself for him popping up.

She sat him at the kitchen table. "Let me get the ice."

He sat, then twisted on the seat as if trying to get comfortable. "No, it's starting to get better."

"Love's the more aggressive twin."

He grunted. "I noticed. Are you okay with her being here?"

She sat in the chair next to him and placed the flowers on the table. Their fragrance immediately transported her back to their night in New York. "I'm taking it one day at a time. She wants to prove she's better, so I decided to keep an open mind."

When they made eye contact, the electric heat the man created with just a look jolted her system. His eyes burned with desire, making it hard for her to breathe.

Faith jerked her eyes away and ran her hands across the tablecloth. She wanted to grin, laugh, jump with excitement that he was there, but the circumstances hadn't changed. "I need to stay here to support her and my parents during this process. We all need to heal."

Irvin put his hand on hers. "Then we'll help her."

"We?"

"Yes, we."

She shook her head. "This is my family's problem. You don't have to do anything. You can't do anything. You're in New York or going to California."

She tried to pull her hand away, but he held firm.

"Who's going to support you through all this? Faith, you deserve so much, and all I want to do is give you everything you deserve."

The look in his eye was so sincere, and the confidence in his voice made her want to accept his offer.

"I appreciate that, but nothing's changed, Irvin. It would have been better if you hadn't come." She stood and went over to the refrigerator. "Do you want some lemonade? My mama made it fresh this morning. She and Daddy went to the grocery store to pick up a few things."

He held the black folder in front of her. She slowly closed the fridge, and with shaky hands, she opened the folder to reveal a charcoal portrait of her and Irvin, signed by Carl.

"Carl says he can't wait to see you again," Irvin said. "He moved into the apartment and started AA. It took some time, but he's healing. I think the same can happen with Love."

Faith smiled. "I'm happy to hear that." She wanted Carl to overcome his demons, just like she wanted Love to overcome hers. Hope for them both filled her. As she stared at the picture, her hope for them blossomed into hope for Irvin and herself.

"I didn't come here to just bribe you with gifts." Irvin turned her to face him. He took a deep breath and stared into her eyes. "I came here to tell you that I love you."

It took a second for what he said to wiggle through her mind. She blinked several times, trying to make sense of words she'd only imagined hearing.

"You love me?"

"Yes. I knew it was happening for a long time, but it wasn't until you left Canada that it really hit me. I would have told you then, but we were always interrupted."

"That's part of the problem. Someone is always going to interrupt us. Most women would jump at the chance to be your girlfriend. For the apartment in New York and the offer to have their parents moved. But I can't live that life. I can't do the constant cameras, fight the crowds everywhere I go or have Kitty organize every move I make. My life is here. My parents are here—"

"What if I told you that I'm taking the rest of the year off, and that I called Kitty on my way here to let her know while I appreciate everything she's done for me, she's free to find another upcoming actor to make a star?"

"The rest of the year off? Irvin, you'll go crazy."

"No, the old Irvin would go crazy. The one who came to New York in order to reinvent himself and forget what he left behind. I don't have to hustle anymore. My fortune is built, my career bigger than I ever expected." He wasn't bragging. She knew that. In fact, he gave a self-effacing shrug. Then a huge grin lit up his face. "I struck a deal with Kevin to back my screenplay. I'll be directing, Faith. But I made the deal with the caveat that we won't begin work until after the New Year."

"You did all of that?"

"All of that. Faith, I was growing tired of the hustle before I met you. I checked my email constantly, waiting for Kevin to call and give me an excuse to take a step back. Then I met you, and like so many of the heroes I played, I fell for the girl in a weekend. I love you, but I know what fame can do to a relationship. I don't want my stardom to ruin us before we get started. We'll take the next year to get this thing right. Right for us, your parents, even your knee-happy twin."

She tried to think of something to say. It should definitely be cute, or funny, or profound, but the only thing she could think of was how much she loved him and how she couldn't imagine he actually was willing to take a chance on loving her.

"Why? Why would you do this?"

"It's like I told you in New York. I believe in fate. It told me it was time to leave my family and go to New York. It made me wander into an audition for a small role in a play that in turn grabbed Kitty's attention and made her introduce me to all the right people. Fate is the reason I got the role that made me a star after I lost another role that everyone swore would make my career. And fate pulled your name out of thousands and brought you to New York. I trust that, and I'm not going to just let it go."

Her heart beat so fast, she wondered if it was going to short-circuit. Love and excitement filled her from head to toe. "I love you, too. Man, Irvin, I love you so much, but I was so afraid to say it. So afraid to trust it. Life kept throwing me curveballs, and I couldn't believe that this thing between us was actually happening."

The words rushed out of her, each one making his smile bigger and brighter. "It really happened." He lowered his head to kiss her. "And I've got several months to show you how much I love you."

Chapter 20

Irvin's leg shook so hard next to Faith that the seats vibrated. She placed her hand on his tuxedo-clad thigh and gave a gentle squeeze. He looked her way and mouthed *Sorry.* Her show of calm was just that, a show. The Dolby Theatre was packed with all of Hollywood royalty, as usual for the Academy Awards. That same royalty held their collective breath as the top awards were about to be announced.

After two years with Irvin, Faith was pretty good at containing her fangirl squeals when she met new celebrities. But tonight she'd nearly fainted when some of the legendary members of Hollywood's elite came over to wish Irvin well.

She'd been excited and petrified about the red carpet. Years of watching the fashion critiques after the awards shows had her freaking out from the moment it was announced that Irvin and his film were nominated for best director, best screenplay and best picture. Thankfully, Kitty agreed to help and ensured Faith got the most beautiful gown, an aquamarine, one-shoulder Vera Wang creation that wowed on the red carpet.

It had taken almost a year for the media to calm some of its constant attention on Irvin. Him moving to a rural county in South Carolina and building a sweeping estate around the private airfield had generated its share of buzz. And by the time that died down, word of his partnership with Kevin Lipinski caused another rush of media excitement. They'd thought it was finally mellowing out when he'd got the nomination.

They'd become extra diligent at keeping their relationship private. Both to protect their relationship and to keep her family out of the spotlight. For Faith and Irvin, there were no more scheduled appearances, constant partying or intense schedules. They'd found a balance, and thanks to having a private airfield, she was able to dart across the country to visit with Irvin when they'd begun shooting. She still couldn't believe she was living this life.

"And now the nominees for best director..." Selena said from the stage.

Unable to contain her nervousness, Faith squeezed Irvin's hand. "No matter what happens, I'm proud of you," she whispered.

She didn't hear the names of all the nominees for the blood rushing between her ears. Her palm became increasingly sweaty in his, and her heart pounded so hard, she thought it'd burst from her chest. It wasn't until he went rigid beside her, then squeezed her hand, that she snapped out of it. She saw heads turned in their direction, smiles everywhere. In what seemed like slow motion, she looked at Irvin and found him grinning.

"I won." Disbelief sounded in his voice.

"You won," she breathed.

He grabbed both sides of her face and kissed her senseless. She laughed and cried at the same time.

"You'd better get up there," she said.

He kissed her again and stood to sprint up the aisle to the stage. Faith joined in with the thunderous applause filling the theater.

Irvin hugged Selena, who kissed his cheek. Then he held out the Oscar to look at it. He slapped a hand over his forehead and turned back to the crowd. "I can't believe I'm actually up here," he said. "I've imagined this moment all of my life, but until you're actually up here... Yeah, it's brilliant. Of course, I want to thank my agent, and my publicist, Kitty Brown, who stuck with me through my voluntary exile." That drew a few laughs from the crowd. "Thanks to the cast and crew, who did such a fantastic job. You guys made directing almost easy. Thank you to Kevin Lipinski for taking a chance on an unproved director and on a screenplay that long before I approached him, I wasn't sure I would ever finish. Many of you know that Eric's story is my story, and it took a lot for me to get the words on paper." He held up the award and shook his head. "Wow, this is completely real."

Several people clapped and cheered.

"I know I'll forget people, so I won't try to remember anyone else, but I'd be remiss if I didn't thank the most important person in the world to me. Fate brought her to me for a reason. I don't have much of a family, but she became my family. And her parents have been wonderful in welcoming me into their midst. Faith..." He looked in her direction. "I love you and can't imagine celebrating this award with anyone else. The only thing that would make this better is if you marry me. So, please, say you'll be my wife."

A gasp, then applause went through the crowd. Tears blurred Faith's vision as the voices of everyone around her became a distant hum. Irvin had brought up marriage only a few times. Even though he'd built the estate, asked her and her family to live there with him and shown the world that she was the woman in his life, she hadn't expected a real proposal. They'd just found the relationship balance that worked for them.

It didn't stop her from making her choice.

"Yes!" she yelled back as the music played and Irvin was ushered off the stage. She hurried across the aisle and ran backstage. She pushed past other celebrities, makeup artists and members of the television crew to the postacceptance interview area.

Kitty and her team were prepping him for all of the usual *how do you feel?* questions. The instant he saw her through the crowd, he left the interview area and ran over to her.

"You're crazy," she said as he swept her up in his arms and swung her around.

"Then you'll be married to a crazy Oscar winner," he said.

He set her down, and they both grinned.

"I can't believe you did that," she said through her smile.

"I can't believe you haven't answered me yet."

"You didn't hear me? I screamed yes." She wrapped her arms around his neck and kissed his cheek repeatedly. "Yes, yes, yes, you wonderful, crazy man."

"I hear you now, cutie," he said, laughing. "I love you so much, Faith." Happiness, excitement and tenderness were written all over his face. "Fate selected you, and I always trust in fate."

She kissed him, and cameras flashed everywhere. For the first time, she didn't care. They could post these pictures all over the internet. It was the happiest day of her life, and she wanted everyone to see it. Finally, fate hadn't played a cruel trick on her. It had brought her the love of her life.

* * * * *

SMALL-TOWN CINDERELLA

STACY CONNELLY

To the staff at The Red Garter Bed & Breakfast in Williams, Arizona. Thanks for answering my questions about running a small-town bakery.

Chapter One

"To the newlywed and the two brides-to-be," Debbie Mattson said as she raised her margarita to her friends. "May you always be as lucky in life as you have been in love."

Darcy Dawson, the bachelorette of their party, lifted her green-apple martini. "To luck and life and love," she echoed.

The four women—Debbie, Darcy, Sophia Pirelli Cameron and the newest member of the group, Kara Starling—had gathered at The Clearville Bar and Grille for Darcy's final send-off as a single woman. The rustic bar was a favorite locale for tourists and townies alike with its flat-screen televisions for the sports lovers and small dance floor for music lovers. Had Debbie been in charge of the bachelorette party, she might have tried for something a little more exciting than dinner and drinks, but Darcy was clearly having a good time, and that was all that mattered.

Six months pregnant, dark-haired Sophia sipped at her own cranberry juice. If Debbie had ever seen a woman with a pregnancy glow, it was her friend, who looked adorable in a floral skirt and long-sleeved pink peasant blouse draped over her round belly. Of course, it just as easily could have been a newlywed glow, as Sophia had married Jake Cameron the previous summer.

Love clearly agreed with Sophia and seemed to be first and foremost on her mind as she exchanged a glance with Darcy and Kara before looking over at Debbie. "With the three of us already finding our guys, you know what that means, right? It's your turn now."

Debbie held on to her smile even though she groaned inside. How many times had she heard that over the past few months? Ever since her friends had met their soul mates, they'd set their sights on the only single member left in their circle. At times, she felt very much the lone sheep about to be set upon by wolves. Cunning, devious, *matchmaking* wolves.

Show no fear, she thought to herself, knowing if she wavered even slightly she was dead meat.

"I'm happy for all of you, I really am. But I'm nowhere near ready to settle down. I'm finally at a place in my life where I have time to look for a little adventure and excitement."

"And romance?" Darcy chimed in slyly.

"I wouldn't be opposed to having, oh, say…a red-hot fling." Debbie took another sip of her margarita, the salty, tart combination making her taste buds tingle while the alcohol warmed her to her subject. "With a guy who's dark and mysterious and exciting, who'll ride into town and sweep me off my feet. Someone who'll take me completely by surprise and keep me on my toes."

"Now you're talking," the gorgeous redhead said with a grin.

"Excuse me?" Kara protested, using a look her friends had dubbed her "professor glare." "Need I remind you that you're getting married this weekend?"

Lifting up her hands in an innocent gesture she couldn't quite pull off while still holding her martini glass, the bride-to-be retorted, "All the more reason to live vicariously through Debbie's escapades. So tell us more about this mystery man."

Feeling heat rush to her face, Debbie set aside her margarita. "Well, I can tell you one thing. I'm certainly not going to find him here," she said wryly.

"At the bar?" Kara asked.

"Not here at the bar. Not here in Clearville." A quick glance around their section of the restaurant confirmed what Debbie already expected.

She knew every single guy in the place. More than that, even; she'd known them all for years. If she thought back, she could picture any number of their embarrassing, awkward moments that were part and parcel of growing up in a small town.

Billy Cummings, the sheriff's son, had gone on a football kick after seeing his first professional game and had worn a miniature helmet 24/7 for weeks on end. Mark Thompson had had the biggest crush on their freshman English teacher, and his brother, Bruce, swore the garage band he was in would make it big even though none of the members could actually play an instrument. Then there was Darrell Nelson and the cruel pranks he used to play, bullying anyone who was smaller and weaker than he was.

She remembered it all, and if that wasn't bad enough, she was well aware they remembered all the awkward growing pains she'd gone through, too.

Mystery? Romance? Excitement?

Not a chance, she thought with a sigh.

"Look, just forget everything I said. This is what happens when a milk-and-cookies girl starts hitting the tequila and lime," she joked, hoping her friends would be as willing to laugh off her comments.

She should have known she wouldn't be so lucky.

"There's nothing wrong with wanting some romance in your life," Kara told her.

At first, Debbie had wondered about the quietly serious college professor marrying Sophia's fun-loving, outgoing brother Sam. But over the past few weeks, Debbie had gotten to know Kara and to see the warm heart behind the classy blonde's cool exterior.

"And I highly recommend having a gorgeous guy sweep you off your feet." Darcy grinned. "But why are you totally discounting the whole Clearville male population? I speak from personal experience when I say my guy is anything but boring."

"I'll drink to that," Kara said as she lifted her glass of chardonnay to tap against Darcy's appletini.

Their smiles shone with newfound love, though Debbie had a hard time picturing Nick and Sam Pirelli as romantic, sweep-a-girl-off-her-feet types. They'd always been more like big brothers to her—sometimes sweet, sometimes annoying, always overprotective big brothers.

That was something Sophia as the youngest Pirelli and only girl could certainly understand. After exchanging a look with her friend, Debbie argued, "It's different for the two of you. Neither of you grew up here, so to you, Clearville guys are mysterious and exciting. But for me, these are the guys I've known forever. The boys next door. No mystery, no excitement, no sparks."

All that was bad enough. Worse was knowing the male

population of the town viewed her the same way. The girl next door. The buddy, the pal, the friend whose shoulder they cried on when the popular, pretty girls turned them down.

She winced at the memory when she thought of the name that had followed her since her days at Redwood Elementary School, thanks in part to the bakery her mother owned and the sweets that had filled her lunches and helped fill out her waistline. She'd never been "little" anything, and while she'd known the nickname was mostly a lighthearted tease, it had hurt all the same.

Now she was the owner of Bonnie's Bakery, and the years of taking care of her mother after she'd fallen ill and spending all her free time at the bakery had toughened her like overkneaded dough. Her feelings weren't so easily injured anymore, though she'd suffered a setback thanks to her last boyfriend.

She and Robert Watkins had dated casually for several months earlier in the year, and things had finally started to get serious over the summer. Serious enough for them to sleep together.

Debbie still wasn't sure which was worse, the pain of heartbreak or the pain of humiliation as she remembered that fateful weekend, and how he'd picked the very next day to tell her he thought they'd be better off just being friends.

It wouldn't have been so bad if the breakup hadn't dragged her back to her high school insecurities. To being every guy's friend, the buddy they could talk to about the prettier, more popular girls they liked. She thought she'd gotten over that. She *was* over it. But Debbie couldn't pretend the split with Robert hadn't brought back a lot of bad memories.

Memories she was determined to overcome. She was

woman enough to have confidence in herself, to know what she wanted and to go after it.

"I'm not sure you're giving these guys enough credit," Darcy argued. "There are some nice men around here who'd be thrilled to know you're looking for a boyfriend." Her eyes lit suddenly. "What about Jarrett Deeks? He and Nick have gotten to be friends working together at Jarrett's horse rescue. We could set up a double date if you want."

Debbie cringed slightly at the thought. "No, thank you, Darcy. I'm sure Jarrett's great and all, but a double date isn't exactly what I had in mind."

Her friend's brow furrowed. "But if you're looking for a relationship—"

"I'm not," she interrupted. "Not really."

"A not-really relationship?" Kara echoed.

"I'm not looking for anything that serious." Debbie stabbed her straw at the ice cubes lingering at the bottom of her glass. "I just want to have some fun." Leaning back against the padded booth, she said, "I feel like I missed out on so much growing up, you know?"

"Actually, we don't." Kara leaned forward, her expression open and interested. "You talk a lot without saying much about yourself."

Debbie blinked, startled by her friend's comment. "I don't do that...do I?" She knew she liked to talk, and the more nervous she became, the more she said—often without saying much at all. But she didn't like to think she fell into that pattern even with her friends. It sounded...selfish. Like she expected them to open their hearts and spill their guts while she kept all her emotions inside. "I'm sorry. I didn't realize—"

"Sweetie, it's not a criticism. Just a comment."

"And I do know what you mean, Deb," Sophia interjected as she shifted forward in the booth as far as her pregnant belly would allow. "So many of us grew up together that we don't go around talking about past history because everyone knows everything."

"But we're new." Darcy's nod included Kara as she added, "So you can tell us all your old stories without worrying that we've heard them before."

"Well, okay, but just because you haven't heard it all before doesn't mean it isn't still boring. My dad was in the military and was killed overseas when I was really young, so growing up, it was just me and my mom. I was still in high school when she was diagnosed with cancer."

Debbie could still remember walking into the bakery after school that day, the scent of vanilla and chocolate strong in the air. She'd been so excited. Posters had decorated the hall for the homecoming dance, and she'd been so sure that that year someone would ask her to go. She even had the perfect dress picked out, her teenage head filled with plans for the future.

"I could tell right away something was wrong, and when she told me— It was like a nightmare. Something that couldn't be true. But it was."

Clearing her throat, she said, "Anyway, my mom always was a fighter, so she went through all the tests and surgeries and treatments, all while still trying to run the bakery. For a while, I thought about dropping out of school, but she wouldn't hear of it. I took as few classes as I could to get by, quit all extracurricular activities, and I worked in the bakery every spare second I had. A few hours before school and then from the minute I got out until close."

She'd never bought that dress. Had never attended that homecoming dance or any other dance in high school. The bakery became Debbie's life the way it had always been her mother's before that.

"It was all I could do.... I couldn't make her better, but

I could make the cupcakes," she concluded with a watery laugh.

Shaking off the sorrows of the past, she protested, "This is not the conversation for a bachelorette party! Here I'm talking about wanting to have fun, and yet I'm the one bringing everyone down."

"You aren't. I think what you did was amazing, and I know a little of what you went through," Darcy confided.

Debbie knew her friend had lost her mother a few years ago. It was that loss that had prompted Darcy to move to her mother's hometown and open the beauty shop the two of them had always dreamed of owning. Darcy had shared that with Debbie not long after they met, and yet she hadn't thought to confide in her friend about her own past, despite what the two of them had in common. Was it like Sophia said, and Debbie simply expected everyone to already know her life story, or was there more to it?

Saving that thought for another time, Debbie said, "Thank you, but it didn't feel like much. Still, I knew how much the bakery meant to my mom, and I did all I could to keep the doors open so she could concentrate on getting better. And for a while, she did. The cancer went into remission for a few years before it came back, but the second time there was no fighting it."

And after her mother had passed away, it was just Debbie and the bakery. Working long hours to numb the sense of loss and to slowly accept the bakery now *was* her future. The dreams she'd had in high school of attending culinary school and becoming a chef had slipped way as she'd kneaded dough and rolled out cookies and decorated cupcakes. But somehow, as those hours turned into days and weeks and years, a minor miracle had taken place.

The reputation of the small-town shop had grown.

Business had increased thanks to Debbie establishing

an online presence. Now her loyal customers didn't have to wait for their yearly trip to the tourist town to order her desserts. They could cater to their craving for something sweet with a few clicks of a mouse, and Debbie could ship her cookies and cheesecakes straight to their door.

She'd even gained the attention of *Just Desserts* magazine. The article had praised her double-chocolate cake and strawberry-filled vanilla cupcakes. As pleased as she was with the recognition, Debbie couldn't help feeling like, well, a fraud. Those were her mother's recipes, and Bonnie should have been the one to bask in the glow of the reporter's praise.

But the article, along with the increase in business, had inspired Debbie to hire on more help. Over the years, she'd frequently paid local teens to run the front register. But Kayla Walker, a young mother who'd moved to Clearville with her boyfriend after she'd inherited a house from her late grandfather, was the first employee Debbie had trained to do the actual baking.

Thanks to Kayla, Debbie now had the chance to expand the menu a bit. To offer her mother's tried-and-true recipes as well as some not-so-vanilla recipes of her own. And with the rush of engagements lately, she was also getting the opportunity to shift her attention from everyday cupcakes and muffins to once-in-a-lifetime wedding cakes.

Working with the bride and groom to find the perfect flavor and filling combinations was a challenge she enjoyed. And then there was the decorating—the literal icing on the cake. The creativity and artistry of building the multiple layers, of designing the perfect flowers and ribbons and scrollwork… She loved every step of the detailed work.

And while she might be a complete flop when it came to love and romance, that didn't mean she wasn't a believer in other couples' happily ever afters. Her friends were all proof that loves of a lifetime did exist, and while Debbie couldn't be more pleased, she wasn't looking to join them.

For the first time in nearly a decade, she had time. Time to think, to breathe, to hang up her apron and have some fun. And if her mother's death had taught her anything, it was that life was short, and Debbie was determined to make the most of it.

"So maybe that's why I'm not looking to settle down," she concluded. "I've been too settled already, too serious and dedicated throughout what should have been the best years of my life. I know the three of you have found the guys of your dreams, and I'm happy for you all, but that's just not what I'm looking for."

"Debbie wants Mr. Excitement," Sophia said with a wink.

"Mr. Mysterious," Darcy seconded.

"Here's to finding Mr. Tall, Dark and Handsome," Kara added.

Still feeling a little ridiculous for spelling out her dream man to her friends, Debbie lifted her glass. "I will definitely drink to that."

Draining the last of her margarita, she admitted finding an exciting and mysterious man was only half the wish. Finding a man who thought *she* was exciting and mysterious…now, *that* would be a fantasy come true.

Drew Pirelli was not a man given to eavesdropping. Living in Clearville his whole life, he was very familiar with its grapevine and the wildfire spread of small-town gossip. He preferred to mind his own business with the somewhat vain hope others would do the same. Neither was he the type to spy on his sister and future sisters-in-law.

If he'd known drinks at the bar and grill were part of the plan for Darcy's bachelorette party, he would have stayed away. Far away. But he'd been somewhat out of the Pirelli family loop recently, something his parents had commented on more than once. He'd used work as a handy excuse, and he *was* busy running his construction company, but that was only part of the reason why he'd avoided family gatherings recently.

How was it, he wondered, that he was the last unattached Pirelli sibling?

Ever since the custom-home side of his business had taken off, Drew had started each project with his own future family in mind. He pictured his wife and family gathered together in the kitchen. His kids watching television or playing games in the den. The woman he loved welcoming him to bed in the spacious master suite.

And yet at the end of each project, he turned the keys over to some other man who would live with his wife and children in the house Drew had painstakingly built.

The nagging dissatisfaction of giving away a piece of himself in each of his houses had convinced him to start building his own place. But that had created another frustration. His attention to detail, the dream of making a house into *his* home, had helped Drew cement his reputation as one of the most sought-after contractors in Northern California. Because of that, he was having trouble finding time to work on his own project while managing the custom-home business as well as the rental cabins he was currently building for Jarrett Deeks.

Not that it was all bad. Professionally, he was as rock solid as the houses he built. On a personal level, though, he couldn't seem to find his footing.

And that was the real reason he'd been keeping his distance from his family. He was tired of being the third, fifth, heck, even the ninth wheel, depending on how many of his relatives showed up.

Which was how he'd ended up completely out of the loop when it came to Darcy's bachelorette party.

When he'd first recognized the female voices coming from the other side of the half wall separating the two rows of booths, he'd slid across the padded seat, ready to slip away unnoticed. Though no expert at bachelorette parties, he knew enough to realize guys weren't allowed.

But before he could push to his feet, the words drifting over from the other side of the booth nailed him to the spot.

I wouldn't be opposed to having a red-hot fling with a guy who's dark and mysterious and exciting, who'll ride into town and sweep me off my feet. Someone who'll take completely by surprise and keep me on my toes.

It wasn't the words that had knocked his feet out from under him. It was shock at the swift, unexpected kick of desire he felt when he heard them.

Drew had known Debbie Mattson her entire life. His earliest memories of her were of her standing on tiptoe to peek up over the counter at her mother's bakery, her big blue eyes sparkling as she flashed her dimples at every customer to walk through the door. She was the typical girl next door. Sweet, friendly, cute. She was his kid sister's friend, but her words pointed out a truth he'd been denying for the past several months.

Debbie wasn't a kid anymore.

His knuckles whitened around the cool glass bottle, and he couldn't remember the last time he'd had to fight so hard not to follow his first instinct. An instinct logic told him was completely irrational. If he did what he longed to do, opened his mouth and spouted off like some kind of idiot about nice girls staying home and waiting for the right kind of guy to come along, Debbie would likely knock his block off, and he'd deserve it.

Debbie was a grown woman now. A beautiful woman,

he was reminded as he thought back to Sophia's wedding a few months earlier.

The wedding had been a small affair, with the reception held in their parents' backyard. Already a few months pregnant at the time, his sister had wanted to keep things quiet and low-key. She'd still felt a little insecure about returning home after leaving town five years before following a break-in at The Hope Chest, the local antiques shop she now managed. Though Sophia hadn't been involved in the burglary and vandalism, she'd taken the blame. Feelings of guilt had kept her away until their parents' anniversary party brought her back—with her former boyfriend, Jake Cameron, hot on her heels.

Like the rest of the family, Drew had been happy his sister had fallen in love with a good man who was clearly in love with her. The day of the wedding, Sophia had looked beautiful in her off-white gown with pale pink roses woven into her dark hair, and her new husband hadn't been able to take his eyes off her.

But it was Debbie, Sophia's maid of honor, who kept drawing Drew's attention. Something she'd evidently noticed as their gazes met before she made her way across lush green lawn. The pale pink gown hugged her curves and left the fair skin of her shoulders and arms bare. Her blond hair was caught up in a cascade of ringlets, and her blue eyes glittered in the white lights strung between the trees. "You should know, Drew, my money's on you."

"Excuse me?"

"The bet on whether you or Sam will be the next to fall," Debbie said, referring to his younger, footloose brother.

"Seriously? People are placing bets?"

"You better believe it," she retorted. "And my money's on you all the way. Sam's not the type to settle down while you, well, you're about as settled as any guy I've ever met."

"Sorry, Debbie, I couldn't tell. Was that an insult or a compliment?"

Tipping her head back, she gave a boisterous laugh guaranteed to turn every male head her way. "Oh, that was a compliment. If I decide to insult you, trust me when I say you'll feel it."

"So you think I'm settled?" he asked, falling back on the teasing, brotherly attitude that had long marked their relationship, even as he felt that balance start to shift in a way he couldn't explain.

"You're as grounded as a man can be and still manage to move both feet."

At the time, her teasing comments hadn't bothered him. Much. But now Debbie's voice reached inside him and threatened to shake something loose. The excitement, the anticipation, the "what if" underscoring her words struck a chord inside him that had been still and silent far too long.

But Debbie wasn't the woman who should be striking those notes. She was a friend, a good friend, and thinking of her in any other way just seemed...wrong. For Drew, dating had always been something of a game, a battle of the sexes he only engaged in on a level playing field. He liked women who were sophisticated and experienced and not the type to have their hearts easily broken. Women very unlike Debbie, who, despite the girl talk going on one booth over, had a tender and innocent heart she hid behind a smart mouth and sassy smile.

The hell of it was that he liked her. A lot. Too much, maybe, for him to ask her out and risk Debbie getting hurt. And getting hurt was exactly what might happen if she was serious about going after her mysterious stranger.

Judging from the sounds coming from the other booth, the women were getting ready to leave. Drew set his beer aside and half rose, ready to circle around to the other side of the restaurant and tell Debbie—what, exactly? That she shouldn't—couldn't—go after the adventure and excitement she was looking for?

She was young, beautiful, single. After the years of caring for her mother and running the bakery, she had every right to go after what she wanted. Any man would jump at the chance to fulfill the longing he'd heard in Debbie's voice.

Or more like any *other* man because Drew just didn't think of Debbie that way.

Did he?

"Are you sure you don't want us to give you a ride?" Sophia asked as the four women stepped out of the bar onto the quiet street. For obvious reasons, she was the designated driver and was in charge of seeing Darcy and Kara safely home.

"I only live five minutes away." She'd lived her entire life in a small apartment above the bakery. As a teenager, she'd longed for more space and room of her own, but after her mother passed away, the two-bedroom unit had been more than large enough, at times seeming far too empty. "The night air will help clear my head."

Debbie knew her limit and had stopped after her second margarita. The first had loosened her tongue more than she wanted to admit. She could only hope the drinks the other women had enjoyed would help them forget some of the foolish things she'd said.

"All right. But if you meet up with any dark handsome strangers on the way home, don't do anything I wouldn't do."

No such luck with her perfectly sober best friend. "Can you please forget I said anything?"

Sophia grinned impishly, reminding Debbie of when

they'd been kids, always looking for some kind of trouble. "Not a chance."

With a put-upon sigh, Debbie looked over at the bride-to-be. "Have a good night, Darcy, and just think, the next time we're all together, you'll be a few hours away from becoming Mrs. Nick Pirelli."

The redhead's beaming smile could have lit the sky. "I can't wait!"

Leaving her friends with a wave goodbye, Debbie walked the quiet street toward the bakery. The night was cold with a definite hint of fall in the air, along with woodsmoke drifting from a nearby chimney. Halloween decorations lurked in the shadows behind the darkened windows, reminding Debbie the holiday was less than a month away.

She wasn't sure when she first noticed the sound of footsteps behind her. With the bar only a few doors back, it wasn't that unusual to think someone else had decided to walk off a beer or two. But the late hour and emptiness of the stores around her was enough to quicken her pace. Most nights she would have circled around to the alley-way behind the bakery and the outside staircase that led directly to her apartment. But tonight, the security lights inside the shop beckoned with the promise of safety.

Reaching inside her oversize bag, she fumbled for her keys. Why couldn't she be one of those women who carried a purse the size of a cell phone case? Instead she'd fallen in love with a tapestry-style tote and stuffed it to the zipper with every item she might ever need. Her finger brushed a metal ring, but her relief was short-lived as she identified the extra set of measuring spoons she'd some-how misplaced. Swearing beneath her breath, she looked inside her bag and spotted the pink enamel cupcake-shaped key ring Sophia had given for her last birthday.

Her heart skipped a beat as she heard a sound behind her—
"Debbie! Wait up!"

Stumbling, she glanced back over her shoulder toward
the familiar voice. "Drew? What do you think you're
doing!" she demanded as he jogged toward her. Her heart
still pounding, she reached out and socked him on the arm.
The muscled bicep felt rock solid against her knuckles, and
he didn't even flinch. "You nearly gave me a heart attack!"

The dim lighting from the shop windows illuminated
his frown. "I called your name like three times."

He had? "Oh, sorry. I guess I wasn't paying attention."

"And that's the problem. You should be paying attention. Walking home by yourself—"

Swallowing a sigh, she tuned out the rest of what he
was saying. Clearly with Sophia now married with a husband to take care of her, Drew had decided to move his
big-brother act down the road and to her door.

Debbie had long thought Sophia's middle brother was
the most handsome of the three very good-looking men.
She'd even had a crush on him once upon a time when
she'd been a starry-eyed kid experiencing her first rush of
romance. Or hormones, she thought ruefully, still slightly
embarrassed by the tongue-tied, blushing preteen she'd
once been. But that was a long time ago, and she was
over him.

Still, that didn't stop a few of those long-buried feelings from shaking off a bit of dust as she gazed up at him
in the moonlight. Even casually dressed like just about
every local guy, in a gray henley shirt tucked into faded
jeans and a denim jacket to ward off the chill stretched
across his broad shoulders, something about Drew made
him stand out from the crowd. It was more than looks—
although he was...so...good-looking. Totally unfair, in
fact, for a man to be that gorgeous.

How many times had she imagined running her fingers through the waves in his dark hair? Pictured how his brown eyes would darken with passion in the seconds before he kissed her? Wondered what it would be like to feel his body pressed against hers?

How many hours had she wasted, her mind taunted her, since Drew would never think of her in the same way?

Slapping those old memories aside, Debbie cut off the rest of his lecture, insisting, "I can take care of myself, Drew. I'm a big girl now."

Was it her imagination or had his gaze dropped slightly at her words, giving her a subtle once-over? She didn't have many opportunities to dress up, and the bachelorette party had given her an excuse to wear her new cream slacks and the wide-necked gold sweater that hugged her curves and, yes, she'd admit it, showed off a fair amount of cleavage. She'd pulled on her leather jacket before leaving the bar, but the blazer style only had a single button, which emphasized rather than hid her figure.

Not that Drew would notice. Her heart skipped a beat. Would he?

"All the more reason to be careful," he warned, his voice gruffer than a moment before. Enough to make her wonder. "A woman like you—"

"A woman like me?"

"A beautiful woman like you needs to be careful. There are guys out there who would take advantage."

Debbie's mind was too caught up on his first words— Drew thought she was beautiful?—to pay attention to whatever else it was he was so intent on telling her. And as he walked her the rest of the way home, a solid masculine presence at her side, she couldn't help wondering what it would be like if Drew was one of those guys. The kind to take advantage at the end of a date by pushing for a good-night kiss and maybe even more.

Her skin heated, and she could only bless the moonlight for hiding her reaction to the thought. Because of course this wasn't a date, and as they reached the bakery door, she reminded him, "This is Clearville, Drew. I know pretty much all the guys 'out there.'"

His jaw clenched as if holding back whatever else he wanted to say. And despite her claim of knowing all there was to know about Clearville guys, his dark eyes were glittering in a way that was completely...unfamiliar.

"Maybe," he finally conceded as he reached out for her keys, "but you never know what might happen...even in a small town like this."

His hand closed over hers, and Debbie's breath caught in her chest. The stroke of his thumb against her skin combined with the deep rumble of his voice sent a shiver down her spine. Surely not what he intended. He was warning her, wasn't he? Trying to scare her...not trying to seduce her.

Heart pounding, her mouth was suddenly too dry to swallow and her tongue snuck out to dampen her lips. Drew tracked the movement, the small amount of moisture evaporating as he leaned closer...

Turning the key in the lock, he pushed the door open and stepped back. "Good night, Debbie. Sweet dreams."

His parting words stayed with her long after she'd climbed the stairs to the safety of her apartment and locked the door behind her. Sweet dreams? With her hand still tingling from his touch, Debbie knew Drew had just about guaranteed he would play a starring role in hers!

Chapter Two

"Don't they make such a lovely couple?"

Debbie looked away from the just-married couple in question to meet Vanessa Pirelli's smiling expression. Nick and Darcy were supposed to be posing for pictures beside the three-tiered wedding cake, but from what Debbie could see, the two of them appeared completely oblivious as they gazed into each other's eyes. The love between them radiated as brightly as the antique chandelier glowing overhead.

The bride and groom had decided on a small wedding, and friends and family had gathered at Hillcrest House for their reception. The sprawling Victorian with its peaked turrets and dormer windows sat elegantly atop a bluff overlooking the ocean. The upper two floors had been converted into hotel rooms while the first-floor dining room was now a high-class, intimate restaurant. The ballroom had mostly remained untouched, still in use after 125 years. With its intricate mahogany wainscot, hand-carved moldings and coffered ceilings, the location added to the romance of Nick and Darcy's wedding reception.

Debbie nodded at the older woman's words. "They do," she agreed. "It was a beautiful wedding."

"Mmm-hmm. It's always a pleasure to see young people in love. Nick and Darcy, Sophia and Jake, Sam and Kara…" The mother of the groom's gaze turned speculative. "And you and Drew certainly make a good-looking couple."

Debbie should have seen it coming. This was the second wedding where she and Drew had walked down the aisle together as part of a wedding party. The matchup made perfect sense, as they were both single. What didn't make as much sense was the rush of heat to her face as she fought to squirm beneath his mother's speculative gaze. Praying her cheeks weren't as bright as the burgundy bridesmaid's dress she wore, Debbie shook her head.

"Mrs. Pirelli—"

"Now, how many times have I asked you to call me Vanessa? You know you're practically family."

"You're exactly right, Vanessa. All of your sons have always been like big brothers to me. There's never been anything romantic between any of us. Including me and Drew."

Not even the night of Darcy's bachelorette party.

In the days since, Debbie convinced herself whatever she thought had happened between her and Drew within the faint glow of her shop windows…hadn't. Drew had simply been looking out for her, same as always, his parting words a brotherly warning and not a sensual promise.

With that in mind, she'd gone out of her way to treat him the same as always. She'd met his gaze with a big smile and had taken his arm for their walk down the aisle with a friendly tug. She had *not* noticed the strength of the bicep linked with her own any more than she'd felt a shiver race across her shoulders when that muscled arm brushed against her. And she most certainly did not keep sneaking looks at him out of the corner of her eye to see if he was sneaking looks at her.

Because he wasn't, and that was that.

Vanessa sighed. "You can't blame a mother for trying to find the right girl for her son. After all, you're a beautiful, strong, confident woman."

Though the trim brunette with sparkling green eyes didn't have any resemblance to Debbie's own well-rounded, blond-haired, blue-eyed mother, the warmth and kindness of the words surrounded Debbie like one of her mother's vanilla-scented hugs. "Thank you, Vanessa. That means a lot to me."

"And, if I do say so myself, my son is not such a bad catch, either."

Tipping her head back with a laugh, Debbie couldn't help but agree, and not just because she was talking to Drew's mother. "You're absolutely right. Drew is a good man. One of the best, which makes him a wonderful friend."

But not the man for her. Drew was as grounded and stable as the houses he built. Not at all the type to rush headlong into adventure and excitement. Worse, Debbie thought as pinpricks of heat stabbed at her, he had known her for her entire life. He'd probably be able to recall every fashion disaster, every bad hair day, every extra pound that haunted her past. She wanted a man who would look at her and see her *now,* as the strong, confident woman Vanessa described and not as the chubby, awkward girl she'd once been.

Debbie glanced over her shoulder at Drew, knowing right where he was standing even while pretending not to. Her breath caught as their gazes met and held. He wasn't looking at her like he was remembering her fashion disaster/bad hair days. If she didn't know better—

A flush started at her painted toes and made a slow, sensual climb. If she didn't know better she might have thought he was looking at her the same way a dieting man always looked at her buns—her sugar-glazed cinnamon buns, that was—like he wanted to devour her and not stop until they were both satisfied. But that was crazy, wasn't it?

After all, this was *Drew* she was thinking about. Even-keel, think-things-through Drew Pirelli. He wasn't the kind of man to devour desserts. More the type to savor a meal, to take things slow and—

How exactly is this helping? she demanded of herself even as she tore her gaze away.

"Well, it's not unheard of for friendship to turn to something more," Vanessa remarked. "If you keep an open heart, you never know what might happen."

The echo of the words Drew had spoken the other night spurred Debbie into action. This was *not* happening. After asking Vanessa to excuse her, she grabbed a glass of champagne on her way across the floral-patterned carpet. If she decided to have some kind of reckless affair—and she had to admit, that was way more talk than action on her part so far—she had the right kind of man in mind. That was not Drew Pirelli.

Drew was the kind of man a woman committed to wholeheartedly and for her entire life. Debbie wasn't ready for that. Just the thought sent a suffocating panic pressing down on her chest. She was ready for fun. So no matter how great of a guy Drew was, and he was the greatest, he was her friend. And the sooner they got back on friendly terms, the...safer she would feel.

And how's that kind of thinking fit a daring woman out for reckless affair?

Ignoring the mocking voice in her head, Debbie smiled as she reached Drew's side. It was what she called her Bonnie's Best smile, the one she'd put on for her mother all those years ago to show Bonnie she could focus entirely on her own health because her daughter was doing just fine. The same smile she'd used to greet neighbors and friends when they asked about her mother's health and later when they inquired about Debbie in the weeks and months after Bonnie's death.

Doing just fine! Thanks so much for asking.

The smile had gotten her through much tougher times than a sudden and inappropriate infatuation with Drew Pirelli.

Pointing her champagne flute at him, Debbie spoke before Drew had the chance. "I have a bone to pick with you!" Her smile felt a little less forced as she went on the offensive. The teasing, confrontational tone was just right for their relationship. It was as comfortable and familiar as Drew himself, and only their surroundings at the posh hotel ballroom kept her from giving a lighthearted pop on the shoulder. "You cost me fifty bucks."

His dark brows rose, and he met her mock anger with a smile. But was there something different there? Something other than his usual, almost patronizing expression? He waited, biding his time, until she reached his side. His breath teased the bare skin of her neck as he leaned close and asked, "How did I do that?"

Debbie fought off a shiver threatening to shake her down to her shoes. "The bet, remember? I thought for sure you would be the next Pirelli to fall and yet Sam's already engaged. How the heck did that happen?"

He frowned as if seriously weighing her words. "Maybe you don't know me as well as you think you do."

His espresso eyes challenged her, and Debbie's confidence started to tremble right along with her suddenly weak knees. Swallowing, she countered, "More like I don't know *Sam*. After all, he's the one who got engaged when I never thought he would."

"And *I'm* the one who's still single. Maybe I'm not as settled as you seem to think."

If anyone was *unsettled,* Debbie decided, it was definitely her. She should walk away now, while she still could, while she still had any hope of getting back on equal footing with Drew again. But that was ridiculous because she did know him. She knew him well enough to realize he was messing with her, giving her a hard time, same as always. *She* was the one who was overreacting thanks to her foolish decision to give voice to her fantasies. She was the one who'd let the crazy thoughts out, and it was going to be up to her to put them back where they belonged.

"Come on, Drew. Tell me you don't see yourself married with a couple of kids." A look of admission flashed in his eyes, and Debbie pressed her point. Nodding in Nick and Darcy's direction, she said, "Tell me you don't want that."

He glanced over at the happy couple, who were busy staring into each other's eyes. "Sure, I do," he agreed readily enough for Debbie to think she'd been right all along about him playing her. "Someday. But there's something else I want right now."

She didn't realize what Drew meant until he took the slim flute from her, set it aside on a nearby table and pulled her onto the dance floor. Her hand rose automatically to rest on his shoulder and her feet quickly found the rhythm of the slow, romantic ballad. It was hardly the first time she and Drew had danced together, and as he pulled her closer, she caught scent of his cologne. The woody fragrance with its hint of cedar was the same brand he'd worn for years—a yearly Christmas gift from his sister. Sophia knew her brother wouldn't bother to buy something he'd consider unnecessary. Debbie knew it, too. She knew Drew. He was as comforting and familiar as the smell of his cologne, except—

The trip in her pulse as he spun her beneath the crystal chandelier wasn't the slow, steady pace of comfort, and she found no familiarity in the tingle of goose bumps chasing across her chest when her breasts brushed the starched front of Drew's tuxedo shirt. His eyes darkened—whether as a result of the intimate contact or in reaction to her own, Debbie didn't know, but there was no denying the heat in his gaze.

The rush of unexpected and unwanted desire took Debbie back to her teenage years and her helpless, overwhelming crush on Drew. To the unrequited longing mixed with the heartbreaking knowledge that he would never see her as anything more than his kid sister's friend. A part of her, that small part that had never lost hope even in the most hopeless of situations, longed to believe everything she was seeing in Drew's expression, longed to believe that maybe, just maybe, he did view her as more than the girl next door.

A decade-old memory drifted through her thoughts. The door to the bakery had been open, letting in the warm summer air and allowing the scents of fresh-baked breads and muffins to drift out onto the sidewalk, to lure tourists and locals inside. Standing behind the counter, she'd caught sight of Drew through the front window. He'd been away at college, but her pulse had taken that same familiar leap as if he'd never been gone a day. He'd smiled at her as he'd stepped inside and the warmth in his gaze had threatened to reach inside and pull her heart straight from her chest.

She'd cut her hair since she'd seen him last, straightening the life out of the curls she hated and taming the locks into a more sophisticated style. She'd been on yet another diet and had dropped to a smaller size. Was this the day when Drew would finally see her for who she really was? Anticipation hammered through her veins until she'd caught sight of the tall, leggy brunette on Drew's arm.

Debbie had kept her smile firmly in place as he introduced her to the girlfriend he'd met at school. She asked all the appropriate questions, showed just the right amount of friendly interest until the moment the couple said goodbye. As the two of them walked out of the shop, Debbie had heard the other girl teasingly ask if she was one of Drew's ex-girlfriends.

Nah, that's just Debbie.

She could still feel the ache of a broken heart as her dreams of Drew being her boyfriend slipped from her fingers and into the gorgeous brunette's hands. But she'd wised up after that, too, forcing herself to get over her pointless crush. She didn't want to be "just Debbie," and she refused to follow the vain hope that Drew might see her any other way.

Lifting her chin, she met his gaze head on. "If this is wedding fever, you should know I'm immune."

"Wedding fever?"

"You know," she answered. "Sympathy pains brought on by too much contact with the crazy-in-love bride and groom."

"I wouldn't call anything I'm feeling right now pain."

Debbie stumbled slightly at his words only to have Drew pull her even tighter against his chest. How many times had she dreamed of a moment like this? A moment when Drew would hold her close and finally, finally claim her mouth with his own? If he kissed her now—

Oh, if he did, Debbie had no doubt she'd fall for him all over again, wrapping herself in foolish hopes and dreams that had no place in the real world. Gazing up into his eyes beneath the chandelier's glittering lights, the promise of the longed for kiss made the risk almost, *almost* seem worth it....

Fortunately, the song came to an end, giving her the excuse to step back and take a sanity-saving breath. "That's the fever talking. You're delirious, but don't worry, it won't last."

"Debbie—"

"I need to check if Darcy needs anything. Bridesmaid's duty and all."

Quickly slipping away, Debbie ducked between the guests gathered along the edges of the dance floor, but she didn't stop to look for the bride amid the crowd. She escaped through the first doorway she found. The sound of music and laughter faded as she stepped out onto a secluded balcony overlooking the historic bed-and-breakfast's manicured grounds. The cool, ocean-scented night air touched her warm cheeks, and as Debbie gazed up at the night sky, she couldn't help thinking all the stars she'd wished upon for all those years were laughing down at her now.

As her mother had often warned her... "Be careful what you wish for," she whispered.

Drew quickly lost sight of Debbie as she darted out the French doors at the back of the ballroom. Forcing himself to let her go, he headed over to the bar and ordered a beer. He clenched the cold bottle in his hand and took a long swallow of the malty brew. She had every reason to run away from him, and he had no right to go after her until he figured out what the hell was going on.

Was Debbie right? Was he suffering from some kind of wedding fever? The explanation made as much sense as anything he could come up with to justify why he was suddenly tempted to throw caution aside when he was with her. Which was crazy, since reason had always trumped emotion in every hand he'd ever played. His head always ruled his heart. How many times had his last girlfriend, Angie, told him to stop thinking and start feeling whenever the inevitable "where is this relationship going?" talk came up?

He'd tried telling her how he felt—he found her attractive, he enjoyed spending time with her, their common interests made a good foundation for a relationship—but none of those explanations satisfied her. She'd wanted something more...just like Debbie did.

He'd overheard the words from her himself. Debbie wanted adventure, excitement, mystery—not a guy she'd known her whole life.

You're as grounded as a man can be and still manage to move both feet.

The memory of the accusation she'd made at his sister's wedding grated on his nerves, and he didn't even know why. The truth was, he prided himself on making solid decisions, on not rushing into situations without being able to predict the outcome. If he crossed the line from friendship to something more with Debbie, he had no idea where that might lead.

Yet knowing all that hadn't stopped him from asking her to dance, or from wanting more than a dance....

She was right about one thing. If their names ended up

linked by the local grapevine, assumptions would immediately be made.

Drew snorted. With the rate his siblings were getting hitched, his parents would be sending out wedding invitations within a week.

He hadn't missed the little conversation between his mother and Debbie earlier. He could only hope his mother had been a little more subtle than she'd been after the rehearsal dinner a few nights before. A dinner he'd attended alone. He'd made excuses about work and the custom house he was building keeping him too busy for a relationship, but his mother had quickly called him out on it.

"Do you think I haven't noticed how many family dinners you've missed recently?" she'd demanded. And then softer, she questioned, "And do you think I don't know the real reason why?"

Okay, so maybe he had been feeling like the odd man out, but he wasn't about to admit that to his mother. "I've been busy. That's the *only* reason."

His mother sighed, giving him the look that could still make him feel like he was six years old. "I have to say, I never thought you would be the child I would have to worry about."

Drew winced in memory.

His mother would love nothing more than to see him settle down.

All the more reason *not* to follow Debbie out onto the secluded balcony. He almost had himself convinced when he spotted her shawl draped across the back of the chair she'd abandoned. Leaving the half-finished bottle of beer at the bar, he crossed the room to the table that had been reserved for the wedding party. And just as he'd been unable to stop himself from pulling her onto the dance floor, he reached for the softly woven shawl. The scent of her perfume, a mix of spicy and sweet that perfectly captured Debbie's personality, drifted over him. Pulling him in when he knew he should be walking away.

As he moved toward the balcony doors, he was stopped several times along the way by friends and neighbors. He took their ribbing about being the only unattached Pirelli with good humor even if the phrase "last man standing" was already getting old. He knew it would get worse after Sam's wedding. Still, he pushed the thought aside. He was a man on a mission, out to find a certain bridesmaid.

She turned as he opened the door, her arms crossed tightly to ward off the night air. For Drew, the chill was a relief after the ballroom's crowded interior. But it wasn't exactly a cold shower, and not nearly cold enough to keep his body from heating when he noticed the swell of flesh above her dress's neckline.

All brides were supposed to be beautiful, and Darcy was undeniably gorgeous. But it was Debbie who had knocked the breath from Drew's lungs when he'd caught sight of her walking down the aisle.

He should have been better prepared, seeing her now, but maybe he hadn't recovered from that first blow. Her blond hair was caught to one side, her golden curls tumbling over her shoulder. The bridesmaids' gowns reflected Darcy's taste, and Debbie looked amazing in the halter-style burgundy dress. Tiny beads highlighted the bodice, and the rich fabric fell to the tops of her strappy sandals with a slit in the side guaranteed to blow his mind with revealing flashes of her shapely calf and thigh.

Her blue eyes gazed at him warily. "Drew…"

He heard the protest in her voice and held up the shawl. "I thought you might be cold out here."

"Oh."

Was it his imagination or did she sound disappointed that he'd followed her for such an innocent reason? "Well, thank you," she said as she reached for the pink material, "but I can take care of myself."

Drew didn't doubt it. Debbie had been on her own since her mother died. Before that, really, with the care Bonnie Mattson had needed during her illness. He'd long admired Debbie's independence and the way she'd scoffed at the idea of needing a man. But for the first time, that toughness seemed to soften something inside his chest. He held on to the shawl, keeping their hands tangled together in the wispy fabric. "I know you can. But once in a while, it's nice to have someone take care of you."

Sliding the shawl from her hands, he draped the material over her shoulders, keeping hold of both ends. "Maybe," she conceded, though her slightly stiff posture wasn't giving an inch. "But I don't need—"

"This isn't about need," he interrupted. "It's about want."

Debbie swallowed. "Want?"

"It's like…dessert. Not something you need, but certainly something you crave."

"And let me guess. You're craving something *sweet*." The sardonic twist on the word told Drew what Debbie thought of that description—one he'd been guilty of using in the past. She'd nailed it when she complained to Darcy and her fellow bridesmaids about the local guys treating her like a little sister or a platonic buddy.

Standing so close to her now, feeling the heat from her body and breathing in the vanilla-and-spice scent of her skin, he wondered how the male population—himself included—could have been so deaf, blind and stupid. He had no doubt Debbie would taste sweet and yet— Suddenly he thought of the sheer temptation of her chocolate-raspberry cake. "I was thinking more along the lines of something rich, decadent, a little sinful even."

Debbie's eyes widened, huge and sparkling in the faint light streaming through the French doors. He'd gone too far, he thought. Pushed too hard for something he shouldn't even let himself want. The smart thing, the logical thing to do was to walk away now while they still could. "Debbie—"

"Seriously, Drew, has anyone ever told you that you talk too much?"

"Uh—" Before he had a chance to say anything else, she reached up, clasped her hands behind his neck and pulled his head toward hers. At the first touch of her lips, Drew was lost. Walk away? How could he when a single kiss had knocked him off his feet?

He'd been right about the sweetness, but had seriously underestimated just how rich, just how decadent she would taste, with just a hint of champagne and the piña colada wedding cake she'd made flavoring the kiss. The combination was addictive, but it was a taste uniquely her own. His tongue hungrily traced her full upper lip from corner to corner, spending an extra second at the enticing peak in the center. Diving deeper when she made a soft, indistinct sound that still managed to convey the intoxicating blend of demand and desire.

Drew might have smiled at the demand—Debbie had never been shy when it came to speaking her mind—but the desire overrode all else. He pulled her closer, her softness and curves melding against his body in a perfect fit. Blood pounded through his veins, and his hands tightened on her hips. The thin, slippery material of her dress hardly seemed like much of a barrier. With a few deft moves to push it out of the way—

The thought had barely crossed his mind when he froze

at the sound of voices drifting over from the parking lot on the other side of the evergreen hedge. The night chill seeped in as Debbie broke the kiss and slipped from his arms.

"You sure about this? Your brother is going to kill you for messing with his ride."

"I know. Great, isn't it?"

"You know what they say about payback, and your wedding is less than two months away."

Drew immediately recognized Sam's voice along with his friend Billy Cummings's. The three of them were supposed to decorate Nick's truck. Even though the newlyweds were spending their first night together at the bed-and-breakfast, their vehicle would proudly announce their just-married status for the trip home. Sam had gathered the appropriate mix of tin cans and shaving cream along with some leashes and dog toys as an homage to Nick's profession.

It wouldn't be long before—

"So where is Drew anyway? Are we doing this without him?"

"No way! He has to be part of this so I can tell Nick it was all his idea." The faint crunch of gravel followed Sam's words. "You go get the stuff, and I'll track him down."

Nick might have been the veterinarian, but Sam could be like a dog with a bone. He wasn't going to give up until he found Drew.

His looked over at Debbie, who'd already taken a few steps back. Her arms were once again crossed over her chest, but Drew didn't think this time was because of the cold. "Debbie, I'm sorry. I— That was—"

The awkwardness of the moment grew in rhythm with the silence as he tried to put the kiss and the past few minutes into words. But she clearly had her own ideas about what had taken place. "Wedding fever," she stated flatly. "But don't worry. You'll forget all about it by morning."

Then she turned and went back into the reception, leaving him alone on the balcony.

Chapter Three

Debbie took one look at the bold black letters on the whiteboard in front of The High Tide restaurant and immediately wanted to turn around and make the forty-minute drive back home from Redfield.

Singles' Night—Meet and Greet!

Nerves somersaulted through her stomach, whirling fast enough to make her feel sick. This was what she got for opening her big mouth in front of her friends. Ever since making that silly claim about wanting someone to sweep her off her feet, Sophia and Kara had been bombarding her—in person and via phone calls and emails—with ways to meet Mr. Tall, Dark and Handsome.

She'd escaped a three-way tag team only because Darcy was in Paris on her honeymoon with Nick. Though if her friend did come across any possibilities, Debbie wouldn't be surprised to receive a message touting Monsieur Tall, Dark and Handsome.

Sophia had been the one to send her the info on the singles' night. Debbie wondered what her friend would think of the sign—one she was sure normally listed the catch of the day. As if she could just order up the perfect guy to go.

Not that she was looking for the perfect guy. But she'd told Sophia she'd give it a try. She had nothing to lose, right?

Memories of the moonlit balcony swarmed her senses—the brush of Drew's lips, the subtle hint of champagne, the murmur of her name spoken against her skin. Okay, maybe she'd caught him off guard, kissing him the way she had, but he'd done a heck of a job kissing her back. It had been enough to make Debbie think that maybe he was right. Maybe she didn't know him as well as she'd always thought. Then he'd deepened the kiss, and she'd stopped thinking at all....

Debbie slammed that mental door shut. As far as she was concerned, those were all reasons *to* go to the singles' night. Drew had gotten caught up in the moment only to immediately regret it. She knew it by the what-the-hell-am-I-doing-kissing-her look in his dark gaze and the apology that had followed. And in his total absence over the past week. Not that they normally saw each other every day, but it was a small town. You couldn't avoid running into someone unless you were avoiding running into someone.

Not that she *expected* him to seek her out, but that he *hadn't*... Well, it only showed that she was right. Temporary insanity brought on by wedding fever and nothing more.

So, fine. She wasn't interested in Drew anyway. She wanted adventure, excitement. She wanted to meet someone new, and she was going to check out the daily specials on offer tonight at The High Tide.

Breathing in a deep, hopeful breath, Debbie climbed from the car and headed toward the restaurant. Redfield also catered to the tourist crowd, and the restaurant had a quaint bait-and-tackle-shop vibe—weathered wood exterior, netting and fishing rods hanging below the sign.

The scent of fried seafood was enough to make her stomach grumble even as she mentally calculated the number of calories. And while she wasn't positive her willpower would persevere, it was a sure bet that her fashion sense would win hands down.

The waistband on her floral skirt didn't have nearly enough give for her to even think about fish and chips. She'd be lucky to squeeze in a salad, but the fitted skirt was the perfect match for her favorite pale pink cashmere sweater. The purchase had been a splurge even on sale, but the savvy saleswoman had told her she looked like a cross between Marilyn Monroe and Jayne Mansfield in the figure-hugging, sinfully soft top, and Debbie had been sold.

You can do this. Sophia's voice echoed in her mind. *Just think, tonight you might meet your own Prince Charming!*

Debbie hadn't tried to explain, again, that she wasn't interested in some love of a lifetime. A relationship would only be another commitment when most days she already felt stretched too thin. Another responsibility when she already longed for more freedom. Another potential for loss when fate had already stolen so much....

But she couldn't expect Sophia, still basking in the glow of her own happily ever after, to understand that. So she'd agreed that yes, tonight might be the night.

As she stepped inside the restaurant, Debbie wondered if she hadn't underestimated the possibilities. She'd feared everyone who would go to such lengths to meet someone—herself included—would reek of desperation. But the good-looking guy standing at the bottom of the steps leading up to the reserved section of the bar met her gaze with a friendly and confident smile. He shifted the clipboard he was casually holding and held out his right hand.

"Welcome to The High Tide. Are you here for the meet and greet?" His green eyes sparkled beneath shaggy blond hair, and deep dimples bracketed his smile.

Definitely cute, and while the touch of his hand against hers didn't set off any fireworks, his grip was strong and warm. Maybe tonight could be the beginning of something after all.

"I am," she agreed, hoping she didn't sound too eager.

After taking her name and email to keep her up to date with future events, he said, "Here's a badge. We'd like you to write your name and an interesting or fun fact about yourself on it."

Debbie reached out but her gaze locked on his hand. His left hand and the shiny gold band on the fourth finger. "You're married?" she blurted out, the words escaping before she had time to call them back.

He glanced down at his wedding ring and flushed slightly. "Oh, yeah. I'm, um, not part of the singles' group," he explained. "I manage the restaurant and like to be here to make sure everything runs smoothly when we have events like this. Sorry if I—"

She waved his words aside. "No need to apologize." After all, it wasn't like he'd kissed her or anything. Withholding a sigh, she asked, "I don't suppose you and your wife met at one of these events, did you?"

His eyes lit in memory. "No, we met while backpacking along the California coastline. We were supposed to travel all the way up to Canada and at the end of the trip go our separate ways. But we realized we'd fallen in love and decided to stay together. Just goes to show that you can find love anywhere along the way. Good luck tonight."

Backpacking across the country. Now, that was a fun

and interesting fact, Debbie thought as she filled out her name badge. She got the first part done okay, but then came to a complete halt. The whole point of going to an event like this was to break out of a rut. She'd lived in the same town, in the same apartment, worked the same job and had known the same people her whole life. If her world was filled with fun and interesting facts, she doubted she'd *be* at a singles' event. No, she'd be backpacking along the coast or jetting off to Paris....

Sighing, she glanced over to the other side of the bar. She'd be sitting across the table from a good-looking guy who looked a lot like— Who looked exactly like— Oh, good grief, it *was* Drew Pirelli!

Sitting in a secluded booth, Drew and a beautiful brunette were engaged in an intense conversation, their heads bent so close together the table between them almost disappeared. As she watched, he reached over and stroked the woman's arm, and a layer of goose bumps rose along her own skin....

Abruptly turning away, Debbie nearly crumpled the name tag in her hand. She had to leave now before he saw her and— And what exactly? Who cared if he saw her out tonight?

She wasn't going to sit at home, waiting for Prince Charming to sweep her off her feet. She was taking charge and going after what she wanted. She wanted to go out, to escape the pressure of duty and responsibility for once in her life. She wanted some fun and interesting facts to write down on her stupid name badge!

Picking up the pen, she printed a few words beneath her name, capping them off with an exclamation point before slapping the sticky tag to the front of her sweater. Now, time to actually meet a single guy at this singles' event.

Within minutes, she'd done just that. Gary Tronston

was in his early thirties by her guess. He had blond hair and wore wire-framed glasses. He was a dentist, and while Debbie wasn't sure how interesting that fact was, he had added on his name tag that he was a dentist with a sweet tooth, which at least showed an attempt at a sense of humor.

But talking to him, Debbie couldn't help feeling he'd somehow slipped her a shot of Novocain.

"I like helping people. Seeing them smile," he added with a smile of his own. "It's not saving the world, but I like to think I've made a difference."

"That's great, Gary. Really."

Debbie might not have always been the best judge of men, but he seemed like a nice guy. If only she felt even the slightest spark…

She didn't, though, and it was all Drew's fault. No matter how hard she tried, she couldn't keep from glancing over poor Gary's shoulder at Drew on the other side of the bar.

His dark hair gleamed even in the bar's muted lighting, and the red T-shirt he wore, the long sleeves pushed back to reveal his tanned, muscular arms, was the perfect contrast. His eyebrows were pulled together in a frown, and though she was too far away, she knew just how rich and warm his eyes were. After a moment, his features relaxed, the lines around his eyes crinkling slightly as he flashed his perfect white teeth in a smile at his date. Debbie tore her gaze away, but it was too late. He looked so vibrant, so virile, that Gary with his blond hair and somewhat pasty skin seemed ready to simply fade away.

Not that Gary was to blame. When she and Drew had kissed, the whole world had faded away. How was the poor guy supposed to compete with that?

"Would you like a drink?" he asked before waving their waitress over and requesting a wine list as if they were at a five-star establishment instead of a casual, family-friendly restaurant. She tried to ignore that it made him seem more than a little pretentious. But once she spotted that chink in his armor, she couldn't help noticing a few more less than attractive details. Like when he mentioned for the third time that he drove a Mercedes. And that he'd graduated with honors. And that he was working with a group of investors to build an exclusive resort in the area.

Debbie supposed it would have been hard to fit all that on a name tag.

Suppressing a sigh, she smiled as the waitress returned with their drinks and took a sip of the white wine Gary had ordered for both of them. She fought to keep her attention on the man in front of her instead of on the one across the bar. But that focus only brought more details to light. Like…wasn't Gary's blond hair combed a little too neatly? His clothes too perfectly pressed? And she'd bet the bakery that the shine on his nails came from a manicure.

Good hygiene was one thing, but that was just…weird, she decided, reaching for her wineglass again. Drew would never—

Debbie tried to stop the hopeless comparison, but suddenly the floodgates were open. There was nothing overstated about Drew, nothing that said he was trying too hard or that he was too hung up on his own good looks. Just a quiet confidence and yes, he was gorgeous enough for Debbie to be hung up on his looks. Of course, he was more than a pretty face and a drool-worthy bod.

He was…Drew.

The boy who'd stood up for her when some of the other kids in school had teased her about her weight and the outrageous desserts her mother always packed in her lunch. Of course, he'd been thirteen at the time and helped her in typical boy fashion—by stealing huge bites out of her cupcake or éclair or torte when Debbie wasn't watching and then flashing her a cocky grin. In typical girl fashion, Debbie had protested, calling him names and probably sticking her tongue out a time or two, even as warmth bloomed inside her.

At nine years old, she'd known he was saving her from pigging out in front of the rest of the class or from hurting Bonnie's feelings by refusing to take those desserts to school or, heaven forbid, throwing out the food her talented mother made with such love.

And then there was the day of her mother's funeral. Just about everyone in town had stopped by to tell her how much her mother would be missed and how they would be there for Debbie if she needed anything.

She'd smiled through it all, reminiscing about her mother, talking about how much she loved to bake and to share her gift of sweets with the town. Only later did Debbie break down in the back of the bakery, crying over a batch of éclairs that she had never, ever been able to make as well as Bonnie, as it hit her that she would never taste her mother's baking again. It was then, after everyone else was gone and she was alone, that Drew knocked on the bakery's back door. He hadn't said much, simply holding her as she cried and then helped her to clean up the mess she'd made of the kitchen.

He'd told her everything would be okay, and though countless others had offered that same platitude, wrapped in Drew's arms, breathing in the familiar scent of his aftershave and listening to the quiet confidence in his deep voice, she'd believed him. And she'd held on to that belief deep in her heart, pulling it out when life got rough and she'd had her doubts about running the business on her own or during the holidays when at times she felt so alone. And somehow she knew everything would be all right. Because Drew had told her so, and he would never go back on his word.

This time, she couldn't keep her glance from straying over toward his booth. Her heart slammed against her rib cage when his dark-eyed gaze snared hers. His date had disappeared, and he was looking back at her without a hint of surprise. A wash of heat crept up her face. How long had he been watching her while she'd been trying so hard not to watch him? And was he really going to sit there the rest of the night, studying her as she pretended to have a good time? Because, yes, by now she was past the point of convincing herself she actually *was* having a good time.

She reached for her glass, surprised to find it almost empty, but thankfully the waitress quickly stopped by with reinforcements. She started when Gary reached out and grabbed her hand. "I'm so glad you came to this event. It's hard to meet the right person, isn't it?"

The right person? Oh, good Lord, she really hoped he wasn't talking about her! "Um, yeah. Look, Gary—"

"I knew as soon as I saw you that you were the one."

Debbie swallowed. "Gary, that's so…sweet of you to say. But the thing is…" Oh, jeez. She hated doing this. She'd been on the other side of the "it's not you, it's me" speech too many times not to feel badly about delivering it. "I'm not really looking for anything serious. I just want to meet some new people, to go out and have a good time."

His sincere expression quickly morphed into one that was far more interested. "Well, in that case, why don't we get out of here? I've booked a room in a hotel just down the street where we can really have some fun."

"Whoa, there, Gar! I think you still have the wrong idea about me. But, you know, good luck with all that!"

Grabbing her glass, Debbie downed half the wine in a single gulp as she made her escape.

Speaking of which… Yep, Drew was still in the corner booth. Still watching…which meant as much as tonight was starting to look like a bust, she couldn't go home yet. She didn't want to give Drew the satisfaction of thinking that he'd run her off or worse, that he was right and that she should be spending her nights at home alone like a good girl.

She was going to have fun tonight, she thought grimly, even if it killed her.

She was killing him.

Drew's hand tightened around the soda he'd been downing all night. He hadn't come to the bar to drink, though that was the invitation he'd issued to Cassidy Carter. It had been strictly business, and he didn't drink on the job. Of course, Cass had left over an hour ago, and he still hadn't switched to anything harder than pure sugar and caffeine. He was a little afraid of what he might do if even so much as a beer went to his head. Hell, the rate the night was going, he should probably switch to diet and caffeine-free.

Every time Debbie laughed, every time she touched another guy—even if it was just to shake hands—every time she leaned closer to hear what one of them said, every damn time the guy's gaze dropped to the rounded curves on display beneath a sweater that looked like it was made out of cotton candy, Drew had to fight to keep his butt in the booth.

He'd always considered himself a patient man, but he was quickly running out. Still, he kept waiting. Waiting for Debbie to realize none of these losers were good enough for her. He could see it at first glance. What was taking her so damn long?

He'd thought overhearing Debbie at Darcy's bachelor-ette party was bad. But that had only been words, and he'd done his best to convince himself it was just talk. That she wasn't serious about wanting some stranger to sweep her off her feet. Clearly, he was wrong. Not only had Debbie meant every word, she was backing them up with actions.

And it was killing him.

Drew didn't want to look too closely at the reasons why. Debbie was an old family friend, and he was worried about her. That was reason enough, right? He didn't want to think that he was jealous or that he wanted to be one of the men standing close enough to her to know if that sweater could possibly feel as soft as it looked. He certainly didn't want to think about any of those men kissing her the way he had on the balcony last weekend because he shouldn't have been the one kissing her, either. Tonight only drove that home more than ever. How could he be the one to protect her if he had to worry about protecting her from himself?

But when the waitress brought Debbie yet another glass of wine and when the introduction handshakes turned into nice-to-meet-you hugs, he couldn't stand by any longer.

He was saving her from herself. When she came to her senses and forgot all about this whole adventure and excitement streak she was on, she'd realize that, too. She'd probably even thank him for it.

A burst of mocking laughter that sounded just like his brothers' echoed in his head.

Yeah, sure she would.

Debbie wasn't sure how long she'd been talking to the brown-haired guy standing in front of her before she realized she no longer held his full attention. His gaze kept flicking toward a point over her shoulder. She might have feared she was too boring to hold his interest, but boredom didn't put a look of fear in a guy's eyes.

"I think I should, um…" He was already backing away before he blurted out, "Nice meeting you, Debbie."

She didn't have to turn around to around to know Drew was behind her. "What are you doing, Drew?" she asked as she drained the last of her wine and motioned to the waitress for another glass.

"I was going to ask you the same thing."

"I am here for singles' night." She turned to face him, feeling herself wobble slightly in her new shoes. She should have gone with the boots instead of the heels, but the pumps had the cutest bow on the toe…. "And you should be with your date."

A frown pulled his dark brows together. "I'm not on a date."

"I'm pretty sure I didn't imagine the brunette you were with earlier."

"That wasn't a date. She's a coworker on a custom house I'm building in the area."

"You always hold hands with your coworkers? I bet your subcontractors love that."

"We weren't holding hands. Cassidy was upset and I was trying to reassure her. The client we're working for is a real nightmare, and Cass is ready to quit. None of which explains what you're doing here."

"I told you. It's singles' night, and I'm single," she said, crossing her arms and meeting his scowl with a smirk.

He mimicked her actions, minus the smirk, folding his muscular arms over his broad chest, as he replied, "Well, so am I."

"You're not signed up for this event," she protested.

Glancing over at a nearby high-top table, he spotted the clipboard and a few leftover name tags. Within seconds, he'd scrawled his name across the sign-in sheet and slapped a tag to his broad chest. His name in bold, block letters with the word *contractor* written beneath. "It's not supposed to be a business card, Drew," she said as she reached out and poked him right in the name tag.

He caught her hand and held it for a moment as his gaze dropped to her chest. Or at least to the name badge on her sweater. "Obviously."

Debbie blinked, for a second having forgotten what she'd written on her own tag. "Oh, yeah. That."

Hungry for the taste of adventure....

It had sounded like something fun to write down at the time, so why did she suddenly feel embarrassed, like a teenager caught by her mother making out with a boy on the front porch? She didn't know. She couldn't even be sure how a moment like that would have felt. She'd never dated as a teenager. She'd never had the opportunity to do so many things.

And that was why she was willing to take a chance on this singles' group. Okay, so tonight had been a bit of a disappointment. There were other events planned. This night was only the beginning. She smiled her thanks and handed the waitress some cash in exchange for another glass of wine.

Lifting her chin, she met Drew's gaze head on. "You're not my big brother, Drew. I don't need you to rescue me."

A flash of guilt flickered across his expression, and Debbie realized she'd nailed it. He really did think of her like a little sister, someone to look out for, someone to protect. She took a swallow of wine to wash away the ache in her throat. So much for thinking he might have been jealous. So much for the foolish hope that he'd approached her because he wanted to be the guy she was talking to instead of the half a dozen or so men whose names she'd already forgotten.

Catching her by the wrist, he took the wineglass from her hand and set it aside. "I think you've had enough."

"You've got that right," she muttered. She'd certainly had enough of him!

Pushing past him, she headed for the exit. The cool, quiet night air brushed her heated cheeks, a welcome relief from the noisy, crowded restaurant. Her heels crunched unevenly across the asphalt, but she didn't get far before he caught up with her again.

"You shouldn't be driving."

"I didn't have that much to drink."

"You had four glasses of wine."

"You were counting?" Debbie snorted, only to realize maybe that was a good thing since she seemed to have stopped keeping track after two. No wonder the asphalt was rocking beneath her feet, and the stars were shooting like a pretty kaleidoscope overhead....

"Let me take you home."

Oh, why did Drew's murmured words have to sound so much better than any of the invitations she'd heard from potential dates that evening? Not that he meant anything by it. Just like he hadn't meant anything by the kiss they'd shared. "You can't fool me."

He was playing the role of the white knight—offering rides home and apologizing for kisses when he should have been kissing her again.

"What?"

"What, what?" She hadn't said anything. Oh, crap, what had she said?

Frowning, Drew asked, "How is asking to give you a ride home trying to fool you?"

Relieved she hadn't spilled anything too embarrassing, yet still annoyed, she snapped, "You didn't offer to drive me home. You asked to take me home. As in, 'Let's go back to your place.' You think I don't know a come-on when I hear one, Drew Pirelli?"

Just like she knew very well when she *hadn't* heard one, but she found herself entirely unwilling to let him off the hook so easily.

"That's not— I didn't—" A pained expression crossed his face, and he ran a frustrated hand through his hair. Blowing out a breath, he started again, "Debbie, I—"

Feeling another apology coming on, she threw up a dismissing hand and started walking. Not that she would risk driving home, but she had a coat in her car and if she had to wait who knew how long for a cab, she'd rather not have to stand around shivering.

But she only made it a few steps before the ground slipped out from beneath her feet. And not because she'd fallen. Her startled gasp ended in a mousy squeak as Drew swept her up into his arms. The stars spun wildly overhead, and without thought she clung to his shoulders. Their gazes collided for a heat-filled second before his mouth crashed down on hers in a stunning kiss.

If that night on the balcony had been wedding fever, this was a different level of heat altogether. The kiss tasted of frustration and passion, a fight-fire-with-fire kind of burn that promised so much more—

The earth may well have moved, but Debbie didn't realize Drew had until he plopped her into the passenger seat of his car. His breathing still ragged from the kiss, he repeated, "You're not driving home."

Despite the way the world was still tilting around her, every ounce of independent woman roared inside her. Realizing her hands were still fisted in his shirt, she pushed him away. "I can*not* believe you just did that!"

Drew's jaw tightened as he leaned closer, until she could

catch a hint of his aftershave mixed with the woodsy night air. "Believe it."

The vehicle's dome light wasn't very bright, but in its faint glow, she saw something in his hardened expression. Something that made her pulse pound even harder. Something that made her wonder if she was seeing Drew in a different light...or if something had changed in the way he was seeing her.

And she had the feeling that as surprised as she was by his actions, he'd surprised himself even more.

Chapter Four

I cannot believe you just did that!

Debbie's outraged words rang in his head on the silent drive back home. Drew couldn't believe it himself. His hands tightened on the steering wheel as he glanced over at Debbie. She was looking out the side window, giving him little more than a view of the back of her head, but he could imagine the fire in her blue eyes. She had every right to be pissed and to give him the cold shoulder, but her silence at least allowed him the time to get his emotions back under control.

Damn if he couldn't hear Angie laughing at him now.

His former girlfriend had accused him more than once of not *having* emotions. *If I walk out this door right now, you won't even try to stop me, will you?* she'd demanded during the fight that led to their breakup. Truth was, he had tried to stop her. He'd talked about how good they were together, how much they had in common. He brought up the time they'd both invested in the relationship and asked if she really wanted to throw that away.

But even as the words were coming out of his mouth—logical, sensible words—he'd known it wasn't enough. Whatever Angie wanted, he didn't have it within himself to give it to her. And that was the reason why he hadn't stopped her when she did finally walk out that door.

Never once had it occurred to him to physically pick Angie up and kiss her to try to convince her to stay. Watching Debbie walk away...that instinct had been undeniable.

And it didn't make sense! Debbie wasn't his girlfriend. She was his friend. And while he wouldn't have let her drive home even if he hadn't known her her entire life, he could have stopped her another way. Hell, all he'd had to do was take her purse and the keys inside. Simple, easy, logical. And yet that solution had never occurred to him.

Drew shifted in the driver's seat. He didn't know what was going on, but he didn't like it. He wanted things to go back to the way they used to be when he didn't know how it felt to have Debbie's soft sweater and softer curves pressed against him. When he didn't have the memory of her kiss replaying again and again through his mind. When he didn't have to fight his imagination to keep the kiss from becoming more than a kiss as his lips moved lower to taste the curves of her breasts....

He'd stopped, or if he were totally honest with himself, he'd been interrupted, that night on the balcony before he could take things further. And yet his fingertips tingled with the thought of tracing the soft, pale skin beneath the burgundy dress she'd worn. He could hear her trembling sighs as his touch became more intimate, more arousing.

Swearing beneath his breath, he pushed the fantasy aside and focused on the headlights cutting through the darkness beyond the windshield. As the winding mountain roads gave way to the gentler slopes leading into town, he glanced over at the woman beside him. "Debbie?"

No response.

"Look, I know you're angry, but you have to understand..." His voice trailed off, at a loss to explain something he couldn't figure out for himself.

The silence from the other side of the SUV continued, and he leaned forward for a closer look. Okay, so she wasn't pissed off and ignoring him. She was sound asleep.

Drew sighed and dropped his head back. Great. Just great.

He didn't want to leave her alone like this, but he couldn't stay if he took her back to her place. Debbie lived in the apartment above the bakery right on Main Street. Someone was bound to notice his truck parked outside her shop all night.

That made his place the better choice, though he doubted Debbie would think so.

Drew lived just outside of town. The Craftsman-style homes in his neighborhood would be hitting the century mark soon, but all were well cared for with nicely maintained yards. Columns and pillars bracketed wide porches marked with front swings and whiskey barrels and hanging pots filled with mums and pansies and petunias.

He'd rented the house for the past several years, liking the consistency of knowing the people who lived around him in the established neighborhood, but he'd always known it was temporary. His dream home had existed in his mind for years, and before long it would be a reality.

Debbie hadn't stirred by the time he'd parked in the driveway and circled around to open the passenger door. The dome light glowed from behind her, illuminating her blond hair and giving her an almost angelic halo. He smiled wryly when he thought of how she might take that comparison. Why she wanted to make a break with the person she was and try to be someone else, he didn't know. Not when she was already perfect.

God, she was pretty. Her dark eyelashes fanned against her cheeks and, even without her bold and sassy smile, he could see the faint hint of the dimple that flashed every time she laughed. The smell of her sweet and spicy perfume tempted him to lean closer, to find the exact spot of ivory skin she'd touched with the scent. Whatever lipstick she'd had on earlier that night had worn away, leaving her mouth a natural pink he hadn't been able to resist.

How was it that he'd known her all her life without really knowing her at all?

She stirred suddenly as if roused by his stare—or maybe even by his earthshaking thoughts—and blinked those bright blue eyes at him. "Wake up, Sleeping Beauty," he murmured.

"Drew— What—" Her gaze focused over his shoulder. "What are we doing here?" She sat up straight, and he could see the moment all that wine went to her head. Her eyes closed again, her face paled and her throat moved as she swallowed hard.

"Are you gonna be sick?"

"If I am, you might want to step back."

Drew laughed even as he leaned closer to unhook her seat belt. She needed someone to look after her, and that was a role he felt comfortable with—even if the idea of Debbie sleeping under his roof did send a pulse of heat through his veins. "Come on. I'm not leaving you alone like this, and I've got a Pirelli family secret recipe, thanks to Sam, guaranteed to take away the worst of a hangover."

He helped her inside, figuring he could judge how poorly she was feeling by her total lack of resistance. It struck him then that Debbie had never been to his place even though she was a common fixture at family gatherings at his parents' house. Now wasn't exactly the time for a tour, not that there was much to see. The living room, with its man-cave style furnishings of oversize recliners and couch, well-worn coffee tables and wall-mounted flatscreen TV, branched off into hallways on either side. One led to the master bedroom, the other to the secondary bedrooms and guest bath.

He guided Debbie through the arched doorway to his tiny dining room. She sank into the chair he pulled out for her and sat with her head in his hands. A short peninsula countertop separated the dining nook from the rest of the kitchen, so he could easily keep an eye on her as he proceeded to fix what really amounted to watered-down hot tea mixed with some lemon and honey. The drink was ready within minutes and he carried it over to her.

She looked miserable, a far different girl from the one who'd tied his guts into knots as she laughed and flirted through the night. A very small part of him was enjoying her discomfort as payback for what she'd put him through, but at least now it was over. Certainly after tonight, she'd have learned her lesson and this would be the end of her ridiculous search for some stranger to come along and sweep her off her feet.

"Careful. It's hot," he said as he set the mug in front of her.

Okay, that warning at least earned him a glare, but she did blow on the surface of the steaming liquid before taking a sip. "Hmm, this is good. Thanks."

"You're welcome," he said as he leaned back against the counter. "As soon as you finish that, I'll get you some more comfortable clothes to change into, and you can crash in the guest room."

"You really don't have to do all this, you know." She

lifted her chin to a stubborn angle even as she laced her fingers around the warm mug—like holding on with both hands would somehow keep her steady. "I've been taking care of myself for a long time."

And she'd taken care of her mother for many years before she'd been on her own. A pinprick of guilt stabbed him. Despite his earlier thoughts, Debbie deserved to go out and have a good time. Why did it bother him so much that she wanted to? She was perfectly capable of taking care of herself. That independent streak was something she had in common with Angie. But unlike with his last girlfriend, Drew was having a hard time fighting his own protective instincts.

"I know. Your mother would be proud of you."

Looking up from the mug of tea, her eyes widened—big and blue and beautiful. Drew felt a moment's panic when they started to fill with tears. Debbie never cried. Or at least, not that he'd ever seen—except that one time.

Nearly the whole town had turned out for her mother's funeral, and everyone who attended had taken the time to speak to Debbie and offer their condolences. Drew wasn't sure what had made him slip away from the crowd or why he'd gone to the bakery later that evening. But he'd taken one look at Debbie's face and the tears she was trying so hard to hide and pulled her into his arms.

They'd never talked about that day, but he had to wonder if she could see the memory reflected in his gaze. She blinked her eyes quickly as she pushed away from the table, her movements slow and careful. "Drew…"

She reached out toward him, and time seemed to stand still. He was caught in the moment, spellbound by the intimate silence of the late night. It was as though he was standing on the brink of two worlds. The one he knew where he and Debbie always had been and always would be friends and a new, uncertain world where anything—*anything*—could happen. His blood heated at the possibilities, and when she touched him, placing her hand against his chest, he felt as though she'd given him a violent shove. One that had him teetering on the edge of crossing that line between friendship and so much more....

She whispered his name again, the longing in the single word grabbing hold of a need inside of him and refusing to let go. He reached up, cupping her face in his hands, and his thumb brushed against a tear. Damp and salty between his rough, calloused skin and the softness of Debbie's. Her eyes still had a watery cast, and he was taken back once more to the day of the funeral. A day when he'd wrapped Debbie in his arms to comfort her.

There'd been nothing sexual about it—one friend offering comfort to another.

But that wouldn't be the case tonight. If he crossed that line, it may never be the case again....

Reining in the desire raging through him took every ounce of the self-control that had deserted him earlier. Kissing her without thinking his actions through had been a mistake he wouldn't repeat. He wouldn't let himself rush into this. Not when Debbie might regret the decision in the light of day. She talked a tough game, but her guard was down right now, revealing a vulnerability her bright smile and smart mouth normally disguised.

Touching his lips against her forehead when he wanted the taste, the texture, the temptation of her mouth beneath his more than he wanted his next breath, he pulled away. Her pale eyebrows pulled together, her confusion a contrast to the flush of arousal coloring her cheeks and painting her parted lips. "Drew, what—"

"Time for bed, princess. I'll go get those clothes." He hurried from the kitchen, half expecting to feel the ceramic mug crash against the back of his head. The patronizing nickname might have taken things too far, but he needed to find his footing and the familiar teasing brought him back to solid ground. And he wasn't moving from there until he'd given serious thought to the direction he was heading.

Debbie squinted against the early-morning sunlight and fought the urge to hide under the covers and sleep for a few more hours. Rolling to her side, her head spun in protest. Ugh, make that a few more days.

She tried to swallow, but her throat was so dry her tongue felt like sandpaper against the roof of her mouth. Oh, she was never going to drink again. Pushing aside the covers, she slipped out of Drew's bed. Okay, technically it was his guest bed, and you'd think if she was going to suffer the physical effects of too much alcohol that she'd at least have the mental relief of not recalling everything that happened the night before. But no, there it was—the memory rearing its ugly, embarrassing head...

Lifting a hand to touch his chest.... Seeing the look in his eyes and foolishly thinking he wanted to kiss her as badly as she wanted to him to.... The way she'd practically begged him to....

And then the touch of his lips against her forehead before he shooed her off to bed like she'd been an eight-year-old guest at one of Sophia's slumber parties.

Heat burned in her cheeks. How was she ever going to face him again?

It's never too late to leave town, she thought grimly.

But one thing was for sure, she decided as she caught a glimpse of herself in the mirror above the dresser. Her blond hair had turned corkscrew wild from all the tossing and turning the night before, and what was left of her makeup was smeared beneath her bloodshot eyes. And she was wearing his clothes—the dark blue, sinfully soft T-shirt and black drawstring shorts he'd left for her outside the bathroom where she'd taken refuge after humiliating herself in the kitchen.

She was not facing him like this.

Cracking the bedroom door, she listened for a moment. She didn't hear any sounds from the rest of the house. Biting her bottom lip, she stepped out into the hall. If she could make her escape while Drew was still sleeping, she could save at least the tiniest bit of her pride. Yes, that would mean doing the walk of shame through town to get back home since her car was still in The High Tide parking lot, but she couldn't think of anyone she'd rather see less at that moment than Drew. And, of course, it wasn't a real walk of shame since that expression was reserved for slipping away the morning after sleeping with someone and she hadn't slept with Drew...which made the whole thing...that...much...worse.

Mentally calling herself and Drew every name she could think of and longing to be in the bakery where she could bang cookie sheets and baking pans as loud as possible, she tiptoed into the bathroom where she'd left her clothes and purse the night before. She eased the door closed behind her, careful not to make even the slightest sound, then hurriedly glanced around for her things. The neatly folded pile sitting on the vanity caught her eye, and Debbie swallowed. In her best moments, she didn't fold her clothes once she'd already worn them. She certainly wouldn't have done so on a night where she was hungover and humiliated.

Reaching out, she touched the cashmere, her heart skipping a beat when she thought of Drew running his work-roughened hands over the soft fabric. But then she remembered he hadn't wanted to run his hands over *her* and she tossed the borrowed clothes aside and jerked the sweater on with far less care than the delicate material deserved.

It took some doing, but thanks to the tiny brush, compact and mini tube of lipstick she carried in her purse, she managed to look halfway decent. Now she just needed her shoes. She had a vague recollection of slipping them off as she sat at the kitchen table. Pressing her feet flat against the cool tile had been a relief after standing around in heels all night.

Another peek through the doorway confirmed Drew was nowhere in sight, and she literally tiptoed down the hall and into the kitchen. Yes! Spotting one of her beige heels beneath the table, she ducked underneath to pick it up. She was glancing around for its mate when she heard Drew's voice coming from outside.

For a split second, she froze. Good Lord, who was he talking to? She'd thought he was still sleeping, but that was definitely his voice coming from the porch. In the next moment, she heard the front door open and sprang into action. Scrambling backward, she tried standing too soon and cracked her head on the underside of the table. Her eyes stung at the sharp pain, but she ignored it as she glanced around wildly one more time for her missing shoe.

Drew spoke again, but she was in too much of a panic to pay attention to the words. There was no way she could slip by and hide out in one of the bedrooms, so she took the only escape route available.

Holding tight to her lone shoe, she ducked out the back door and onto the porch overlooking the backyard. Her pulse was pounding in her ears even as she tried to hear what was going on inside. She'd probably been fooling herself when she thought she would walk home in the early-morning mist, and she couldn't even pretend like she'd be able to make the trek barefoot. She heard Drew's voice again, and this time the words penetrated.

"Hey, Debbie?"

Her heart slammed against her chest. What was he thinking? Didn't he know what anyone would assume after finding her at his house first thing in the morning? She didn't have time to formulate any kind of excuse before the back door opened, and Drew was gazing at her in confusion from the doorway.

"What are you doing?" he asked.

"What am I doing? What are you doing?" she demanded, her voice a harsh whisper. "Why would you bring someone into the house? What if they figure out that I'm here?"

His expression cleared, a slight smile tilting his lips. "Oh, she already figured that out. She's got a really good sense of smell."

Smell? The absurdity of the conversation made Debbie question whether or not this was real. Maybe she was still asleep in her bed at home, and none of this had ever happened.

Drew stuck his head back inside the door and called out, "Come here, Rain!"

A second later, a black streak of fur darted out in a beeline for Debbie's bare toes. *This* was who Drew had been talking to? Relief and reaction to the puppy's sheer cuteness soon had a wry smile tugging at her lips. The exuberant licking tickled, and she tried not to do some ridiculous dance to escape the puppy's quick-moving tongue. She'd already made a big enough fool of herself in front of Drew this morning. Never mind her humiliating behavior the night before.

Focusing on the dog was much easier than focusing on the man standing in front of her, looking good enough to eat in faded jeans and a red sweatshirt. The early morning breeze had ruffled his dark hair and brought out a ruddiness in his cheeks. His dark eyes sparkled, and he looked awake and energized. Unlike Debbie who felt tired and rumpled and, yes, hungover.

"Dog-sitting?" she asked as she bent down to rub the puppy's silky ears. Rain gave up on Debbie's toes and jumped on her back legs, trying to reach her face with that warm, darting tongue.

"Nope," he said. "This one's all mine."

"Really?" Debbie asked as she glanced up.

She knew Darcy had taken in a stray a few months ago, unaware the dog was about to give birth. She'd called Nick, the local vet, and that had been the start of their relationship. The last Debbie had heard, Maddie, Nick's daughter, had been pushing to keep the mama dog and the four puppies, much to Nick and Darcy's dismay.

"Kara and Sam took one of the boys for Timmy," Drew said, referring to Sam's recently found four-year-old son who also happened to be Kara's nephew. "A friend of Maddie's took the other girl. I think Maddie's going to get her way, though, and they'll end up keeping the last boy. Unless you're interested?"

"Oh, no, not me!" Debbie straightened abruptly as if she expected him to try to foist the other puppy on her right that minute.

"Why not? You clearly like dogs."

"I do. What's not to like? They're cute and cuddly and loving, but they're also a lot of work."

"Yeah, but it's worth it," he said with a grin as Rain turned her attention toward him. The puppy was clearly smitten with her new owner, and not just because of her fascination with the laces on his tennis shoes. The affection was mutual as Drew picked up the squirming puppy and held her in his arms. His big palm just about covered her small back, and as he rubbed her silky fur, the puppy groaned in bliss.

Smart girl, Debbie thought, figuring she'd do the same if Drew buried his fingers in her hair.

Goose bumps rose on the back of her neck at the very thought. Debbie wished she could blame the reaction on the cool breeze and overcast fall morning, but she knew better. It was all Drew—the memory of his kiss and the unfulfilled promise of his caress the night before.

Crazy that the puppy snuggled in his arms didn't detract from that oh-so-masculine sexiness. Crazier still that it only added to it.

"So what exactly are you doing out here?"

"I heard you talking and thought you were bringing someone inside. The last thing I need is anyone thinking I spent the night with you."

His dark brows pulled together. "You did spend the night."

Heat touched her cheeks. "You know what I mean." Dropping her focus to her shoe, she said, "I couldn't find my other shoe."

His frown morphed into a sheepish expression as he said, "Yeah, um, about that…Rain's still teething, and she's been doing really well but—"

"No! Seriously?" Her shoulders slumping, Debbie clutched her sole surviving pump to her chest. "They were so cute."

And though she'd had them for months, they were brand-new. She'd been saving them for a special occasion, and wasn't it a sorry testament to her life that a few dozen or so weeks could go by without a special occasion in sight?

"Would it help to know it made a really awesome chew toy?"

"Oddly, no." She sighed.

"How about if Rain said she was sorry?" Drew held out the puppy as if prompting a five-year-old to remember her manners. Rain rolled her head toward Debbie, draping her neck over the crook of Drew's elbow. With one ear flopping over, her tongue hanging out the side of her mouth and her eyes bright and happy, she didn't look the least bit repentant. She did, however, look absolutely adorable, and any irritation Debbie might have felt disappeared. Toward the dog and toward the man holding her.

She'd been angry and hurt and humiliated when Drew had turned her away the night before, but in the clear light of day, she could see now that he'd made the right decision. Sexual chemistry aside—assuming, that was, that it wasn't just on *one* side—she and Drew were at different places in their lives. He was four years older than she was, and while that age difference was minimal, they'd taken very different paths to get where they were.

Though Drew had worked odd jobs as a teenager, he'd still had plenty of time for sports and extracurricular activities as well as parties and hanging out with his friends. He'd been one of the cool kids who'd gone to every high school dance, run for class office and had been nominated for homecoming king. He'd never been short on friends or girlfriends, and she assumed his years at college had been the same way.

He'd had his fun. He'd done all the things he wanted to do, including opening and running a successful business in his hometown. No matter what he said to the contrary, it only made sense that he would soon be looking toward the future—a wife, a family, a dog…

One down, Debbie thought as she reached out to stroke one of Rain's silky ears, *two to go.*

She was looking for fun and freedom, not extra responsibility, even if that only meant taking care of a dog. She'd accused the puppy of being a lot of work when, really, what she'd been thinking was how the little thing was such a huge commitment. A commitment Drew was clearly willing to make.

So staying friends was obviously the logical choice, even though her heart ached a little at the thought of Drew Pirelli never kissing her again. "No hard feelings, Rain. I know sometimes it can be really tough to do the right thing."

"Can I make you breakfast as part of that apology?" Drew offered. "Or do you need to get to the bakery?"

"I wasn't sure how late I'd be out last night, so I asked Kayla Walker to open up this morning."

"So…breakfast?"

"Do you even know how to cook?" Debbie asked as she followed him back into the kitchen. Vanessa Pirelli, Drew's mother, was known for her skill in the kitchen, but Debbie wasn't aware if the woman had passed those talents on to her son.

His expression was somewhat wry as he set Rain down on the kitchen floor where she scurried away, hopefully going off in search of a teething-approved dog toy. "I think I can manage frying an egg and working a toaster."

"Right. Okay, buster, move aside, and I'll show you how it's done."

"Really?"

"You think I only know how to bake?" Baking was her profession, but cooking— Cooking was her passion, one she so rarely indulged because she'd never enjoyed fixing an extravagant meal with no one to share it with.

Debbie wasn't sure what to make of Drew's expression as he stepped closer. He smelled like the outdoors—woodsy with a hint of ocean mist that rolled in every morning with the tide. Her pulse picked up its pace at the look in his dark eyes. A look that last night she'd thought meant he wanted to kiss her again. But that had been four glasses of wine talking, and this morning she had no excuse.

"I think," he murmured, "that you can do anything you want."

Her heart stumbled in her chest, and she turned toward the stove before Drew could read by the longing in her expression that what she really wanted to do was... well, *Drew*.

Chapter Five

Drew stared with a critical eye at the bare-bones structure in front of him. The early-morning chill formed a cloud as he exhaled a satisfied breath, and he took a drink from the steaming cup of coffee warming his hands. The framed house barely hinted at the layout and the details to come, but he could already see the finished product in his mind's eye. After all, he'd been designing and redesigning the plans for years.

He could picture the large foyer opening into the great room. A stone fireplace and rough-hewn mantel would be the room's centerpiece. And okay, yeah, a flat-screen TV, too. The oversize arcadia doors would offer a view to the mountains and pines beyond the property and lead the way to a redwood deck. Maybe he'd add an outdoor kitchen and built-in grill. A hot tub, too, while he was at it.

With the open floor plan, the flow led into the kitchen. A huge island took center stage with white cabinets and stainless-steel appliances all around. Smooth-as-glass black granite countertops would be a cool contrast to the warmth and character of the multicolored flagstone slate on the floors.

The rest of the house was dedicated to bedrooms—four of them. Three smaller rooms and a master suite. The master bedroom faced the same direction as the great room, and a wall of windows would take full advantage of the view. A view he looked forward to waking up to for the rest of his life.

Of all the homes he'd built over the years, Drew had to admit, this one was special. This one was his. Even though he put his heart, his soul, his sweat and sometimes even blood into every house he built, there was something about ownership, about possession, that gave him an extra sense of pride when he looked at the newly framed house. This time, when the house was complete, he wouldn't be handing the keys over to some other family. The house would be his, and the family...

Yeah, he wanted that, too.

The crunch of tires coming down the gravel lane caught his attention, and he whistled for Rain. The puppy was smart but still had a lot to learn, and Drew wasn't taking any chances. She bounded over to his side, tail wagging, a large stick clamped between her jaws. She sat and dropped her new toy at his feet, her expression bright and eager to please.

"Hey, cool stick, girl." Picking it up, he tossed it in the opposite direction of the approaching vehicle.

Drew didn't recognize the rugged SUV, but he grinned when he caught sight of the man behind the wheel. He walked over to the vehicle, Rain trotting faithfully at his side, the stick forgotten in light of a new person to love.

"Ryder, I'd heard you were moving back to town," he

said as he greeted the brown-haired man climbing from the driver's seat.

"You heard, huh?" Ryder Kincaid winced slightly as he shook Drew's hand. "Gonna take a while to get used to the whole small-town mentality again."

While Ryder was two years younger than Drew, both he and Nick had been friends with his older brother who still lived in town. Ryder had left Clearville after his senior year to attend college on a sports scholarship. Drew had heard the other man had taken a job at a prestigious construction company in San Francisco—working for his in-laws. He'd also heard that Brittany, Ryder's wife, was not moving back with him. Judging by the circles beneath the other man's eyes and the rough-around-the-edges stubble and overgrown hair, the separation had hit Ryder hard.

"So." Drew cleared his throat. "How have you been?"

Giving a short laugh beneath his breath, Ryder said, "Something tells me you've heard all about that, too."

"Sorry, man."

"You know what they say, it's for the best and time to move on."

From what Drew recalled, Ryder Kincaid and Brittany Baines had been high school sweethearts, prom king and queen their senior year, and both families had long expected them to marry. They'd been Clearville's golden couple, and Drew was aware of a subtle divide when it came to Ryder's return.

Half the town had welcomed the hometown kid back, taking his side on whatever had caused the split with Brittany. The other half, people who were still in touch with Brittany and her family, thought Ryder was clearly the one to blame.

It was part of small-town life—feeling that connection to the people around you. Oh, sure, sometimes little more than nosiness and boredom were at work, but most times the townspeople had a genuine investment in the lives of their friends and neighbors. They truly cared.

Suddenly, an image of Debbie came to mind—a common occurrence since bringing her home the other night. Her feminine scent, a combination of sugar and spice, of sweet and sexy, still lingered in his truck. And when he'd gone to change the sheets in the guest bedroom, he'd caught himself holding on to the pillow far longer than necessary, as if somehow holding on to the idea of her sleeping under his roof, in his bed—even if it was just the guest bed.

But she was his kid sister's best friend. Hell, she was *his* friend! He'd done the right thing in walking away. Even if she hadn't had too much to drink, even if he hadn't seen the vulnerability softening her blue gaze, pursuing Debbie would be like running through a minefield. Talk about causing a rift if things didn't work out! He could see it now—his sister and sisters-in-law on one side with his brothers on the other.

Or not.

Was he really so sure Nick and Sam would have his back if it meant being at odds with the women they loved? Drew wasn't sure he wanted to know the answer, but just the possibility of causing any kind of dissent in his close family should have been enough to shut down any thoughts he had of crossing the line from friendship with Debbie into…something more. Playing it safe made perfect sense, so why did he feel like he was going to regret not taking that chance for a long time to come?

Ryder gave Rain a final pat and stood. "Moving on to something new is actually why I'm here. I wanted to know if you're looking to hire on any help."

Drew had had the feeling Ryder's visit wasn't purely a

social call. "Things might have changed around here in the years since you've been gone, but not that much. There isn't exactly a need for commercial construction around here."

"Yeah, I noticed the lack of high-rises, but I'd just as soon get out of that work anyway. I'm more interested in home building." He jerked his chin toward the unfinished house. "This looks like quite the place."

"Yeah, it's a custom I'm working on." Other than family, Drew had told few people that the house he was building was his own. He didn't know why, but he wanted the house finished, or nearly so, before showing her off to the rest of the town. And he wanted to finish it on his own. "Ryder—"

Seeming to hear the apology Drew was about to deliver, the other man interrupted. "Or I can take on remodeling jobs that come your way. I've had a ton of experience. I put myself through college working as a handyman."

"But that's something you could do on your own. Start your own business, be your own boss," Drew suggested.

"Yeah, I'd like that. Someday. But until the divorce goes through..." Ryder shrugged, but the tension he carried in his shoulders made the effort look as easy as lifting the weight of the world. Starting up a new business while in the middle of splitting assets probably wasn't the best idea. "For now, I'm just looking for a job."

In the early years of his business, Drew had started with remodeling projects. Soon his focus had changed toward building custom homes, and as that side of the business began to take off the smaller jobs had fallen to the wayside. But with the number of old houses and businesses around town, homeowners were always needing repairs and upgrades on the turn-of-the-century Craftsman-style and even older Queen Anne and Victorian homes.

"If we put the word out," Drew said, "I bet it won't be

long before we have some clients looking for remodeling estimates."

"I can begin right away," Ryder said, a little light sparking in his tired eyes. "I'm looking for a fresh start, and this could be just the thing. I can send you references from San Francisco and my resume."

"Email them to me when you get a chance," Drew said.

The two men talked a little more about the jobs Drew was currently working on and his plans for the future before Ryder left. If things worked out, the other man would have plenty of projects to keep him busy and he might also take some of the work off Drew's shoulders.

A sense of anticipation filled him. Maybe he could move up his time frame for completing the house. He'd felt stuck in such a holding pattern lately. Maybe finishing it would give him the push to start moving forward, even if he wasn't entirely sure what he was moving toward.

You're as grounded as a man can be and still manage to move both feet.

Was Debbie right? Was the restlessness he felt not a symptom of the slow process of building his dream home to his standard of perfection but of being stuck in a rut in his personal life?

She'd told him with dead certainty that he wasn't the man for her. That he was too settled, too staid, too boring. Okay, maybe she hadn't spelled it out that baldly, but it was how she thought of him. One of the guys she'd known her whole life who could never challenge or surprise her.

The desire to prove himself to Debbie—hell, maybe even to himself—made no sense, especially not on the heels of his conversation with Ryder and his awareness of the ripple effect of a broken relationship in their close-knit town.

"Come on, Rain. Time to get to work." The puppy

barked in response to her name and bounded over to his side, her tail wagging for all she was worth.

One good thing about being the boss—it meant making the rules, and as of a few weeks ago, Pirelli Construction was a dog-friendly workplace. Taking Rain along with him to the office and to job-site inspections kept the smart and curious puppy from being stuck at home by herself—bored and getting into trouble.

Which reminded him... Looking Rain in the eye, he said, "We owe a certain lady a new pair of shoes."

"What do you think?" Debbie asked Kayla as she stepped back to admire her handiwork.

"Frightfully delicious."

Debbie matched her assistant's grin. "Just what I was hoping you'd say."

The two of them were taking advantage of a midafternoon lull to decorate the bakery for Halloween. It was one of her favorite holidays, right up there with Christmas and Valentine's Day and—

Oh, who was she kidding? She loved any holiday associated with food, as the decorations throughout the bakery—black cats and witches and the occasional skeleton—would attest. But in keeping with the bakery, the silhouette of the arching cat taped to the front window was perched atop a black-and-white cupcake. And instead of stirring a caldron, the green-faced cartoon witch was whisking her potion in a mixing bowl.

The "spooky" decorations were a sharp contrast to the bakery's typically cheery atmosphere. Pink-and-white-striped valances hung over the front window and matching cushions decorated the tiny white bistro set, the only seating available within the small space. White bead board wainscoting lined the lower half of the walls, and the front of the checkout counter was topped by white marble. Frothy pink-frosted vanilla cupcakes floated across the white walls—murals Debbie had painted while her mother was recovering from her first round of chemotherapy.

Looking at them now, Debbie suffered a twinge of embarrassment. She felt like an adult who still had her kindergarten artwork displayed on the refrigerator. But her mother had loved the whimsical cupcakes so much, she couldn't bring herself to paint over them. It would have been too much like wiping the memory of her mother's happiness away.

"Why don't you drape some of the black streamers across the front counter and display case, and I'll hang the rest of these from the ceiling," Debbie said as she gathered up the orange, yellow and white candy-corn cutouts.

"What about these?" Kayla wrinkled her nose as she waved a hand at the black plastic spiders.

Debbie laughed at the look on the younger woman's face. "Sam's son, Timmy, inspired me there. He's got a thing for bugs. I'm going to add them to just a few of the cupcakes in the display case. They'll be great decorations to go along with the sugar cookies shaped like witches and black cats. And the severed ladyfingers—those have always been such a hit."

The rolled, oblong cookies fit their name, and for the spooky holiday, Debbie added a touch of pink to one end for a painted fingernail and then dipped the other side in red food coloring. "The adults usually refrain, but the bloodthirsty boys love them."

Faking a shudder, Kayla grabbed the roll of black crepe paper. "I am so glad I have a girl."

"Are you taking Annabel to the Fall Fest this year?"

Kayla flashed Debbie a smile over her shoulder as she knelt down to tape the twisted lengths of crepe paper to the front of the counter. With her slight build, light brown hair and pale blue eyes, Kayla Walker had a quiet, unassuming personality that hid the determined, hardworking woman inside. When Kayla had come in looking for a job, Debbie had hired her thinking she would be doing Kayla a favor. But after only a few months, Debbie knew she'd gotten the better end of the bargain—an honest, loyal employee determined to learn as much as she could.

"Are you kidding?" The younger woman laughed. "Devon wouldn't miss it. I keep telling him Annabel's too young for trick-or-treating, but he insists she'll have a great time. Which makes me think he's going to eat all the candy."

Maneuvering the ladder into place, Debbie climbed the rungs to hang the dangling candy-corn decorations. "Have you found a costume for her yet?"

"We did! It's the cutest sunflower outfit. Of course, it's really just a green jumpsuit with a hood designed to look like a sunflower, but it's so adorable! I had to take half a dozen pictures of her just when we were trying it on in the store."

"I can't wait to see. The kids and their costumes are my favorite part, and I love the way the town goes all out for the festival. There is something for everyone. Games, pumpkin carving, music, more food booths than you'd think could fit in such a small space. It's a chance for all the families to get together and have a good time."

Families... Even as she said the word, Debbie felt the slight ache in her chest. Oh, sure, she had great friends. Important, meaningful friendships, but family was something missing from her life.

We always wanted more children, her mother had told her once. Or maybe Bonnie had been talking to Debbie's father as she gazed with a lingering sadness at the picture of her late husband.

Debbie still had that photo on her coffee table, the last one taken of her dad, an image of a brown-haired man in a Nirvana T-shirt and faded jeans leaning against the hood of his truck and laughing into the camera. Looking so young…as if he had his whole life in front of him.

Debbie didn't know what affect her father's presence might have had, but she'd grown up under the weight of his absence. The feeling that life was short and could pass by all too quickly. So even though she might have felt a twinge or two when she thought of Kayla's adorable daughter, she pushed that longing aside.

Selfish as it may sound, she was going to focus on herself. She was going to have fun and enjoy a life free of commitment and responsibility while she still could. No one was going to tie her down until she was 100 percent ready. If taking over the bakery had taught her anything, it was that important lesson.

Bonnie's hope had been that her daughter would love running the bakery as much as she had, but as hard as she tried, Debbie didn't. And all the guilt in the world wasn't enough to smother the resentment that crept over her every now and then. The thought of settling down too soon and feeling that same resentment toward her husband or child… That fear alone would help her stand firm against any baby cravings.

Drew's dark eyes and sexy grin flashed through Debbie's mind, and a slight shiver raced through her body. A different kind of longing than the warm fuzzies she got when picturing little Annabel in her Halloween costume, for sure, but one she was just as determined to ignore.

Cooking breakfast for Drew the other morning had tugged hard at old dreams. She'd made him a massive omelet filled with diced ham, onions and peppers, enjoying every moment in his kitchen and well aware of his eyes following her every movement. She'd felt sexier there than she had ever felt with a man in the bedroom, and his over-the-top praise as he dug into the meal left her glowing with a far greater satisfaction, too.

Despite her acknowledgment that they were wrong for each other, her awareness of him on the ride back to The High Tide for her car had heightened her senses to an almost fevered pitch. She couldn't draw a breath without inhaling his scent. Couldn't stop herself from babbling inanely simply to hear the sound of his deep voice in response. Couldn't help resenting the seat belt that kept her on the opposite side of his SUV instead of pressed against him like she wanted to be.

But when she walked into work later that morning, she'd ruthlessly shoved her dreams of cooking for hungry guests—and other just-as-dangerous fantasies of making breakfast for Drew on a regular basis—aside.

Looking for something more than running the bakery— or for something more than friendship with Drew—would only led to heartbreak.

Pushing the thoughts aside, Debbie concentrated on the decorations. She and Kayla had just finished with the last of them when the timer from the kitchen buzzed. "Oh, those will be the cupcakes! I can't wait to try them. I bet they'll be amazing."

The younger woman led the way through the swinging door to the kitchen while Debbie followed at a slower pace. She had learned years ago how to tell when she'd found the perfect recipe. Long before she placed a cupcake or Danish or pie on display, she knew if the creation was just right or not. And it wasn't just a matter of taste that determined whether a new recipe was up to her standards.

It had to do with how the ingredients came together in the bowl—the texture, the color, the consistency. Even the scent of eggs, flour, vanilla and whatever other flavorings she might add. It was those "other flavors" that challenged her the most. She'd never been content, as her mother had once been, to simply offer the tried-and-true recipes she knew would sell.

Oh, sure, she always had those on hand, recipes she'd learned from her mother so long ago. Her chocolate-lovers' double-chocolate cake. Her traditional apple pie. Her always delicious vanilla cupcakes. And even though her mother had never been big on experimenting, it was while writing new recipes that Debbie best recalled standing at her mother's side enjoying the newness and wonder of learning to bake.

This afternoon, the experiment had been with more savory flavors as she tried to incorporate some of the fall-harvest vegetables into her cupcakes. The flavors of butternut squash and pumpkin combined with cinnamon and nutmeg, and she knew before she pulled the first tray from the oven just how they would taste.

"They're, um, different," Kayla said after she bit into one of the cakes before it had completely cooled. "But, you know...good," she clarified quickly.

"No, Kayla." Debbie sighed. "They're not."

"Sorry," Kayla ducked her head sheepishly. "It's not bad, but something's a little off. Or maybe I just like the traditional stuff—you know, vanilla and chocolate."

"Don't knock traditional stuff. It's what keeps us in business." And maybe she was only fooling herself in experimenting with bolder, more unusual recipes. Return customers came to Bonnie's Bakery with cravings for the familiar flavors they'd been savoring since her mother was alive. They weren't longing for different or exciting or unique—*she* was.

"Did you want me to stay and help with the prep work for tomorrow?" Kayla asked as Debbie slid the cupcakes onto one of the shelves on the stainless-steel cooling rack. She'd think on the recipe for a day or two and maybe come up with an answer for what was missing. A hint of cloves, maybe? More nutmeg and less cinnamon? Something sweet to balance the savory?

Pushing the thoughts aside for now, Debbie shook her head. "You've been covering for me in the mornings. I'll do the prep." Much of the dough—for cookies, pies and pastries—could be made the day before, cutting down on the predawn hours needed to keep the "baked fresh daily" promise. "Go spend time with that cute baby of yours."

Once Kayla left for the day, Debbie moved through the kitchen, performing tasks she could handle with her eyes closed. Creaming the softened butter and sugar, cracking the eggs, measuring out and adding the dry ingredients, transferring the dough to the butcher block counter and cutting into smaller sizes for easier handling.

The constant movement of her hands allowed her mind to wander to her plans for the bakery. If her extra promotion led to more orders for wedding and specialty cakes, would that help take away some of the monotony of her daily routine? Or would she only end up feeling overwhelmed by the more time-consuming, highly detailed work?

The piña colada cake for Nick and Darcy's wedding had been a specific request by the bride and groom. The tropical flavors were not traditional or for everyone, but Debbie thought the combination of coconut cream, pineapple and a hint of rum in the filling had been spot-on.

She'd spent hours on the painstaking work of piping

the basket-weave pattern, decorative flowers, bows and ribbons, wanting to give her friends the perfect cake, and she had received numerous compliments at the reception. Of course, most of the guests were friends and neighbors, people like Kayla who would be too polite or afraid of hurting her feelings to say anything negative. Other clients wouldn't be so kind.

She tried to stay focused on wedding cakes, but just the mere thought of weddings brought images of Drew to mind. His dark eyes sparkling as he met her gaze during her walk down the aisle. His tall, muscular body looking that much more masculine in the elegant tuxedo. The flash of his smile beneath the twinkling chandelier as he pulled her into his arms during their dance. His kiss on the balcony—

Debbie slammed the door on the memory. Hadn't she decided they were better off friends? That they were at different places in their lives and wanted different things? Wasn't that why she'd printed out the flyer advertising the next singles' event—karaoke night at The High Tide? She'd never dared to sing in public before, but she was ready to step out from her comfort zone. She wanted that hint of daring, of risk, of excitement in her life. She wanted—

A quick knock sounded at the back door, and her heart skipped a beat as Drew stepped inside. He'd clearly come from a job site—he looked rugged and outdoorsy in his work boots, faded jeans and a red-and-black-checkered flannel shirt over a gray T-shirt.

"Drew! What are you doing here?"

"I saw the kitchen lights were on from the front of the store and figured you were back here."

Sure enough, the late-afternoon sunlight had faded into darkness as she'd worked. But that really didn't explain why Drew had stopped by when the shop was already closed.

Not that she was afraid to be alone with him, but *knowing* that they were alone fired her awareness until she could feel each beat of her heart. He stepped closer and her breath caught on an inhale that drew in his scent—a mix of pine, fresh-cut wood, a hint of cool ocean air and warm, enticing man.

Reaching up, he brushed his thumb across her cheek. A slight stroke she felt down to her toes and every inch in between. "Drew…"

"You have some flour right here."

"I— Oh!" Flour, right. Of course. Why else would Drew be touching her? Ducking her head, Debbie scrubbed at her face, her skin suddenly hot with embarrassment and so much more. She'd hung a mirror behind the swinging door that lead to the bakery so she wouldn't end up greeting clients with flour on her face or chocolate around her mouth. But the mirror did little good when people surprised her by showing up at the back door.

Distracted, she didn't notice Drew reaching for the pumpkin cupcakes until it was too late. She started to protest, but he'd broken off a piece and popped it into his mouth before she could say a word. Served him right, she thought, hiding a smug smile, for sneaking treats from her kitchen.

He swallowed the bite, but not without pulling a face. "Sweetheart, you know I think you bake like a goddess, and your double-chocolate cake can bring a mortal man to his knees. But that—it needs some work."

"The recipe isn't ready yet," she admitted as she brushed by him. She pulled out the tray and focused on transferring the desserts into an airtight container so he wouldn't see how his words had affected her. She'd half expected him to try to spare her feelings by telling a white lie. She should have known better. His response had been simple and straightforward and honest. Funny, wasn't it, that his criticism made it easier for her to take his compliment to heart?

Drew thought she baked like a goddess.

And wouldn't she just love to believe she could bring him to his knees—only with something other than her skills in the kitchen? "I would have told you that had you actually asked to try them."

"Next time I'll remember. I'll even say please," he promised with a teasing grin just sexy enough to make a woman agree to anything—whether he said please or not.

A crumb clung to the corner of his mouth, and Debbie reached out before she could stop herself, brushing it aside with her thumb. He caught her hand with his, and for a moment, time hung suspended. Tension held her motionless even as she sucked in a quick breath. She caught a hint of coffee and chocolate—her cupcakes clearly weren't the only sweets he'd been sampling—and had the inane thought that she knew just how to fix the recipe.

A Drew-flavored cupcake... The product would fly off the shelves—if she didn't devour them all herself. Pulling her hand away, she took a step back and cleared her throat. "You do that, but for now, why don't you tell me why you're here. Assuming you didn't just stop by to steal cupcakes."

"I, um... No. I stopped by to bring you a present. Or maybe it's more of an IOU."

"Why would you owe me a present?" she asked as he ducked out the back door and came back in carrying a rectangular box.

"You'll see when you open it. Go on," he added as she hesitantly reached for the package.

The wrapping didn't give any clue as to what was inside,

but when she saw the box with the logo of her favorite shoe store hidden beneath the brown paper, she couldn't hide her smile. He hadn't! Debbie lifted the lid and brushed aside the crinkling white tissue paper. Oh, but he had! Reaching inside, she pulled out a pair of heels. They weren't the same as the ones Rain had turned into a chew toy the other night—with crisscrossing straps over the toe instead of the small bow—but it didn't matter.

The beige leather was butter soft to the touch, and it was all she could do not to kick off her practical white tie-ups. She already knew they would fit. Drew, being Drew, had of course bought the right size, and she couldn't wait to try them on.

"You didn't have to do this."

"They're not a perfect match for the other pair, but I hope they're a perfect fit."

"I love them. Thank you," she said, holding the shoes to her chest.

Of all the men in the world who she never thought could surprise her, Drew kept knocking her for a loop every time she turned around. Her resistance was melting, but Debbie couldn't let herself weaken. Drew Pirelli might be Clearville's perfect catch, but he was not the man for her.

"And Rain promises not to eat this pair."

"I'm sure she won't." Because, of course, the puppy wouldn't get the chance. After all, it wasn't like Debbie would be spending the night at Drew's again. And even if she did… She couldn't stop herself from remembering how she'd practically begged him to kiss her and how he'd teasingly turned her away.

Time for bed, princess.

She couldn't pretend the rejection hadn't hurt. He'd treated her like a kid when she longed to be treated like a woman. After playing the role of honorary big brother for so long, he couldn't see her any other way—their few exceptional kisses merely proving the rule.

"Thank you, again, for the shoes."

Drew frowned as Debbie nestled them back into the box. At first, she'd really seemed to like the gift, but now he wasn't so sure. He could have simply offered to pay for the shoes—that would have been the logical decision, but he'd wanted to do something more. Something that would make Debbie smile.

When he'd first walked in and seen her with her hair pulled back into a ponytail, a dusting of flour on her cheek, ten years had disappeared in a blink. Just seeing her looking like the adorable teenage girl he remembered had eased some of the pressure from his chest, the uncomfortable weight having settled there since the night of Darcy's bachelorette party. This was the Debbie he knew, the Debbie he was comfortable with, and he'd thought maybe she was right. Maybe the attraction he'd felt, the desire, had been nothing more than a lingering case of wedding fever and things between them could go back to normal now.

He'd even felt a little relieved at the thought, at the rational explanation that would keep his life moving forward on an even keel. And then she'd touched him....

Desire had slammed into his gut, knocking the breath from his lungs. All from her stroking her thumb across his mouth, and he knew he was only fooling himself if he thought life would ever be the same. He wanted her more than any woman ever before. Still coming to grips with the unexpected yet undeniable reaction, he'd tried to play it cool. Was still trying to play things cool when he glanced over her shoulder and saw a familiar-looking flyer stuck to the whiteboard beside the wall phone.

"What is this?" he demanded as he pulled the piece of paper out from beneath a teaspoon-shaped magnet.

Debbie gave a casual shrug as she placed the lid back on the shoebox. "It's an invitation to karaoke night with the singles' group. I thought it sounded fun."

"You've got to be kidding me! You still haven't changed you mind about—" Biting his tongue, Drew cut off the rest of his words. Debbie didn't know he'd overheard her wish the night of the bachelorette party and blurting it out now would not be the way to tell her. "After what happened last weekend, you're going out with that crowd again?"

"*Nothing* happened last weekend," she retorted, and was it his imagination or did she stress that first word a little too much?

Feeling the need to defend himself for turning away from the almost kiss, he said, "You had too much to drink. You weren't in any kind of shape to—"

"You don't have to worry about that," she interrupted. "I did get carried away, but I've learned my lesson. I won't drink, and I'll be perfectly sober when I decide who takes me home."

The flyer crinkled as his fingers tightened into a fist. No one was taking her home but him! "Debbie—"

Huffing out a sigh, she grabbed the now-wrinkled paper from his hand. Color brightened her cheeks and annoyance deepened her eyes to sapphire. "Give me a break, Drew! I'm just kidding. I want to go out and have some fun. I want to listen to horrible renditions of 'My Heart Will Go On.' I'm tired of my whole life revolving around work. I'm not like you. I'm not—"

"Not what?"

She sighed again. "It doesn't matter. This isn't about you. It's about me, and how I feel like my life is passing me by!"

"You're twenty-six years old! Your whole life is still in front of you."

"Is it? I turned twenty-six last month, and you know what? My dad never made it past twenty-five. I bet he thought he had his whole life in front of him, too, but then it was gone. Like that." She snapped her fingers in his face, but despite the defiant angle of her lifted chin, he could see the sorrow and lingering sadness in her gaze.

"Debbie, it's not the same thing."

"I know he had a dangerous job in a dangerous place, and I live and work in safe little Clearville, but that doesn't change knowing that life is short. And for the first time, I have the chance to go out and live it. Karaoke might sound stupid to you, but it's something I want to do. For me. Just because I can."

Listening to Debbie, that feeling was back—the urge to step out from his own comfort zone. To say the hell with playing it safe, to looking before he leaped, to weighing risk against reward. Maybe this was his opportunity, too, to go out and live life to the fullest. With Debbie by his side…because he couldn't imagine another woman who would inspire him to take such a chance.

His mind made up, he stepped closer, crowding her against the stainless-steel countertop until she had to tilt her head back to meet his gaze. "You aren't the only one who wants to have a good time, sweetheart, and you aren't the only one who signed up for the singles' group last weekend."

Her jaw dropped so comically he couldn't help reaching beneath her chin to guide it shut. He should have been better prepared, but her smooth skin against his work-roughened fingers packed as much punch the second time, and when she shivered in response… The faint tremor nearly knocked him to his knees, and he jerked his hand away before he embarrassed himself.

"What—what are you talking about?"

Playing it cool when he was feeling anything but, he answered, "Turns out I'm feeling hungry for the taste of adventure, too. I can't promise I'll sing any Celine Dion songs." Reaching out, he flicked the edge of the invitation she still held. "But I will see you there."

He backed out of the kitchen with a smile, enjoying the stunned look on Debbie's face. He figured he should escape while he still could before she came to her senses and smacked him upside the head. Or maybe before *he* came to his own and did it himself.

Karaoke? He *hated* karaoke. But he couldn't remember a night he was looking forward to more.

Maybe it didn't make any sense, but he still couldn't wipe the smile from his face. Debbie wanted a man who could take her by surprise? Well, he was pretty sure he'd succeeded. He had her off balance, but he was willing to bet he'd captured her curiosity, too. The longer he could stoke that flicker of interest and anticipation, the better.

His conscience dug at him a little, a reminder of the unfair advantage he had—having overheard Debbie's at the bachelorette party—but he pushed the concern aside. He would tell her the truth…just not yet.

Chapter Six

"So do you think he'll be here tonight?"

The words had been echoing on such a constant loop since Drew had left the bakery the night before that it took a moment for Debbie to realize they weren't just in her head. Glancing over to her right, she met the curious gaze of a brunette who looked to be in her early thirties. Recognizing her, Debbie said, "It's Marcy, right? You were here for the meet and greet."

The other woman nodded. "I figured I'd give it another shot even though last weekend was a bit of a bust. Well, for everyone but you. So is he coming tonight?"

"I don't—"

"Oh, come on! Don't pretend you can't remember the tall, dark and gorgeous guy who couldn't take his eyes of you?"

Tall, dark and handsome… The night of Darcy's bachelorette party, that was exactly the way she'd described her fantasy guy—the one who was supposed to take her by surprise and fill her life with romance and excitement. Funny, wasn't it, that those same words so perfectly described Drew?

"He, um, said he would be," she responded.

"Thought so by the way you're looking over at the door every thirty seconds."

She wasn't, was she? Debbie mentally groaned. Okay, so physically Drew met the criteria of her perfect man, but as for the rest— "I really don't think he's my type," she told Marcy.

The other woman gave a snort of laughter. "In that case, I'd be afraid to see who *is* your type."

Debbie fought back a sigh. The whole point of joining the singles' group was so she could meet someone new and exciting...but wasn't there something different about Drew lately?

The Drew she knew—the Drew she *thought* she knew— wouldn't have kissed her on the balcony the night of Nick and Darcy's wedding. He would never have gotten so carried away by the moment that he forgot where they were or that half the town was gathered on the other side of the French doors. Never would have picked her up off her feet, kissed her and carried her off to his SUV.

And the Drew she knew wouldn't be walking into The High Tide on karaoke night, looking gorgeous enough in a pair of dark jeans and slate-gray sweater to stop her heart and steal her breath...

No, this just wasn't the Drew she knew at all.

His dark eyes scanned the corner of the restaurant reserved for the singles' group, and she could tell the moment he spotted her. He stopped looking, stopped everything, freezing as their gazes met and held, and she could almost believe he was struck by the same jolt of attraction that she felt for him. He smiled then, the tilt of his lips a little wry as if he too was surprised he'd shown up.

"Oh, no," Marcy murmured at Debbie's side, "you two aren't into each other at all."

Debbie didn't try to explain to the other woman something she didn't understand herself. But as she watched Drew stride toward her, she couldn't help wondering if she was so wrong about him...could that mean he was so right for her?

"Well, someone's gotta get this party started," Marcy said with a nod toward the DJ manning the karaoke machine. "You're singing, too, aren't you?"

For a split second, Debbie broke her focus from Drew and glanced over at the blue television screen waiting for the first brave soul to step up to the microphone. "I haven't decided on a song yet." A huge three-ring binder sat on the table, offering just about every well-known and not-so-well-known single ever recorded.

"Ah, don't overthink things. Just go for it," the other woman advised with a wink as she pushed away from the table just as Drew approached, and Debbie had to wonder if the brunette was still talking about finding the right song.

"Don't tell me I already missed your solo." Sinking into the chair beside her, he leaned back, his long legs stretched out in front of him. He looked totally relaxed and comfortable, as if the two of them were buddies hanging out at the bar, while she felt ready to jump out of her skin.

Was she only imagining that Drew felt something more? Setting herself up to fall for a guy only to have him tell her they were better off friends? It wouldn't be the first time.

She swallowed hard, but the ache in her throat and the pressure in her chest didn't go away. Bad enough Robert had dumped her following their one night together. How much worse would it be if Drew did the same thing?

Maybe she should quit while she was ahead. So she and Drew had shared a few kisses. It didn't have to mean anything. She could keep those good memories and not have to worry about them tarnishing later.

Drew moved closer as the music kicked up and Marcy started to sing—a decent rendition of Adele belting out that they could have had it all. His dark eyes snared hers as he said, "Don't tell me you've changed your mind."

Had she? Caught by her own indecision, Debbie wished she had some kind of sign from Drew that she wasn't alone in this longing.

"I'd hate to think I missed you promising that your heart will go on." He raised an eyebrow in challenge. "Or were you waiting for me?"

Debbie managed a laugh. "Waiting for you? I didn't think you'd even show."

"Yeah," he murmured, leaning in until she could feel the warm caress of his breath against her ear. "You did."

"What makes you so sure?" She made the mistake of turning to face him as she issued her challenge, and her breath caught as she realized his face was mere inches away, his mouth within easy kissing distance.

"You're wearing my shoes."

Her face heated, and she couldn't pretend she hadn't been thinking of him as she'd dressed for the evening. Couldn't pretend she hadn't been thinking of him almost nonstop since Nick and Darcy's wedding. Striving for some semblance of cool—without giving away her sanity-saving need to retreat—Debbie leaned back in her chair. "Seeing as you gave them to me to replace the ones I bought, I think that makes them mine now."

"Whatever you say, sweetheart. I'm still willing to bet you were counting on me showing tonight."

"Yeah, well, I'm starting to think I'm not the betting type."

"Oh, we both know that's not true. You've always been the type to take risks."

"Me?" She laughed again, this time the sound filled with unbelief. "Since when?"

"For as long as I've known you. You were always the one to go against the pack, to speak your own mind, to stand up for the kids in school who wouldn't defend themselves. I think you were the only one of Sophia's friends to stick by her when all that business with vandalism at Hope's shop went down."

Five years ago, his sister had been convinced by a friend of hers to sneak into The Hope Chest—the local antiques store owned by Hope Daniels. Sophia hadn't known her supposed friends had planned to rob and ransack the place once they were inside. Nor had she known that Hope was staying in the small apartment above the shop. The older woman had been injured when she'd gone down to investigate the break-in. The rest the teens had scattered, but Sophia had stayed behind until the paramedics arrived to help Hope, even though it meant getting caught red-handed and taking the blame.

"I knew Sophia wasn't responsible for that. She never would have done anything to hurt Hope."

"A lot of people probably believed that, but none of them were as vocal about their faith in her as you were. Sophia always appreciated that. So did the rest of us."

The rest of us... Drew meant the rest of his family. In many ways, the Pirellis had been like family to Debbie since her mother had become ill and especially after her death. They looked out for her, inviting her to family get-togethers and holiday parties as if she was one of their own. As an only child, she'd often envied her friends' large and loving family. A family just like the one Drew no doubt wanted for himself—sooner rather than later.

"I never saw any of that as taking a risk, but even if it is, I'm not—"

"Willing to take a chance on me? On us?"

Us... Debbie swallowed. She'd asked for a sign, and that was a pretty big one, lit up in glowing green letters that had her hormones wanting to charge full speed ahead. But still she hesitated. "I don't think— We don't want the same things, Drew."

"And yet we're both here tonight."

"I'm not talking about tonight. I'm talking about the future. I'm not interested in settling down right now. I don't want a relationship. I just want to go out and have fun and be free to live *my* life."

Tilting his head, he studied her until she fought to shift under the intense scrutiny. "Weren't you the one to remind me that you can't count on the future? That you never know what might happen today?"

Debbie didn't know why she'd brought up her father the other day. She rarely talked about him. He was little more than a memory, and she'd never been certain if the memories were her own or just stories told so often by her mother that they'd become almost real.

For other people, turning twenty-six might not have been such a milestone, but it had hit her hard. Hard enough to make her question what she was doing with her life. Or, more specifically, what she *wasn't* doing with it.

As long as she could remember, she'd lived with the awareness that life was short. Yet somehow she'd still let some of the best years—her teens and early twenties—pass by while she struggled just to get through one day and onto the next.

She half expected to see pity in Drew's dark gaze, but

instead saw only understanding, as if he knew exactly what she was thinking and why she'd set out on this mission to seize the day. And rather than trying to talk her out of it, he was waiting…for her.

But that wasn't possible. Was it?

"You want me to take a chance on us, but there is no 'us,' Drew," she pointed out, almost desperately. "There's me and the woman I really am, and then there's you and the kid you still think I am."

"I admit it took a while for me to see how much you've changed. You've been my kid sister's best friend for as long as I've known you, and it was easier for me to keep you in that role. Safer."

Right! Debbie barely swallowed a sarcastic laugh. Like she posed any danger to a man like Drew. No matter what he said, she was the girl next door, not the femme fatale. All the karaoke in the world wouldn't change that.

"You're wrong, though, if you think I still see you as a kid or that my feelings for you are platonic. And you're wrong if you don't think I want to kiss you right now more than I've ever wanted anything."

Her pulse pounded so wildly in her throat, she couldn't swallow, couldn't breathe. *Simple, straightforward, honest.* The words she'd used to describe Drew the other day still rang true. If he said he wanted her…

"It's your turn," he said softly.

Her turn to do what exactly? To spill her feelings like he'd just done? Or maybe… Debbie dropped her gaze to his lips as she wondered if his words were an invitation to do what she'd wanted to do since he'd sat down beside her.…
Her heart was still pounding, but over the raging beat, she heard someone call her name. Blinking, she jerked out of the fantasy of kissing Drew and realized half the people around her were staring at her. "My—what?"

"Come on, Debbie!" Marcy called out. She still held the microphone but was pointing it in Debbie's direction. "It's your turn." The brunette's grin was broad, and Debbie could see her name printed in bold letters across the screen.

A wave of sheer panic washed over her. Oh, no. She couldn't do this. All those people staring at her as she opened her mouth to sing... What if she screwed up? What if her voice went flat and the words came out all wrong? Or worse, what if she froze and couldn't make a sound? Heat crawled up her face, and she didn't think she could breathe, forget trying to sing. Suddenly light-headed, she struggled to pull in a gasp of air. "I don't think—"

"Don't think," urged Drew. "Just go up there."

The irony of Drew's advice was enough to shake off some of the terror. "Funny, coming from you. When do you ever act first and think later?"

His grin was wry as he pulled her off the stool and to her feet. "You'd be surprised. Now go do this."

A tiny stage had been set up in the corner of the room, complete with a spotlight ready to showcase her utter humiliation. "Drew—"

His large, warm hand gripped the back of her neck and kissed just long enough to leave her breathless and just short enough to leave her longing for more. "I promise you, I will be thinking about that later. Now go knock 'em dead."

"That was so much fun!" Debbie grinned as she stepped out into the night air, her arms thrown out wide as she spun to face him. "I can't believe you didn't get up and sing!"

"Maybe next time."

Whether she realized it or not, tonight hadn't been about him. This had been her night, and man, had she shone. Drew still couldn't understand why she'd hesitated to go up on stage. How had he not known Debbie had such an amazing voice, and watching her on stage *watching* him as she performed—

He'd never seen a sexier sight.

It didn't matter that the songs had been pop tunes— "Girls Just Wanna Have Fun," her opening number and a theme she clearly embraced. What counted was seeing the light in her eyes and the confidence she gained as she broke away from the past and reclaimed a piece of herself that she'd lost along the way.

"Marcy was really good, too, wasn't she?" Debbie asked as she waved at the brunette from across the now-deserted parking lot. The two women had pretty much closed down the place, and only a few cars remained. "Kurt asked her out," she said of the sandy-haired man walking with the other woman. "I think they make a cute couple."

"Mmm-hmm." Drew wasn't really interested in which of the singles had paired up that night. He was just glad the other guys had given Debbie a wide berth after he'd sat down beside her. After he'd kissed her, they'd backed off entirely.

If he'd known that was all it would take— Hell, he should have kissed Debbie a long time ago, and not just as a way to warn off other single guys.

Her eyes had deepened to sparkling sapphire and her hair gleamed almost silver in the misty moonlight. A pair of white jeans hugged her hips, and she was wearing a red sweater that reminded him of the candy apples from his youth. Debbie might not care for the description, but just looking at her had his mouth watering for something sweet. Her gaze softened as she gazed over at Marcy and her new potential boyfriend, Kurt.

Drew's gut tightened at the wistful smile tilting her lips. Was she wishing she'd met someone tonight? That some new, not-Clearville guy was walking her to her car, getting her number and making plans to see her again?

She noticed him watching her and glanced away, her expression somewhat guilty. Was she embarrassed that he'd caught her daydreaming about the kind of guy she had yet to find?

Debbie had complained that the guys in town only saw her as a little sister. Could it be that she only saw him in that same platonic light? Every masculine muscle in his body tensed at the idea. Yes, she'd returned his kiss tonight and at the wedding, but both times he'd caught her off guard, ambushing her even. He knew he was the exact opposite of everything she said she wanted—but could he change her mind?

"Do you ever wonder," she began, only to send her blond hair tumbling back over her shoulders as she shook her head. "Never mind."

"Wonder what?" he pressed.

"Do you ever wonder what might have happened if we'd met on a night like tonight? If we hadn't practically grown up together but instead were brought together by singles' night like Marcy and Kurt. Two strangers whose eyes meet across a crowded bar." Debbie laughed at the cliché, but the question lingered in her expression.

Strangers meeting in a bar... That was the fantasy she'd described during Darcy's bachelorette party. On that night, he wasn't supposed to have heard her wish, but tonight— Drew's heartbeat quickened. Did he dare see her words as encouragement, that she was putting *him* in the role? Taking a chance, he said, "I don't have to wonder."

"You don't?"

"I know what would have happened."

"You do?" Debbie made a face as if acknowledging the way she'd taken to echoing everything he was saying.

"First I would tell you how amazing you were on stage tonight and what a great voice you have."

Her lips twitched a smile she gave him a sideways glance. "You already did that."

"Good. That means I'm right on track."

"And what comes next?"

"Well, I'd offer to walk you to your car, of course," he said just as they reached her lime-green VW Bug.

"Very chivalrous of you."

He made a soft sound of agreement. "See, if you knew me better and if I wasn't a total stranger, you'd realize that I am very much a gentleman."

Her smile glowed even brighter as he played along with the game of pretend she'd established. "And once we reached my car..." She placed a hand on the shiny hood as she turned to face him. "What would you do then? Would you ask for my phone number? Would you kiss me good-night?"

Drew stepped close and then closer until he could feel the heat from Debbie's body calling out to his. "Oh, yeah," he answered, his voice dropping an octave as his gaze fell to her lips, parted and waiting beneath his. "I would definitely want to see you again. And only an idiot wouldn't kiss you if he had the chance."

Her eyes widened at his reference to the weekend before when he hadn't kissed her and had turned away instead. But that was then and this was now. Tonight Debbie hadn't had anything stronger to drink than iced tea. And after tonight, he better understood what was motivating her to go down this path.

This wasn't some whim that had struck Debbie during the bachelorette party, even if that was when she'd first given voice to her longing for something more. This was important to her, and for reasons Drew couldn't completely understand, it was important to him to help her fulfill that wish. He didn't bother trying to fool himself into believing he was simply trying to look out for her, and though that protective instinct was still on guard inside him, somehow the feeling had changed...grown.

Keeping Debbie safe wasn't as important as making her happy.

Drew's conscience gave a snort of laughter. All the logic and reasoning he came up with might help justify his actions and keep him from feeling too guilty about coming on to a woman he'd always treated like family, but logic and reason carried little weight against one simple fact.

He wanted to kiss her more than he wanted to draw his next breath.

But despite her bold and flirty words, the moonlight touched on the hesitation in her expression, and Drew could have kicked himself for the way he'd rejected her before. He'd had his reasons, good ones he'd thought, but he'd hurt her, and that was the last thing he ever wanted to do.

Settling his hands on her shoulders, he bent his head and put his whole heart in making this kiss everything their first should have been. A slow study as he experienced the warmth and sweetness of her mouth. A learning curve as he discovered the shape of her lips with his own and sought to determine what she liked—but then slow and sweet seemed to slip from his fingers along with his control, and he found himself wrapping his arms around her and holding her tight.

They were both breathless by the time he stepped back. He might have felt a sense of masculine satisfaction at the unfocused look in her eyes if he wasn't having so much trouble seeing straight himself. Blinking, she lifted a hand to touch her lips. "That, um, that was some first kiss."

He tried to answer, barely managing a grunt in response.

Still partially hidden by her fingers, Debbie's mouth curved into a smile. A confident smile, one that erased any sign of the vulnerability he'd sensed in her earlier. The sight was almost enough to make Drew overlook that she'd recovered faster than he had from that mind-blowing kiss. Who exactly, he wondered, was seducing whom?

"You know, if we had met tonight for the first time, I think I just might give you my number."

"Might?" he bit out in a disbelieving laugh. "You *might* give it to me?"

"Yep," she answered with a saucy wink as she opened her car door and slid behind the wheel.

Reaching out, Drew caught the edge of the door and leaned down until they were face-to-face. "And what if I gave you mine?"

Her husky laughter hit like a sucker punch to his gut. "Oh, I think we both know I've already got that."

Chapter Seven

The knock at the bakery's back door was the answer to her prayer, and Debbie let the soaking-wet mop fall into a pile of soggy towels as she rushed across the kitchen. "Thank goodness you're here!"

Drew greeted her with a cocky grin, one hand braced against the jamb, the other carrying a toolbox. "You know, when you said you had my number, I didn't really think you'd be using it so soon."

Her face heating, she tried to act cool and knew she was failing miserably as he stepped inside the disaster that was now her kitchen. "Trust me, neither did I."

At least not like this. She'd had a nightmare of an afternoon and Drew—Drew looked like every red-blooded woman's fantasy man come true. He could have stepped right out from a "Men at Work" calendar. A leather tool belt hung low on his lean, denim-clad hips and a faded green henley T-shirt embraced his broad shoulders and flat abs. But Drew was the real deal, and the scarred belt and work-worn boots were more than simple props.

So unfair, when she was almost as big of a mess as her bakery kitchen.

"I just went to adjust the sprayer on the faucet," she said, waving at the double-bowl industrial sink, "and the whole thing came off in my hand and water started shooting out all over the place! I tried the shutoff valve but it was too tight to move, and by the time I'd grabbed a wrench, water was everywhere, and it was all I could do to move the flour and sugar out of the way to keep it from getting ruined."

The fifty-pound bags were hard enough to lift under the best of conditions. Hauling them out from the pantry during a sudden flood had left Debbie a tired, sweaty, *soggy* mess. Her first thought that didn't involve a dozen or so swear words had been to call Drew.

Only now that he was here, she wished she'd called someone—anyone—else. She wanted him to see her as the woman she'd been the other night. Confident, bold, sensual. Instead she felt like reality had once again come crashing down on her dreams, reminding her that this— the bakery, life in Clearville and her role as Drew's kid sister's friend—was all there'd ever be.

"You didn't have to come over. I thought you'd just recommend someone," she said finally. "I'm sure you have bigger projects to bother checking on my faulty plumbing."

"No job is too small, and I still like getting my hands dirty."

Okay, that should not have sounded so sexy, but feeling like she did, she couldn't come up with a witty comeback. His teasing grin faded at her silence, and Drew set the toolbox down before stepping closer. He cupped her face in his hands, and it was all Debbie could do not to duck away from his searching gaze.

She didn't want him seeing her looking like this. Didn't want to watch the realization *she'd* just had steal across his features. And his expression did change—but not into one of pity or regret. A warmth and caring filled his dark eyes, so strong she could feel it in the brush of his thumbs against her cheeks, in the massaging fingers that tunneled into her hair.

"And I didn't want to send someone else. I wanted to be here. To be the one to play the white knight and ride in to save the day."

Debbie managed a smile as he turned the words she used the night of the meet and greet against her. "Sorry, Drew, but I'm not exactly feeling like a fairy-tale princess right now."

"And I can't think of a better moment to come to your rescue."

She knew she was a total mess, and yet the look in his eyes— He'd looked at her the same way the night before— when she'd spent an hour on her hair and makeup. Desire and awareness swirled through his eyes....

This time she did duck away, too afraid Drew would see the tears in her eyes at his murmured words. But that only made it easier for him to pull her into his arms and tuck her head beneath his chin. She felt the brush of his lips against her hair, but the sweetness of the kiss only made her feel cherished. She didn't know how long he held her. All she knew was that she could have stayed in his arms forever.

"So are you going to let me help you clean up this place? Please?"

"Well, since you did say please," she said with a watery laugh. She pulled out of his embrace, blinking back tears, and glanced around at the mess in the kitchen that suddenly didn't seem so bad. With Drew working by her side, they had the wet towels spinning in the washer and the last of the water mopped up from the floor within minutes.

"How badly do you need water right now? Are you right in the middle of anything?"

"No, actually. I was just cleaning up when the faucet broke." She waved a hand at the covered bowls of batter waiting to be poured into muffin tins and baked. "Those are all ready to go."

"Uh-oh." Drew warily eyed the orange batter. "Those aren't the same cupcakes from the other day, are they?"

"No. I told you those weren't ready yet."

Before the broken faucet and minor flood, she'd been elbow deep in fixing the recipe she'd tried out the other day. With the disaster averted and her breakdown under control, anticipation surged through her as she thought of the cupcakes waiting to be baked. Waiting to be tasted. Her pulse picked up its pace as she anticipated Drew's reaction.

Building on the base foundation of the recipe, she'd taken it in a half a dozen different directions. She couldn't wait for him to sample them all, couldn't wait to see his expression as she teased his taste buds with minicupcakes that were little more than a bite and guaranteed to leave him wanting more....

"Okay, then. I'll replace the faucet while you throw those cupcakes in the oven, and when they're done..."

"I'll let you try them," she promised even as she wondered at the excitement brewing inside her. Was this the spark, then, that had been missing from the bakery these past few years? Simply having someone to share it with?

Debbie wished the answer could be so simple. But she and Kayla had sampled plenty of recipes, new ones and old favorites as she taught her young apprentice, and it hadn't been enough to light this kind of fire in her oven. The idea that only Drew could stoke the flames of passion in her was too troubling to contemplate, so she shoved the thought aside.

"But I want you to tell me the truth. These are still new recipes, and if you don't like them, I want you to say so. I would never expect you to love everything I make. And I'd much rather you tell me the truth than convince me those cupcakes were wonderful when they're not."

"Really?"

"Really. If you're honest about what you don't like, then I know I can trust you when you say you do like something. It might sound funny, but that means a lot to me, Drew."

She'd been on her own for so long she'd learned to trust her own judgment, but would it really be so bad to have someone else to count on? Not all the time, but just every now and then?

Drew broke her gaze, and Debbie wondered if she'd embarrassed him with her praise. "Debbie, I—" Cutting himself off, he shook his head. "I'm gonna go grab a faucet. I'll have the old one replaced in no time."

"Okay, you go do your job while I do mine."

"I should warn you, I tend to work up an appetite doing hard, manly labor like this."

Debbie grinned. "I'm counting on it."

I know I can trust you... That means a lot to me, Drew.

After making a run to the hardware store, Drew returned to the bakery and tried staying focused on the job. But the hardest part was maneuvering his large frame into the cramped space beneath the sink. The work itself wasn't nearly challenging enough to keep his mind off Debbie— or to keep the guilt from burning away inside him.

The trust shining in her eyes as she gazed up at him hit hard. Not that he was lying to her, exactly. He was just— Drew swore as the wrench slipped off the bolt and his knuckles scraped against the plaster wall. Who was he trying to kid? He was lying to her. By omission, but lying all the same.

He should have come clean by now about overhearing her the night of the bachelorette party. He *would* tell her, before they took things any further, or the guilt would eat him alive. But he had to find the right moment when she'd be open to listening to his explanation and not jump to the conclusion that he'd manipulated the situation. That he'd used her own words against her or—even worse—used her.

A mouthwatering, fresh-from-the-oven smell—a hint of spice and sweetness that reminded him of Debbie's own scent—filled the kitchen. She'd finished baking the cupcakes while he was at the store and had stuck them in the freezer to cool quickly while she made the frosting.

"These are just about ready," she said as she drizzled something across the top of the cupcakes. "Are you at a stopping point?"

"Nope. I'm all finished." He turned on the new faucet with a flick of the handle.

"Oh, perfect timing!"

She flashed a smile at him, and Drew had the thought that his timing wasn't the only thing that was perfect—*she* was. He knew she hated the girl-next-door image, but there was a sweetness and friendliness about her that couldn't be denied. And for too long, that was all he had seen. But beyond the blond hair, blue eyes and bubbly laughter, Debbie was tough. Resilient, a fighter who'd battled through life's hardships and hidden so much of what she was feeling behind a smile. Maybe too much. She was right when she said she could take care of herself, but he wanted to be the one to take care of *her.*

"Come on. I can't wait for you to taste this."

His gaze automatically dropped to her lips, and he swallowed. Hard. "Yeah, um, give me a second to clean up." He washed his hands quickly, wincing slightly at the sting of water and soap against his scraped knuckles. Less than he deserved, his conscience berated him, for not *truly* coming clean.

But one look in her sparking blue eyes and his plan to tell the truth stalled. The words got caught behind the lump in his throat as he realized how much *he* wanted to be the one to put that spark in her eyes. The one to keep her on her toes when he wasn't sweeping her off her feet—and no short-term fling was going to do.

"Drew? Are you okay?" Debbie asked.

A frown knit her eyebrows together, and he realized he'd been standing motionless even as the earth shifted beneath his feet. "I, um, yeah. I was just—making sure the faucet's running right." Reaching out, he shut off the tap. "You should probably have all the plumbing checked out." Logic may have deserted him, but at least he still had the job to fall back on. "The wiring, too. You know how old these buildings are."

"As long as the faucet's no longer acting like a fountain, everything's good. Rattling pipes and flickering lights are all part of the turn-of-the-century charm. Now come on! I can't wait for you to try this new recipe."

Still stunned by his realization, when Debbie reached out and grabbed his hand she could have led him straight into traffic and he wouldn't have put up a fight. Thankfully, she simply led him to the counter where she had arranged several different plates. Each one showed off a minicupcake with carefully piped frosting swirled over the top. He'd seen her do something similar before—when she'd offered Nick and Darcy a taste test for their wedding cake.

The ground shifted beneath his feet again even though the plates held cupcakes and not slices of wedding cake. Bracing a hand against the stainless-steel counter, he sucked in a deep breath and prayed the world would quickly right itself once more. Fortunately, Debbie seemed completely unaware of the earthshaking, life-altering moments as she reached for the first plate.

"Now, the batters for all of these are mostly the same, but each one has some slight differences. I already know which one is my favorite, but I want to see what you think. And remember, be completely honest."

At first, Drew wasn't sure he'd be able to swallow a single bite, but that wasn't giving Debbie nearly enough credit. With the first taste, he knew the tiny dessert would never be enough. Unlike the cupcake he'd tasted the other day, which had been heavy and dense, this one was light and moist with flavors that perfectly captured the rich flavors of an autumn day. The pumpkin-spice cupcake was filled with bits of walnut and dried fruit and topped with butterscotch icing so good that he wanted to lick the last crumb from the plate.

"That's it. That has to be your favorite."

Debbie shook a teasing finger at him. "No fair choosing until you've tasted them all."

"I don't know what you did with the recipe, but as far as I'm concerned, it's perfect now."

"Hard to tell they're somewhat healthy, too, isn't it?"

"Seriously?"

"Yep. I've been experimenting with an entire line of health-conscious desserts for my online menu. Did you know in some of the bigger cities, there are bakeries that sell cakes that are one-hundred-percent gluten-free? They use rice flour for people with allergies that make eating the typical desserts impossible. Some places have gone organic, too, or even vegan, using applesauce in cakes rather than eggs."

"So why are you only offering those desserts online?"

"Oh, come on, Drew. You know what it's like around here. No one wants to see Bonnie's Bakery change."

Bonnie's Bakery. It was odd after years of knowing one another to realize there were things about Debbie he didn't know. Things he'd never thought to ask—like why she'd kept the name of the bakery. "Is it Clearville that doesn't want the bakery to change," he asked gently, "or is it you?"

"What do you mean?" Wariness and a flash of something buried deeper rippled beneath the surface of her expression.

In anyone else, Drew would have labeled the expression fear, but he'd never known Debbie to be afraid of anything. Wasn't protecting her from charging off into adventure and excitement what started him down this road?

"The front of the bakery, the uniform..." Reaching out, he tugged on the collar, and then couldn't resist brushing his thumb against her jaw. Her cheeks heated until the color almost matched the pink of the shirt. Her soft-as-silk skin made him forget why he'd reached out in the first place. Made him forget everything but the urge to cup her face in his hands and bring her mouth to his. To have a taste test of his own and determine once and for all what was most irresistible—the flavor of her parted lips, the delicate curve behind her jaw, the hidden valley between her breasts...

"The uniform?"

Her echoed words dragged him back from his heated thoughts, and a decade-old memory surfaced. How Debbie had complained to Sophia not long after she'd first started working behind the counter.

I look like a strawberry ice cream cone, she'd said. *Pink on top and tan on the bottom.*

Ten years on, and Drew doubted her opinion of the shirt and pants had improved, and yet she still wore them every day at work. "The uniform. Even the name," he finished. "You haven't changed any of it."

"This was my mother's dream, and keeping the name is my way of keeping that dream alive. It was her bakery long before I took over, and she loved it."

And Debbie didn't.

The thought startled Drew, but he realized it was true. Just because she baked like a dream and greeted every customer who walked into her shop with a smile, he'd assumed running the bakery was all she'd ever wanted to do. He'd never asked, never even considered, that she might have wanted something different—something more….

Could the excitement and adventure she was seeking in her personal life be due in part to feeling so stifled professionally? If Debbie felt free to branch out at the bakery, might she then be more willing to settle down into a relationship? Say, a relationship with him?

To Drew, it all made sense, though he couldn't help wondering if he wasn't twisting logic so Debbie's vision of the future would dovetail into his own. One thing he knew was that trying to force those pieces to fit wouldn't work. He'd have to be patient, something that had never been a problem for him in the past. So why did he already feel so restless?

Maybe because wanting Debbie, wanting that future, was so much bigger, so much more important than anything he'd wanted before….

For now, he'd settle for seeing that spark back in her eyes, one that had dimmed as they talked about her mother, so he was glad when she responded by teasing, "And when I thought about changing the name, I got stuck on the whole alliteration thing and I just couldn't get around Debbie's Donuts."

"Debbie's Donuts...Mattson's Muffins," he supplied.

"So you see my dilemma."

"I do," he agreed. But solving it would have to wait for another day. Once he'd considered how he could encourage Debbie to reach for her own dreams while still holding true to her mother's. "I hope you understand my dilemma, too."

"What's that?"

"How I'm supposed to pick just one favorite," he said as he reached for another plate.

The spark was back as Drew quickly devoured three more minicupcakes—one with chunks of toffee inside and a matching frosting, another with macadamia nuts and a white-chocolate icing and the last with a hint of orange. Though they all were delicious, none could beat the first one, but Debbie was wearing a secret smile as she reached for the final plate.

"I probably shouldn't say anything since I don't want to influence your opinion but...this is my favorite." She lifted the minicupcake, stepping close enough for him to feel her body heat and to catch a hint of her scent—as delicious and tempting as anything she'd ever made in this kitchen. Did she know, he wondered, that she was doing so much more than influencing his *opinion?* From that seductive, secret smile, he'd bet she did.

And what was that old saying? If you can't take the heat...

Well, they were already in the kitchen.

Drew raised a hand, but instead of taking the cake from Debbie, he wrapped his fingers around hers and guided her hand to his mouth. The combination of flavors—a hint of pumpkin and spice mixed with chunks of dark chocolate and a shot of coffee—was to die for. But it was the mix of emotions on her face—awareness, anticipation, desire—that had him coming back for more. He savored the tiny dessert, making it last bite after bite, until there was nothing left to do but lick the last traces of frosting from her fingers....

The tug and pull of his mouth against her skin send a rush of sweet, rich heat pouring through Debbie's veins. The sensation pooled in her belly and sapped strength, turning her bones to molten chocolate. Her legs trembled and her head tipped back. All that from his mouth against her fingers. Just the thought of those skilled lips teasing and tormenting more intimate flesh...

A delicious shiver racked her whole body. Drew's dark gaze held her captive—watching and knowing just what he was doing to her—and yet she couldn't look away. "Drew."

His name was little more than a gasp for breath and his answer little more than a wicked grin. "Looks like you were right."

"I was?" She swallowed hard, trying to gather her scrambled wits. "Oh, good. I always like being right. What is it I'm right about again?"

His grin grew even bigger and even more wicked. "This is my favorite."

Debbie didn't know if he was talking about tasting the cupcakes or tasting *her,* but then he was kissing her and she couldn't think at all. He framed her face in his hands as he deepened the kiss, his fingers splayed wide, as if he felt the same desperation to touch, to taste, to experience all he could in a stolen moment of time.

She slid her hands up his back, the material of his shirt denying the skin-against-skin friction she craved. She fisted her hands, but warm cotton was no substitute for hot skin. He pulled her tight, and she no longer cared that her bones were melting because it made it so much easier for him to meld her body to his. Her curves met the hardened planes and angles of his masculine form—softening, conforming, blending with a sense of perfection she'd never experienced before.

The panicked feeling came out of nowhere, a cold splash of reality. She didn't want perfect or permanent or lasting. She wanted— Drew's mouth trailed across her cheek, his breathing as ragged and gasping as her when she moaned his name.

She wanted Drew.

No. Well, yes, she wanted him. But she couldn't— wouldn't—fall for him. Not because it would be hard, but because it would be all too easy.

"This is crazy," she breathed, knowing it wouldn't take much more for her whole body to break from the sheer pleasure. She was barely aware of speaking the words. She certainly hadn't meant them as a criticism, but Drew stilled, caught on the razor's edge that gripped them both.

Oh, please, let this be happening to both of them.

His breath was hot, rasping, against her shoulder. The tension held his body tight to hers, but Debbie's awareness gradually expanded from the circle of Drew's arms to their surroundings—the batches of cupcakes she still needed to frost, the icing likely hardening in the bowls, the kitchen Bonnie had treated like sacred ground. Her mother would be scandalized.

Drew slowly straightened away from her, humor banking some of the heat in his gaze. "I'm starting to think crazy is a good thing."

The so un-Drewlike statement startled a laugh from her. "Since when?" she asked as the moment of levity eased the pressure on her chest and cooled some of the raging desire.

At least until he answered, "Since I haven't been able to

get you out of my head. Since I can't stop thinking about the next time I'll have you in my arms again."

A hint of a question lingered in his words. Asking for a next time? Or was it a subtle proposition that they find someplace to better continue *this* time? Her tiny apartment, a dozen steps away up the staircase...

Her heart pounded so loudly, she wondered if Drew could hear it beating its way out of her chest. "We could—"

The ring of the phone cut off whatever Debbie might have said, and she exhaled a dizzying breath—half relief, half disappointment—as she didn't even know what her answer might have been. The machine picked up almost immediately, and Sophia's voice filled the space.

"Hey, Deb!"

And just like that, Debbie's awareness reached even further, far beyond the intimate circle she and Drew still created, beyond the kitchen and bakery, to Clearville and the outside world. A world that included loving and nosy friends and, in Drew's case, family who would have their own ideas of what her next step with Drew should be. And the step after that and the step after that, all the way to a walk down the aisle.

"Just wanted to let you know we're having a get-together this weekend and you have to come," Sophia's happy voice continued. "I want to hear all about karaoke night! Did your amazing voice knock some gorgeous guy's socks off—or maybe some other article of clothing?" Her teasing laughter ended with "Call me!"

Judging by Drew's frown, he wasn't amused. "I think I need to have a talk with Jake about my little sister. Married life is supposed to be settling her down."

"It has. Now she's trying to live vicariously through me. She's the one who sent me the info on the singles' group."

The frown darkened to a scowl. "Definitely going to have a talk."

"I doubt it will do much good. I keep telling her I'm not interested in a serious relationship, but your sister is on a mission. Ever since she got married, she's been pushing me to find someone of my own. It's that whole happy-couple-in-love thing where they want everyone else to be part of a happy couple in love, too."

"You think I haven't had my share of that? We're going to have three weddings in my family within a year. My mother would like nothing more than to see me matched up. The odd number is playing hell with her seating chart at family dinners."

Debbie could easily picture Vanessa Pirelli's exasperation. "Well, there's always Maddie."

"Ah, you're forgetting about Timmy. My niece and nephew are the cute couple at the kiddie table. I'm surprised my mom hasn't kicked me out onto the back porch."

His words brought Sophia's invitation to mind, along with memories of dozens of other Pirelli gatherings Debbie had attended over the years. They were as close to family as she had and Sophia was her best friend. If things didn't work out with Drew and if it ended up costing her that connection, that friendship…

"All of which makes this thing between us that much more complicated. If your family finds out about us—"

"I don't kiss and tell, Debbie."

"Still, it's not too late, you know."

His brow furrowed as his eyebrows pulled together. "For what?"

"To forget all of this and pretend none of it ever happened."

"Oh, yes it is. I'm going to remember your kiss for the rest of my life."

Her breath caught at his roughly murmured words. Words that said exactly what she was thinking, how she was feeling. Years from now, when she did look back, did she really only want to have kisses to remember?

Not a chance!

Drew was right. It was too late to go back. Too late to do anything but go forward.

"We're really going to do this? Have a fling?" Her face heated as she blurted out the word. It sounded so silly, but *affair* had too much of a negative ring to it, and Debbie just couldn't bring herself to ask if he wanted to have sex with her. "So…how are we going to do this?"

A sexy glint entered his gaze. "Oh, I figure the usual way."

Judging by the way he could jump-start her heart with something as simple as a smile, Debbie doubted there'd be anything *usual* about it. Still… "That's not what I meant."

"I know." That killer grin was back. "I'll take care of everything."

Not exactly an answer. At least not one she could blindly accept after taking care of herself for so long. "But—"

He silenced her with another quick kiss. "No questions or you'll ruin the surprise. Where's your sense of adventure?"

Adventure, excitement, mystery… Wasn't that exactly what she'd wished for at Darcy's bachelorette party? Drew was offering all that and more. She'd never imagined he would be the man to sweep her off her feet, but now that he had, all she could do was hold on tight and enjoy the ride…for as long as it lasted.

Chapter Eight

Drew had never claimed to be an over-the-top romantic. If he had, he was sure his former girlfriends would have quickly disabused him of that notion. In all honesty, he'd never put himself totally on the line when it came to women. Oh, sure, he'd asked out plenty, but he'd always been relatively assured of a positive response. Pursuing an uninterested woman had always struck him as a waste of time and, well, somewhat unnecessary when far more receptive members of the opposite sex could be found.

Not that Debbie was uninterested. He had no doubts about the chemistry between them. But he wanted more than a physical relationship. He wanted *Debbie* to want more than a physical relationship. More than the secret "fling" she'd proposed. Sure, he'd agreed. What red-blooded man in his right mind wouldn't? And he'd admit he wasn't ready to put his feelings on display for all of Clearville to see, especially when he knew Debbie didn't feel the same way. At least, not yet.

He'd always been one to keep his emotions close to the vest, to play things safe. But safe wouldn't do in the relationship he wanted with Debbie. He wanted the scary, reckless, no-holds-barred kind of love he used to think was out of his grasp. She'd pushed him out of his comfort zone, made him question everything he thought he knew when it came to the line between friendship and love.

After his breakup with Angie, he'd realized their relationship lacked that intrinsic connection he sensed bound his parents together. A connection Nick had found with Darcy, Jake with Sophia and Sam with Kara. He'd been ready to believe his ex was right, and he simply didn't have the necessary depth of emotion inside. But Angie had been wrong. His feelings for Debbie were beyond anything he'd felt for another woman, and going there was a giant leap for Drew, one he was ready to take.

He'd made reservations at an upscale restaurant located inside a newly built five-star hotel in Redfield. He thought he might hear from Debbie after sending her his "invitation" but she hadn't called, leaving him to wonder if she would show.

Taking a seat at the bar, he ordered a beer but barely raised the bottle for than a few swallows. His attention and his cravings were all focused on the door to the restaurant as he waited.

He hadn't realized exactly how nervous he was that Debbie might not show until the moment she walked into the restaurant. His breath escaped in a rush and he sank back against the padded back of the leather bar stool. From his vantage point in the bar, he had a perfect chance to study her unnoticed. She looked...breathtaking.

The restaurant's décor was a combination of rustic and elegant with its rough-hewn, exposed-beam ceiling and river-rock fireplace illuminated by bronze sconces and blown-glass chandeliers. Her blond hair glinted in the ambient lighting, and her soft skin was awash in a golden glow. His blood heated at just how much of that skin was revealed by her pale blue strapless dress. Black lace outlined the bodice and flirted with the hem, splitting his gaze between the curves of her breasts and shapely legs. She walked with confidence despite the spiky black heels she wore, but Drew could see a hint of nerves as she pushed her hair back behind one ear.

After thanking the hostess and taking a seat at the table, she glanced around the restaurant, but her gaze didn't travel toward his corner of bar. Seeming to come to the conclusion that she'd arrived first, Debbie glanced at the leather-bound menu. The waiter stopped by, and though Drew was too far away to hear the conversation, he watched her wave to the opposite side of the booth and figured she'd told the waiter she would wait for the rest of her party to arrive before ordering.

Her patience played into his plan perfectly. Catching the bartender's eye, he waved the younger man over. "I'd like to send a glass of champagne to the woman in the corner booth."

The bartender grinned. "Yes, sir. Anything else for you?" he asked with a nod to his lone beer.

"No, thanks," he responded.

When the bartender delivered the flute of champagne to Debbie, she took another look around the restaurant. This time, she spotted him in the bar. Her eyes lit up, and the smile she sent him hit his chest with the force of a sledgehammer.

Leaving some cash on the bar for the beer and champagne, Drew walked over to the small booth. His heart pounded, and he felt like a kid at his first school dance. It was crazy to feel so nervous about approaching someone he'd known almost his whole life. Then he caught sight of the tiny pendant she wore on a delicate gold chain around her neck, and some of the tightness in his chest eased.

She offered him a small smile so different from the bright grin she normally wore. "Hi."

"Hey. I see you got my invitation."

Her hand rose to finger the crystal slipper nestled at the hollow of her throat. "I did. Thank you. It's beautiful."

"If the glass slipper fits…"

Even in the faint lighting, he could see the blush coloring her cheeks. She glanced around the restaurant, evading his gaze, as she said, "I've never been here before. Have you?"

"No, but from what I hear, the food's great and the atmosphere is…intimate and quiet. Perfect for getting to know each other."

"Right." She gave a soft laugh. "Because you haven't known me since birth."

"I've known you as my kid sister's friend and as one of my friends. But this—this is different. And I bet there are hundreds of interesting things I don't know about you."

Doubt raised one of her eyebrows. "Like what?"

"You tell me. Tell me something I don't know about you."

"My favorite color?" she teased. "The first boy I kissed?"

"Blue," he answered. "And no, you better not tell me about the first boy you kissed, because I probably know him, and if you told me, I'd be tempted to go kick his ass."

"For a kiss that happened over a decade ago?" She laughed.

"Hey, you still remember it."

"Yes, and I remember thinking it was gross. Which is not at all what I've been thinking about more recent kisses. But I suspect that is something you already know." Their gazes caught and held as memories played between them of those stolen moments. "Now, for something you don't know…"

A door at the back of the restaurant swung open, and a waiter stepped out carrying a large tray holding steaming entrees for a nearby table. She followed the waiter's progress before looking back at Drew. "My senior year of high school, I was accepted into a culinary school in San Francisco. I wanted to study to be a chef and get a job running a kitchen in a place like this."

He'd asked for a piece of her life, something he hadn't known, but her response was more than that. It was the answer to the question he'd had, the something *more* that she'd longed for. This was the dream working in the bakery wasn't enough to fulfill.

"You're right. I had no idea."

"When I got the news, I was so excited," she said with a bittersweet smile. "My mom's cancer had been in remission for a few years, and I had such big dreams…." Her voice faded away along with her smile, and even though it happened a long time ago, Drew felt like he was watching those dreams fade away, too.

Because while he might not have known Debbie had been accepted to culinary school, he knew why she hadn't gone. Bonnie's illness had returned. And whatever hopes, whatever dreams Debbie might have had during the time when her mother's health was good had slipped away once more.

"I'm sorry, Debbie. I knew about your mom and how you'd taken over for her, but I wish I'd—I don't know… been there for you somehow."

"You were at college most of that time. Besides, there wasn't anything you could have done."

Drew's jaw tightened even though he didn't want to

admit those words hurt a little. He'd known going in that Debbie had an independent streak. And while he knew he couldn't have done anything about her mother's illness, he still could have been there for Debbie. Because that was what you did when you lo— *Cared* about someone. You stood by their side, and he refused to believe that didn't have some value.

Reaching over, he entwined his fingers with hers. "I could have held your hand, and let you know you weren't alone."

For a long time she didn't respond. But when she looked up from their joined hands, he caught the sheen of tears in her blue eyes. "I would have liked that," she said huskily.

"You know, it's not too late. If there's something else you want to do, something other than running the bakery—"

"I can't," she protested. "The bakery was my mother's dream, and with her gone…it would be like losing the only part of her I have left."

"I know how hard that would be, but what about *your* dreams?"

"I let them go a long time ago," she said, as if referring to some old toys a child had outgrown or last year's clothes that were no longer in fashion. Something meaningless and easily forgotten.

Everything inside him rebelled at the thought. Debbie was so bright, so beautiful inside and out, he couldn't stand knowing she'd given up on her dreams. On all dreams. Was that why she was willing to settle for a temporary relationship? Because she wasn't ready to believe they could have anything more?

"Debbie—"

"What about you?" she interrupted before he could say

more. "Tell me something about Drew Pirelli I don't already know."

Something she didn't know… His feelings for her tumbled around inside him, but he wasn't any more ready to put those emotions into words than Debbie was to hear them. So he settled for something far less complicated. "I'm building a house."

"You're a contractor, Drew. No real secret there."

Her teasing smile was enough to heat his blood to the point of making him want to run a finger under his collar. "No, I'm, um, building my own house."

Sitting back in her chair, she said, "You're right. I didn't know that."

"I've pretty much only told my family."

"Why?"

"I don't know. I've always felt like I put something of myself in the custom homes I build for my clients, but this is different. All the decisions, all the planning—" he gave a short laugh "—all the hard work is going into something I'm building for myself, and that's made it all much more personal. And I guess I'd rather wait and have everyone see the finished product. The hard-work part isn't always pretty."

"I think I know what you mean. Wedding cakes are the same way. Even after the crumb coat—that's a first layer of icing used to smooth out the surface of the cake— sometimes I worry that the cake's just not going to come together. That it will be lopsided or the layers will start to sag or even break. I'd never want a bride to see a cake before it's finished down to the last sugar pearl." She sipped her champagne. "So this house? Did you design it yourself?"

"I did."

"I remember at one time you were interested in studying to be an architect."

"That's where I started out. At first, everything was great. I loved the precision of designing a house. Of finding the right blend between a house that looks like a showplace but still feels like a home. Of seeing something I'd imagined take shape on paper."

"So what changed?"

"A few semesters in, I started an internship at an architecture firm. The time there gave me a really good feel for what the job would be like, just how much time would be spent behind a desk, working on blueprints or on conference calls and in planning meetings. It was enough to make me realize it wasn't what I wanted to do for the rest of my life. And it wasn't enough to just see my designs on paper. I wanted to see them come to life as I built them with my own hands."

"Judging by how successful your company is, I'd say you made the right choice."

"I'm glad business has taken off the way it has, but even if the company was struggling, I'd still know I made the right decision."

Because he'd had the opportunity to follow *his* dreams. Debbie had given up her own without complaint to care for her mother.

"I think you're incredible, you know that?"

Debbie blinked at the left-field compliment, a soft blush covering her cheeks. "I don't know about that."

"Well, there you go—something about *you* that you didn't know."

He was pretty sure she also didn't know how much he wanted to reach for her across the small table. To kiss her until they were both breathless and wanting more. But then her blush deepened even more, and he wondered if maybe she did....

The waiter cleared his throat, and Drew cursed the interruption as Debbie pulled her hand from his to smooth the napkin at her lap. After reciting the evening's specials, the young man asked, "Can I start you off with an appetizer tonight?"

"Anything sound tempting to you?" Drew asked. The only thing he was in the mood for was room service and, with any luck, breakfast in bed, but that was pushing things.

And yet Debbie seemed willing to skip some steps as she said, "You know, the best way I've found to judge a restaurant is by their desserts. What do you say to splitting the raspberry cheesecake?"

Drew grinned. "I'd say life is short. Eat dessert first."

Once the waiter left with their order, Debbie leaned closer. "Are you sure this won't spoil your appetite?"

"I don't think that's possible."

The hunger inside him wasn't the least bit satisfied by the cheesecake. Especially not when they ended up not just sharing the dessert but the same fork. When Debbie fed him a bite, all he could imagine was tasting the same sweet raspberry flavor straight from her lips.

Desire swirled between them as rich and decadent as the dessert. "I can't tell you how much I want to kiss you right now."

Her lips parted at his murmured words, drawing even more of his heated attention as she ran her tongue over the upper arch, as if already tasting him there. "Then why aren't you?"

"Because once I start, I won't want to stop."

Pulling in a deep breath that lifted her breasts against

the bodice of her dress and weakened his control even more, she said, "What if I don't want you to stop?"

"Then I'd say we should find someplace a little more private than the middle of a restaurant."

"Someplace like a hotel room?"

The key for the room he'd checked into earlier was burning a hole in his pocket. All he had to do was take Debbie's hand in his and lead her to the bank of mirrored elevator doors across the restaurant. But there was something he had to do first. Something he knew full well might ruin everything.

Sucking in a deep breath, he said, "Debbie, there's something I have to tell you. The night of Darcy's bachelorette party, I overheard your conversation with the girls."

As a kid, Debbie had fallen off her bike once and had the wind knocked out of her. She felt the same way—dizzy, panicked and unable to breathe—as Drew's words reached across the table and sucker punched her. "You heard me.... So this was all some kind of joke, then? Give poor, lonely Debbie a quick thrill, right?"

"No! No." Reaching out, Drew grasped hold of her arm when she would have otherwise jumped up and run from the booth. His grip was firm enough to let her know he didn't want her to leave yet not so tight that she'd have any trouble breaking away. But it was the warmth of his skin against hers rather than any amount of force that kept her seated. "It's not like that."

"Then tell me how it is, Drew. Tell me how you took something I said in confidence to my *friends*—" she stressed the word, making it clear she no longer considered him one of that group "—and used it to play me."

"I wasn't playing," he muttered.

"Then what were you thinking? No, let me guess. This

was all some misguided effort to save me from myself, right?" Because even as angry as she was, Debbie couldn't believe Drew would do anything purposefully cruel or hurtful. He wasn't that kind of man, and even though he hadn't been acting like himself lately, she still knew that to be true.

"You heard me say that I was looking for adventure and excitement—" her face heated at the thought of what else he'd overheard "—and you thought to yourself that couldn't possibly be good for me. Good girls are supposed to sit at home and wait for some nice boy to come calling, right? So you thought you'd step in and play superhero."

Drew's jaw tightened, but she could read the truth he was trying to hide in his dark gaze. And it hurt. So much that she felt the sting of tears at the back of her eyes. Biting down on the inside of her cheek, she willed the emotion away.

"Dammit, Debbie, will you just listen for a minute?" His shoulders rose on a deep breath as if he was struggling for calm, though why he even thought he had a right to be upset was worlds beyond her. "When I overheard you talking with Sophia and the other girls, I have to admit, I didn't like the idea of you going out and finding some stranger. The whole idea seemed—"

"Desperate?" she supplied, hopefully with enough sarcasm to mask the fact that she'd thought so herself a time or two.

"Dangerous," he argued. "The thought of you and some stranger bugged the hell out of me. And then the more I thought about it, the more the idea of you and any guy— didn't matter if it was a stranger or someone you'd known for years—started to bug me just as much."

"You're trying to tell me you were jealous," she scoffed.

"I'm trying to tell you that if any guy was going to sweep you off your feet, I wanted it to be me."

"So why not just ask me out? Why this whole ruse?"

"Because you didn't want just some everyday, average local guy to ask you out for dinner and a movie. You said so yourself."

"You really expect me to believe after all these years of *not* asking me out, all it took was overhearing that one conversation to make you suddenly realize how much you wanted to go out with me? Forgive me if I find that hard to believe." Almost as hard to believe as the jealousy undercutting his voice earlier when he spoke about the affair she'd thought she wanted to have with her tall, dark, handsome stranger.

"It wasn't just what you said. It was the way you said it."

"How? With a drunken slur?"

"You weren't drunk," Drew responded flatly. "Listening to you, I could hear the anticipation in your voice, a longing for excitement."

Her cheeks heated as her mind scrambled to think back to what else she might have said when she thought she'd been alone with her friends. "It was girl talk at a bachelorette party, Drew. Not something to take seriously and *not* something you were meant to hear."

"But I did," he argued. "And it was enough to make me realize how much excitement and mystery has been missing from my own life. Is it really so hard to believe that you're not the only one looking for something more than small-town life?"

Was it so impossible to believe? Or did she just want to believe it so much?

"Debbie—"

"I need a minute," she said as she slipped away from his touch and out of the booth.

Drew nodded and didn't try to stop her, but she read the disappointment in his gaze. He didn't think she'd be back, and as she made her escape to the restrooms, she wasn't entirely sure he was wrong. The lit sign above the exit beckoned, and she imagined herself escaping through the door and pretending this whole night had never happened.

Instead, though, she found the ladies' room and slipped inside. She'd told Drew she needed a minute, and she felt she at least owed him those sixty seconds to think about what he'd said. As she gazed into her reflection above the granite vanity, every instinct was still urging her to leave.

"You're a lucky lady, you know," a tall brunette said as she washed her hands in the sink next to Debbie.

"Excuse me?" She was hardly in the mood to engage in small talk, but the odd opening line captured her attention.

"Your boyfriend," the other woman explained. "I bumped into him at the bar earlier. I should have realized right away a guy that gorgeous had to be taken. He could barely pull his gaze away from watching the door and waiting for you to arrive." Her assessing glance traveled from Debbie's head to her toes. "You make a good-looking couple."

The woman slipped out of the restroom before Debbie had a chance to respond, but her words had already painted a picture in her mind. An image of Drew waiting for her, of him planning this night, and everything else he'd done in the past few weeks. Watching out for her at the meet and greet, showing up for karaoke night, kissing her when she looked her worst and gazing at her as if she looked her best. Did it really make a difference what had inspired Drew to arrange a night like tonight? All that really mattered was that she wanted to be with him and he wanted to be with her....

Or at least he *had* wanted to be with her. Walking back

into the restaurant, she saw the booth was now empty. Had Drew left, thinking she'd changed her mind about coming back? The few bites of the cheesecake they'd shared settled like a rock in her gut. Had she blown this one chance?

But no, he wouldn't just leave. Not without making sure she was okay and likely following her back home. The gentleman in him went far too deep for him to walk out.

"Miss?"

Debbie started as their waiter appeared at her side. "Yes?"

"Your date asked me to give you this."

"Thank you." Unfolding a piece of paper, she expected to find a note. Instead the paper was folded like an envelope around a key card with a room number written inside.

No words were really necessary, were they? Drew had already stated his case. Now the choice was up to her.

And wasn't that all she'd ever really wanted? A chance to live her own life? But from the moment her mother was diagnosed with cancer, Debbie's future had been cast in stone—or shaped in a copper mold. She'd made a success out of following in her mother's footsteps, yet it had always been out of necessity and never by choice. But now Drew was giving her that choice. This next step was entirely up to her.

Did she really want to look back on tonight as something that might have been?

Denial rose up inside her, swift and sure, propelling her feet toward the elevator. No way was she letting this opportunity slip through her fingers. And no way was she going to miss this chance to get her hands on Drew. The ride up to the fifth floor seemed to take forever.

Debbie rushed toward the room, walking as fast as she could in her high heels. Her knuckles had barely rapped against the door when it was yanked open from the inside.

Moments earlier, Drew had been impeccably dressed. His pale blue dress shirt had been properly buttoned and tucked into slate-gray slacks. Now the tails hung down over his lean hips, the sleeves were pushed back to his elbows and the top buttons were undone, giving her a glimpse of the muscled chest beneath. His hair was mussed from running his fingers through it, bringing out a hint of the normally tamed curl.

The man she'd shared dessert with, who'd eaten from her fork and looked at her as if he was imagining licking the creamy cheesecake right off her, the man who normally looked so calm, so cool, so sexy was nowhere to be seen.

She liked this man even better. The relief washing over his features erased her lingering doubts. Tonight mattered to him. Almost as much as it mattered to her. "Can I come in?"

Drew stepped aside and opened the door wide. Glancing around the room, she noticed the burgundy-and-gold comforter was folded at the foot of the bed and the sheets were already turned down invitingly. Her pulse picked up its pace even as she saw the unopened bottle of champagne on ice. Her eyebrows rose as she looked back at Drew. "Pretty confident that I'd show up, weren't you?"

"Not at all," he said with a completely self-deprecating laugh. "I was hopeful that you would come and figured if you didn't, that bottle of champagne would keep me company tonight." He sobered as he crossed the room to stand in front of her. He ran his palms down her bare arms until he reached her hands and linked their fingers together. "If you're not sure about this, we can go back downstairs for dinner. We can share that champagne and then I can follow you home."

"Still trying to play the white knight, Drew?"

"It's getting harder," he confessed, and then winced at the unintended double meaning to his words.

"Then let me make it easier for you and remind you that I don't need rescuing. You don't need to save me from myself. I'm old enough to know what I want...and I want you."

Reaching up, she twined her arms around his neck and kissed him. For Debbie, it was like no time had passed between this moment of being in his arms and the last. One kiss, and she was ready for more. One touch, and she couldn't get enough.

She tasted the sweetness of raspberry and the sexiness that was pure Drew. He held her body tight to his own, leaving no doubt to how much he wanted her...wanted this. The heat pulsing through her left her weak, and when his kisses found the column of her throat, her head fell back. And when his lips traced the skin above the bodice of her dress, her bones melted like heated sugar.

He found the tab of the zipper and he made the slow slide that much more seductive by tracing his fingertips along every inch of skin he exposed. Goose bumps stood at attention, and her breasts tightened with need. She felt only a moment's hesitation as the dress fell to the floor, leaving her with nothing but her black strapless bra and matching panties. But every doubt she ever had about her hips being too round, her stomach too soft, her breasts too big was burned away by the heat of Drew's touch.

Suddenly everything that had always seemed too much or not enough was just right. A perfect fit, and Drew the perfect man...

"You are so beautiful," he breathed, and Debbie believed him. It was impossible not to when the words were spoken against her skin in a rough whisper and the hands that stripped away the last of her clothes were not quite steady.

Lifting her up in his arms like he had that night in the parking lot, he laid her down in the middle of the bed. He followed her down, but only after he'd tossed aside his own clothes, revealing a body made lean and strong by hard work—broad shoulders, muscular arms, rock-hard abs and long, powerful legs. A lock of his hair had fallen over his forehead and desire darkened his eyes to the deepest, richest chocolate.

He swallowed her gasp with his kiss at the first unrestrained contact of his body, so hard and hot above hers. She arched into his every touch—from her throat to her breast to her belly and her thighs.

It was at the same time too much and never enough, and when the rising, building pleasure broke over her, scattering pieces of her heart and soul, she knew she would never be the same.

Debbie woke in the middle of the night. She didn't need to check the clock to know sunrise was still hours away. Working at the bakery had set her internal alarm clock to a ridiculously early hour, but after so many years, she was used to it.

What she wasn't at all accustomed to was waking up in a man's arms. *Drew's* arms. He held her from behind, his body curving perfectly around hers as if the two of them were made for each other, as if they were meant to be together....

No! That was not what tonight was about. They'd agreed! *Both* of them! This was to be a fling and nothing more. And now, after one night, for her to start thinking about forever—

No! No, this wasn't happening. She wasn't falling for Drew when he'd made his own feelings more than clear.

Nah, that's just Debbie.

In high school, they'd been friends, yet in her young, foolish heart, she'd longed to be his girlfriend. Now they were lovers, and she wanted to believe making love was the same as falling in love when she was old enough to know better.

She had to get a grip on her emotions, and that wasn't about to happen while she was still wrapped in the oh-so-tempting warmth and strength of Drew's arms. She carefully pushed the covers away with one hand and tried to slip out from beneath the heavy weight of his forearm at her waist. His muscles automatically tightened, trying even in sleep to keep her close, and Debbie felt her willpower—if not her heart—fracture the tiniest bit.

It would be so easy to stay, so easy to fall even deeper, to let him get too close. Under her skin and into her heart—

Slapping a mental bandage over the break in her self-control, she eased away from Drew and out of the bed. Finding her way in the zero-dark-thirty hours of the morning was one thing. Maneuvering her way around an unfamiliar hotel room was far more difficult.

Where had all her clothes gone? Drew had been so eager to strip them away—

She slammed her mind shut on the memory, feeling her way across the plush carpet, pulling on each article of clothing as she found it—strapless bra, shoe, dress, underwear—freezing at the slightest sound coming from the bed, until she was almost fully dressed.

Almost.

What was it with her and shoes lately? She was missing a black heel, and searching for it in the darkness she couldn't help remembering the morning at Drew's house. How ruggedly handsome and yet adorable he'd looked holding the puppy in his arms. How proud and *possessive* on karaoke night when he'd called her out on wearing the shoes he'd bought to replace the ones Rain had used as a chew toy. How excited she'd been to read his invitation to meet him at the hotel and then touched to find the tiny crystal pendant inside. The pendant that had been the only thing she hadn't taken off when they made love....

There! Was that— Her fingers brushed against leather near the foot of the bed, and she almost wilted in relief as she grabbed the missing shoe. Drew's low voice came from tangled sheets, and she froze. Not an indistinct murmur, but a single word—her name. Her pulse pounded as she waited for him to ask where she was going, why she was leaving, but no other sound came from the bed. He was still asleep, her presence lingering in his dreams.... The temptation to crawl back into his arms pulled at her, her senses already craving his touch, his taste.

A shiver racked her from head to toe. She needed to go, needed time and distance to put the foolhardy dreams out of her head and out of her heart. But she couldn't escape without leaving something behind to let Drew know she was fine. That she was every bit the woman he'd overhead the night of Darcy's bachelorette party. A woman looking for adventure and excitement. A woman mature and sophisticated enough to know sex didn't equal love.

Aided by the glow of her cell phone, she found the embossed stationary and pen on the hotel room desk. After scribbling out her message, she slipped out as quietly as she could manage and closed the door behind her.

Chapter Nine

Seated on the small bistro table outside the bakery, Sophia leaned back against the white wrought iron chair and groaned dramatically around a bite of pumpkin-spice-and-chocolate-chip cupcake. "Oh, my gosh! These are *so* good. How long have you been hiding these from me?"

Debbie managed a smile and tried to smother another yawn. Her friend looked so fresh and energetic, her pregnancy glow putting Debbie to shame. She was accustomed to waking up early, but normally that meant she went to bed early, as well. Making love with Drew and spending the rest of the night alone in her bed reliving every moment she'd spent in his arms had robbed her of all but an hour or so of sleep.

She'd picked up the phone half a dozen times to call him, but she didn't know what to say. *Sorry I'm such a coward?* Or maybe *I know we agreed to a no-strings fling but after one night, I already want more?*

And she was terrified by just how *much* more. Wasn't she the same girl who didn't want to end up trapped by responsibility? Who wanted her freedom and fun? It was what she'd told her friends. It was what she'd told Drew. So why did those words sound so hollow? So…lonely?

Frustrated by the endless questions circling her mind, she'd been glad when Sophia had stopped by during her break from The Hope Chest, the antiques store just down the street from the bakery. "I haven't been hiding them. I've just added them as part of a fall menu."

"Tell me you plan to keep them on the menu. They're too good to only have for a couple of months."

"I don't know," Debbie said lightly. "Maybe what makes them so good is knowing they'll only be around for a short time."

Sophia shook her head as she dug her fork in for another bite. "No way. They're too good and too addicting to give up. Nothing else is going to compare."

And that was what she was afraid of, wasn't it? Debbie thought. Of being spoiled for life? Knowing from now on everything else would see like second best?

Pressure built in her chest, almost like feeling the need to cry, and she had to remind herself that they were only talking about *cupcakes,* for goodness' sake! She huddled deeper into the oversize cream sweater she'd grabbed before joining her friend outside in the cool, fall-scented morning.

"I left you a message and you didn't call me back," the brunette scolded once she'd finished the cupcake and reached for her herbal tea. "I hope that means you've been too busy to keep in touch with old friends," she continued with a spark in her dark eyes.

"You only left that message the day before yesterday," Debbie pointed out. But then again, a lot could happen in two days. A lot could happen in twenty-four hours. Things like meeting Sophia's brother at a hotel and spending half the night making love with him.

"Which doesn't answer the question. Did anything happen on karaoke night?"

"Karaoke night?" she echoed, feeling like so much time had already passed since then.

Sophia frowned as she crossed her arms over her pregnant belly. "You chickened out, didn't you?"

"I did not!" she protested. "I went and I even sang a couple of songs! I had a great time and—"

Drew had kissed her good-night.

She'd had a great time that night because Drew had shown up. She'd sang those songs because Drew had encouraged her. He believed in her, and that had made her want to believe in herself....

"You met someone!" Sophia exclaimed as Debbie's voice trailed off.

"I— No. No, I didn't meet anyone."

Guilt twisted Debbie's gut for not being completely honest with her friend. She'd known keeping a relationship with Drew secret would be difficult, but she hadn't thought of this part. The lying part. Although technically, she'd told the truth. She and Drew hadn't met that night. She'd known him her whole life.

But it's different now, isn't it? Different knowing him as a man instead of just as a friend....

"Gee, that's too bad," Sophia said in a voice far too innocent for Debbie to believe. "So I guess you don't have plans for tonight?"

"Why?" she asked, not bothering to hide her suspicion.

"Because," her friend drawled, "Kara's best friend, Olivia, is in town, and we're getting together for dinner. You should come with us."

The last thing Debbie wanted was to go out, but staying at home meant having nothing to do but relive each and every moment she'd spent in Drew's arms—something she'd already determined was not good for her heart. "Sure, I'll go. Sounds fun."

"Perfect! Why don't you wear the sweater you bought the last time we went shopping?"

Debbie's eyes narrowed. The sweater was the very same one she'd worn to the singles' meet and greet and was not something she would typically choose for a casual girls' night out. "Why would you want me to wear that?"

"Because you look amazing in it."

"When I bought it, you told me my boobs looked amazing in it."

"And they do!"

"And you want me to wear it tonight…why?"

"Because Sam might have run into Ryder Kincaid the other day and invited him along."

"Sophia!"

"What? Think about it. He's a Clearville guy, but he's been living in San Francisco for ten years, so you can hardly say you know everything about him."

"I know he's going through a divorce." Debbie had heard that much about the hometown boy's return.

"I know, but you keep saying that you're not interested in anything serious. I doubt he is, either."

"So you want me to be his rebound girl?"

"No, I want you to go out with a nice guy and have a good time." Heaving a sigh, Sophia leaned back in the chair and folded her arms over her round belly. "You know, for all your talk at Darcy's bachelorette party, I'm not so sure that a wild fling is really want you want at all."

Picking up her coffee, Debbie dropped her gaze to the

rich, warm brew—just the color of Drew's eyes—and tried
to tell herself her friend's words weren't all too true.

As Drew drove back home, his mood was at odds with
the crisp, clear fall afternoon. He'd known as he'd made
his way out to the job site that today was not a good day
to be working at the custom house. He was in the mood to
tear things down—preferably with his bare hands—and
not focused enough to keep his attention on the work next
on his schedule. Sure enough, by midday he had plenty to
tear down—pretty much the whole series of stairs leading
to the front deck. The stringer, steps and treads weren't up
to his standard, and he'd wasted time and material building them.

Three hours later, when he found himself snapping at
Rain as she nosed around his toolbox, chewed on an elec-
trical cord—one that thankfully wasn't plugged in—stole
his one of his leather gloves for the third time and basically acted exactly the way a puppy should act, he knew
it was time to call it a day.

Fortunately, thanks to her happy-go-lucky personality, she willingly forgave him for his bad mood and had
burned off enough energy to ride back on the seat next to
him with her head tucked against his thigh.

The hell of it was, he should have been in a great mood,
an awesome mood, after the previous night. He was more
ticked off than he wanted to admit at the way Debbie had
snuck out of the hotel room like they'd done something
wrong. It was one thing to keep their relationship secret;
treating it like something to be ashamed of was something else.

He'd agreed to the no-strings clause in their affair. He'd
orchestrated the night at the bar, doing all he could to ful-

fill her fantasy of a stranger sweeping her off her feet, because she wasn't interested in an ordinary guy like him.

But this morning, he'd thought—what? That Debbie would change her mind about what she wanted...just because he'd changed his? Maybe, Drew admitted, feeling like a fool. At the very least, he'd expected to wake with her in his arms and to spend some time together before they had to head back to Clearville and the real world Debbie found so mundane. What he sure as hell hadn't expected was to wake up alone.

And that—*sucked,* was the first word that came to mind, but it was more than that. Lifting his hand from Rain's silky fur, he rubbed at the ache in his chest. It flat-out hurt, but that was his problem, wasn't it? Debbie was simply playing by the rules—a secret affair away from town, out of sight of friends and family. He was the one who already wanted to change the game.

As if sensing his mood, Rain sat up with her front paws on his denim-clad thigh and licked the side of his face. "Thanks, Rain," he said with a sigh, "but you're not the girl who can kiss it and make it better."

A few minutes later, he arrived home. With the puppy trotting at his heels, he led the way into the kitchen over to the puppy's water bowl. He'd just grabbed a beer for himself when his cell phone rang. A picture of his sister flashed across the screen. "Hey, Sophia. How's it going?"

"Drew! Oh, good. I'm so glad I caught you."

Sophia's chipper voice took him back to when they were kids, and he couldn't help using her childhood nickname as he asked, "What's up, Fifi?"

Ignoring his use of the despised nickname, she demanded, "Tell me you don't have plans for tonight."

"Why do I not have plans for tonight?"

"Because…Kara's best friend is in town, and I thought it would be fun if we all went out together."

"Forget it, Sophia," Drew protested.

"What? I've seen pictures of her and she's really pretty. And besides that, from everything Kara says, she's nice and funny and smart."

"I'm sure she is, but I'm not interested in any of your matchmaking."

"What matchmaking? It's going out with a friend of the family."

"It's a setup, and not a very good one. Doesn't she live in San Diego?"

"That doesn't mean you two can't hang out while she's here. And if things work out…"

She left the unspoken words dangling, but he refused to take the bait.

"Oh, come on! Say yes! I don't want her to feel weird being the only one there who's not part of a couple. Not that it makes you a couple if you show up. And of course Debbie and Ryder aren't a couple, either, though my fingers are crossed…."

"Wait! What did you say?" He'd almost turned out his sister's matchmaking ramblings until that last part. The untouched beer clunked against the counter. "What was that about Debbie and Ryder?"

"Sam invited him, and I thought it would be the perfect opportunity for Debbie and Ryder to get reacquainted."

"Jeez, Soph! His divorce isn't even final yet!" Yeah, like *that* was his only objection.

"No, but it will be soon, and since Debbie's not looking for anything serious, I thought he'd be someone she could go out and have a good time with."

"And Debbie—" He cleared his throat. "She agreed?"

"Sure. Just like you should agree to go out with Olivia. Come on. It'll be fun!"

"Right. Fun." Drew could think of a lot of words to describe the upcoming night, but that would not be one of them.

Debbie had tried to get out of the "date that wasn't a date," but the more she argued with Sophia, the closer she came to blurting out the truth about her and Drew. And not just the truth that they'd slept together but the whole truth—that she was terrified she was falling in love with him. And once she spoke those words out loud—even if it was just to Drew's sister—there would be no going back. Her feelings would be out there and she'd no longer be able to deny them. Not to herself and, she feared, not to Drew, either.

She had put her foot down on a few points, though. Ryder didn't need to pick her up. After all, they were meeting at the bar and grill only a block away from her shop. And Sophia would not go out of her way to force the two of them together. This was simply a group of friends having dinner together and not a date.

Sophia reluctantly agreed, but Debbie still found herself seated next to Ryder Kincaid. That she truly did believe was more by default than by design. They were simply the only two single people in the group.

While she wouldn't call the atmosphere romantic, their corner of the bar was dimly lit. Most of the illumination was provided by a few neon signs, the flash of the large-screen televisions, a chandelier made out of empty beer bottles, and the love-struck couples were taking advantage. Sophia was cuddled up to her husband, Jake, and Kara was seated next to Sam. The engaged pair had their heads bent together—maybe trying to hear each other over the mix of laughter, music and sound from the TVs, but somehow Debbie doubted the noise even penetrated their own private world. She had yet to meet Kara's friend, Olivia, and thought perhaps the other woman was running late.

"So..." Ryder began, and Debbie turned her attention to the man at her side. Wearing black trousers and a button-down black silk shirt, part of his San Francisco wardrobe no doubt, he leaned back in his chair and raised a questioning eyebrow. "How hard did Sam have to twist your arm to get you to come tonight?"

"Oh, it wasn't Sam. It was—" Debbie cut off the words, feeling her face heat as she realized what she'd just admitted.

But Ryder merely laughed, a bit of the teenager she remembered from high school coming back. He had been two grades ahead of Debbie, but she still remembered how he used to walk the halls like he owned them—star quarterback, prom king and half of Clearville High's golden couple. Ten years was a long time, and Debbie had expected him to have changed. But despite the familiar reddish-brown hair and sharp green eyes, she saw little of the carefree boy she recalled thanks to the shadows in those eyes and the new lines bracketing the sides of his mouth.

"What I meant was that Sophia is the one who invited me tonight, not Sam."

"Either way, I'm glad you came. I'd be feeling like a fifth wheel for sure in this group," he said, tilting his head toward the couple on the opposite side of the table. "And Sam was right about me needing to get out."

"What are your plans now that you've moved back?" she asked, careful not to stick her foot in her mouth again by bringing up his soon-to-be ex, Brittany, or the life he'd left behind.

"I'm going to be working with Drew Pirelli for now."

"Really? He didn't— I mean, I hadn't heard that."

"Well, it's not official since a remodeling job hasn't come up yet, but I have some appointments lined up next week for job estimates."

They spoke for a few more minutes about the remodeling jobs he would handle while Drew concentrated on the custom building when Ryder glanced over her shoulder. "There's my boss man now."

Startled, Debbie followed his gaze to the doorway leading to another area of the bar where patrons could play darts or a game of pool. Her heart skipped a beat when she saw Drew and then plummeted toward the floor as she noticed the brunette at his side.

The woman was overdressed for the small-town bar scene in a burgundy wrap dress that highlighted her slender curves. With her curly hair caught up in a messy twist and a pair of dark-framed glasses perched on her upturned nose, she had the sexy professor look down to a science. Wearing faded jeans and a navy T-shirt stretched across his wide shoulders, Drew looked that much more masculine, that much more ruggedly handsome in contrast to the beautiful woman laughing in response to his teasing smile.

"I take it that's Olivia," Debbie said, barely able to push the words past the lump in her throat.

"Yeah. Seems we're not the only setup tonight."

Catching the last bit of their conversation, Sophia leaned across the table. "I think Olivia is just perfect for Drew."

As they neared the table, Drew's gaze locked on Debbie. But while shock was still flooding her veins like ice water, he didn't appear the least bit surprised to see her seated with Ryder.

"I think they're really hitting it off. Isn't that great?" her friend gushed.

"Oh, sure. Great."

"So." Sam shot a knowing grin at his older brother. "Did Olivia kick your, um, butt in pool?"

Drew clapped him on the shoulder as he walked by. "Ran the table on me."

As Sam hooted with laughter, the brunette held up her hands. "I'm telling you guys—it's all about geometry and physics."

Debbie picked up her glass and stabbed at the ice with her straw. *More like chemistry.* She could just imagine Drew watching the slender brunette's every move as she bent over the pool table. Any guilt she felt for agreeing to go out—even as part of a group—with Ryder was quickly burned away by jealousy that Drew was there with Olivia.

"Debbie, this is my friend, Olivia Roberts. She's one of the professors at the college where I used to teach and my best friend." Kara made the introduction as Drew pulled out a chair for the other woman and then claimed the seat right next to Debbie for himself.

Leaning around Drew, the brunette greeted Debbie with a warm smile. "I've been looking forward to meeting you and stopping by your bakery. Drew says you're the best."

Debbie's gaze shot to the man next to her. He'd talked to Olivia about her?

His dark eyes captured hers, and she couldn't look away. Couldn't do anything but recall the look in those same eyes as he'd watched her come apart in his arms. "Totally addicting," he murmured now. "One taste, and I was hooked."

Hoping the sudden rush of heat to her face didn't give her away, she tore her attention away from Drew and forced herself to return Olivia's smile. "Nice to meet you."

She wasn't sure how long she sat at the table, pretending to enjoy the appetizers being passed around as she sipped at her soda. A cheer went up from the raucous crowd, but the noise, like the various games on the large-screen televisions, hardly penetrated. She could barely focus on what she and Ryder were talking about, uncertain and yet unconcerned if her responses even made sense.

All she could do was watch Drew out of the corner of her eye and wait. Wait for him to realize how pretty Olivia was. How much smarter and funnier and more interesting than Debbie was.

But as the night went on, she realized Drew had maneuvered his chair closer to hers. Close enough where his knee brushed against the outside of her thigh, robbing her of her breath while he casually participated in the conversations around them.

The first time, Debbie thought it might have been an accident. With eight people crowded around the two small tables they'd pushed together, the seating was cramped. By the fourth or fifth time, she knew he'd purposely made each move. Even through two layers of denim, she could feel the heat from his body, and it was impossible not to remember their legs tangling together with nothing in between....

Reaching for her glass, she gulped down a large swallow of diet soda, but it did little to cool last night's memories or the desire burning through her veins right then. And when Drew pressed his leg closer and *left* it there, she couldn't take it another second. After setting the glass aside, she slid her hand beneath the table and immediately realized her mistake. Because the second she touched his thigh, she was the one who couldn't pull away.

The shape and size and strength of the muscle beneath the warm, faded-to-soft denim fascinated her. Her intention to push him away evaporated as her fingertips found the inside seam of his jeans. Her nails scraped along the raised stitching as she inched higher. Drew tensed, and she thought she might have heard him mutter a curse beneath his breath before he reached down and stopped her upward progress. But instead of removing her hand, he held her palm pressed against the rock-hard muscle, teasing and tormenting them both.

Desire heated her veins, almost hot enough to burn away the reminder that Drew's "date" was sitting on his other side. *Almost.*

Some of that heat turned to anger as she pulled her hand from his grasp. "If you'll excuse me for a minute."

Her chair leg caught on Drew's as she tried to push away from the table, locking her in place. She had to wait for him to slide back before she could try to escape. She'd barely made it to her feet before he stopped her. A simple touch on her arm and *everything* stopped—her breath, her heart, the entire world around her.

She jerked back, stumbling against the stupid chair that seemed out to get her—and might have fallen if not for Drew. He caught her by the shoulders, pulling her close, just as he had in the hotel room the night before. She sucked in a quick breath, his familiar scent only adding fuel to her memories, and she could see the desire reflected in his dark eyes....

"Sorry." She forced a shaky laugh, hoping anyone watching too closely would mistake the color rushing to her face for embarrassment. "I'll be right back."

She hurried from the table, Drew's watchful gaze dogging her every step.

"Is it just me or is something up with Debbie?" Sophia asked Kara, almost shouting over the noise in the bar. Once Debbie had rushed off, Sam had challenged Jake to a game of pool, Ryder had gone for drinks and Drew had slipped way to make a phone call, leaving Sophia, Kara and Olivia alone at the table. "She hasn't been herself all evening."

"I haven't really seen her since Darcy's wedding." The blonde pulled a guilty face. "Sam and I have been busy with plans for our own wedding, and then the past few days, I've been spending time with Olivia," she added with a smile at her best friend.

Only then did Sophia notice how the brunette was eyeing them both with eyebrows raised above the frame of her glasses. "You all really don't see it?" she asked.

"See what, Liv?" Kara asked.

"It's Drew."

"Sorry...what's Drew?" Sophia asked.

Olivia gave a quiet laugh. "The *something* that's up with your friend—it's Drew."

"You mean like there's something going on between the two of them?" Sophia gave an incredulous laugh. "As much as I like the idea of my best friend getting together with my brother, I'm afraid you're wrong, Olivia. Debbie and Drew are friends—just like she's friends with Jake and Sam."

The brunette shook her head. "Debbie wasn't avoiding looking at Jake and Sam all evening. And didn't you notice the way she practically jumped out of her skin when Drew touched her? Plus, he talked about her the whole time we were playing pool. I'm telling you, something's going on."

"But if that's true," Kara asked with a frown, "why would they keep it a secret? They'd have to know how happy everyone would be to find out they're a couple."

"It's hard for you to picture the two of them as a couple because you're so used to seeing them as friends. Maybe Debbie and Drew are still getting adjusted to the idea, as well."

"I don't know," Sophia murmured doubtfully. "Deb-

bie's been pretty adamant about not going out with Clearville guys."

Olivia lifted a slender shoulder. "Another reason why
she might be keeping quiet about their relationship."

"If you're right—" Sophia couldn't stop the huge grin
from spreading over her face. "My best friend and my
brother… I've always felt that Debbie was like a big sister
to me, and now we could be sisters-in-law!"

"Whoa! Moving a little fast here, don't you think?"
Kara asked. "We're not even sure they're together yet."

"You're right. So what should we do?"

"Well," Olivia said wryly, "for starters, you should probably stop setting them up with other people."

Sophia threw her hands up in exasperation. "How was
I supposed to know?"

Drew didn't know if anyone bought his excuse of needing to make a phone call seconds after Debbie disappeared
toward the restrooms. Ryder had already headed to the
bar, and Jake and Sam had gone off to play pool. Sophia
and Kara were talking over each other in a conversation
that skipped from baby names to bridesmaids' dresses to
nursery decorations and honeymoon locations so quickly,
even trying his hardest not to listen made his head swim.
But Olivia had given him a studied glance as he pushed
away from the table—like he was some kind of equation
she was trying to solve.

Good luck with that, he thought with a snort. He couldn't
even figure out what he was thinking or feeling or doing
from one second to the next. He still couldn't believe he'd
let Sophia set him up, even if he had his own reasons for
showing up at the bar that night.

He had to admit, though, that Sophia had been right
about Olivia. She really was pretty. Behind the dark-

framed glasses, her eyes were a rich, warm brown, and she had a sprinkling of freckles like gold dust across her upturned nose and fair cheeks. "First Sam and now you," she had commented after Sophia made the introduction. "I can see why a single woman would consider moving to your hometown."

She was smart and funny and charming. But as cute as her upturned nose was, it didn't crinkle when she smiled. And as much as he liked the freckles, somehow he'd missed the sight of a dimple in her cheek when she laughed, and her eyes couldn't nail him to the spot with just a glance because they were brown. Brown and not blue.

Thankfully, Olivia was savvy enough to realize his head—not to mention his heart—wasn't in the game. Hadn't stopped her from wiping the floor with him in pool, but he figured he'd deserved that.

The music and laughter faded a little as he stepped into the narrow hallway leading to the restrooms and the door to the back parking lot. He felt like a stalker, lurking outside the women's restroom. More so when Debbie stepped into the darkened hall and gave a startled gasp. "Drew!" Her blue eyes grew even wider when he took her hand and led the way out back. "What are you doing?"

The cool night air and silence was a relief from the crowded bar, and he pulled in a deep breath. A few lights along the back of the lot illuminated the cars, but moonlight provided most of the glow. Debbie's eyes glittered like jewels and her hair looked more silver than gold, but still as soft as ever cascading over her shoulders. She hadn't dressed up for the evening—something that pleased him probably more than it should—but she still looked amazing to him in faded jeans and a long-sleeved turquoise sweater.

"I wanted to talk to you. To see if you're okay."

He'd never had a one-night stand and wasn't the type

of guy to sleep with a woman and then walk away without a backward glance. Not that he had been the one to walk away.

Debbie had.

She reacted to his concern as if he'd accused her of some kind of weakness, drawing her shoulders back and lifting her head. "I'm fine. I just—didn't expect to see you until—"

"Next week," he finished, trying to ignore the annoyance still buzzing like a relentless mosquito inside him at the memory of the note she'd left behind.

She cleared her throat. "Right. Next week. But since you're here, there are some things we didn't have a chance to talk about after last night."

"The way I remember it, we didn't talk at all."

Her gaze quickly cut away from his. Was she simply embarrassed, or could he hope that she regretted sneaking out the way she had? "Yes, well, I didn't think this conversation would be necessary, but now—" She waved a hand in an all-encompassing gesture. "Obviously it is."

Since Drew didn't find anything obvious about the whole conversation, he asked, "What exactly is it that we need to talk about?"

Debbie took a deep breath. "Seeing other people."

Her words his like a sucker punch to his gut. That was what Debbie wanted to discuss? She wanted to see other people? He'd convinced himself she wasn't really interested in Ryder. That she couldn't be—not after the night the two of them had shared. It was the only way he'd kept from decking the guy when he'd seen his newest employee sitting next to Debbie.

Had he just been fooling himself in thinking the date had been a harmless setup by his sister? Fooling himself in thinking that giving Debbie what she wanted—a no-strings affair—would eventually lead her to realize she wanted more?

"If this is going to work," she continued, "we need to have some—ground rules."

Rules. Probably something along the line of Drew *not* punching the other guy in the face. Uncurling the fists he'd unconsciously made, he said, "Go on."

"As long as we're—together, I expect us to be monogamous." Finishing in a rush, she added, "I don't see how this can work if that's going to be a problem for you."

Relief washed over him, draining away the tension before a feeling of irritation crept in. "For me? You're the one bringing up the idea of seeing other people in the first place!"

"And you're the one who's here with Olivia!" she shot back.

Crossing his arms over his chest, he met her angry gaze and tried to hide a smile. If she was as pissed off about seeing him with Olivia as he'd been about seeing *her* with Ryder—somehow that made his own anger and jealousy drain away. Looked as though Debbie was going to be the first to tie some strings around their no-strings affair. That worked perfectly for Drew, who already felt so tangled up in knots about the woman in front of him he didn't think he'd ever work his way free.

Still, he had to point out, "The chair next to you wasn't exactly empty, sweetheart."

She had the grace to duck her head, and some of the tension eased from her shoulders. "It's not like I'm here with Ryder. I'd already agreed to go out tonight before your sister sprung the news on me that he'd be here, too."

"I know. She set both of us up."

"So you already knew I'd be here tonight?"

"Why do you think I came? And don't say because of

Olivia. Nice as she is, she's not the woman I want, and I don't want to wait until next weekend to have you in my arms again."

For a split second, he thought she might argue, but instead she breathlessly asked, "What about your family?"

"We'll tell them we both have early mornings and need to head out."

When they went back inside, though, their excuses were barely needed. Only Kara and Sophia were still sitting at the table, and Debbie had just made note of the time when Sophia exclaimed, "Oh, you're right! It is getting late, isn't it? We're all about ready to head out, too." She glanced over at Kara, who quickly nodded in agreement as Sophia reached for her purse beneath the table. "Drew, you wouldn't mind walking Debbie home, would you?"

Narrowing his eyes, he looked at his sister, who gazed back—all wide-eyed and innocent. *Yeah, right...* Still, he knew better than to look a perfect excuse in the mouth. "Of course I will."

"Um, what about—" Debbie glanced toward Ryder's empty chair.

"Olivia and Ryder challenged Jake and Sam to one last game of pool before we go," Kara explained.

"Don't worry. We'll let them know you two had to head out early."

"Thanks, Sophia."

"Oh, sure!" His little sister flashed a wink his way. "Told you tonight would be fun."

He had a feeling Sophia was enjoying herself a little *too* much. Still, if she had figured out what was going on between him and Debbie, it felt good to know she was on his side. Leaning down, he brushed a kiss across her forehead. "Thanks again."

Catching his arm before he could pull away, she was

still smiling as she said, "She's my best friend. Break her heart, and I break you."

He managed a smile of his own, his teasing words all too serious as he asked, "What happens if she breaks mine?"

Chapter Ten

Debbie cut the engine on her small VW but hesitated in getting out of the car and entering the Pirellis' large farmhouse. Terra-cotta flowerpots filled with bright-faced pansies and purple snapdragons marked each step on the way up to the wraparound porch, and a fall-inspired wreath made of silk mums and decorated with miniature pumpkins added a splash of red and gold and orange to the front door. The place looked as homey and welcoming as ever, and it was ridiculous to feel nervous.

She couldn't count the number of times she'd been invited over for dinners, birthdays and holidays. But tonight was different. Tonight she worried Drew's parents were going to take one look at her and know what had happened between her and their middle son at the hotel in Redfield... and at her place the weekend before.

When she'd entered into this secret affair with Drew, she'd never imagined inviting him back to her apartment.

Bad enough he already haunted her thoughts when she lay in her bed alone. How would she ever sleep again once she'd experienced sleeping there with him beside her? But from the moment Drew admitted he couldn't wait to have her in his arms again, she hadn't been thinking.

The walk from the bar had seemed to take forever, and the back door of the bakery had barely closed before Drew reached for her. Unlike at the hotel when he'd seduced and romanced her, giving, taking and teasing, that night his kisses had demanded. He'd left her desperate and wanting, begging for more, and she'd been the one to lead them to the narrow staircase to her small apartment. Their clothes had littered every other step along the way, and they'd barely made it to the bed before he was inside her....

She didn't know how she could look at him without every heated memory reflecting on her face, and she already regretted agreeing to come. Sophia had been way too persuasive and she— Well, she hadn't been able to think of an adequate excuse for skipping—other than blurting out the news that she was sleeping with her friend's brother.

So now she was sitting in her car in front of Drew's parents' house, feeling as guilty and self-conscious as if the two of them had been caught making out in the backseat.

"You're being ridiculous," she scolded herself. And despite her fears, a glance in the rearview mirror proved that her attraction to Drew wasn't written all over her face.

She could do this.

"Debbie! Good, you're here!" Sophia greeted her as she opened the front door to Debbie's knock. "And you brought dessert!"

"What else?" she asked somewhat wryly as she balanced the cake box in one hand.

"I'll take this to the kitchen. We're about ready to eat."

"Am I late?" she asked as Sophia led the way through

the living room that held the same slightly worn and comfortable couches and chairs from her last visit, but the family portrait above the fireplace was new. The previous photo had been taken a few years ago. The updated one included the newest members of the family—Jake, Darcy, Kara and Sam's son, Timmy.

Drew's image smiled out from behind the glass, and Debbie wondered if it was only her imagination that his expression seemed a little wry. *Last man standing.* The picture seemed to emphasize the teasing comment she'd heard at Nick's wedding as Drew was the only unattached member of his family.

Saving the best for last, she thought with a small smile of her own.

"No, you're right on time. But you know how it is around here." Sophia rolled her eyes. "The guys are always starving."

With a nod toward the formal dining room, Sophia said, "Go ahead and have a seat. My mom's got everything under control in the kitchen."

"Are you sure I can't help?"

Vanessa Pirelli stepped through the swinging door from the kitchen in time to hear Debbie's question. She held a large pan of bubbling, mouthwatering lasagna in her oven-mitted hands. The scent of oregano, garlic, basil, rich tomato sauce and decadent cheese filled the air. "Sophia's right. I've got this, and you know what they say about too many cooks spoiling the lasagna."

"I don't think anything could spoil your lasagna, Vanessa."

"Hmm, except maybe your chocolate cake. This group would just as soon eat dessert first."

On those words, an echo from the night at the hotel, Debbie stepped into the dining room. Her gaze immediately locked on Drew. He was helping his dad move dishes around on the table—one holding steaming garlic bread, another a tossed salad and smaller bowls filled with dressing, croutons and grated parmesan cheese—to make way for the main dish. At his mother's statement, he looked up and the subtle grin he shot her was enough to weaken her knees.

"Have a seat, Debbie. There's a spot for you right beside Drew."

He rolled his eyes at his mother's pleased statement even as he pulled out the chair. Debbie fought a smile and shot him a warning look as she sat down. His grin only widened in response. Bending low as she slid her chair closer to the table, he whispered, "Try to keep your hands to yourself this time."

"You started it," she retorted with a benign grin.

A shiver raced down her spine when his heated, sidelong glance reminded her just how well he'd finished what he'd started, too.

Pirelli family dinners had always been crowded, noisy affairs, and that was before adding Jake, Darcy, Kara and Timmy to the mix. The result was a constant passing of food and a half a dozen conversations taking place at once. It was completely different from the quiet meals she used to share with her mother at their round, two-person table. As much as she missed her mother, Debbie loved the laughter and chaos of the big group.

Vince Pirelli, an older, heavier version of his dark-haired sons, kept up a running dialogue about sports with the guys while fielding "guess what, Grandpa?" questions from Timmy, most of which revolved around the boy's love of dinosaurs and his excitement over his Halloween costume and trick-or-treating the next weekend.

Vanessa, meanwhile, engaged the rest of the table with

updates on out-of-town relatives as well as local news. "I heard Anne Novak is moving to Colorado to be with her family," she said to Debbie as she passed the garlic bread.

Debbie nodded. Anne had been her "neighbor" for the past few years, running a used bookstore in the space beside the bakery. "She's so excited to be closer to her grandkids."

"I'm sure she is. Still, I know you're going to miss her."

"I will. She's been a good friend, and I enjoyed having the bookstore next door. I hope another business moves in soon."

"Oh, wouldn't it be great if a clothing boutique moved in?" Darcy asked.

"Right. Because it's not like you don't already have enough clothes," Nick said to his fashionable wife.

"Daddy, you can never have enough clothes," his eight-year-old daughter, Maddie, chimed in.

The laugher almost drowned out Nick's groan.

After a few minutes of the women debating what other new businesses they'd like to see, Drew said, "I think you should take over the space, Debbie."

Barely managing to swallow a bite of lasagna without choking, she sputtered, "Me?"

"Sure. Think of how you could branch out and do so much more with the extra space—add some sandwiches and salads to the menu. You could turn the bakery into a café."

Debbie caught her breath at the unexpected suggestion. Pressure built in her chest at his words, along with the sting of tears behind her eyes, and she didn't even know why. Okay, so years ago she'd had hopes of going to culinary school and opening a restaurant. For Drew to bring up that long-denied dream now, well, it hurt.

She felt as though he'd dismissed the past four years

she'd spent working to make the bakery a success. The hard work she'd done to *forget* that she'd once wanted something bigger than the bakery.... But that was before the heartbreaking reality of her mother's illness had crashed down on the both of them.

Her voice sharpened by the jagged memories, she echoed, "More than the bakery? Because you don't think that's enough?"

His eyebrows rose slightly at her tone, but his voice was calm as he asked, "I don't know, Debbie. Is it?"

It had to be enough, because what else was there? She couldn't turn her back on the bakery any more than she could have turned her back on her mother to follow her own dreams.

"The bakery is more than enough to keep me busy, and speaking of which—" she pushed back her chair and glanced around the table "—is everyone ready for dessert? I brought everyone's favorite—double chocolate!"

A loud cheer went up, lead mostly by Sam's four-year-old, Timmy, who started a chant of, "Cake, cake, cake!"

Standing, she turned toward the kitchen, relief inching through her as she thought she might make good on her escape. But Drew, ever the gentleman, stood as well, effectively blocking her exit.

"Debbie..." He placed a hand on her arm, and something about the look in his dark eyes grabbed hold of her heart and wouldn't let go....

But she still pulled away from his touch and brightly promised, "I'll be right back with that cake!"

"So was it my imagination, or did I see some sparks flying?" Sam asked Drew. After dinner and dessert, the guys had split off on one side of the living room with the women on the other as Darcy regaled them with her tales of love at first sight—for every shoe store and ultrachic boutique she'd set foot in during the trip to Paris. She'd also brought back gifts for her friends, and they were all currently oohing and aahing over the silver frame she'd given to Sophia with her soon-to-arrive baby in mind.

"Sparks?" Drew echoed, his gaze automatically shifting toward Debbie. She was laughing at Darcy's effusive storytelling, looking happy and relaxed with no sign of the tension twisting between them earlier.

It had been a mistake to push. He'd known that as soon as he'd opened his mouth. Debbie had a stubborn streak to go along with her independence, and there was no way he could force her in a direction she didn't want to go. Which should have kept him from talking to her in front of his entire family. He didn't know why he'd tried except that it still bothered him that he'd never questioned her reasons for not changing the bakery. Never wondered if stepping into her mother's footsteps was enough to make her happy.

"You and Olivia."

Drew barely stopped himself from repeating the woman's name. If he kept mindlessly echoing everything his brothers said, they were bound to notice. But his distraction wasn't thanks to Kara's best friend.

"Sam says you went to dinner together when she was here in town."

Olivia had gone back to San Diego, but Nick was clearly getting caught up on what had been happening while he was on his honeymoon. "A whole group of us went out to dinner. It wasn't a date."

"It could have been if you'd ask her out after that," Sam pointed out. "I gotta say, no one thought you'd be the last of us to get married."

"That's because no one ever thought you'd get married at all."

"All it took was meeting the right girl." Sam's expression softened as he glanced across the room at his fiancée.

It still felt weird to see his little brother so in love, and a hell of a lot more like jealousy than Drew wanted to admit. He might have thought Sam, who had a reputation for avoiding commitment and never taking life too seriously, would have some major doubts about settling down with one woman for the rest of his life. But Sam being Sam, he seemed to take the upcoming wedding as one big adventure, with his typical exuberance and good humor.

He looked over at Nick. "When you know, you know. Right, Nick?"

"Right, Sam," he echoed with a grin. He sobered slightly as he met Drew's gaze. "It's like suddenly your eyes are open and you realize the woman you've been waiting for your whole life is standing right in front of you. And you know."

Drew swallowed as his brother's soft-spoken statement lodged in his chest. The words fit Debbie perfectly. He'd known her her whole life and that entire time, she'd been right there. Right in front of him, and all he had to do was open his eyes.

He'd always cared for Debbie, but his feelings were—different now. And not just because of the sex. He'd been in enough relationships to know that sex didn't necessarily lead to love. More often than not, the opposite was true. Sex came first and nothing followed. Making love with Debbie had made him realize just how empty those previous relationships had been.

"I'll tell you what I know," he ground out once he was sure he could speak around the lump in his throat. "Olivia's a great girl, but she's not the one. Just as well, since I'm not looking to settle down."

His brothers exchanged a look and then burst into laughter. He couldn't remember the last time he'd made them laugh so hard…especially when he hadn't said anything so damn funny. "What?" he demanded, irritated by their reaction and just irritated in general.

"Dude, you are so ready to settle down. You were like born ready."

Nick nodded his agreement. "Just look at the house you're building."

"It's an investment," Drew argued, wondering if he could sound any more lame.

"It's a home for a family," his older brother stressed.

"That—" Sam gave a soft snort "—or a really big doghouse."

"Rain will have plenty of room to roam," Nick agreed with a smug smile, clearly still feeling he'd somehow conned Drew into taking the puppy off his hands.

"Think whatever you want," he said testily, "but the only walk I'm going to be taking down the aisle is as your best man, Sam."

Nick's gaze swung toward their younger brother. "You told me I was going to be best man."

"He's just saying that. I haven't decided yet. You're both my brothers." Sam's wide shoulders lifted in a shrug. "How am I supposed to choose?"

"Easy. You pick me. I'm the oldest anyway."

"What? And that means you automatically get to be my best man or just that you automatically get to tell me what to do?"

"Both!"

Leaving them to the argument that had been going on since the minute Sam had gotten engaged, Drew used the opportunity to slip away. He was heading toward the kitchen when another outburst caught his attention—this time from the female corner of the living room.

A catcall and a few whoops went up as Debbie held a clinging black negligee against her body. Drew's mouth went dry. It didn't matter that the only thing he could see through the sheer lace was the cream-colored sweater and floral leggings she'd been wearing all evening. He knew what was beneath those leggings and that sweater and could imagine what her creamy skin would look like draped in black lace as easily as he could picture himself slowly stripping the negligee away from her gorgeous curves.

"As soon as I saw that nightgown, I thought of our conversation the night of my bachelorette party and knew I had to get for you...just in case."

Just in case Debbie found a handsome stranger to sweep her off her feet. Darcy might not have known Drew had overheard that conversation, but Debbie did. He waited, caught in a mix of anticipation and dread, for her blue eyes to swing his way. And when they did—

Jerking his gaze away, he stalked off into his parents' kitchen. He doubted his mom had any hard liquor on hand, but maybe he could stick his head in the freezer and at least cool off part of his body. Even if it wasn't the half ready to explode. He'd downed a glass of ice water and was going back for a refill when the door behind him swung open and Debbie stepped inside. Just like that his heart rate jumped into high gear and his blood heated. At least she'd left the nightgown back in the living room.

"Drew—"

"Debbie—"

They both broke off with a short laugh, some of the tension easing as they spoke at the same time. "Ladies first."

"I'm sorry about snapping at you earlier," she blurted out. "It's been a long time since I seriously thought about doing something other than running the bakery. I never told anyone about applying to culinary school. No one except you, that is."

"You didn't tell Bonnie?" The two of them had been so close, Drew couldn't imagine Debbie keeping such a big secret from her mother.

"When I first applied, I didn't really think I'd get in."

"But once you did—"

"Once I did, my mom's cancer had already come back. Telling her about the school, about what I was giving up to stay with her, would have only made her feel bad."

"Just like me bringing it up again made you feel bad," he guessed.

Debbie ducked her head, but not before he saw the lingering hurt shining in her eyes. Swearing beneath his breath at his own stupidity, he pulled her into his arms and felt the rest of the tension leave his body when she nestled willingly into his chest.

"I'm sorry, sweetheart. And I swear that wasn't my intention. I just thought this might be an opportunity for you to branch out, to go after what you really want." He hated the idea of her settling for less. She deserved a career that left her fulfilled instead of empty. And an open, honest relationship instead of one she felt the need to hide.

Or was that just what *he* wanted?

"I know, and that's why I'm sorry for reacting the way I did. But I'm finally at a point where I can relax a little. Where I have a bit of freedom to go out and have a good time and—"

"Find some tall, dark stranger to have a secret fling with?" Drew filled in.

Still holding her, his chin resting against the softness of her blond hair, he could feel as well as hear her laughter. The vibrations settled into his chest, into his heart, the same way Debbie had.

"Some tall, dark, *handsome* stranger," she stressed. "I don't want to give that up...." Lifting her head, she met his gaze as she hesitantly asked, "Do you?"

"Give it up? Not a chance." He wanted more, not less. "I just don't see why it has to be one or the other."

"Because that's the way it's always been," Debbie confessed. "The bakery comes first and everything else a distant or nonexistent second. And sometimes I get so tired of it that I just want to quit, but how do you quit when you're the boss and it's your business and my mom— She would be so disappointed in me if she knew I felt this way."

"I think you're right."

His words stabbed at her, and her startled gaze flew to his. "That's not what you're supposed to say. You're supposed to tell me I'm wrong and my mother would never hate for me for feeling like this."

"Okay, *now* you're wrong. Your mother would never hate you, but I do think she'd be disappointed that you aren't following your own dreams. That you aren't doing what *you* love. I can't imagine that she would have left you the bakery if she didn't think you'd be happy."

"*She* was," Debbie admitted. "She was so happy to run the bakery, and sometimes I wonder what's wrong with me that it's not enough...that I want more. But you already figured that out, didn't you? And I jumped all over you because just hearing you suggest it made me feel so guilty."

"There's nothing wrong with you, and there's nothing wrong with wanting more. With wanting...everything."

Gazing into his dark eyes, Debbie almost forgot to breathe. She could so easily get lost in the caring and compassion she saw there. In the undefined *everything* he was promising. "I, um, do want to make some changes at the bakery. Now that I've hired Kayla, it's given me time to focus on expanding the menu—"

"Like with the fall cupcakes," he said, the deepening of his voice telling her he was remembering more than tasting the pumpkin spice and chocolate cakes.

"Exactly. And I—I've done some more promotion for wedding cakes. It's not totally new for me. I've made several over the years, but just locally for friends and acquaintances. It's never been a big part of the business."

"Everyone raved about the cakes you made for Darcy and Nick and for Sophia and Jake."

"Well, I don't know that everyone did—"

"Then you just didn't hear them, because believe me, sweetheart, people couldn't stop talking about how beautiful they looked and how great they tasted—kind of like the woman who made them."

Sputtering a laugh, Debbie said, "Well, I hope you're right—about the cakes, at least. I asked Darcy and Nick's photographer to take some extra shots of the wedding cake. As soon as I get those back I'm going to redesign my website with a page just for wedding cakes, as well as doing some advertising in bridal magazines. I'm kind of excited to see what the response might be." As she said the words, Debbie realized it was true. "It's a part of the bakery that could be all mine, you know?"

"Yeah, I get that. It's like the house I'm building. I work just as hard and pay just as much attention to detail on every house, but it still feels different knowing this one is going to be my own."

The sound of voices from the living room carried into the kitchen. "What? I'm just going for drinks."

The door swung open, but not before Debbie had a split second to step out of Drew's embrace. The platter of leftover cake sitting on the kitchen island caught her attention, and by the time Sam stepped inside with Sophia following close on his heels, she was calmly slicing the dessert. "I'm cutting the leftovers into smaller pieces. Do you both want to take some home?"

"Probably shouldn't." Sophia placed her hands on her expanding stomach. "Jake will eat it all and yet I'll be the one to end up gaining weight."

"Are you kidding?" Sam asked. "Timmy would eat cake for breakfast if we let him. Drew, pass me a couple of beers, will you?"

As he tossed Sam the cans, Sophia looked from Drew to Debbie and back again. "So what were you two talking about in here?"

"My new house," he answered before Debbie could even come up with an excuse.

"It's going to be amazing, Debbie. You should see it—" Her dark eyes lit suddenly. "In fact, that's a great idea! Drew, you should take Debbie out there and give her a tour."

"Oh, I don't know, Sophia," Debbie protested, remembering his comment that he wanted the house finished before showing off the place.

But he was already pulling his keys from the pocket of his jeans. "Let's go."

Chapter Eleven

"Are you sure you don't mind taking me to see the house?" Debbie asked as Drew climbed behind the wheel. "I remember what you said about wanting to show off the finished product."

"I figured you could maybe use a break from my family." Drew glanced over at her as he guided the oversize SUV away from the Pirellis' home.

"Are you kidding? I love your family."

"Well, then, maybe I'm the one who needed a break from them," he said wryly. "Especially if it means being alone with you."

A small shiver raced through her at his words, and she grinned as he reached over and took her hand. Too bad the cab had bucket seats with a gearshift preventing her from sliding up against him. Instead she had to settle for twining her fingers through his and feeling the pressure of his knuckles against her leg.

For a few minutes, they sat in easy silence, driving

down the highway cutting through the towering pines, until Debbie asked, "What were you, Sam and Nick talking about earlier? It looked pretty serious."

His broad shoulder lifted in a shrug. "Usual stupid stuff. Arguing over who would be Sam's best man."

She wasn't sure why, but she didn't think his explanation was 100 percent true. "You're lucky, you know, and I've always been a little envious."

"Why? Do you want to be Sam's best man?"

"Very funny. What I meant is that growing up I used to wish I had brothers and sisters. Not that I told my mom that. She wanted more kids, but it wasn't meant to be."

"I always liked your mom. I remember her sneaking me and my brothers cookies while my parents pretended not to notice. The thought that we were getting away with something made those bite-size treats taste even better."

"Forbidden fruit," she teased even as she recalled her conversation with Sophia at the bakery the other day. Was the newness and the secrecy of her relationship with Drew what made it so sweet? she wondered. But then Drew moved his thumb, stroking her skin through the thin fabric of her leggings, and she couldn't imagine the rush of desire ever growing old. Couldn't imagine her feelings ever fading.

Drew pulled the SUV off the paved road and slowed to a bumpy crawl over a long, graded driveway. As they rounded a curve, Debbie glanced through the front windshield. "Oh, Drew."

When he climbed from the truck and came around to open her door, she slid from the passenger seat and got an even better look at the house he'd built. Nestled in a wooded grove, the towering pines and the fading rays of sunset were the perfect back for the beautiful house. Even though the raw, unfinished wood was still exposed, the solid shape and style of the house was apparent. The front had a traditional Craftsman porch and entry with two columns on either side of the steps. But the house spread out, far larger than the typical turn-of-the-century homes.

"It doesn't look like much yet. The siding still needs to go up and eventually the base of the columns will be covered by stone veneer. I'm planning to stain the porch and stairs to match," he said as he led the way up those same stairs.

"It's incredible," she breathed as he opened the door and ushered her inside.

"With the exposed wires and piping, sometimes it can be hard to imagine what it will look like with actual walls and floors made of something other than concrete."

Despite the typical construction dust and debris, Debbie didn't have any trouble at all picturing the home when it was finished. The foyer opened into a large great room. The far wall was almost all windows, giving a view of the mountains and trees backed up to the property. Room had been left for a large deck, and she could almost smell the scent of grilled burgers filling the air along with the sound of laughter as the Pirellis gathered in Drew's backyard.

To the right of the living room was the kitchen, a huge expanse, empty now but with plenty of room for state-of-the-art appliances. Debbie could see the outline on the bare floors, marking the location of a large center island. The open floor plan would make it possible for whoever was in the kitchen to still interact with family and guests. A formal dining room was framed in on the other side of the great room, but Debbie knew most meals would be shared around the island. Another room with the same view of the mountains was reserved for Drew's study. And then he showed her the bedrooms.

Lots of bedrooms.

"This is really a big house," she said as they stood in one of the secondary bedrooms. A child's bedroom—one that would start out as a nursery and then grow from there along with the child who slept within its walls.

Drew's child. A quietly serious, dark-haired, dark-eyed boy. Or maybe a sweetly shy daughter who would have her daddy wrapped around her little finger. She could almost hear the childish laughter filling the room.

"I figured if I was going to go through all the work of building my own place, it should include everything I want."

Everything he wanted… He'd told her that he, too, was looking for adventure and excitement when they started out on their affair, but what was that saying about actions speaking louder than words? This house, this home Drew was building with his own hands, this was the reality he truly wanted. A wife, kids, a family to go along with the dog he already owned.

He'd encouraged her to go after her dreams, but how was she supposed to encourage him to go after his when it meant letting him go? And not just losing what they had, but losing him to another woman?

The ache in her chest grew until she could barely breathe. She turned away from the room, from the image of the child who would one day sleep inside it, but Drew was right there. Waiting…watching… His gaze caught hers and something…happened. Those dreams of the future, Drew's dreams, were written in clear detail in the longing on his handsome face. The wife, the kids, the family. Only suddenly Debbie saw herself in the reflection of his dark eyes. Saw herself as his wife, his children as her children, his family as her family….

And the feeling that surrounded her wasn't one of pressure, of responsibility closing in and trapping her on every side. Instead the embrace was filled with hope, with possibility and with love.

"Follow me home?" Debbie asked as Drew pulled his SUV next to her small VW parked in his parents' driveway. Her heart was pounding as if she was asking Drew to make love to her the first time. She couldn't pretend tonight wouldn't be different. Admitting how she felt— even just to herself—would only leave her heart that much more open to Drew. She'd no longer be able to hide behind the pretense that their relationship was some kind of no-strings affair.

But looking at the heat in Drew's eyes, she couldn't help wondering if the only one she'd been fooling was herself....

"I might just beat you there."

Laughing, she was reaching for her purse when her cell phone rang. She didn't recognize the number but swiped the screen to accept the call. "Hello?"

"Debbie, this is Andrea Collins."

"Andrea, hello." Debbie hoped her voice didn't reveal her surprise. Andrea was the town's Realtor, and while Debbie knew the older woman by sight and reputation, they weren't close enough to have exchanged cell phone numbers. "How are you?"

"How am I? I'm desperate, that's how I am. I need your help."

"Help with what?" Catching her side of the conversation, Drew raised his eyebrows, but Debbie could only shrug.

"Saving a wedding and the lives of my unborn grandchildren."

"Um, okay. Wow. How can I help with that?"

"My lovely daughter is getting married. This weekend. And her husband-to-be, man that he is, gladly left all the details up to her. 'It's your day, dear. Whatever makes you happy makes me happy.'" Andrea quoted her future son-in-law's voice with a heavy dose of sarcasm. "Yeah, right."

"I take it he's not happy?"

"No, he is not. Evidently, he's allergic. To strawberries— as is half of his entire, anaphylactic family."

Starting to get a feel for where the conversation was going, Debbie said, "Let me guess. Your daughter's wedding cake has strawberries on it?"

"On it. In it. With berries carved into tiny flowers topping the whole gorgeous, inedible thing."

"Did you contact the bakery?"

"Oh, sure, as soon as we realized the problem. But it's too late. They book their weddings months in advance, and while they are very sorry for our problem, it's very much our problem and they have no solution to offer. Debbie, please, I am desperate. Caroline is my only child and she is thirty-five years old. My window of opportunity for becoming a grandmother is closing fast, and I will not have it slam shut because of a food allergy."

"I doubt your daughter and her fiancé would call off the wedding just because of the cake."

"You'd be surprised. Caroline has a serious case of cold feet. She's looking at any negative as a sign that she's not supposed to go through with this wedding, even though her fiancé, despite his allergies, is an amazing man who adores her. Please, Debbie. I tried telling my daughter we could get a cake from the grocery store, and I thought she was going to pass out. You are my last hope. I heard all about the cake you made for Nick and Darcy's wedding. I know you can do this."

After asking Andrea to send her a photo of the type

of cake her daughter had in mind, Debbie explained the trouble to Drew. "Jeez, I'm not sure who I feel more sorry for," he said, "Caroline, her fiancé or Andrea."

"I can't believe Caroline's fiancé didn't tell her about his allergy."

"Ah, give the poor guy a break. His mind was probably focused on the honeymoon."

"Not sure it was his mind," Debbie muttered, but Drew only grinned in response. He climbed from the SUV and opened the door for her. A second later, her phone beeped and an image of the cake glowed on the screen.

"Oh, wow." She'd seen her share of amazing cakes—even made a few herself—but the photo was of a masterpiece. The graduated round layers were covered in white fondant and decorated with a diamond-shaped quilted pattern. Small gold sugar pearls dotted each point, and the dreaded, delicately carved strawberries waterfalled from one level to the next. And if all that wasn't challenging enough, the tiers didn't stack one on top of the other. Instead they were offset, almost defying gravity, with an impressive height.

Even Drew let out a low whistle. "That is some cake."

"I don't think I can do this. I mean, if I had *days,* maybe, but by tomorrow? I don't know... And besides, we have... plans."

"It's only one weekend, Debbie."

"But that's just it. It's not. It's been every weekend for the past ten years," she said with a sigh. "The bakery comes first and everything else is second."

"It's not the same thing. This is your chance, sweetheart. You told me you wanted wedding cakes to be a bigger part of the business, and you know Andrea Collins. She has connections all over the place. You do this for her, and she'll be all the advertising you need."

"Yeah, and if I blow it—"

"You can do this." Lifting her hand, he held the screen and the image of the cake in front of her. "You can do *this*."

"Drew...you don't understand. I've never made a cake like that before. The cakes I've made have always stacked on top of each other with dowels or decorative pillars to support the layers above. This—this is—"

"It's a spiral staircase." He pointed to the cake. "There's a center column, just like on a staircase, and each layer of cake is like one of the treads. As long as the column is solid and secure to the base, it'll support the treads with no problem. Or in this case, the layers of cake."

He was right, Debbie realized, and even if she wouldn't have described the cake in those terms, the structures were the same. If she used a larger dowel in the center, could she attach the layers to create the same cascade effect as Caroline's original cake? "I could always add extra support beneath each of the layers, too. Ones that would go down to the base at the bottom. You'd be able to see it from the back of the cake, but not from the front."

"And you could always scale this down a little, too. This thing has—what? Seven layers? You could cut back to five and still have the same look overall."

"No, I think I could still do all seven. Because, look, if I had the layers overlap a little more, I could still use regular dowels hidden inside the cake to support the tier above. And I—I can do this, Drew."

"I never had a doubt."

"But—what about tonight? I'd have to start baking right away to give the cakes time to chill before I can decorate and stack them."

"There will be other nights. I promise you that. But

right now, it's time for you to play heroine, to ride to the rescue and save Caroline's wedding day."

Fueled by half a pot of coffee and the challenge of recreating the original wedding cake, Debbie was up at four in the morning leveling the first and largest layer of the cake. She'd baked the seven layers of chocolate cake the night before after checking with Andrea to make sure the family had no chocolate allergies to worry about. The cakes had chilled in the refrigerator while she'd grabbed a few hours' sleep, making them slightly less fragile and easier to work with.

A soft knock at the back door took her by surprise. She wasn't expecting Kayla for another hour, but it wasn't her assistant who greeted her with a smile.

"Vanessa! What are you doing here?"

"My son has called me in for reinforcement. He says you have a wedding cake to make and no time to do your usual baking, so he asked me to lend a hand." The older woman's eyes sparkled, and Debbie didn't even want to guess what Drew's mother was thinking about her son's request. "I'll be the first to admit, I've never been paid for any of the meals I've made over the years—unless you count the praise and gratitude of my hungry family—but I can say with all honesty that I am an amazing cook."

"Of course you are!" Debbie readily agreed, but she never would have thought to ask for help. "Part of me can't believe Drew did this, but the other part knows I shouldn't have expected anything less."

"He is a rather remarkable boy, if I do say so myself."

Debbie might have argued the "boy" part, but as for the rest— "I couldn't agree more."

"Now, Kayla and I are going to do the baking and run the front of the shop and finish all the prep work for tomorrow. You focus on making a dream wedding cake for that poor couple, and we will do our best just to stay out of the way."

Debbie wasn't sure what it would be like to have another cook in the kitchen, but she was too grateful to Vanessa and to Drew for thinking about her to do anything but agree. She shouldn't have worried. Kayla and Vanessa worked together as seamlessly as if they'd done so for years, leaving Debbie to focus solely on the wedding cake. She crumb coated the cakes with buttercream icing, adding a layer of Bavarian cream between, and covered each one with fondant. She used a diamond-shaped cutter to press the quilt pattern into the thick frosting. She built one tier on top of the other until all seven formed the perfect spiral. She replaced the strawberry flowers with ones made of fondant in the same pinkish-red color.

By the time she was done, her back and shoulders ached, but being tired and sore wasn't enough to keep her from smiling at the cake—a darn close replica to Caroline's original choice if she did say so herself, minus the offending fruit.

"Oh, Debbie. It's just beautiful," Vanessa said, her proud smile once again reminding Debbie of her own mother.

"I just hope Caroline likes it."

"How could she not?"

Andrea had arranged for the caterers to pick up the cake in their van, and Debbie followed them to Hillcrest House, the site of the wedding and reception. The ballroom's darkly paneled walls and rich furnishings made for a perfect backdrop for the white cake. She made a few touch-ups once the cake was moved to the serving table and then stepped back to let Caroline and Andrea see the last-minute replacement.

"It's perfect. Just...perfect. I don't know how you did

it, but it's amazing. Thank you!" Caroline gushed. The blond bride looked gorgeous in a sheath-style gown with her hair caught up in a simple twist. Tears filled her eyes as she gazed at the cake, and Andrea quickly started to hustle her away before she could ruin her makeup.

"You are a lifesaver," the older woman vowed. "My future grandchildren thank you."

"Mom! Seriously?"

Debbie laughed at the exasperation in Caroline's voice even as she took another moment to look at the cake. She'd done it. Made a beautiful cake in a short period of time, but more than that, she'd silenced her own doubts. *This* was what she wanted to do. The creativity and challenge of making wedding cakes would never get old. Neither would seeing the joy in a bride's eyes when she saw her cake for the first time.

It was late by the time Debbie returned to the bakery, past closing time, so she was surprised to see the lights still on in the back. She hoped Vanessa and Kayla hadn't thought they needed to stick around until she returned. The two of them had already gone beyond the call of duty to have taken over for her the way they had.

But when she opened the door, it wasn't the two women who were waiting for her. Instead Drew sat at the butcher-block island with a couple of disposable take-out containers in front of him. "Drew, what are you doing here?"

"My mom told me that you worked all day with no more than a few minutes' break. I figured you were probably starving but wouldn't bother to eat if you had to make dinner for yourself."

"You're right." Debbie dropped onto the stool he pulled over for her and closed her eyes. The scent of barbecue teased her senses and made her mouth water, but she was so tired she didn't know if she could stay awake long enough to eat.

"Hey, come on, Sleeping Beauty. You've got to eat something. Brides are going to be beating your door down when word gets out about that cake you made, so you've got to keep your strength up."

Smiling, Debbie opened her eyes. "You should have seen the cake, Drew."

He laughed. "Do you really think my mom didn't take a ton of pictures and send them to me? She was so thrilled to help out today."

"Thank you for that. She was a lifesaver. I don't know what I would have done without her."

And she didn't know what she would have done without Drew. He'd encouraged her to go after her dreams, to believe they could still come true. And if she wasn't so exhausted, she would have loved to show him just how grateful she was.

But she barely managed to eat half of the barbecue sandwich he'd picked up for her before her eyes started to close. After packing up the leftovers and stashing them in the refrigerator, Drew pulled Debbie up from the stool. He wrapped an arm around her shoulders as he led her up the stairs to her bedroom.

Gazing with longing at her bed, Debbie sighed. She was torn between sleeping...and sleeping with Drew. A giant yawn came out of nowhere, seeming to give her the answer she needed. "I'm sorry, Drew. I'm just—exhausted."

"I know. Which is why I'm putting you to bed and not taking you to bed."

True to his word, Drew guided her to the bathroom and waited while she stumbled through changing into her pajamas, washing her face and brushing her teeth. He had the covers on her bed turned back for her, and Debbie had to smile as she remembered the night at his house when he'd sent her off to bed with nothing more than a kiss on the forehead.

Exhausted or not, she wasn't letting him get away with it a second time. Slipping between the sheets, she held out a hand to him. "Stay with me?"

Drew froze for a split second before taking her hand. "Are you sure?"

She smiled sleepily. "Stay."

Two nights with too little sleep should have left Debbie feeling exhausted, but she couldn't keep the smile off her face or a softly hummed tune from her lips as she opened the bakery the next morning. She wasn't sure what time it had been when she and Drew had awoken and reached for each other, but the inky darkness only added to the intimacy as they explored each other using other senses— touch, taste, sound. And she hadn't needed to see the satisfied smile on Drew's face to know she'd put it there.

She couldn't recall a time when she'd been so happy, and if at times a worried whisper slipped through her thoughts, questioning how long such happiness could last, Debbie brushed it away.

The bell above the door rang, and Debbie looked up to see Evelyn McClaren step inside. The fiftysomething woman owned and ran Hillcrest House, and she glanced at the Halloween decorations scattered throughout the bakery as if wondering if she'd entered the right shop.

Debbie had only met the other woman a few times, and she was as stylish and businesslike as ever in her straight red skirt and matching jacket. Her auburn hair was caught up in a twist; her makeup and jewelry were understated and impeccable. She was also extremely thin and fit, looking at least a decade younger than her age, and not someone who normally—if ever—visited the bakery. "Mrs. McClaren, good morning. What can I get for you?"

A small smile curved the woman's lips as if she'd guessed Debbie's thoughts. "I'll have a cup of coffee, please."

Curious about the reason for the businesswoman's visit, she lifted the pot of freshly brewed dark roast and poured a cup. After accepting the steaming mug, Evelyn got right down to business. "I have a proposition for you, Ms. Mattson," she said, eyeing her over the rim once she'd taken a sip. "Hillcrest House has a reputation locally as the place to go for special occasions—engagement parties, weddings, anniversaries. But it's always been my goal to reach outside of our little town." The slightest hint of sarcasm touched the woman's last words, giving away the fact that Evelyn McClaren clearly still thought of the big city as her home—despite living in little Clearville.

"Now more and more of the couples who come to Hillcrest to get married are from out of town. And as many opportunities as that presents, it also can present problems—like what happened last weekend with Caroline Collins's wedding."

"But Caroline's from Clearville," Debbie pointed out.

"True. But the bakery she chose was up in Portland, and the flowers came from Sacramento and the band she hired was from San Francisco—" Evelyn waived a dismissive hand. "Getting married might be a wonderful, romantic event for the bride and groom, but for me, it's business. And in business, the closer the relationship you have with those you work with, the better off you will be. Which is why I'm interested in offering all-inclusive wedding packages for tourists and locals alike. The resort will handle everything—from the music, to the photographer, to the flowers and the cake. And that is where you come in."

"Me?" Debbie kept her jaw from dropping, but just barely.

"Andrea Collins thinks you are a lifesaver, and I agree. Her daughter was a tissue or two away from calling off the whole wedding, and the inn's cancellation policy wouldn't have come close to covering the losses at such a late date. The cake you made was gorgeous—and delicious, from the comments I overheard. I would expect that from any baker, but the way you worked under pressure and stepped up to help simply because someone asked, that's what truly impressed me."

"I— Thank you. I was happy to help." And Drew was right—it had felt good to ride in and save the day. She'd never imagined it would lead to this kind of offer from the biggest resort in town. A buzz vibrated beneath her skin, and she could barely hold still. And the more she and the other woman talked, the stronger that feeling grew until she felt ready to bounce off the ceiling like a kid on a sugar high from too many of her Halloween cookies.

"I'll want your input regarding the different flavors and fillings to offer in the packages, and I'll need photographs of the designs that will be available. Of course, the size of the cake and number of layers will depend on the number of guests. Once the holiday rush is over, we'll be ready to focus on spring weddings, so I'll want everything finalized in the next few weeks. I assume that won't be a problem."

"I could have some tasting cakes ready by this weekend. If you have any of the menus set for the reception dinners, I could see if there's a certain flavor of cake that would complement the entrees."

"I'll send you what our chef has come up with so far." They spoke for a few more minutes before Evelyn said, "I think this partnership will benefit us both, and of course, all the credit for the wedding cakes will go to you and your bakery."

Debbie accepted the businesswoman's card but waved aside her offer to pay for the coffee. Promising to be in touch, Evelyn turned and walked out on her three-inch heels. With echo of the bell still ringing in her ears, Debbie held tight to the small card—proof that the past few minutes hadn't been an illusion. Evelyn wouldn't be an easy woman to work for, but the opportunity was still too incredible to possibly pass up.

It was exactly what she wanted—a chance to find her own success in the bakery that still bore her mother's name. After so many years of keeping her mother's dream alive, this was her one shot to live her own, and she couldn't let anything stand in her way. The partnership with the inn would mean a lot of hard work and sacrifice, but that at least was nothing new.

After all, the bakery had always come first.

Drew wasn't sure what to expect when Debbie asked him to come over that evening. She'd told him she had some exciting news to share, but something in her voice was off. Something that sounded more nervous than excited.

When he walked into the bakery, he could see she'd been baking up a storm. The sink was filled with mixing bowls and cake pans and a dozen or so cakes lined the cooling racks. She was whipping something in a stainless-steel bowl, the whisk moving so fast it became little more than a metallic blur in her hand.

"Give me just a second. This whipped cream is almost ready."

"You've been busy. Is this another round of taste tests for the new menu?"

"Not exactly." Seeming satisfied with the peaks in the cream, she set the bowl aside to face him. She took a deep breath, and a bad feeling settled in Drew's gut. Whatever news she had to share, he already knew he wasn't going to like hearing it.

"Evelyn McClaren stopped by today."

As she filled him in on the conversation she'd had with the inn owner, Drew thought maybe he'd misread the situation. Maybe it was just Debbie's nerves he was picking up on and he'd imagined the rest.

"That's great, Debbie! I'm so proud of you." But when he stepped closer, he knew it wasn't his imagination that she took a small step back. The movement was slight. Just the tiniest step, but Drew swallowed, seeing it for the chasm it truly was.

"The thing is, I'm going to be really busy the next few weeks coming up with the perfect cakes and decorations, and then I have Kara and Sam's wedding cake to bake on top of all that. If this partnership with Hillcrest House takes off the way I hope it will, I'll have to hire on more help. But that won't be for several months."

"What are you saying, Debbie?"

"I just think it might be time for us to take a step back."

A step back? Most days he felt like he barely had a toehold into her life as it was. "Back to what, exactly?"

She hesitated. "Just being friends."

He couldn't believe it. "Because you've let me so far in already."

Her chin rose at his burst of sarcasm, her expression so stubborn and so beautiful it hurt him to look at her. "We agreed. This was just supposed to be a fling."

Drew swore beneath his breath. "Don't give me that! It's been more than a fling from the start, and you know it."

Crossing her arms over her apron, she said, "I told you I wasn't looking for anything serious. You agreed."

"I don't agree with you kicking me to the curb because you're scared to realize how serious our relationship already is."

"I am not scared! This is my chance to go after my dream, and I'm taking it! This time I'm not going to let anything stand in my way."

The blow she landed hit him square in the chest, knocking more than just the wind out of him. Somehow it shattered what was left of his hope. "Is that what you think I do? Stand in the way of your happiness?"

"No, not— No. But I need to focus and not leave myself open to…distractions."

"Distractions. Right." Because that was what she was reducing their relationship to. The distraction of a meaningless fling.

Hurt and frustration boiled up inside him, and the hell of it was Drew couldn't even say that she hadn't warned him. Debbie had always said the bakery came first. But he'd never expected to find himself so completely out of the running.

Chapter Twelve

"What's this I hear about you not staying open for Halloween night?" Sophia demanded as she walked through the bakery's back door and into the kitchen.

"Who told you—" Debbie didn't need to finish the question as Kayla guiltily ducked her head and muttered something about making sure everything was locked up out front.

Planting her hands on her hips, her friend looked just like she had when they'd argued as kids. Well, except for her expanding belly. But the stubborn lift to her jaw and flashing eyes were still the same. "You always stay open late on Halloween for the kids to trick-or-treat here before they head over to the Fall Fest in the town square!"

"I've just been too busy this year to even think about it. The other stores on Main Street will still be open—including The Hope Chest—so it's not like the kids will be disappointed."

"It's not the kids I'm worried about. You love dressing up every year almost as much as you love seeing the kids in their costumes and passing out miniature cookies for them to eat!"

She *did* love dressing up. So much so that she'd bought a costume a few weeks ago. An ice-blue ball gown complete with white, elbow-length gloves, a sparkling tiara and glass—well, clear plastic—slippers. Her hand lifted to a real glass slipper—the tiny crystal pendant Drew had given her—and the one she hadn't been able to take off.

"I just—can't." To her horror, her eyes filled with tears, and she couldn't look away fast enough to hide them from Sophia.

Sympathy softened her friend's expression for a split second before her typical drill-sergeant personality took over. Grabbing Debbie's arm, she practically dragged her from the kitchen to the stair that led to the apartment above.

"The bakery—"

"Kayla will finish up anything that needs to be done. That's why you hired her." Marching her over to the living room's small, shabby-chic love seat, Sophia settled Debbie against the cushions before raiding her bathroom for a box of tissue and her kitchen for a pint of mint-chocolate-chip ice cream and two spoons. "Now tell me," she said with a sigh, "how badly do I have to beat up Drew?"

Almost choking on her first frozen bite, Debbie stared at her friend. "You—knew?"

"Of course I knew! You're my best friend and Drew's my brother. Did you really think I wouldn't notice something going on between the two of you?"

"You never said anything…"

"Because you weren't talking! But I did warn Drew

that I'd hurt him if he hurt you. So tell me, how badly do I need to beat him up?"

Her eyes burning with tears again, Debbie stuck the spoon back into the ice cream, unable to eat another bite.

"That bad, huh?"

"No, and that's what makes it so sad." Pressing the heels of her hands against her eyes, she admitted, "It wasn't Drew. It was me."

"Well, I guess I should be glad about that, at least. Don't tell Nick or Sam, but Drew's always been my favorite brother." That got a short laugh out of Debbie as Sophia pulled her hands from her face and passed her several tissues. "So I guess my next question is how badly did you hurt *him?*"

"Oh, Sophia. I never meant to." And just like that, the whole story came pouring out—from the moment Drew had overheard them at the bachelorette party to when he'd walked out a few days before.

"He was right, too. I am scared. I don't know how to handle this opportunity with Hillcrest House and still make time for a relationship. If I blow this chance with Evelyn, what if I end up blaming and resenting Drew? And if I focus too much on the bakery, then he'll just end up resenting me."

She took a deep breath and looked over to her best friend for comfort and support and—

Sophia lifted a shoulder in a casual shrug. "Other couples juggle jobs and relationships all the time."

"What?"

"Well, they do. Jake and I manage even with all the work he does out of town. Nick and Darcy. Sam and Kara. We've all made it work."

"Okay, well, thank you very much for the pep talk that's made me feel like an even bigger failure."

"You're not a failure, but I don't think you're being totally honest with yourself about what it is you're truly afraid of."

"This partnership with Hillcrest House is a really big deal. What else would I be afraid of?"

After setting the ice cream on the beat-up steamer trunk Debbie used for a coffee table, Sophia picked up the framed photograph sitting there. The last picture taken of her father before he died. "He's the only other man you've ever loved, and you lost him," Sophia said softly.

Tracing a finger over the cool, smooth glass, Debbie argued, "I was just a kid. I don't even remember..."

Except that wasn't true. Not entirely. A memory, far more faded and faint than the picture in the frame, lingered in her mind. Her birthday party the year she turned four. She'd invited friends from preschool and had worn a new dress. The cake her mother made had been enormous in her childish mind—bigger than she was—with layer after pink layer reaching to the ceiling.

Her father hadn't been there, but a calendar had hung on the refrigerator, and each day she and her mother had marked off another day. First counting down to her birthday and then to the day when her daddy would be home. And she'd been so excited... She'd closed her eyes tight when she'd blown out those candles, wishing so hard that when she opened them, her daddy would already be there—

Opening her eyes over twenty-two years later, he still wasn't there.

Maybe it was that moment when she was a little girl—or maybe it was years later when her mother was diagnosed with cancer—that she'd stopped wishing, stopped hoping, stopped believing. And in place of wishes and hope and faith, fear had taken root. The fear that nothing good could last and that *temporary* was all she could count on.

She'd been right about Drew all along. He wasn't a temporary kind of guy. He was the kind of man a woman could love forever—if she was brave enough to trust in a forever love.

"You're right. I'm afraid of how much I already love Drew. I did my best to minimize what we had and to keep him at a distance and it still didn't work. I still fell in love with him, and if I lost him—the way my mom lost my dad—"

"Sweetie, you know how much your mom loved your dad and how much she missed him, but don't you think if she had the chance to do it all over again, she would? In a heartbeat? Because that's what love is. It's a celebration of the time we do have together—whether that's decades or even only days."

"She would have lost him a hundred times as long as it meant she had the chance to love him first." Wiping at her eyes, she looked at her friend. "So what do I do? How do I fix things with Drew?"

"Well, first off, you're staying open late for Halloween and you're coming to the Fall Fest."

"Seriously?" Debbie fell back against the cushions with a faint laugh.

"Yes, I take all holidays very seriously. Now tell me—because I know you already have one—what's your costume for this year?"

Heaving a sigh, she admitted, "Cinderella."

Sophia's clapped her hands together. "Yes! That is just perfect."

"Why?"

"Because," she said with a matchmaking twinkle in her dark eyes, "I am your fairy godmother."

* * *

True to her word, Sophia arrived the afternoon of Halloween to help with the magical transformation of turning Debbie into a princess. She had to admit her friend had done an amazing job with her makeup and hair, sweeping her blond curls into a cartoon-perfect twist.

The only change Debbie made to the costume was passing up the glass slippers for the heels Drew had bought for her. Not that anyone could see them beneath the gown's full skirt, but she felt a little more hopeful simply knowing she was wearing them.

And she could use all the hope and all the help she could get.

No matter how many times she asked Sophia, her friend had refused to tell Debbie how she planned to get Drew to come to the Fall Fest that night.

"Trust me," Sophia promised when she stopped by the bakery looking adorable in green leggings and an orange sweatshirt with a grinning black jack-o'-lantern face over her pregnant belly.

"Drew will be there. Just make sure you get to the square before midnight," she teased with a wink.

"I'm closing up at seven. I think I'll make it," she said as she handed out another bite-size cookie, this time to a toddler dressed in the cutest black-and-red ladybug outfit. She couldn't help smiling as the delicate little girl tried to shove her whole fist, cookie and all, into her mouth, much to her mother's embarrassment.

The festival was in full swing by the time Debbie arrived. The cool evening air was filled with the scents of fried food, kettle corn and the hay bales scattered around for seating and ambiance. The town square was decorated in the orange and black of Halloween along with the rich, vibrant colors of fall. Music drifted above the sounds of talking and laughter, and she saw that the local cover band had taken its place on the stage.

Looking around for her friends, she spotted Sam Pirelli first. Dressed in full Captain Jack Sparrow regalia, complete with hat, eyeliner and dreadlocks, he was hard to miss. Kara stood alongside him, looking at once embarrassed and yet proud to have such a good-looking, if outrageous, fiancé. Jake Cameron, Sophia's husband, hadn't dressed up, but he stood behind his wife, his arms wrapped around their "pumpkin" in the oven.

Debbie knew Kara hadn't wanted Timmy out too late and figured his grandparents had already taken him home. Nick's daughter, Maddie, had stopped by the bakery earlier with a group of friends, giving Nick and Darcy a night alone.

Which left only one Pirelli unaccounted for.

As Debbie made her way through the crowd, the band switched to a ballad. First Sam and Kara, and then Sophia and Jake stepped onto the makeshift dance floor. Debbie's footsteps slowed as the couples wrapped their arms around each other and gazed into one another's eyes. As much as she loved spending time with her friends, did she really want to play the part of the fifth wheel throughout the evening if Drew didn't show?

She pulled the white shawl she'd added to help ward off the October chill a little closer. Her pale blue skirt rustled against her legs, and while she certainly wasn't the only one in costume, she was starting to feel all dressed up with no place to go.

Drew had done some foolish things in his life. A man could hardly reach the age of thirty without having more than a few what-the-hell-was-I-thinking moments, but he was pretty sure tonight might end up taking the cake.

Walking toward the square, he stopped short as he caught sight of himself in a darkened store window. In a small town like Clearville, businesses shut down in the early evening on most nights. They certainly did on nights when the town had an event like the Fall Fest planned.

The event would run for hours, starting with little kids trick-or-treating throughout town rather than trying to go from house to house where neighbors were separated by several acres of land. After that, families would head toward the town square. Costume contests and pie throwing and pumpkin carving were all scheduled, and he could already hear music from a local band playing. A cheer rose as they switched to a classic-rock song with a pulsing beat guaranteed to get the crowd jumping and bounce the slow dancers off the floor.

But it was still early. Early enough for him to go home and change.

The wavy image in the storefront window seemed to urge him to do just that. To change his clothes and change his mind and maybe not make a total ass out of himself.

Why had he listened to Sophia in the first place? For all he knew this was some kind of setup, payback for him pulling her pigtails one too many times back when they were kids. Except his sister wasn't the type to kick a man when he was down, and there was no question that was how she'd found him when she'd stopped by his house the day before.

He'd crashed on the couch, Rain by his side, as he'd tried to watch the midweek football game. By the third quarter, the contest was a rout, but that had little to do with his lack of attention.

Had he really read Debbie so wrong? He'd been so sure she wanted more than casual, more than temporary. Had he only seen what he wanted to see?

He heard the knock on his front door a split second before the sound of it opening, signaling it was a member of his nosy family. Rain jumped down to welcome the visitor, and his sister greeted the dog in a high-pitched voice guaranteed to set the puppy shaking with excitement.

"The point of knocking," he told her as she carried the ecstatic puppy back into the living room, "is to wait for the person inside to let you in."

Dropping onto the couch beside him, she lifted her chin out of the way of Rain's darting tongue. "Thought I'd save you the trouble."

After circling a few times, the puppy settled into what was left of Sophia's lap, both of them looking like they planned to stay there awhile. "What do you want, Soph?"

"To tell you that I talked to Debbie."

"Well, then, you know you don't have to worry about me breaking her heart anymore, do you?"

"You know she loves you, right?"

Drew could stand to hear a lot of things, but that wasn't one of them. Pushing off the couch, he glared down at his little sister. "Give me a break. You were there the night of Darcy's bachelorette party. You heard what Debbie wanted. Some guy to have a fling with. And that's all it was."

That was all *he* was.

"You don't really believe that."

"She made it pretty clear."

"She's afraid of how she really feels. So maybe she was looking for an easy out, and what did you do but take it?"

Drew tossed up his hands in exasperation. "How did this end up being my fault?"

Sophia struggled to get to her feet but couldn't quite manage thanks to the low-slung couch and the puppy in her lap. She set the puppy back on the floor and pushed up from the cushions. "Because, Drew, when the woman you love walks away, you don't let her go. You go after her!"

Maybe it spoke to his desperation that he'd been so quick to listen to Sophia, to believe he and Debbie still had a chance. Why else would he have agreed to show up to the festival in costume? He never dressed up, leaving that to Sam, who always went all out without the slightest bit of embarrassment. Drew felt as self-conscious as hell, but he'd promised he would attend the event and that he would try to convince Debbie to give their relationship another try. An *honest* try.

Making his decision, he continued walking toward the square. As the sounds of the music and scents of fried foods grew stronger, he slipped through the crowd gathered near the food booths.

"Well, if it isn't Prince Charming!"

Drew's face heated and his temper started to burn at the hoot of laughter as he turned to face his younger brother. Or at least he thought it was Sam. It was a little hard to tell under the eyeliner and black dreads. "That's the guy from Snow White. I'm supposed to be the one from Cinderella."

"Oh, well, yeah. 'Cause that makes it so much less lame."

"Shut up, Captain Jack."

Drew took a deep breath, reminding himself what was at stake and why he'd been willing to put on the blue uniform with its bright gold buttons, red sash and epaulets. Gold-freakin'-tasseled epaulets.

"Why don't both of you chill. This is a party, remember? And I'm ready for a good time." Ryder Kincaid was wearing his football jersey from high school and had his Wildcat helmet tucked beneath his arm. Exchanging a look with Sam, he asked, "So you really think I should I ask her out?"

"Oh, yeah! Why not, right? She's pretty, sexy, funny—available."

Still searching the crowd, Drew barely paid attention to the conversation between the other two men until one word jumped out at him and he froze. Turning back, he demanded, "What did you say about Debbie?"

Ryder grinned. "That she's turned out to be pretty hot. I mean, I don't really remember her that well from high school, but when your sister set us up the other night, I thought I hit the jackpot. I figure it's time for me to dive back into the dating pool."

Grinding his back teeth together, Drew gritted out, "Find another girl."

"Why? I mean, we're both single. Or at least she is, and I will be as soon as the divorce goes through, so—"

Drew didn't stop to think. Stepping closer, he repeated, "Find another girl, Kincaid."

"Wow, dude!" Sam threw an arm across Drew's chest and pulled him away from Ryder. Drew braced himself, waiting for the other man to retaliate, but the tension slowly eased from his body as he realized Ryder wasn't angry. Instead he and Sam were grinning like a couple of idiots.

"I wouldn't have believed it if I hadn't seen it for myself," his brother said.

Holding out a hand, Ryder said, "Pay up, man."

Drew watched as Sam passed his newest employee twenty bucks, the last of his jealousy and anger dissolving into confusion. "What's going on?"

"Ryder told me you had a thing for Debbie, and I didn't believe it."

"I don't have a thing for her."

"Yeah, what would you call it?"

"I don't know, Sam. How do you describe the way you feel about Kara?" Drew shot back.

His younger brother sobered almost instantly. "It's that serious?"

Drew sighed. "It is for me."

"Then why are you standing around with the two of us?" Ryder asked.

"Ryder's right. Go get her, Cinderella Man!"

"Sam, I swear…" Drew was shaking his head as he walked away. But he was smiling, too.

Debbie did eventually join her girlfriends on the edge of the dance floor. She was doing her best to try to have a good time, but her heart wasn't in it. She wondered how long she would have to stay before she could slip away and head home.

"Don't worry. He'll be here," Sophia promised.

"How can you be so sure? Maybe he changed his mind. Maybe he doesn't think I'm worth it after the way I pushed him away."

"I'm sure." Her friend's smile grew wider. "Fairy tales always end happily ever after."

"My life has never been much of a fairy tale, Sophia."

"It is tonight," Sophia whispered as she placed her hands on Debbie's shoulders and tuned her toward the dance floor.

Debbie gasped as she caught sight of Drew cutting his way through the crowd. He was here. Making his way toward her. The sights and sounds of the festival faded away. The distance between them lessened until she could feel the heat of his gaze wash over her.

A trembling smile crossed her face as the crowd finally parted, and she caught sight of what he was wearing. The classic prince costume—the royal blue coat, the gold buttons, the red sash. He looked incredible, if completely uncomfortable, which only made her love him that much more.

He moved toward her without breaking stride, not stopping until he stood a few feet in front of her and held out his hand. Placing her gloved hand in his, she followed him onto the dance floor. The band started to play, and she couldn't help but give a small laugh as she recognized the first few notes of the classic Celine Dion soundtrack.

"I know tonight is all about fantasy and make-believe," he told her, "but what I want is real. A real relationship. One that's out in the open, for all our friends and family to see. One that's important enough to come first in both of our lives."

"Drew, I'm so sorry for everything I said. For pushing you away. I don't want to hide how I feel anymore."

Grinning, he said, "Well, that's a good thing considering the cat's pretty much out of the bag now."

She laughed, tears shimmering in her eyes, and then a playful grin lit up her face. "Well, considering half the town seems to be watching, I think we might as well give them something to see, don't you?"

Pulling his head down, Debbie pressed her mouth to his, relishing the freedom to kiss him and not care who was watching. A few catcalls came from the crowd, and she felt his smile before he backed away. "Let's not give them too much to see."

Drew wasn't sure when he became aware of a sound beyond the crowd of people around them, beyond the music from the stage. The sound of shouting and the faint wail of sirens growing louder. Closer.

He saw people around him exchanging worried looks as a ripple moved through the crowd. He caught only a couple of words, but they were enough to send a shiver of concern racing through him.

Smoke...Main Street...fire department...
And a word he hoped Debbie hadn't heard.

Grabbing his arm, color faded from her face as she whispered, "The bakery."

Chapter Thirteen

In the harsh light of morning, the destruction of the bakery was even more apparent than it had been the night before. The plate-glass window had been broken out, the shelves and register inside nothing more than charred ruins. She didn't know the extent of the damage to the kitchen or her apartment upstairs. The fire department had yet to declare the structure safe to enter.

"Are you sure you want to be here, Debbie?" Sophia asked gently.

Jake and Sophia had brought her home with them the night before. Drew had wanted to take her back to his place, but even in her dazed state, she'd heard Sophia's whispered reminder that Debbie wouldn't have anything else to wear. Her whole wardrobe was now limited to a Halloween costume.

Tonight is about fantasy.

Drew's words echoed in her head, and she fought the

crazy urge to laugh. Well, today was just chock full of reality, wasn't it?

"This isn't a good idea," Drew muttered. "Come on, Debbie. Let's go."

Sympathy filled his dark eyes, and she had to look away. She couldn't face it, couldn't face him, with the ugly, destructive mass of guilt building up inside her. How many times had she felt like she was trapped by the business her mother had loved, by the legacy Bonnie had left behind? How many times, in the darkest places of her heart, had she secretly resented it? She couldn't believe that bitter acid of resentment had eaten away at the ancient wiring, but that didn't mean this wasn't some kind of a sign.

She'd wanted her freedom, and now she had it. She'd felt shackled to the business, and now that it was in ruins, those chains slipped way.

"It's all my fault."

"Don't!" Grabbing her shoulders, he turned her away from the building. "Don't say that. We don't even know what caused the fire."

"You warned me about the wiring, and I didn't listen."

He swore under his breath. "Even if it was the wiring, I didn't honestly suspect there was a problem. If I had, don't you think I would have insisted on checking it out myself? And doesn't that make this more my fault than yours?"

His grip eased as he slid his hands down her arms. He linked his fingers with hers, but Debbie was too numb to feel it. "We're going to fix this, Debbie. It'll only take a few weeks, and everything will be back to the way it was."

Debbie gave a rough laugh. The way it was. The way it would always be if she didn't take the chance fate had handed her. "Maybe I don't want to fix it."

"What are you talking about? You can't just leave it—"

"Why not? Those 'few weeks' will make it too late for

me to take the partnership with Hillcrest that Evelyn offered. You can't fix that, Drew, any more than you can fix the bakery. Bonnie's Bakery is gone. I wanted freedom and now—" She waved a hand at the smoke-scarred, water-stained building. "There's nothing left for me here."

Drew flinched as if she'd struck him. "Nothing?" he echoed flatly. "What about us, Debbie? Or is that nothing, too? I love you. Can you really still not see that? I'm in love with you."

Pain clutched her throat, each word jagged and cutting as she tried to get them out. "I don't— I can't—"

Sophia wrapped an arm around her shoulders and led Debbie away. "Come on. Let's go."

Jake clamped a hand on Drew's shoulder and quietly advised, "She's still in shock. Give her time."

Drew nodded, but he knew all the time in the world wouldn't matter if Debbie didn't love him back.

"You do realize that one of these days you're going to have to leave this room," Sophia said as she walked into the guest bedroom where Debbie had been staying since the fire. A guest bedroom Sophia was gradually turning into a nursery.

Along with the small twin bed where Debbie had holed up, a white crib, matching dresser and a bookshelf filled the room. Sophia's baby already had an accumulation of toys lining the shelves, with more to come once Sophia had her shower in a few weeks.

"I figure I'll wait until your little guy or girl comes along."

"That's not for another two months."

Debbie nodded as she tucked a stray curl behind her ear. She knew it was only her imagination because she'd thoroughly washed her hair since the fire, but the stench of smoke still seemed to cling to everything she touched. Even food tasted like ash. "Two months sounds about right."

"Deb…" Sophia sank onto the bed beside her, pulling away the cream-colored ruffled pillow she had been holding to her chest like some kind of shield.

"I just—can't. It's like the days after my mom died all over again. With everyone being so sympathetic and so nice, and I just don't have the strength to pretend everything's fine."

"Good grief, Debbie! Everything is not fine, and no one expects you to pretend that it is! You've lost your business and your home, and people want to help. That's what we do around here. You know that."

"Everything's—gone. There's nothing anyone can do about that."

"You're so sure about that?"

Unable to hold Sophia's steady gaze, Debbie glanced down at the sea-green comforter. She knew her friend had overheard Drew's heartfelt declaration and her own cold, empty silence.

Huffing a sigh, Sophia reached into the pocket of her flowery maternity dress. "Well, at least listen to your messages. Your phone hasn't stopped ringing in the past two days."

Her phone. She'd forgotten that it, too, hadn't been lost in the fire, having thrown it into her small evening bag on Halloween night at the last minute. Swiping the screen, she blinked, startled to realize Sophia hadn't exaggerated about the number of calls.

The first was from Kayla, and Debbie cringed. She should have been the one to call her employee. In the background, she could hear Kayla's baby girl's sweet babbling, but the young woman didn't say anything about her job or ask when she might be able to come back to work. She simply said how sorry she was and asked Debbie to call if she needed anything.

The next message was from Vanessa Pirelli, who volunteered to help at the bakery again anytime Debbie might need her. Andrea Collins reminded Debbie that she worked in real estate and could help her find a temporary rental space until the bakery was up and running again. Hope Daniels offered her a place to stay in the apartment above the antiques store.

And another message was from Evelyn McClaren, who offered her the use of Hillcrest's kitchen for her baking, not wanting Debbie to fall behind on wedding cake selections they still needed to finalize for the inn's all-inclusive wedding packages.

Other messages were from friends and acquaintances— all telling her they couldn't wait for the bakery to open again and offering their help just as Sophia had said.

How had she missed that? How had she become so focused on what muffins she made or what cupcakes she sold that she stopped thinking about the customers and friends she saw—sometimes every day. And had she really believed that the *bakery* was the only thing tying her to Clearville?

She couldn't leave this town she loved any more than she could leave the man she loved. But of all the messages she'd played back on her phone, not one of them had been from Drew.

He told you he loved you, and you just walked away.

He'd already come back to her once after she'd pushed him away. Did she really think he'd chase after her again?

It was definitely her turn.

Drew stared at the under-construction house and wondered if he'd ever be able to finish it. What would be the point when the family he'd built it for—the family of his dreams—seemed more out of reach than ever? He couldn't stand the thought of living there alone. And yet the idea of another family moving in made him want to tear the place down with his bare hands. Board by board, nail by nail, until there was nothing left.

When he'd been a kid, he'd broken a rib once while roughhousing with Nick. He still remembered the stabbing pain with every breath he took. That pain was back. Only now it was his raw and bruised heart aching on each and every breath, and no tightly wrapped bandage was going to take that hurt away.

This was different from the first time, though he still couldn't believe he was fool enough to have let Debbie trample his heart *twice*. The night in the bakery, they'd argued. They'd both lost their temper, hurling accusations and saying things they didn't mean. Deep down, though, he'd still had hope that he could fix things.

You can't fix this.

Debbie's broken, aching words added a dull throb to the already stabbing pain, and he hunched his shoulders beneath the leather jacket he wore. She was right, of course. His offer had been stupid and meaningless. The bakery was more than a building. More than new floors and walls and windows. She'd told him once that keeping the bakery the same as it was when her mother was alive was a way for her to keep Bonnie's memory alive.

Did he really think he could recreate those memories by slapping up a new coat of bright and shiny pink paint?

He kicked his work boot at the loose rocks along the driveway. That was as stupid as thinking if he built this house that the family he'd always imagined would come.

He should turn Ryder loose on the place. Let the other man finish it and put the house up for sale.

There's nothing left for me here.

Yeah, he was starting to know the feeling.

The crunch of gravel alerted him to a car's approach, and he hoped it wasn't Sophia or another member of his family—but the familiar lime-green Bug didn't belong to Sophia. And his stupid heart started pounding against his chest, ready and willing to throw itself out there to get trampled a third time.

He soaked in the sight of her, as if it had been two years instead of the two days since he'd last seen her. She looked tired. Her hair was caught back in a low ponytail, her face washed clean of makeup and she was wearing his sister's borrowed clothes. And he'd never seen her look more beautiful. Because despite all those things, when she met his gaze she lifted her chin, holding her head high. Still strong, still a fighter, still the girl he'd fallen in love with—hell, maybe as far back as the day of her mother's funeral.

"I was wrong." Her voice carried across the cool, crisp morning air, her misty breath forming a cloud around her words. A bit of color came to her cheeks as she closed the space between them. "I want you to rebuild the bakery."

"So you're here looking for a contractor?"

She nodded. "A contractor, a white knight…the man I love."

Her voice caught on the last word, but it didn't matter. Drew still heard it. Still felt it shining in the bright blue of her eyes, in the warmth of her smile, and he realized he'd been wrong. As that feeling wrapped tight around his heart, all the pain *did* go away.

"God, Debbie, I am so sorry," he whispered as he pulled her into his arms. He breathed in the sweet smell of her shampoo as he held her tight. "About the fire. About acting like I could just ride to the rescue and make everything better."

"You can. You have."

"No, you were right. Offering to rebuild the bakery as if I could make it as good as new was stupid. I can't give you back all the memories you lost in the fire."

"Maybe not," she agreed as she pulled back just far enough to gaze up at him. Tears swam in her eyes, making the blue that much brighter, but he had no doubt that they were tears of joy, of hope. "But you can help me make new ones. I thought the fire was a chance to break free of the past, and maybe it is. But more than that, it's a chance for me to embrace the future. I want you to rebuild the bakery and to help me make it mine. The way you've built this house to be yours."

"This house isn't mine," he confessed with a shaky laugh. "It never was. It's always been ours. Whether I knew it or not, from the moment I broke ground, I was building it for us. For our family."

"I like the sound of that."

"Well, I hope you like the sound of this even more. I love you, Debbie Mattson. I love that you've been my friend all these years and that you know me so well and yet you never cease take me by surprise. I love that you were willing to give up your own dreams to take care of your mom and that you still have courage to go after them now."

"I'm glad you see me that way, but the truth is I've been a coward. I tried to tell myself that having a fling with you was my way of living in the moment, but instead it was just me hiding from my feelings. I think the best way to seize the day is to hold on to the people you love and never let them go."

"Where am I going to go when the woman I love is right here?"

"Well, you can't just stand around for too long. We have a future to build, remember?"

"That we do," he promised. "And you know, if you're going to rebuild the bakery of your dreams, you're going to need a new name."

"You're right. It's something I should have done a long time ago. Something my mother would have wanted me to do."

"Well, I've been thinking long and hard about this, and I've come up with the perfect choice."

Judging by the smile tugging at Debbie's lips, he wasn't doing a very good job keeping a straight face. "And what is that?"

"I was thinking…Pirelli's Pastries."

Debbie's laughter filled the morning air, and Drew didn't bother trying to hold back his smile as she threw her arms around his neck. "Is that a yes?"

"To marrying you? That's an absolute yes! To renaming the bakery? I think we need to give that one another try."

* * * * *

SILKEN EMBRACE

ZURI DAY

Sometimes the goal is worth the chase
Vying with many in the race
When you're heart to heart and face-to-face
Forever enjoying his silken embrace.

Chapter 1

"Good morning, Terrell." The attractive Drake Community Center employee's eyes sparkled with admiration and interest while traveling the length of his body.

Terrell Drake returned her greeting with a smile and a wink, aware of but unaffected by the blatant flirtation. He wasn't cocky. At least not more than the average Drake man. He was simply used to it; he'd affected the female species this way his entire life.

"Hey, Tee, what's up, man?"

"It's your world, Luther, I'm just trying to navigate it."

He bumped fists with the community center's executive director and kept it moving. Months ago when his mother had asked him to volunteer at the center as one of its assistant directors, he'd balked at what he thought would cramp his style. He'd been wrong. The joy that came from seeing a struggling student solve a math problem, or properly knot his tie, or curtailing a would-be bully's antics and have him see reason was beyond anything Terrell could have imagined. He actually looked forward to the three days a week he spent at the center. Walking into this after-school and summertime haven for more than a hundred children always made him feel good.

He reached the T-shaped end of the hallway and turned right toward the gymnasium. What he saw next made his heart skip a beat and wonder who owned the booty that, like sunshine, had just brightened up his world.

"Wow."

The owner of said gluteus maximus stopped, paused for a beat, then turned to look at him.

Wait, did I just say that out loud?

If he were to judge by her reaction and the look at her face? That would be a *yes*.

But that his slip caused her to turn was worth whatever was about to happen. The woman looked as good from the front as she did from the back. Better even. Her heart-shaped face was almost totally devoid of makeup, natural, the way Terrell preferred. She had big brown eyes, a pert nose and pleasingly plump lips to match her generous cleavage. All kinds of sexy oozing through that frown. Time to turn on the Drake charm. Terrell whipped out a smile that could sell toothpaste and closed the distance between them with a confident stroll.

"Good afternoon."

Her perfectly arched brow raised a notch. "According to whom?"

He had the decency to look sheepish. "Sorry about that."

"You should be." Her voice remained stern but he noticed a spark in her eyes.

He determined that he could get lost in those eyes. Holding out his hand, he said, "Terrell."

She paused just long enough to make him nervous, and then extended her hand. "Aliyah."

"Like the singer?"

Her scowl deepened as she shook her head and pulled back her hand. "No. Like myself."

"I meant no offense, was a real fan of her music." Terrell could deliver spot-on compliments in his sleep. Not today. From the look on her face, he'd just added insult to injury. He shifted his position to regroup and was just about to unleash his arsenal of amorous acclamations when he noted that Aliyah's weren't the only eyes watching him intently. He looked to her right, and down.

"Hello there, little man."

"Hi."

"What's your name?"

"Kyle."

Terrell held out his hand. "Nice to meet you, Kyle. I'm Mr. Drake."

The kid sized him up openly with a face that would do any poker player proud. "Are you my teacher?"

"I work with teenagers. How old are you?"

"Five."

"Five? Are you sure?"

He looked at Aliyah, who nodded. "He's big for his age."

"You might be raising a football player." She shrugged at his observation. "Are you here for the Progeny Project?"

"Is that what the mentorship program is called?"

"Yes, the Progeny Project."

She nodded. "We're here for that, and perhaps some of the activities the center offers. Kyle's young, but he's smart and easily bored. I'd like to get him enrolled in as many as are available to him."

"I can help with that. Follow me." He noticed that she hesitated. "Do you have another question?"

"I'm waiting to follow you."

She said it with just the hint of a smile. Terrell nodded his understanding. Any other brother would have assumed her hesitancy was because of what had happened moments earlier. Terrell knew the truth—time for her to check him out.

He placed a hand on Kyle's shoulder, encouraging the young boy to walk beside him. "Are you as smart as your mother says you are?"

Kyle nodded. "Yes."

"Confident, too," Terrell said with a laugh. "I like that."

They reached the end of the hallway. He led her to a set of double doors, and followed her into the general office area, where registrants were enrolled and files were kept. This area also housed three offices, including the one Terrell used when he was at the center.

"Hello, handsome!"

"Good afternoon, Miss Marva." Terrell walked around the counter and embraced the slight, older woman with graying hair tucked into a neat bun. The powder blue pantsuit she wore was topped off with pearl earrings and a matching necklace. Very classy. "Thank you for the compliment."

Marva laughed, entwining her arm with Terrell's as she looked into his eyes. "I'd say you're welcome if the compliment was meant for you. It wasn't." She looked at Kyle. "It was for this handsome young man standing by the pretty lady."

This statement won smiles from both Aliyah and her son.

"Whoa!" Terrell grabbed his heart. "You wound me!"

"You know what they say about assumptions. You brought that on yourself."

"I guess I did." He looked at Kyle. "She was talking to you, handsome young man."

Aliyah encouraged her son. "Say hello to Miss Marva, Kyle."

"Hello," he said shyly, before hiding his face behind his mother's skirt.

"Aliyah is here to enroll her son in Progeny, and to learn more about what our center offers."

"Wonderful! We'll get this young man signed right up."

"I will leave the two of you in Miss Marva's capable hands." He pulled out a card and presented it to Aliyah.

"If you have any other questions about the center or our programs, anything at all, please feel free to contact me."

She nodded curtly, then smiled as she returned her attention to Miss Marva.

Terrell reached the door and turned. "One more thing."

He watched her shoulders rise and fall before turning sideways to face him. "Yes?"

Their eyes met. The air sizzled, all but crackled between them. An unspoken, as yet unacknowledged attraction existed in each gaze.

"Never mind. Have a nice afternoon."

A little over an hour later, Terrell returned to the office. He walked behind Miss Marva, grabbed her by the shoulders and smushed her hair with his chin. "Get on away from me with that foolishness," she playfully chided, swatting blindly behind her while Terrell dodged and laughed. With a final squeeze, he let her go and walked to a set of file cabinets. Opening one, he began browsing through folders.

"May I help you, Mr. Drake? I know you think you own the world, but this office is my domain."

He retrieved a file, set it on top of the others and opened it. "You're absolutely right about that, Miss Marva. I'll soon be out of your way." Finding the desired document, he pulled out his phone. "I had to run earlier and just want to follow up on our latest registrant, Mr. Kyle—" a glance at the paperwork "—Robinson."

Miss Marva folded her arms, her mouth now as twisted as her lovely chignon. "And just what kind of follow-up do you think is needed?"

"The general kind, you know, answering any questions his mother may have regarding our program."

"Mmm-hmm. I've known you since you were crawling, Terrell Drake. And I am sure that the questions you want to ask that pretty lady have nothing to do with this center."

He tapped a button on his phone, placed the paper in the folder and placed the folder back in the file cabinet. "They absolutely do." He struck a professional pose—chin up, back straight. "And if those questions get asked over, say, a glass of wine or two, well—" he shrugged "—all the better, wouldn't you say?"

Marva's mouth untwisted into a lovely smile. "I'd say you're full of it and then I'd tell you to take her out and have a nice time. She seems like a sweet girl."

"Thank you, Miss Marva." After a quick look around, he lowered his voice. "And...let's keep this between us, okay?"

"I appreciate your stating the obvious, but this old trap has never sprung a leak."

Terrell went into his office, closed the door and tapped the number he'd entered into his phone.

"Hello?"

"Hello, Aliyah. It's Terrell, from the community center." There was a pause. "Yes?"

"I had to rush out earlier and wanted to call and make sure everything regarding your son's enrollment went smoothly."

"Oh." Another pause. "Yes. The administrator, Miss Marva, handled everything just fine. Gave us a little tour and explained the program. We're all set."

"Good, that's real good."

A second ticked by. And then another.

"Is there...anything else?"

"Actually, Aliyah, there is. I'd like you to help me do something. Though it isn't very difficult, it doesn't happen often."

Suspicion coated the words she delivered. "Like what?"

"I'd like you to give me a second chance to make a first impression."

"That's really not necessary."

"I know. But I'd like to do it anyway—prove I'm not the cad my comment may have led you to believe. Something simple, say, dinner tonight. Casual. Jeans."

"I guess I can do that."

Terrell sat back with a satisfied smile.

"As long as regarding one thing we're perfectly clear. The part of my anatomy you found so intriguing will not be on the menu."

Chapter 2

Later that night Terrell was still thinking about Aliyah, surprised and a bit annoyed that she'd stayed on his mind. Sure, she was fine, but so were all the other women he'd dated. She was intriguing, but it was something more. An indefinable trait Terrell couldn't quite identify. He shrugged, focusing back on the computer screen and the news website he'd pulled up. It was just dinner. No big deal. That's why he'd suggested they meet at the Cove Café, the town's family-friendly diner, instead of the more upscale Acquired Taste or the always remarkable Paradise Cove country club. He didn't want to come off as trying to impress or anything. Why would he? Good looks aside, she was the parent of a student at the community center, with attitude to boot. Not mixing business with pleasure was Playboy Rulebook 101. With all of the women constantly trying to hook up with him, was a get-to-know-you dinner with her perfectly formed buns worth the messiness to his personal life that decision could potentially cause?

Yes.

Terrell ignored this answer that popped into his head, and the excitement that flowed through his other head as well. He wasn't in the market for a girlfriend and had enough friends with benefits to keep him more than satisfied.

So why was he taking Aliyah to dinner?

By the time he'd broken out his favorite pair of jeans, paired them with a navy button-down complemented by a platinum bracelet and thin chain, whipped out his solitaire diamond stud, removed his five-o'clock shadow and splashed on an exclusive blend of designer cologne, he'd convinced himself that he was just being a nice guy. That and he was hungry. Everyone had to eat, right?

He gathered his wallet and keys, and was heading to the door of his west wing suite when the estate's intercom sounded in his room.

"Terrell?"

"Yes, Mom?"

"Are you joining us for dinner, dear?"

"No. I'm heading out."

"Dinner meeting?"

He paused. "Something like that."

"Oh, I see. Have fun on your date, dear."

"Who said anything about a date?"

The sound of Jennifer's light chuckle made him smile. "Indirectly, you did. 'Bye now."

"'Bye, Mom. Love you."

"I love you more."

Aliyah pulled into the crowded parking lot, found a space and cut the engine. Grabbing a sweater from the backseat to ward off the slight October chill, she was pleasantly surprised to see the café Terrell had suggested was a homey-looking diner and not a swanky five-star restaurant. After getting Kyle enrolled in the community center's fall program she'd returned home, gone online and typed *Terrell Drake* in the search engine. What she'd seen there would impress most women. She was no exception. But it hadn't made her excited to meet him. She was all too familiar with men like him. Those who had the world by the tail, and thought they ruled it, from a family that practically owned the town or at least helped build it. One brother a grape grower and rancher and another one the mayor? Elite affiliations and country clubs for sure. The more she'd read, the more she'd been tempted to cancel their meeting. When he'd called and boldly requested dinner, and she accepted, it was to possibly secure a west coast casual who could periodically scratch her sexual itch. It had been months, she had been busy and a woman had needs. But now? With his lifestyle sounding so much like the ex whose family made it clear that she didn't and could never fit into their world? Why pull the scab off of a sore still healing? Because the attraction she'd felt in the community center office earlier was greater than her fear. So here she was.

She saw him right away, standing in a bar area with a group near the hostess stand. As she neared them he turned and reached for her, forcing the two women standing in front of her to step aside and let her through. Two men greeted her cordially and then walked away. The two women remained: appraising, waiting.

He made the introductions. Greetings were exchanged. He looked at Aliyah. "Shall we?"

"Yes."

"Ladies." With a nod goodbye in their direction, he placed a hand on the small of Aliyah's back as they followed the hostess to a corner booth.

But the ladies followed, hot on their heels.

"Did you have any trouble finding the place?"

Aliyah shook her head. "Not at all. Have GPS, will travel."

"That system does make it easier."

The woman closest to her, a cute brunette with expressive gray eyes, cleared her throat. "Where'd you drive from?"

Aliyah looked at Terrell, then turned to address the woman behind her. "Davis."

"You live there?" asked the woman who'd been fawning over Terrell when she walked in, and when introduced had offered a smile about as real as a three-dollar bill. The obvious competition, had Aliyah been in the hunt for a handsome, wealthy, well-built, charismatic, sexy example of male magnificence. She wasn't. So Nosy Nancy had nothing to worry about. And no need to know her business.

They reached the booth. Aliyah sat without answering. The server immediately came over. "Is this who you were waiting for, Terrell?"

"Yes, it is."

She placed menus in front of Aliyah and Terrell, then looked at the women. "Do y'all need menus?"

"Yes."

"No."

The server looked between Terrell and Nosy, from whom the simultaneous answer had come.

"It will just be Aliyah and myself tonight," Terrell said. "My friends were just leaving."

"Oh, okay." Expressive Eyes gave a general wave. "I guess I'll see you guys later." She walked over and joined the two men who'd left Terrell to sit at the bar.

"Speak for yourself," Nosy Nancy said, before looking at Terrell. "Are you going to scoot over or get up and let me in?" He didn't move, just looked at her. "This isn't a date, is it? I mean, you're at the Cove Café for goodness sake, so obviously—" she looked at Aliyah "—it's no big deal."

So this was how it went down in Terrell's hometown? Girlfriend didn't know but the poised, polite chick in front of her was east coast all day long, where people kept it real. She could switch it up and hurt her feelings. But instead, Aliyah ignored her. Why spar with someone trying to crash into where she had been invited? She casually picked up her menu and began to browse.

Terrell's voice remained low and casual, but his eyes

were those of someone who'd had enough. "You have a nice evening...okay?"

"Oh. Okay." She flung long black hair over her shoulder and adjusted a nice designer bag over store-bought boobs. "Sorry I upset you, Alicia. Terrell and I go way back, to preschool almost."

The misspoken name was intentional, and catty. Aliyah knew that, and offered advice instead of correction. "Don't be sorry."

Terrell's brief but knowing smile did things to her insides. The man was dangerous, too sexy for her own good. With no man in her life for the past few months, she wished he were on the menu she held. He had her so distracted she barely noticed Nosy mosey away.

"Sorry about that."

Aliyah's eyes turned devilish. "Don't be—"

"Stop it!" He laughed. "You know you're wrong. Clever, though."

"I learned from the best—been dealing with girls like her since I was fourteen."

"In Davis?"

"No. On Manhattan's Upper East Side, where I went to private school on a scholastic scholarship."

"You're from New York?"

She nodded. "Brooklyn, more specifically. Born and bred in Prospect Heights."

"But smart enough to go to school with the rich and privileged."

"Yes, and at times that was most unfortunate. I watched girls who had everything become jealous of one who had nothing."

He sat back, observing her keenly. "That's not true. You've got a lot."

"Yes, well, there's that."

"I'm not talking about your physical generosities..."

"Ha!"

"I'm talking about you."

"You don't even know me."

"But you make a brother want to know you. And that's what I'm talking about."

"Looks like you're a brother who knows everybody, and who everybody knows."

"It's one of the downsides of living in a small town. And one of the reasons I don't eat here often even though the town's dining options are limited. Everybody thinks they know you well enough to get all up in your business, even uninvited."

"Most women who act like that have a reason for doing so."

"She doesn't."

Aliyah shrugged. "Not my monkey, not my circus."

"Meaning?"

"Meaning whatever is between you two is not my concern. I just hope this place serves a good burger."

"It's not the best one in town but you won't be disappointed."

As if on cue, the server came over to take their orders. Conversation halted as Aliyah perused the menu. Terrell watched. She noticed. "Clearly you've already decided what you want to order."

"Absolutely," he said, his eyes narrowing slightly. "I already know exactly what I want."

She rolled her eyes. He didn't know, but the action matched the roiling of her stomach as she took in the curly long lashes that framed chocolate-brown orbs, his cleanly shaven angular face and cushy lips. He smiled when she ordered the Cove Classic: double-patty cheeseburger, coleslaw and fries.

"Make that two," he told the server, letting her walk

away before he refocused his attention on Aliyah. "I love it. A woman with a healthy appetite and not afraid to show it."

She fixed him with a sultry look of her own. "Oh, yes. I have a very healthy appetite."

Check, and checkmate.

"So tell me about yourself, Aliyah Robinson."

"What would you like to know?"

"Since you live in Davis, how'd you learn about our center here in Paradise Cove?"

"A good friend recommended it. Her youngest son is enrolled there. She watches Kyle for me. So it works out."

"What's her name?"

"Lauren Hensley. Do you know her?"

"No. But I'm only there three days a week, tutoring and mentoring teenaged boys between thirteen and sixteen years old. A buddy of mine named Luther works with your son's age group."

"I wouldn't have pegged you as a guy who tutored teens."

"Why not?"

"I don't know. You just don't look the type."

"What type do I look like?"

Like the type of man I need to take home. Tonight. "Let me think about that." The honest answer remained unspoken, but a hint of it showed in her eyes.

"Is UC what brought you to Davis?" She nodded. "With all of the great schools on the east coast, why that school?"

"The residency program."

His brow rose in surprise. "You're a doctor?"

"Not for at least another two and half years. I'm in residency as an anesthesiologist."

"Impressive. Fine, smart…and you wonder why those girls were jealous."

"Things look much differently when you're fourteen."

"Indeed."

The server brought their drinks. Aliyah took a sip of her frothy root beer. Terrell had opted for real beer, and took a healthy swig from the bottle.

"Ever been to New York?"

"I've spent a little time there. My younger brother is going to NYU."

"What's he studying?"

"He's getting his doctorate in psychology."

"Oh, so you'll have a doctor in your family as well."

"We already do. My cousin's wife is a doctor in San Diego. But yes, Julian, hands down, is the brains in my family."

"Are you the brawn?"

He smiled. "Is that your answer for my type?"

"No, but if forced to fight I think you could hold your own."

"Ha! Thanks, I think. My family owns a realty and consulting company. I handle sales."

He was being humble. Due to her internet sleuthing, Aliyah knew he was a director in what appeared to be a very profitable company, heading up the sale of corporate and commercial properties throughout the state. A rich, successful, confident man who was also unassuming? Maybe he could scratch her itch after all.

"Is that how you ended up in Paradise Cove?"

"My grandfather settled here after leaving the military, went in with a partner and bought up a lot of land at a time when it was a buyer's market. After college, my dad correctly predicted that metropolitan expansion would push the population this way. So he acquired more land in this area, got his real estate license and partnered with a contractor to build homes. Thirty years ago, where we sit now was nothing but farmland. Now, we've got Paradise Cove and, next to it, Paradise Valley, where my brother Warren now manages and co-owns that initial land my grandfather purchased."

"Not many people of color can claim such historical ties and land ownership. You must be proud of what your grandfather and father have done."

"I'm proud of my entire family."

Conversation continued. The flow was easy. The food was good, the flirtations continuous. She told him a little more about Kyle, and about the teacher/mentor-turned-friend, Lauren, who'd encouraged Aliyah to choose UC Davis for her residency. She also let him know that while her body was in California, her heart still bled Brooklyn. She was a New York Jets fan for life. Aliyah ascertained that Terrell's extended family was a close-knit one, that he was a member of the Raider Nation, but—that glaring offense aside—there was substance behind the sexiness. It was clear that neither wanted the night to end. But for Aliyah, it had to. She had a son to pick up and an early surgery to assist with in the morning.

She placed her napkin on the plate. "Thanks for dinner. The food was delicious."

"What about the company?"

She shrugged, reached for her glass. "It was all right."

"Ha! Just all right, huh?"

"Yep." She finished the last of her soda. "Just all right."

"You're something else, you know that?"

"So I've been told a time or two."

"Well, hopefully I made a better first impression the second time around."

She blessed him with a smile. "You did."

"Enough for you to go out with me again?"

She reached for her purse. "Maybe. But tonight's good time has come to an end. I have to be up early in the morning."

Terrell reached into his wallet and tossed a couple bills

on the table. They stood and together walked out of the restaurant. He passed his shiny sports convertible and continued to her car.

"So, what kinds of things do you like to do?"

"I'm pretty adventurous and open to new things. There's probably not many things I wouldn't try at least once."

Her quick once-over suggested he was included in this statement.

"Is that so?" They reached her car. He opened the door. Before she could get in, he cut her off and pressed her against the metal. "What about Friday night?"

She didn't back down. She pressed back. "I have to work this Saturday. I'm off on Sunday, though."

"Then what about Saturday night?" He ran a strong, large hand down her arm, before resting it lightly on her hip.

"Highly likely, if I can arrange a sitter. But not here, in your town. I'm not up to watching you fend off women all night and if insulted again, I might not act as civilly as I did tonight." She pressed a hand against his shirt, and met a chest as solid as steel. "You work out."

"I do. As tight as your body is, looks like you do, too." Their bodies were close, their faces, too, so much so that their breaths mingled.

"Can't say much for crunches and treadmills—" she slid a finger down the side of his face "—but there are certain ways I like to exercise." She gently pushed him away and got into the car.

"Keep Saturday night open."

"Don't keep me waiting. Make a date."

"All right then. Saturday, seven o'clock. I'll text the details later."

"See you then."

She closed the door, started the engine and left the parking lot without looking back. Thoughts of Terrell accompanied her home, though.

Saturday night couldn't come soon enough.

Chapter 3

The days flew. By the time Saturday arrived Aliyah had almost changed her mind again about her date with Terrell. Though this was a woman's prerogative, she was usually more decisive. But he'd been on her mind more than was comfortable, took up more mental space than a potential casual should occupy. Trying to finish a three-year residency in two and a half was the only type of serious she could handle right now and something—okay, keen intuition and a heart that skipped a pitter when his face came to mind—told her that keeping things easy breezy and detached might not be possible. That scared her. So did the potency of her attraction. Yes, he was good-looking and yes, he was rich. She'd dated her share of handsome men and Kyle's father's family was part of the east coast's Black bourgeoisie. Her ex's family had doubted the truth of Kyle's paternity and shattered her self-esteem. She didn't want to go through that kind of scrutiny and judgment again, which is why a friend with benefits was all she wanted Terrell to be. But what if her heart felt otherwise? Did she want to chance a hot, sexual fling blazing into a relationship? Or worse, an inferno?

When she'd pulled up stakes and left the east coast, falling for an obvious heartthrob within a month of arriving hadn't been in her plans. It still wasn't. At least through this year, the only male she planned to focus on was the not yet three-foot-tall, sweet and curious tyke standing in front of her with his ever-present tablet in hand. But unlike most kids, Kyle was as likely to be working math problems from the study modules she'd downloaded as playing video games. The child had an unusual interest in numbers. She'd purchased the kid-friendly program to encourage him. Being good with numbers could take you places.

"Where are you going, Mommy?"

"Out with a friend, sweetheart."

"Is it Mr. Drake?"

Aliyah was stunned, but maintained her composure by putting on her earring before she turned around. "What makes you think Mr. Drake and I are friends?"

"Because."

Aliyah watched as her son held his arms out to the side and "flew" around the room. He could never sit still. She walked over to where he was and placed hands on his shoulders to still him. "Because what?"

"Because of how he was smiling when you came to pick us up."

On Friday Lauren's teenaged son, Conrad, had fractured his arm while skateboarding. On her way to emergency she'd called Aliyah, who agreed to pick up Kyle and Conner from the center.

"Mr. Drake wasn't there, honey, remember? I spoke with your teacher, Mr. Adams."

"I know, but Mr. Drake saw you, too. He stopped in the hallway and started smiling. Like this."

Kyle smiled broadly. Aliyah laughed.

Observant little bugger. *Note to self: watch your actions with Terrell when Kyle is around.*

"I think he wanted to say hi, but this woman came and got him."

A scowl jumped on her face without her permission, before she could stop it. The unconscious reaction surprised her. No doubt Terrell was popular with the ladies. And obviously unattached. Why wouldn't they be swarming around him like bees on a honeycomb? And why should it matter to her? All she wanted from him was some horizontal exercise. She vowed to remember that.

"Do you see Mr. Drake often?"

"Yes. He comes and talks to Mr. Adams. They're good friends."

"How do you know?"

"They laugh a lot."

"Oh."

Kyle sat on the bench at the foot of her bed, tapped the face of the tablet and restarted a numbers game. "I like Mr. Drake."

"Why?"

He shrugged. "Because he is cool."

Great. Even her son was smitten. Well, Mr. Cool made Mommy hot, and glad that Luther Adams was Kyle's main teacher. Not good for her son to get too attached to a man in their lives only temporarily. She walked over to the closet and stood in front of a row of shoes, deciding. She was in no way trying to impress Mr. Drake, but still bypassed the comfy flats and chose a pair of strappy crystal-covered stilettos to pair with her black skinny jeans and off-the-shoulder cream-colored top. "Go get your Power Ranger backpack. It's packed with clothes for you."

Kyle looked up. "Where am I going?"

"Oh. I didn't tell you? You've been invited to Conner's house for an overnight playdate."

"Awesome!"

She laughed as he ran from the room, his interest in Mommy's date, who just happened to be with Mr. Cool, totally forgotten. It had been Lauren's idea to have Kyle spend the night. They were good friends who shared almost everything. Lauren was probably just as excited that Aliyah might get some as she was.

A few minutes later and they were in the car and headed to the Hensleys, whose house was mere blocks away. She only had a few minutes once they arrived, but she still got out of the car to greet her mentor and best friend.

"Hey, girl."

"Hey yourself. Don't you look snazzy!" Leaning in, Lauren whispered, "I especially love those F-me pumps."

Rather than disagree, Aliyah cosigned. "If I'm lucky!"

They laughed and high-fived.

Aliyah had met Lauren during her sophomore year in high school. At that time, Lauren worked as a counselor at the academy Aliyah attended. A raven-haired, free-spirited thirtysomething cutie from California, Lauren quickly picked up on some of Aliyah's classmates' antics. She paid special attention to Aliyah, not only for that reason, but also because she was so smart. And driven, too. When Aliyah announced her plans to become a doctor, Lauren was her biggest cheerleader, helping Aliyah choose appropriate classes and complete scholarship applications. Once Aliyah graduated high school, the two kept in touch and when she got pregnant, it was Lauren that Aliyah went to first with the news, ashamed to tell her mother for fear of being a disappointment. Somewhere between then and the time Kyle was born, mentor and mentee became best friends. A short time later Lauren's husband, a professor, landed a job at the University of California at Davis, a college located close to where Lauren had grown up. She jumped at the chance to move back west and once she found out about the college's residency program, lobbied for Aliyah to finish there.

After pulling out money for Kyle's entertainment, a move that Lauren summarily rebuffed, Aliyah waved goodbye. Before leaving Lauren's driveway, she typed the address Terrell had texted her into the GPS. He hadn't told her the name of where they were meeting. Not that it mattered. Since arriving a month ago, Aliyah's world had basically been work, home and Kyle's school. Wherever they were meeting was likely someplace she'd not been before.

Fifteen minutes later and not only was she somewhere she'd never been before, but it was also some place she never would have guessed he'd ask her to meet.

Terrell exited his car as she pulled up, his eyes sparkling, smile wide. "Hello, beautiful."

"Hey." She stepped into his open arms for a hug. "What is this place?"

"An airport, Aliyah. Small, I know, but all that we need."

She gave him a look. "Thanks for stating the obvious. Where are we going?"

"San Francisco."

"Are you serious?"

"You said we couldn't meet in Paradise Cove. I couldn't think of an appropriate place for this night in Davis. So we're going to San Francisco."

"And we're flying? I heard it's only an hour's drive away."

"More like ninety minutes, depending on traffic. Why get stuck in traffic when you can fly over it?"

The logic of the rich, much like Kyle's father, except without a snobbish tone. Still, every similarity to Ernest Westcott was a strike against Terrell Drake. But given the emotional distance she planned to maintain, that was probably a good thing.

They entered the regional airport hangar and walked over to a sleek private jet where two men, one casually dressed in button-down and slacks, the other wearing a stained gray uniform, stood talking. Mr. Casual saw them approaching and broke away from the worker, who turned and walked into an office.

"Mr. Drake!"

"Stan, my man!" The two men shook hands. Terrell turned to Aliyah. "Stan, I'd like you to meet Aliyah Robinson, an east coast transplant suffering from a case of small-townitis."

Stan smiled as he held out his hand. "San Francisco is a great remedy for that disease. A pleasure to meet you."

Aliyah greeted him. "Likewise."

"Are we ready to go? I saw you in discussion with the mechanic."

"We were just shooting the breeze. We're all set. Inspection completed. Gauges checked. Bar is stocked. Just waiting on you."

"After you." Terrell stepped aside so that Aliyah could precede him up the steps. Midway, she turned quickly. As expected, his eyes were squarely on her assets.

"Hey, it's directly in my line of vision!"

"You're obsessed," she said with a chuckle, and continued up the steps. Ernest's family had chartered private jets on occasion, for events to which she'd not been invited. This was her first time inside one. If its interior was any indication of how the Drakes lived, theirs was a lavish, luxurious lifestyle. She took it all in: buttery leather seats, mahogany trim, crystal this, platinum that. All the discomfort from earlier returned.

Terrell motioned for Aliyah to sit in one of two front seats, watching her as she did so. "You all right?"

She nodded.

"You're not afraid of flying are you?"

"No, but I'm usually on a bigger plane."

"Don't worry," Terrell said, continuing to the bar that was midway back. "This is one of the safest planes out there and when it comes to pilots, Stan is top-notch. He flew fighter jets in the air force. He can do this hop to San Fran in his sleep. What can I get you to drink?"

"What are you having?"

"Let's pop a bottle—make it a celebration."

"What are we celebrating?"

Terrell shrugged. "Life."

"Sounds good to me."

Terrell poured two flutes and returned to his seat. He lifted his glass. "To a wonderful time in the big city."

Aliyah tapped his glass and sipped. "Mmm, this is good. I don't like champagne that's either too dry or too sweet. This is neither." She took another sip. "What brand is this?"

"It's called Diamond, a Drake Wines product."

Ah, yes. The grape-growing brother. "Your family owns a winery?"

"My immediate family is in real estate, for the most part. But my brother Warren, the one who co-owns the land with my grandfather, planted several acres of grapes that are now thriving. He did so on the advice of one of my cousins, whose family owns a resort and winery in Southern California."

"Lots of success in your family."

"We've been blessed."

The captain walked back and asked them to buckle up. Ten minutes later they were above the clouds that had hovered for most of the day, surrounded by brilliant blue skies and a sun that would not be setting before they landed.

"So tell me about your family, Aliyah."

"It's not like yours, that's for sure."

"Few are." This answer got a raised brow. "I don't say that arrogantly, but honestly. It's a lifestyle that is not commonly experienced, one I'm grateful to have. But nothing was handed to us on a silver platter. My family's achievements come from a combination of luck, good timing and lots of hard work."

Aliyah nodded, her mind awhirl with how to respond to his question. She wasn't ashamed of her family, nor the struggles they all endured growing up in a vibrant but gritty section of Brooklyn's Prospect Heights. The drive, resilience and determination to succeed arose from the notorious neighborhood activities she sometimes witnessed, events that left some childhood friends and acquaintances incarcerated too long, pregnant too young or dead too early. Those experiences helped make her who she was today. But she knew all too well how the upper two percent sometimes viewed the working class, since she'd spent twelve years—high school, undergrad and graduate school—surrounded by students of privilege and families of wealth. While dating Ernest, she had a bird's-eye view of how high society operated—the judgments, condescension and exclusivity, and how friends were chosen less by personality and more by zip code and pedigree. Not even her becoming a doctor was good enough to gain entry. "A charity case to fulfill quotas" was how her attending the same Ivy League college as Ernest was described by his parents. As if her high SAT scores and 4.0 grade average—an average maintained even after the baby and while working part-time—had nothing to do with it.

Terrell mistook her silence. "Listen, Aliyah, I didn't mean to offend you."

"Oh, no. It's not that." She took a sip of champagne and gazed out the window a moment before turning back to him. "Kyle's father is from a wealthy family, one into which I was never accepted. They abhorred my background, disapproved of our dating. My becoming pregnant left them petrified. Their vitriol was unrelenting, to the point where even I questioned my worth. It took a long time to rebuild my confidence. There is evidently still some work to do."

"Where was Kyle's father while his family attacked you?"

Her smile was bittersweet. "Mostly, on their side."

"Even after you gave birth to his son?"

"Oh, that was just to trap him, you see, and a determination made only after paternity was proven by not one official test, but three."

"You can't be serious."

"As serious as his parents were when they demanded I take them. After Kyle was born, they ramped up the pressure for him to dump his low-brow girlfriend and find someone respectable to marry. Someone with the right... credentials. That's what he did."

"Then you're better off without him. A man who doesn't have your back, no matter what the situation or who the person is attacking, doesn't deserve you."

"I appreciate that."

"Hopefully he helps out financially, at least."

"The bare minimum, thanks to creative accounting and a savvy attorney. What they didn't understand, and still don't, is that Ernest's presence in Kyle's life would be more valuable than any check he could write. Every child needs a father, but for boys, it's even more important.

"In the end, it's probably for the best. I wouldn't feel comfortable leaving him alone with that set of grandparents. There's no telling how they'd poison his mind, or scar his soul."

Terrell reached over and caressed her face. "Would it sound too selfish for me to say that I'm glad he's not in your life?"

"Yes, that sounds selfish. But I'm still glad you said it."

He leaned. She leaned. Their lips touched, softly, exploring. Soon their tongues intertwined, still bearing the essence of the wine. He kissed her thoroughly. She matched him stroke for stroke.

He pulled back. "I'd better stop while I can. We'll soon be landing."

Terrell's kiss erased yesteryear's heartache. Aliyah relaxed into the comfort of the supple leather, and began to feel the excitement of being in a private plane with a handsome man, soaring to a night of fun. She finished her flute of champagne and turned flirty eyes to Terrell.

"I'm glad Kyle is at your center. All of the men there, at least the ones I've met, seem genuinely invested in the program's success and are great male role models."

"Including me?"

"Especially you."

Terrell extended his arm across the aisle. Aliyah placed her small hand inside his much larger one. "I'm glad he's there, too. We'll do our best to provide him with the mentorship he needs. Meanwhile, tonight—" Terrell raised her hand and kissed it lightly "—I'd like to make sure his mother, the lovely Aliyah Robinson, gets whatever it is she wants and needs as well."

Chapter 4

They landed at San Francisco International Airport and were whisked away to a cozy, upscale restaurant with stunning views of the bay and the Golden Gate Bridge.

Aliyah looked around. "I didn't expect we'd be someplace this fancy. Glad I wore my crystal stilettos or I'd feel out of place."

"You could walk in here wearing a garbage bag and outshine every woman in the room."

Aliyah laughed and sat back in her chair. "Wow, you are a salesman, aren't you?"

"Yes, and a darn good one. But that wasn't a line."

The waiter came over and after describing the evening's special features, took their drink and appetizer orders. After further discussion of the menu and deciding on entrées, the conversation came back around to their continuing to get to know each other.

"So, Aliyah…"

"Yes?"

"What made you decide to become a doctor?"

"Not just any doctor but an anesthesiologist, specifically. The reason? Shannon's mom."

"Was she an anesthesiologist?"

Aliyah nodded. "My seventh-grade summer, I was selected for a math-and-science program that paired students from different schools to work on a project together. I was paired with this geeky, slightly chubby girl named Shannon. We were best friends from day one. So much so that she invited me to her birthday party. She lived on Manhattan's Upper East Side. That train ride took me to another world and changed my life.

"After that day, I spent several more at her house. One time we were in her room and I was asking how her family lived the way they did. Where they got so much money. Her mother was walking by and answered, 'We worked for it.' I asked her what she did and she told me that she was an anesthesiologist. Right then and there, I decided that's what I'd be, too. Of course, had I known that such a declaration was going to cost me twelve additional years of my life after high school, I would have chosen Shannon's father's career instead."

"What did he do?"

"Worked in finance. On Wall Street. He's retired now. They both are. Shannon still lives in the home I visited but her parents spend most of their time in their villa in France."

"Do you like what you do?"

"I love it. Money and the lavish lifestyle I saw at Shannon's house is what sparked my interest. The satisfaction I found during the educational journey to my goal is what's kept me here."

"You've accomplished a lot. As a single mother, it couldn't have been easy."

"I'm not used to easy. Anytime I think of quitting I remember those on the block who chose differently, and are no longer with us. I never want Kyle to experience what I saw growing up. He's my motivation."

Dinner arrived. The conversation changed. From the appetizer to dessert, the food was as decadent as Aliyah's thoughts had been ever since Terrell's promise to satisfy her. They left the restaurant, and just when she thought the night couldn't get any better Terrell surprised her with tickets and backstage passes to see one of her favorite artists, Janelle Monáe. The show was rocking, so much so that Aliyah was almost able to ignore all the attention Terrell received from the ladies. Even if she were interested in a serious relationship, which she wasn't, Terrell wouldn't be on her short list. Relationships were hard enough. One with walking temptation wrapped around fifty shades of sexy would be impossible.

After spending time with the singer backstage, Terrell placed his arm around Aliyah and pulled her to his side. They walked toward the exit. "Ms. Robinson?"

She placed an arm around his waist. "Yes?"

"Have you enjoyed the evening so far?"

"Are you kidding? This has been the most fun I've had in a long time."

"It makes me happy to hear that."

"I'm happy that you're happy."

He stopped and turned to her. "Then only one question remains."

"What's that?"

"Should our next destination be the airport, to take you home and kiss you good-night at the door, or my place here in San Francisco, away from Paradise Cove's prying eyes?"

She leaned into him. "Mr. Drake, I want you to take me wherever you can fulfill your promise of leaving me fully satisfied."

They couldn't reach the Drake place fast enough.

"Wow." Aliyah stepped inside, immediately noticing the city view from their high perch in the hills. "This is beautiful."

Terrell came up behind her, kissing her temple as he wrapped her in his arms. "So is this."

She turned into him, desire in her eyes. The evidence of his desire was a little farther down.

"You know what I've been wanting to do all night?"

"Probably the same thing on my mind."

Their heads moved in unison toward a mutual destination. The kiss was soft, purposeful, their lips rubbing against each other in a casual get-to-know. Terrell's hands went on a journey of discovery, meandering over her shoulders, down her back and to the top of bootyliciousness. Aliyah, who at five-five had always preferred a tall man, relished how her five-inch heels made it possible to easily wrap her arms around his neck. With a swipe of her tongue against his lips, she intensified the exchange.

He sucked it in, an act that weakened her knees.

After a long moment, they came up for air. Terrell mumbled against her hair, "Damn, you feel good."

"So do you."

"You taste good."

"Mmm."

"I want to taste more of you."

"What are you waiting for?"

He grabbed her hand and led them to the couch. Once seated, he pulled her to his lap. The fit was perfect, as if they'd been designed for each other. The kiss resumed—slower, hotter, wetter. Tongues twirling, slow and easy, hips grinding in the same rhythm. Terrell caressed Aliyah's arm, running his hand down the length of it, coming back up to cup her breast. Seconds more, and he eased down the fabric and palmed the warm flesh beneath. His thumb brushed against a rapidly hardening nipple. Aliyah arched her back, encouraging him to move faster, to take more. Instead he stopped, hugging her tightly before sitting back to look into her eyes.

"What?"

"Girl, I don't know what it is about you. You've got me so turned on!"

"And that's a problem."

"No. I just…"

"Just what."

"I just want to make sure that you're ready for this. That this is what you want."

"You gave me a choice. I'm still happy with the one I made."

"I want you, too. But I don't want something done in the heat of the moment to change how we are with each other. I like you. I want you. But I also respect you. I don't want you to feel bad afterward."

Aliyah rolled off of him and stood. "Look," she began, pulling her top over her head and tossing it on the floor. "We are two clear-thinking, intelligent, consenting adults who came here for the same reason." She reached behind her and unclasped her bra. It joined her top on the floor. Her breasts swayed invitingly, nipples protruding in invitation to be licked. She undid her jeans button and unzipped them before sitting on the couch to remove her shoes. "There will be no regrets, no guilt trips and no expectations. I am as uninterested in a steady relationship as I'm sure you are. Now—" she raised her legs to him "—will you help me take off these jeans and show me what that mouth is good at besides talking?"

She watched his eyes light up and become predatory as he reached for first one leg of her jeans and then the other, removing denim to reveal smooth, flawless skin that reminded him of a favorite childhood drink. Hot chocolate. He stood. She watched. His eyes never left hers as he removed his shoes, shirt and pants. Placing his hands on the band of his boxers, he paused just a moment before pulling them down and stepping out of them in one fluid motion.

"Oh, my goodness," Aliyah cooed, staring unabashedly at eight thick inches of penis perfection. "Is that all for me?"

"All for you, baby. Sit back."

He started at her toes. No preamble, no warning. Just sucked one into his mouth. So nasty, yet so decadently nice. Leisurely placed kisses continued from her ankle to her knee, up the outer and inner sides of thigh. She spread her legs in invitation, though there was none needed. His index finger was already working itself between her thong's elastic edge, already teasing her moistening folds as his tongue teased the slip of satin covering her treasure. Aliyah hissed and moaned, swirling her hips against his tongue to increase the friction and douse her desire.

Her actions were rewarded when Terrell slipped his tongue beneath the thong and kissed the satin of her skin. Lapping, nipping, licking, tasting her over and again. Aliyah threw back her head in ecstasy. The man was a maestro, playing her passion with precision and skill. Sweet torture that she wanted to stop, that she hoped would go on forever.

But she wanted more.

"Stand up."

No answer. His tongue was busy doing other things. She chuckled, placed her hands on the sides of his head and gently pulled him away from her. "Stand up."

"What's wrong?"

"Just do it."

He complied. In an instant Aliyah was on her knees, fondling the massive weapon that had made her mouth water. She licked its length, outlined the perfect mushroom tip with her tongue, took him in, slowly, fully.

"Aliyah." Spoken like a promise, or a prayer. "Baby…" He pulled back. "You're driving me crazy. I've got to be inside you, now."

He reached for protection and then sat on the couch. Aliyah climbed on top of him and slowly, oh, so slowly, eased down on his massive shaft, allowing the delicious friction to heat up her insides. He pulled a nipple into his mouth and reverently cupped the butt that began this journey. Squeezing. Kneading. Grinding. Thrusting. Hard and fast, then slow and easy. Riding one wave of ecstasy after another, resting only long enough to ride again.

Later, they moved to the master suite, where the vastness of the four-poster, king-size bed offered a whole new realm of possibilities. They explored them all, each matching the other's voracious appetite with their own unbridled enthusiasm. Each had clearly met their match.

When Aliyah returned to earth from a shattering climax that brought her near tears, she cuddled in the crook of Terrell's arm, listening as his own heartbeat slowed and returned to normal.

"Terrell."

"Yes, Ms. Robinson."

"That was frickin' amazing."

He laughed, pulled her even closer. "So you're saying I took care of you properly?"

"Yeah, you were all right." Said in that lazy, drawn-out way she'd heard the teens do it.

This answer lifted his head from the pillow. "Just all right?"

"Yes." He grunted. She smiled into the darkness, doubting his sexual prowess had been called anything less than amazing his entire life. If indeed it had happened, whoever said it had lied. "Terrell?"

"Yes, Aliyah."

"Can you be all right again in the morning?"

His deep-throated chuckle was the last thing she heard before falling asleep.

Chapter 5

He awoke to her lips kissing his manhood, her glory spread before him like a gourmet buffet.

"Good morning!" he said.

She purred, occupied.

"You sure know how to wake a man up."

She knew how to do more than that. Working magic with her tongue and fingers caused all talk to cease until after they'd showered. After drying off, they strode down the stairs in their toned, naked glory and retrieved the clothes that last night had been tossed aside.

Terrell reached for his boxers. "What do you want for breakfast?" She wriggled her eyebrows suggestively. "Girl, stop!"

"Ha!"

"Dang! I never thought I'd meet someone who liked sex more than I do."

"I would apologize for wearing you out but truthfully, I'm not at all sorry." She zipped up her jeans and reached for her bra. "It had been a while."

"I could tell."

"Shut up!"

They laughed, sharing a comfortable camaraderie that some couples never experienced, even after being together for years.

"Seriously, though. What do you feel like eating?"

"Something quick. I want to spend the afternoon with Kyle."

"Hey, why don't the two of you come over for brunch?"

"You cook?"

He put up his hands. "Oh, no. I'm allergic to the kitchen. I'm talking about coming over to my parents' house, where we have brunch every Sunday."

She smiled. "No, thank you."

"Why not?"

"Um, this isn't a meeting-the-family kind of situation, remember?"

"Oh, no. It's not like that. Friends get invited over all the time."

She gave him a look. "Even more reason not to be woman number whatever showing up."

"Wait! Not those kinds of friends."

"Then what kinds of friends?"

"Friends who I really like. Not just anyone. I don't invite booty calls over to my mama's house, for instance."

"Something tells me that to do that your mama would have to have a really big house."

"Ha!"

"I appreciate the invite but would rather grab something quick and casual on the way to the airport. Are we leaving now?"

"Wow, she uses me all night long, wrings every ounce of strength from my body, then tosses me aside with the first light of morning."

"No, I used you some more at the first light of morning. It's almost ten o'clock." Sliding on her shoe, she walked over and gave him a peck on the lips. "I'm going to use the restroom and then I'll be ready to go."

Terrell reached for his phone to call the pilot, shaking his head as he watched Aliyah leave the room.

A short time later they arrived at the airport, takeout

orders from an organic café in hand. Stan greeted them cheerfully. "Breakfast for me? Terrell, you shouldn't have."

"Good. Because I didn't." They laughed. "Give me a minute to heat this up and get situated, all right?"

"Sure. Just let me know when you're ready."

Ten minutes later they were in the air, speeding toward Paradise Cove...and reality.

"That was delicious." Aliyah finished off the last of her egg white omelet and swiped her mouth with a napkin. "Everything about this weekend was oh-so tasty!" She reached over and placed a hand on Terrell's arm. "Thanks again for inviting me out. It was just the date I needed. The last few months have been busy—securing the job, finding a house, moving across country. And that's after a jam-packed schedule, four years of killer courses to get my degree." She sighed, looked away. "And everything else." A second, and then she turned back to him. "I didn't realize how long it had been since I totally relaxed and enjoyed myself. But I was able to do that with you."

"I'm happy that you're happy, and enjoyed myself as well."

She pulled out her phone and they were both soon busy texting, answering messages and emails that last night had been ignored. Casual conversation flowed in between, making the forty-five-minute flight back home seem much shorter.

They landed. He walked her to her car, shared a quick kiss and hug. Terrell opened her door. "I'll see you tomorrow, right?"

"How so?"

"Your son. The center. Our tutoring and activity program?"

"Actually, no. I came to enroll him and scope out the place. Since everything I saw met with my approval—"

she paused, giving him a slow once-over "—Lauren, his babysitter, will likely handle it from here on out."

"Then when am I going to see you?"

"Soon." She got into her car, gave a quick wave and was gone. He watched her car turn on to the street and speed away, and wondered why his heart seemed to go with her.

He knew just who to call for the answer, and wasn't surprised when just as he thought this, his phone rang. That whole twin-radar, two-halves-of-the-same-whole sort of thing. He tapped the speaker button. "Tee."

"Hey, Tee." It was his sister, Teresa.

"I was just getting ready to call you."

"I know. What kind of trouble have you gotten yourself into this weekend?"

"No trouble, sis."

"That's not the vibe I'm getting. Who is she?"

"The mother of one of the new students at the center. Her name is Aliyah."

"All right, Silky."

"Ha!" It had been a while since Terrell had heard this high school nickname. "What made you call me that?"

"Hearing that Cindy was divorced and living back in PC. Remember that cheer she made up after hearing that was your nickname?" She adopted a high-pitched voice. "Terrell Drake, with all the moves, a voice like silk and twice as smooth."

"Please, sis. Spare me the memory. Crazy that you brought it up, though. I ran in to her while meeting Aliyah for dinner."

"Was she pushy, as usual?"

"She basically invited herself to join us for dinner. What would you call it?"

"Ha! Cindy was in love with Silky."

"Girl, stop."

"What about the rule we made? Don't reach where you teach!"

"I wasn't reaching."

"What, she kidnapped you?"

"She gave me a second chance to make a first impression, which led to a third one."

"What was her first impression? Never mind, just start at the beginning and tell me everything."

"Well, sis, it all started when I turned the corner and saw this wonderful behind."

"Oh, Lord."

"Perfectly proportioned on this amazing body."

"And you just had to have her phone number."

"As one of the center's volunteer faculty, it was my duty to follow up on the new enrollee and make sure all had been handled properly. That's all…"

"Oh, so that's what was on your mind? Duty? I thought it was booty."

Terrell could only laugh at the truth. He continued, filling her in on how he got busted and why he felt he at least owed her dinner. How cool and down to earth Aliyah was and how conversation flowed.

"Before the first date was over, I knew I wanted a second one. She did, too, but not in Paradise Cove."

"With Cindy's tactless antics, who could blame her?"

"I was glad she felt that way."

"Unlike all the others in PC, who'd make sure your date was somewhere public where everybody would know they'd been with a Drake."

"Well, you know."

"Unfortunately, yes, I do."

Terrell chuckled. "Anyway, last night we went to San Francisco. Dinner, concert, a night on the hill. I'm driving home from the airport now."

"Sounds like a top-tier Drake date. What didn't she like?"

"She loved it. Said it was the best time she'd had in a while."

"Oh, so now you're afraid she'll stalk you at the center, wanting exclusivity?"

"No, exactly the opposite. She made it clear that this was just a sex thing, basically—wouldn't even accept my invitation to Sunday brunch."

"Wow, Tee, she sounds like you!"

"I knew you'd say that."

"Because it's true!"

"The way she dismissed me, so casually, made me feel like a used piece of meat. I need to call every girl I sent home after the deed was done and apologize."

"No apology needed if that's all they expected. Clearly that's what your girl thought last night. But from the sound of your voice and the words left unspoken, you might be the one who ends up stalking her!"

"Tee?"

"What?"

"Go wrestle a bear."

"Ha! I love you, too. And for the record while I've grown to love Alaska, I'm still afraid of the wild."

"No matter what, Tee, you'll always be city. I need to run. Tell Atka I said what's up."

"Will do."

Chapter 6

Aliyah signed out of her FaceTime account, happy that she'd been able to see and speak to her whole family. These days, finding her parents and four siblings all home at the same time was rare. It made her miss New York, but it also allowed her to see that all of her hard work was paying off. She hadn't gone to college and blazed a trail of success just for herself. She'd done it so that the four hardheads looking up to her—three brothers and one sister, all younger—could have a clear example of how to avoid life's pitfalls and go for one's dreams. The two oldest brothers were excelling in college. The younger brother and sister still made her nervous, entranced by the smoke and mirrors of quick money and instant success. Gangs constantly courted her six-foot-plus brother. Pretty-boy tough guys wanted to date her gorgeous sixteen-year-old sister. Avoiding neighborhood temptations was hard. But so far, they'd succeeded.

After a final check on Kyle, Aliyah turned out the lights and climbed into a bed that suddenly felt too big and too empty. She'd stayed busy on purpose, had filled her entire day with one project or event after another. All to keep her mind occupied and not think of Terrell. But now, with the house quiet, and her lying down, images and memories of San Francisco assailed her. She couldn't ignore them as she'd done to Terrell's earlier phone call. Thinking of the message he'd left made her tingle and smile at the same time. It was simple. Three words. They'd thrummed like a mantra in her head all day.

I want more.

She did, too. And she planned to get it, as much as she could. Hands down, he was the best she'd ever even dreamed about having. If he were a drug, she'd need rehab. Already. After just a few days. So she needed to find a way to assuage her appetite while guarding her heart. She wasn't looking for commitment. If she were, someone like Terrell Drake would not be a likely candidate. It's why she'd never considered a serious relationship with her childhood friend, turned lover. He was tall, handsome and virile, with enough charisma to fill the Atlantic—characteristics that were great for a good time and a roll in the hay. Not the best for a committed relationship. She never worried about Ernest. Turned out he was an arrogant, superficial, self-centered a-hole. But as far as she knew, he was faithful. Even jerks could have one good trait.

She changed positions, fluffed her pillow and settled down in search of sleep. As it came, the mantra continued.

I want more.

The next morning, Aliyah's phone rang at 7:00 a.m. Given her family lived on the east coast, this was not an unusual occurrence. She reached over, eyes still closed, and answered.

"Hello?"

"Good morning, Ms. Robinson."

Her eyes flew open. "Terrell?"

"I wish I could say I'm sorry for waking you up, but what I really feel bad about is that I'm not there with you."

"You're such a playboy," she said with a chuckle, rolling over and getting out of bed. She left the room in search of tea.

"Is that what I am?"

"Absolutely."

"What makes you say that?"

"Where do I start? It could be that woman-magnet sports car you drive. Or the daggers shot at me by every woman who saw us together in the Cove Café. Or better yet, what about the woman who invited herself to our table?"

"Hey…"

"No, wait, I'm not done. Let's not leave out the lover's lair you own in San Francisco and perhaps in other major cities as well. Lastly, add a handsome face, a killer bod and skills in the bedroom and you have all the attributes of the perfect player."

A pause and then, "Are you done now?"

"Yes, I believe so."

"Good. Because your reasoning is skewed."

"How so?"

"Just because a man takes care of himself and has nice things doesn't mean he's a playboy. As for what happened in the café, that's just small-town nosiness and Cindy being Cindy.

"Yours was a new, unrecognized face in a town where everyone knows everybody, and everyone wants to know my business. Your being with me made you my business. I'm sure the grapevine is still buzzing with questions about who you are."

"Hmm."

"And for the record, the house in San Francisco is not my lair. It is a family property. We all stay there when in town, as do some of our friends and colleagues. However, I do not apologize for being particularly fond of the opposite sex, and especially interested in the one I'm talking to right now, the one who didn't return my call from yesterday."

"Terrell, it's early in the morning. You hardly gave me a chance."

"Whenever you see my number on the screen, you are to call me back immediately."

"Oh, is that so?"

"Yes, it is."

"Or what?"

"Or I'm going to come over and spank you just right, and love you 'til you holler and throw up both your hands."

She laughed. "Don't you have to be at work or something?"

"I'm already here. What about you? Are your hours as erratic as I hear they can be for medical doctors?"

"Right now, even more so. Tuesday through Thursday I'm in residency at UC Davis Medical Center, then I intern at a local hospital, Living Medical, on Monday and Friday. And there's still studying to do on top of all that. Which is why this past weekend was so appreciated."

"Wow. No wonder you're not interested in a relationship. You don't have time for one."

"Exactly."

"Well, guess what?"

"What?"

"You need to make some time for yours truly. I need to finish what I started in San Francisco."

"Which was?"

"Satisfying you."

"Oh, trust me, you did that."

"Baby, that was just the appetizer. I want the whole meal."

"Well, unless you're up for a midnight rendezvous in a hotel near the hospital, your dining will to have to wait."

"Until when?"

"Um...next Sunday?"

"All right."

"All right, fine. I've got to run and wake the kid but

I'll call you toward the end of the week, make sure we're still on."

"See you soon."

Aliyah got Kyle dressed and took him out for his favorite pancake breakfast. While they ate, however, it was Terrell's appetite that was on her mind. He was successful, an expert lover and could charm the panties off most women. She'd love to pursue something with him. But the timing was all wrong. She was at the beginning of at least two and a half years of intense residency training. At the most, she'd have time for a little tune-up every once and again, but real dates? Like the one they'd just had? Unlikely. Something told her Terrell wouldn't be happy with that. To her, he seemed like a man who wanted lots of attention. And lots of sex.

At least they had one thing in common.

Chapter 7

Terrell leaned against the doorjamb, watching his friend since high school, Luther, playfully interacting with a group of five- and six-year-old boys. They used to wreak havoc in the clubs, engaging ladies who wanted to be with them and angering men who wanted to be them. Since getting married and having children, Luther had gone from tough guy to teddy bear. Terrell was proud of his friends and business partners who'd stepped up to the plate and agreed to be mentors and role models for the young men who came to the center, many of whose fathers were absent, deployed or incarcerated. Luther was the perfect one to handle the little ones. Terrell mentored the teens.

All except one young boy, whom he looked for now. Kyle was seated on a mat, surrounded by Legos, using his imagination to create something grand.

Terrell stepped into the room and after a brief chat with Luther walked over to where Kyle was playing and kneeled down.

"Hey, little man."

"I'm not little." This said while remaining focused on the task at hand. "I'm big."

"Oh, all right. Excuse my error." In this moment, Terrell realized just how infrequent he interacted with people under the age of ten and, thinking of his nieces and nephews, over the age of two. Terrell found himself in the rare position of being at a loss for words. But he'd told Aliyah that he'd take special interest in, and mentor, her son. He was a man of his word. So he placed down the deck of math flash cards he'd used earlier with the teens, sat beside Kyle and picked up a bright red block.

"What are you building?"

"A trajectory."

"A what?"

Kyle repeated what he said.

"A trajectory is a direction, Kyle, not an object." To this Kyle remained silent. "Although I am impressed that you know the word." He took the red block he was holding. "May I?" Kyle nodded. Terrell added the block to Kyle's "trajectory."

Kyle looked over at the flash cards Terrell had put down. "What are these?"

"Math quizzes."

"Let me see!"

"Naw, these are for teenagers—a little too much for someone your age. Can you count, though?"

"Of course." Kyle gave him a look that reminded him so much of Aliyah that Terrell laughed. He reached for one of the flash cards Terrell set down and watched Kyle pretend to add the numbers, silently mouthing figures as his fingers tapped the floor. Terrell reached for his vibrating phone. Meeting reminder. Time to go.

"Good talking to you, Kyle. May I have my cards back?"

"Can I keep them?"

"No, those are for the big, I mean older, boys." Kyle returned the flash cards. "Take care, little man."

"'Bye."

The day passed quickly and the next two were a blur. Between work at Drake Realty, mentoring at Drake Center, board meetings and social networking, Terrell barely managed to squeeze in time to sleep. And he hadn't talked to Aliyah. He'd gotten voice mail when he called yesterday and missed her call last night. But he knew she got off work tonight at eleven. And that was why at nine thirty he was in his car and headed to Davis. He would be waiting by her car when she got off work, ready to help her relax.

When it was something or someone he wanted, Terrell was a persistent man.

He surfed the web to pass the time. Unlike the rest of the week, tonight time seemed to pass slowly. Finally at eleven fifteen he saw her, looking tired but lovely. A pair of scrubs had never looked so good. His heart flip-flopped. He ignored it. This wasn't the first gorgeous woman he'd dated. Nor the most successful. The newness of their being together was why he was so excited to see her. That was his story and he was sticking to it.

He quietly got out of his car. She didn't see him. He began walking toward her. She didn't even look up. When he was about three feet away, he spoke to her. "Hey, Ms. Robinson."

She jumped, eyes wide, her hand to her throat. "Terrell?! Oh, my gosh! You scared me to death."

"I didn't mean to." He opened his arms. She stepped into his embrace. "It's a good thing I wasn't the bad guy. You would have been caught totally off guard."

"I just did seventeen hours," she said with a yawn, stepping away from him to look in his face. "What are you doing here?"

"I couldn't get you on the phone so I came over."

"'Over,'" she said, using air quotes for emphasis, "is thirty miles away."

"You know what they say. Ain't no mountain high enough."

She stepped around him and continued to her car. He fell into step beside her. "I wish you'd called first. I'm exhausted. The only thing in my immediate future is a bed and a pillow."

"That's fine. I just want to share it with you."

She looked at her watch. "At this time of night, Kyle is the only male allowed in my home."

"That's no problem. We can do what you suggested earlier and get a hotel room. With a king-size bed."

"Terrell…" She reached for her door handle. He placed his hand on top of hers.

"You don't have to do anything but go to sleep."

"You came all this way to watch me sleep."

"No, but—"

"Exactly. And that's all I'm going to do and even that for only four or five hours. My three days here are always intense. I'm back on the clock at six thirty."

"Dang. That's hard work."

"Sorry."

"Since I'm here, though, I might as well stay—right? We can do your apartment or a hotel. All you have to do is sleep, unless—" he took a step toward her, massaged the nape of her neck "—you get a spurt of energy and want to do something else."

"You forget I have a son to pick up from Lauren's house."

"Didn't you tell me her son was Kyle's age? Ask if he can spend the night."

She eyed him a minute and shrugged. "Okay, but don't say I didn't warn you."

"Where are we going?"

"There's a Westin right down the street. Let's go there. Follow me."

He did and within fifteen minutes they were in the room and in the shower, Aliyah allowing the water to cascade down her hair and face.

"My baby's so tired." Terrell poured a generous amount of liquid soap on the washcloth, rubbing it in a circular motion across her skin. The result was bubbles all over her body, which he began to wash off. When she yawned again, he finished the work quickly, turned off the shower and wrapped her in a towel. "Let's go to bed."

They lay down. Aliyah rolled to her side, adjusting the pillow as she did. "Thank you for coming, Terrell. Good night."

"Good night," he said, spooning behind her, his mind swimming with ideas of how good the night was going to get.

He placed his hand on her naked hip, massaging gently. Her skin was warm and velvety soft. His semi-erection hardened as he rubbed his hand down her thigh, around to her luscious booty and up to her waist.

Aliyah murmured something, reached for his hand to pull his arm tighter around her and nestled deeper under the cover.

Terrell smiled. *Yeah, I've still got it. Sleepy? I'll take care of that.*

He moved in with kisses—neck, back, arm. Rolled her over. She didn't resist. "Um, Terrell…"

"Shh, just lay back and enjoy, baby."

More kisses—tender, feathery, a purposeful trail from her breasts to her navel and continuing on to her hips and thighs. He repositioned himself, spread her legs and French-kissed her pleasure lips. He heard a whimper. Felt he would have her screaming his name in five minutes or less. He licked, kissed and tantalized her with her fingers.

There it was again. That sound.

He stopped. Listened. Looked.

What he thought was a whimper was in fact a soft snore. Aliyah was sound asleep.

Terrell fell back on the bed, stunned. Here he was pulling out all the stops, being Mr. Player, Terrell the Torrential

Lover, and she goes to sleep? In answer, another soft snore and then quiet, as she turned back on her side.

If his friends ever found out about this they'd never let him forget it, and that was why no one save he and Aliyah would ever know. He'd have to pull his player card for real.

Aliyah wasn't the only one who got a surprise tonight.

Chapter 8

Seemed her head had just hit the pillow when the soft chimes of her alarm announced that sleep time was over. Aliyah gently removed Terrell's arm from around her waist, scooted out of bed and headed to the shower. If she hurried, she could get coffee and food, both sorely needed, before her shift started.

The spray of cold water blasted away sleep. She turned it to warm and began a quick shower. Halfway through, her hand stopped in midair. A dream, fuzzy and incomplete, came to mind. An image of Terrell, kissing, teasing, loving her orally. The mere thought caused her nipples to pebble and her core to clench. She shook away the mental picture and turned off the water. A day in bed with her skillful lover wasn't going to happen, no matter how much she wished it could.

"Good morning." Terrell came in and hugged Aliyah from behind.

"Morning." Aliyah wriggled out of his embrace, gave Terrell's lips a quick peck and hurried out of the bathroom. "I hate to rush you but can we leave in five? I'd like to grab breakfast before my shift starts."

"Right away, Doctor."

"Said with a hint of sarcasm." She pulled on her scrubs, pulling her hair into a ponytail as she stepped into the bathroom doorway. "I'm sorry it's so busy. If given the option,

I'd much rather spend the day with you and that weapon poking me in the back last night."

"Please, girl." He left the bathroom and began dressing. "You didn't feel a thing."

"That's because we didn't do anything, even though I dreamed otherwise."

"What did you dream?"

"That you were...never mind. I've got to go."

"Call me from your car. I want to hear about this dream you had."

"Okay." She headed for the door.

"If you don't, I'm coming back to the hospital."

"You're a brat."

"Call me."

Once out of the parking lot, Aliyah called him.

"Okay...back to the dream," he said, instead of hello.

"I'm a little embarrassed. I dreamed that we were having oral sex...well, you were doing it to me and—"

"That wasn't a dream."

"Huh?"

"I came to bed, all prepared to get you relaxed, make you feel good, make long and slow love to you."

"And?"

"And you fell asleep with my tongue in your—"

"No!"

"Passed out. Zonked. It was a wrap."

"Stop playing!"

"I was serious, too, down there getting it in!" Aliyah laughed, not believing him for a minute. "I heard you moaning and I was like, 'yeah, I'm going to tear this up.' Then I listened. I think you're all into it. But I stop, listen again. You weren't moaning. You were snoring."

"Ha!"

Terrell tried to remain quiet but soon he laughed, too.

"Good thing I'm a confident man because a woman falling asleep in the middle of the act is quite the ego deflator."

"Babe, I was exhausted! I told you!"

"I know, but…"

"Oh, gosh! I can just about imagine your face…" Laughter swallowed up the rest of her sentence.

"Gee. Thanks a lot."

"I'm sorry."

"You don't sound sorry."

"But I am." She tried to hold it in but imagining the look on his face when he discovered she was snoring instead of moaning made her burst out laughing again.

"That's alright. Payback will come later. Hey, are you off on Halloween?"

"Yes, why?"

"An event in PC. I'll call you later about it."

After a quick date with a drive-thru, Aliyah returned to the UC Davis Medical Center. At the nurses' station, she checked the charts to confirm what was scheduled, then went to see her first patient of the day.

"Good morning, Mr. Robinson!"

"There's my beautiful wife!"

Said with blue eyes twinkling. Ever since eighty-two-year-old widower Dale Robinson had learned they shared the same last name, he'd insisted she was the one he'd searched for all his life. He was dealing with a debilitating back injury in a place too risky for surgery. The doctor's recommendation had been a positive attitude and pain medication. Dale had loads of the former. The latter was where Aliyah's knowledge of pain management kicked in. If it made this nice old man feel better for a few moments, then she'd gladly be his wifey through every treatment.

"Sounds like someone is feeling better this morning!"

"Always feel better when you're here, hon."

"Aww, that's nice." She reached for his wrist, checked his pulse and body temperature.

"Am I alive?"

"Absolutely."

"Well, praise the Lord."

She smiled at his humor. "How's the pain today?"

"Fair to middling."

"Good enough for us to hold off on treatment for a bit? I can handle a few other patients and come back if you'd like."

"Why don't you do that—as soon as that syrup hits my system it knocks me out, cuts into my flirting time."

"Well, we can't have that now, can we?"

"Looks like I'm not the only one in a good mood today. Is somebody trying to step in and steal you away from me?"

"Who could do that?" Aliyah lightly replied, as her mind brought up an image of what Terrell had said was happening when she fell asleep. And how it felt to walk out and see him waiting: wanting, needing, to see her. In that moment, she knew the answer. Because Terrell made her feel significant.

Later that afternoon, because of a multicar accident, Aliyah got the opportunity to first shadow and later assist the anesthesiologist on duty in emergency. The rest of the day went quickly. For that she was grateful. Fridays at Living Medical were usually slow and easy, aided by the fact that tomorrow she worked the afternoon shift, noon to eight, with a chance of getting off early. With Halloween approaching, she hoped Davis citizens stayed healthy so she could be Mommy and spend the day with Kyle.

Once off work and on her way to pick up Kyle, she called Terrell.

"Hello, Doctor."

She laughed. "That sounds weird."

"Well, that's the title you're busting your butt for so get used to it."

"Earlier you mentioned an event in PC?"

"Yes."

"What is it?"

She listened, skillfully navigating the rush-hour traffic and arriving at Lauren's in no time. After ending the call she walked up the drive, rang the bell and then walked in through a door that during the day was often left unlocked.

"Lauren, it's me!"

Lauren came around the corner. "I thought I heard someone pull up. Come on in. The boys are having dinner, which was delayed a bit because we stopped at the mall."

"No worries."

"You hungry?"

"A little. What'd you cook?"

"Two large supreme with extra pepperoni."

Aliyah laughed. "I'll have a slice." She followed Lauren to the dining room, where Conrad, Cody, Conner and Kyle were debating God knew what between bites. "Hi, guys."

Mumbled greetings from filled mouths echoed around the table.

"Mommy—" Kyle began.

"Don't talk with your mouth full, Kyle." He hurriedly finished his bite. "Don't swallow food without chewing, either."

"Sorry, Mommy. But, listen. I helped Conrad do his homework!"

"Let's have wine with the pizza," Lauren yelled from the kitchen.

"That's nice, son. Mommy's going to talk with Miss Lauren." She walked into the kitchen and was greeted by a full glass of wine and a plate for her pizza.

"Let's go in the other room." Lauren's tone was serious. "We need to talk."

"Ooh, okay."

"No messes, boys, and no fighting."

"Where you going, Mommy?"

"Miss Lauren and I are going to have a grown-up chat."

The two women walked by just as Lauren's professor husband, Calvin, walked through the door. After quick greetings and being informed he was now on kid patrol, he continued to the dining room while Lauren and Aliyah continued to the stylish yet lived-in den of the Hensleys's rambling ranch-styled home and sat on the oversize sectional dominating the far corner.

Aliyah took a few sips of wine. The tone in Lauren's voice made her think that she might need it. "Okay, girl. What's going on?"

"Uh, hello. That's what I'm here to ask you?"

Aliyah was genuinely confused. Then it hit her. "Oh. The date."

"Oh, the date," Lauren mocked. "The date, first one mind you—"

"Second, technically—"

"Not according to you Ms. It's Just Dinner."

Aliyah could only laugh. She was guilty as charged.

"First date with a near stranger where you were flown via private plane to San Francisco and did who knows what since the person who thought she was your BFF hasn't been told a thing!"

Lauren's expressiveness had grown more animated with each word, causing Aliyah to laugh harder. "It's a shame you didn't pursue that acting career. You've could have gone places."

"But not to San Francisco on a private with a hunk."

"I'm sorry. I've been meaning to tell you, really, but you know how busy it's been." Aliyah took another sip of wine, then set down the glass. "So, I told you about the dinner in Paradise Cove, right?"

"Only that some woman tried to invite herself to join you."

"Okay. Well…"

For the next fifteen minutes, Lauren sat spellbound as Aliyah recalled her magical date with Terrell, their steamy phone conversations and his surprising her at work after she'd finished her shift.

Lauren's mouth dropped. "You told me you were working late, that's why you wanted Kyle to stay overnight!"

Aliyah wriggled her brows. "I was."

The ladies cracked up.

"So when do I get to meet this Drake fella?"

Aliyah reached for her phone, went to the internet and pulled up his image. "Here he is."

"Hot damn!" Lauren whooped. "Girl, now I really understand. You were working late!"

"He just invited me to spend Halloween in Paradise Cove, to attend a festival they're having. I don't know if I'm going."

"Why not?"

"Several reasons. One, his family will be there. Two, I'll have Kyle, and three, I don't want to blur the lines and confuse him. He already thinks Mr. Drake is 'cool.'" She used air quotes. "He doesn't need to know that his mommy has the hots for Mr. Cool."

Lauren looked again at his photo. "He is a hottie. I have to agree with you on that."

"You and half the women in this state. All he and I will ever have is a casual, mutually pleasurable…friendship."

"All the more reason to join him on the 31st. Let him be your boo."

"On that really tired note…" Both women laughed as Aliyah stood. "It's getting late. I should go and get Kyle in bed."

Lauren stood as well, and put her arm around Aliyah's

shoulders as they walked out together. "It's good to see you happy, girl. You deserve it. And though you haven't asked, here's a piece of advice."

"Oh, no."

They stopped just beyond the living room, where the boys were now playing video games. Lauren turned to Aliyah. "Don't be so quick to define this situation. I know why you're doing it, and I understand. Just try not to let the past shape your present and impact your future. Okay?"

Aliyah slowly nodded. "Okay."

After sitting and chatting for a while with the family, she and Kyle left the Hensley clan and spent a quiet evening at home. They munched on popcorn while watching a movie and topped the snack off with homemade shakes. After Kyle was in bed and her studying was done, she lay listening to music to fall asleep, Aliyah continued to think about what Lauren said. Ernest was her past. Could Terrell be her future? From her point of view, not likely. But he was her present, so for now, she'd just enjoy the gift.

Chapter 9

A light tap on his office door caused Terrell to look up from the computer screen. It was his brother Ike. He leaned back against the chair. "You out of here, man?"

"Yeah, I think I'm done for the day."

"A rare night that you beat me out of here."

"A rare night that you stay late."

"Hey, I'm efficient, what can I say?"

"You can say what really happened, that you're still here because you were late this morning." Ike stepped into the office and sat in a chair in front of Terrell's desk. "Mom said she thought you were dating someone new."

"Mom thinks and says too much."

Ike laughed. "True that." A pause and then he asked, "It isn't Cindy, is it? I heard she's back in town."

"Unfortunately."

"You've seen her?"

"Briefly."

"Silky, Silky!"

"Ha! What is it about Cindy that makes y'all remember Silky? Teresa did the same thing!"

"Probably because she got on my nerves with it. It's really a compliment, just so you know. Your gift of gab and salesmanship."

"And my way with women, that's mostly how it was used."

"That, too. So who is it?"

"A new friend with benefits."

"Another one? Variety might be the spice of life, but when it comes to those beneficial friends you collect like souvenir shot glasses, there might be such a thing as too many."

"I'm not that bad."

"You're worse?"

"Ha!"

Terrell reached for the water bottle on his desk and rocked back in the leather office recliner. "Actually, between the workload here and activities at the center, I don't have much time to mess around."

"I've been meaning to get over there, put in a few volunteer hours."

"You should. I balked at first but working with those young men feels good. That first week they acted like knuckleheads but I got them in line quick, let them know I wasn't playing and that the rules of the center—mutual respect, nonviolent resolution, circumspect conduct—weren't up for debate. The scowls remained for a little while, but after a few days everything mellowed out. May have been the first time some of them had been man-handled, you know what I mean?" Ike nodded. "I think they appreciate it."

"Coming up the way we did, with both our father and grandfather being such huge influences in our lives, and some uncles even, I can't imagine coming into manhood without that male support, those role models."

"Exactly. That's what makes me feel good about it."

"You sure it isn't that one student's bootylicious mama you've been seeing?"

Terrell's mouth dropped. Busted. "Dang, man! First Mom, now Teresa, too?"

"Don't be mad at her," Ike said amid laughter. "Mom

is the one who pried it out of her. I just happened to be over to the house."

Terrell shook his head, smiling, too. "Can't keep a secret in this family for nothing!"

"It's pretty tough." Ike stood. "Well, man, I'm out of here."

"All right, bro. Oh, and Ike?"

"Yes?"

"You're looking old, man. Looks like you could use a little bootylicious yourself."

His cell phone rang as Ike left the office. Bootylicious was calling. "Hey, you."

"You sound happy."

"I was just teasing my brother. Where are you?"

"In bed."

"So early? You feeling okay?"

"Just tired but that's nothing new. Those three days always leave me exhausted."

"The residency at the medical center, correct?"

"That's the one."

"And then you're somewhere else the other two days."

"At Living Medical, a center for the aging and disabled. I'm always studying, but on Saturdays it's a priority. Sunday is reserved for quality time with Kyle. Though she's a dear friend, I feel bad he spends so much time with his sitter, Lauren, and her family."

"What you're doing is to help secure his future. He'll thank you in the end."

"I hope so."

"Maybe I should come over and keep you company."

"Trust me, company is the last thing I need right now. Unless you want a repeat of last night."

"Go ahead. I hear you laughing."

"I'm not!" She was.

"Make a brother feel bad!"

"I felt awful, I really did. You know if there'd been any energy in me at all, I would not have turned you down."

"Is that right?"

"With that magic wand you're working with? Absolutely not!"

Terrell lowered his voice. "Well, my magic wand wants to perform a trick or two on you. Tonight."

"You're so bad. Terrell, I'm exhausted. Plus, I wouldn't want you to come over with Kyle home. He's very observant and very talkative, if you know what I mean. If he saw you over here tonight, trust me, everyone at the center would know about it tomorrow."

"Whoa, then you're right. Not the best idea."

"I thought you'd see things my way."

"Then what about the Halloween festival? It's on a Sunday. That's perfect, right? We could spend the day together."

"Thanks, Terrell, but no, I'll pass. Like I said earlier, I want to spend more time with Kyle so whatever I do will involve him, too."

"By all means. There's a big celebration planned by the lake. There will be activities and fun for people of all ages." No comment. "Oh, right, can't have Mr. Big Mouth spreading our business."

"Hey, that's my son you're talking about!"

They laughed. Terrell glanced at his watch and fired up his sleeping computer once more. "Look, I'm still at work and need to finish up."

"No worries."

"You need to change your mind and spend Halloween with me."

"Look, don't get dictatorial."

"I thought that's the part you loved about me."

"Ha! You're silly. 'Bye, Terrell."

"Goodbye, Aliyah."

Terrell went back to work, thinking of wands, magic tricks and how he couldn't wait to spend time with Aliyah.

Chapter 10

This year, Halloween fell on a Sunday. A good thing, except if she'd had a choice, Aliyah would have happily spent the day in bed with a remote in one hand and a bag of junk food in the other. But for mothers of hyper five-year-olds, this was not an option. So she sat at the computer, checking out the festivities happening in Davis. Not much. She clicked over to Paradise Cove's website. A list of events jumped off the page. Scrolling down, she saw the Drake Lake event Terrell had invited her to attend. Listed were games, pony rides, a treasure hunt, face painting and more, things that Kyle would truly enjoy. Topping all of that off was a haunted house tour and Halloween costume contest. Was it right to deny her son a good time because of her insecurities and bad memories? There would probably be hundreds of people there. Chances were she wouldn't even see his family. As for his female fan club, which she was sure would be circling, that was more his problem than hers.

She reached for her cell. He answered on the second ring. "I've changed my mind."

"About what?"

"About accepting your invitation."

"That's great, babe. What made you change your mind?"

"The list of activities listed on the PC website. I thought

to also invite my friend Lauren and her family. Her boys will love it and with his best friend there, Kyle will be in heaven."

"Sure, bring them along. The more the merrier."

Three days later Aliyah drove behind the SUV carrying Lauren, her husband, their two youngest sons and Kyle on the ten-minute drive to Paradise Cove. Since hearing he'd have a chance to ride a pony and catch a fish, her son had been bouncing off the walls. It felt good to see him happy. It also reminded her of how little time she had to spend with him these days. Lauren was like family and her boys were like his brothers, so she felt blessed to have them close by. But he was growing so fast. She felt bad for him, but worse for herself for missing precious moments in his life.

Once they'd reached Paradise Cove and taken the lake exit, she called Terrell.

"Hey, baby. Are you here?" he asked.

"Just took the lake exit."

"Then you're less than ten minutes away. Just follow the signs."

"Where should I meet you?"

"Once you've parked, walk back toward the parking entrance and cross the street. All the activities are here, around the lake. To the right of the lake are three large bouncy houses. Do you know what those are?"

"He asks the mother of a five-year-old."

"Hey, I'm proud of myself for being able to describe them because I just found out. Anyway, come to the big yellow one. I'll be waiting for you."

Fifteen minutes later, Terrell turned in her direction at the exact same time she spotted him. He waved them over.

"Mr. Drake!"

Terrell gave Kyle a fist bump. "Hello there, Kyle."

"I'm not Kyle. I'm an Avenger!"

Terrell glanced over at Aliyah. She shrugged and smiled with a look that conveyed the message: you're on your own.

"Why, of course. I knew that."

"Which one am I?"

"Oh, so there's more than one."

Aliyah chuckled. Terrell frowned.

"Yes, Mr. Drake!" Kyle crossed his arms. "Gosh, I thought you were cool!"

"I thought I was, too, Kyle, but—"

"Where's Mr. Adams? He knows all the Avenger names."

"I don't know but he's here, along with other Avengers, probably, otherwise known as your friends."

"Mommy, can I go find them?"

"We'll look for them in a minute, honey." She turned to Terrell. "Hello there."

Terrell held out his hand. "Ms. Robinson."

She accepted his handshake.

A simple, appropriate action except for the tone of his voice, the look in his eyes and how his fingers trailed against her palm ever so slightly. All while maintaining a friendly expression as though nothing was going on. A man shouldn't be able to make a handshake X-rated, but Terrell was about to moisten her panties.

It was all she could do not to jerk back her hand. Instead she pulled and at the same time turned to the people who'd joined her.

"Terrell, these are my friends. This is Lauren, her husband, Calvin, and her sons, Cody and Conner, who attend the center."

"I thought I recognized you," Terrell said, shaking the hand of the ten-year-old. While shaking Conner's hand, he spoke to Kyle. "This is your friend from school."

"And home, and everything! He's an Avenger, too!"

Terrell laughed. "I've seen you two playing together.

It's good to meet all of you. Let me give you a quick lay of the land."

With that, a raucous afternoon of fun, rides, laughter and carnival-style junk food began. Aliyah was relieved to see so many from the center. That she was there, seen with Terrell, did not stand out. At various times the parties split, with the children going one way, accompanied by one of the center's interns, and the couples enjoying some alone time. It was during one such time that Aliyah found herself meeting some of Terrell's family, thereby breaking the rule to not do it.

They'd just left a target game where Terrell won her a large stuffed bear when an attractive, familiar-looking couple approached them.

"I see someone's enjoying the festivities," the woman said to him, before addressing Aliyah with an outstretched hand. "Hi, I'm Teresa. The good twin."

Terrell feigned offense as the ladies shook hands. "Atka, did you not school your wife on how to behave in public?"

"No," the handsome man answered. "She skipped my class."

Everyone laughed.

"Sis, this is my friend Aliyah Robinson. Aliyah, my baby sister, Teresa, and her husband, Atka."

"It's nice meeting you both. Now I know why you looked so familiar," she said to Teresa. "You two really look alike."

"It's why I'm in therapy," Teresa said, deadpan.

"Best thing that ever happened to her," Terrell quickly responded. Through this it was clear to see that the love between these two knew no bounds.

"Where's everybody?" Terrell asked Teresa.

"Let's see. Monique and a few others are over at Warren and Charlie's. Ike and Audrey were playing hosts to some power couple from DC. Niko's busy being mayor. I saw Mom and Dad earlier but I think they left. That leaves all the fun to us."

Aliyah enjoyed all the event had to offer: food, fun, games and seeing her little man giddy with excitement. And sugar. At one point, she let Kyle go with the Hensleys to enjoy rides with Conner and visit the haunted house. Terrell took this opportunity to whisk her away, a few miles farther down the road, to the home of Warren, the grape-growing rancher, and his wife, Charlie, who with her jean shorts, tank top, cowboy hat and boots was the epitome of a 21st-century cowgirl. Had she roped a steer or rode a bucking bronco, Aliyah would not have been surprised. Nice enough, though. And down-to-earth, despite a home that seemed plucked from an interior design magazine, surrounded by land that was postcard perfect. As they left, Terrell drove her by Warren's neighbors, Teresa and Atka, who'd built a home for their many trips back to PC from Alaska, Atka's home state and place of their main residence.

Back at the festival, she met Ike and his date, watched Niko in action and quickly saw why he'd garnered the vote. Though each wielded it differently, every Drake man she'd met had an indefinable quality that was easy to notice and hard to resist. His brief yet passionate speech about the town's bright future made her want to cheer and she didn't even live there.

A fireworks display timed to music was the exclamation point to a perfect holiday. Five minutes after the last Roman candle boom, Kyle was asleep in Terrell's arms.

"We can take him with us," Lauren offered, as they all walked to the parking lot.

"That's okay. I'm heading home, too."

Terrell and Aliyah continued to her car. After Terrell placed Kyle in the car seat, Aliyah made sure he was strapped in securely.

"Thank you for inviting us here," she said, turning to face Terrell. "I couldn't have imagined how much fun this would be. I've never seen Kyle so happy."

Terrell reached out to hold her but she stepped back. "Too many eyes," she explained. "And as it is, I might have to make a stop at UC Davis to remove all the daggers the Tee Drake groupies were shooting at my back."

"Couldn't have been more than I should have thrown at all the men checking you out. But I wasn't worried. They got to look, but I get to touch. So what are we doing?"

"I'm going home."

"Why don't you come over to my house? It's just going to be my fam, a few friends."

"Because I have a son who needs to be put to bed."

"We've got beds at our house."

"Yes, but I'm going to put him in the one in his room."

He opened her car door. She climbed inside. "Then you know what's getting ready to happen, right?"

After starting the car, she looked up at him. "What?"

"I'm going to be in the one in your room. Text me your address." He turned and walked away.

"Terrell!" she yelled softly, if there was such a thing, so as not to wake the little one. She thought about simply not sending her address. That was an easy enough solution to not doing what she said she'd never do, and break another rule.

Except one should never say never. And that the prerogative of a woman to change her mind was a well-known fact. And it had been a long time since San Francisco.

So she texted him her address, and hurried home to welcome her guest.

Chapter 11

Once home, Aliyah lay Kyle on top of his bedcovers and took a quick shower. After spritzing her body with an organic concoction of vanilla and jasmine oils diluted in distilled water, she brushed back her hair, wrapped her body in a satiny, flowered kimono and returned to Kyle's room. She'd barely managed to remove the costume from her sleeping Avenger and tuck him into bed before her message indicator vibrated.

"That can't be Terrell," she mumbled, looking at her watch as she crossed over to her room and the nightstand where her phone lay.

There's a special delivery at your door. Come open it.

She did, and was immediately enveloped in a bear hug followed by a kiss so long and deep it threatened her breathing.

"Wait," she panted, finally breaking away, a hand to her chest as she stepped around him to close the door.

"You all right, babe?"

She put a finger to her mouth and used the other to direct him toward her bedroom. Once there, and with her door firmly shut, she took a deep breath. "Kyle's a pretty sound sleeper but I don't want to chance him hearing you.

That Mr. Drake came to visit Mommy is a story I don't want spread."

"I can understand that."

"To answer your question, yes, I'm all right. Though that was some kiss. It almost left me short of breath."

"Baby, that's what I'm here for. To take your breath away."

"Oh, Lord. Is that what's his name making a comeback? Silky?"

"Which family member opened their big mouth?"

"My lips are sealed."

"It had to be Teresa. I'm going to get her for that."

Aliyah watched Terrell unbutton and remove his shirt, then sit on her bed and begin unlacing his sneakers. She joined him on the bed. "By all means, make yourself comfortable."

"Oh, I'm going to do more than that." He stood, then unzipped and removed his pants.

She rested back on her haunches, her eyes lowered to half-mast. "Just what are you going to do, Mr. Drake?"

He lowered his voice even more. "I'm going to get rid of any and all obstructions between us." He pulled down and stepped out of his underwear. His dick—thick, long, hard, ready—sprang up like a cobra ready to strike.

He placed a knee on the bed, reached for the kimono belt and loosened the knot. "Like this." His eyes never left hers as he pushed the fabric away from her body, leaving her exposed, wanting. He ran a finger down the side of her face, continuing to her chest and over to flick a nipple.

Fully on the bed now, he lowered his head. "Then," he whispered, his breath flowing across her nipple now pebbled with lust, "I'm going to kiss." His lips caressed her skin. "Lick." His tongue—slow, wet—laved across one nipple, then the other, trailed to her stomach and around her inward navel. Lower, to the triangular paradise now moist with desire, her pearl plump and exposed, ripe for the plucking...and he did, with relish. He nipped with his teeth and lapped with his tongue, parting her folds and lavishing her with all of the desire he'd held at bay all day.

He spread her legs wider, pushed his tongue deeper, branding her spot with the precision of a tattoo artist, and just as lasting.

"Mmm, baby, you taste so good."

And on and on he went, licking, laving, lapping, loving, lower and lower still.

To a part of her body that no man had ever touched.

"Ooh, Terrell..."

"What? You don't like it?"

"No. I mean, I don't know. I've never—" She gasped, words lost to this foreign, excruciatingly maddening touch of his tongue. Hot. Wet. Licking her there.

He guided her over, onto her stomach. Her body quivered, goose bumps appearing at the heat of his gaze. His dick, already swollen, became even more engorged.

"This right here," he whispered softly, almost reverently, as he squeezed her cheeks apart. And together. And apart again. "This is my favorite part of your body." He kissed it. "Perfect." He kissed it again. "The best I've ever seen."

He ran a finger down each crease. Back and forth. Making her wetter with each long swipe. "Damn, you're so wet for me. So instead of telling you what's about to happen... I'll show you."

He turned her over, grabbed her thighs, buried his head in her sweet spot and thrust his tongue in deep.

Aliyah yelped, the sudden delicious invasion making her come with abandon. She grabbed a pillow to absorb the screams as on the waves of the seismic orgasm he positioned himself over her and sheathed himself inside her tight core. For minutes, or was it hours, he moved inside her, taking her over the top once again. Still hard, still hungry, he flipped them over. Laced his hands behind his head and watched her slide down his shaft, her breasts swaying in time with her hips, her eyes fluttering closed at the hypnotic feel of him inside her. Later, bodies glistening with sweat, tendrils of hair clinging against her neck and back, she rode with him once again over the edge. His groan deep and powerful, her body completely spent.

Collapsing on top of him she had breath enough left for only one word. "Amazing."

It was a little after midnight. They lay naked, spooning, in her queen-size bed.

"You're dangerous."

Terrell pulled her tighter, nudged her with his package. "How so?"

She gave him a look. "You have to ask?"

"I'd never assume anything."

"I now understand why you have such a large...female following." He laughed. She joined him. "Not the comment you expected?"

"It's why I don't assume. But don't think everybody gets what you got tonight. That was special. Just for you."

She eyed him again. "Really?"

He turned on his side, the gaze meeting hers that of a very satisfied man. "Yes, really. You've got me feeling you on a deep level. For real."

She looked away from him. "Don't get mad at your sister. The nickname fits."

"So it was Teresa. I knew it."

"Says that it's what makes you such a successful businessman. Can sell honey to bees she told me. A gift of gab that is as smooth as silk."

"She said all that?"

"No, I added the last part."

"My spiels work because they are honest, and come

from the heart. When I say something, I mean it. Besides, for you I'd rather be thought of as silky for other, more personal uses of my mouth and tongue."

Aliyah took a deep breath and tried to slow the heartbeat that his words had increased. Not to mention how her pussy just quivered. This conversation was getting into scary territory. And her feelings were following suit. "You've got me breaking rules, dude! Rule one, no serious anything."

"Oh, so this is serious now?" he said, chuckling.

"No! But meeting your family makes it feel serious." She turned her head toward him even though the room was dark. "Have you ever met the parents of a booty call?"

"I'm more than a booty call."

"No, you're not." His confident, disbelieving laugh was slightly infuriating. "You're a friend with benefits."

"If you say so."

"Rule two," she continued, ignoring his smugness. "No male sleepovers, except for Kyle's friends."

"No worries. I'll make sure we stay awake all night."

This earned a swat on his exposed thigh. "No, you won't. I have to work tomorrow."

"What time do you have to be there?"

"Not until noon," she answered with a grateful sigh. "But don't expect pancakes for breakfast. You'll be leaving shortly."

"You're putting me out?"

"Yes."

"What, it's screw and through?"

"Absolutely."

"Ha!"

"Shh! Quiet, before you wake Kyle, and I have to explain what Mr. Drake is doing in Mommy's bed."

He turned, and settled on his back. "Aliyah."

"Hmm?"

"Is that the real reason you were so against meeting

my family, because to do so would change your views of our relationship?"

"It's not a—"

"Okay, friendship. My bad."

A second passed, and then another.

"No, not really."

"What's the reason?"

Aliyah repositioned herself to lie on her back, too. "Because being around families like yours reminds me of Ernest's family, Kyle's father. As I've already shared, that was not a good experience."

"Made worse because your ex did not stand by your side."

"That hurt the most, but it wasn't the only thing."

"Explain that."

She let out a sigh. "It's not important."

"It is to me."

"Why?"

He reached out in the darkness, ran a gentle finger down the side of her face, and down her arm, before resting it on her hip. "Because I like you, Aliyah Robinson. And I'm trying to get to know the person beneath the scrubs, and the tough, screw-and-through exterior. That's all."

Several seconds passed, to the point where Terrell doubted she'd answer. But she did.

"Being around Ernest's family often left me feeling insignificant. Not just because they were wealthy, not just the materialism. It was also their societal recognition, their knowledge of a family lineage they could take back generations and their amazing ability to simply ignore that which they did not believe in or think important. Huge matters, like world hunger, or global warming, or race relations or an economy spiraling out of control. Situations that sometimes impacted me and my family. It was as though if they didn't talk about it, it didn't exist.

"The Westcotts are native Rhode Islanders whose fore-fathers were prominent members of the larger community since, if they are to be believed, the ink began to dry on the Emancipation Proclamation. His father, a lawyer, has been a councilman for years. His mother is a socialite." Said as though cotton were stuffed up her nose and eliciting the laughter she intended. "Their daughter, Jane, is married to a banker, whose Boston-based family is also part of the elite. So Ernest holding a conversation with me, much less dating and, gasp and sputter, getting me pregnant, was akin to murder in the first degree."

"How'd you meet him?"

"At Brown University. He was a senior. I was a freshman minding my own business when he stopped my stroll across the campus and asked me on a date."

"That just goes to show you how fine you are because many of those brothers don't socialize outside their circle."

"I don't think he had plans for me beyond the sheets. My intelligence surprised him."

"A woman with a booty and a brain!"

"You're silly. One date turned into several and before you know it, we were official. After six months or so, he invited me to a dance. Big mistake. One look at me and his parents knew I wasn't upper crust. I think he'd hoped my becoming a doctor would get me a pass, but no. His mother was not having it. She didn't like me and made no attempt to hide it. His father was friendlier. His sister, cordial enough. Shortly after this, I got pregnant. Totally unexpected. Was on the pill and everything. Thought about not having it. That was a really tough time."

"Why did you?" Terrell asked, with a comforting squeeze.

"I loved Ernest, and wanted to be with him. Yes, the baby presented a huge challenge, but I thought that together, we could get through it. He did, too. Until the ultimatum, when he was told to break off all contact with me or else. I think a part of him wanted to break out of the roles he'd been handed by his parents, to live a life that was driven more by the heart than the head and what's considered socially acceptable. I think a part of him really loved me. But that wasn't enough to risk defying his parents and losing a hefty inheritance. By the time the you-know-what hit the fan I was four months along and out of options."

"You've had to be strong."

"Yes."

She turned and laid her head on Terrell's shoulder. He wrapped an arm around her. "How did you feel around my family today?"

"I felt fine. They all treated me nicely, didn't act too uppity."

"What do you mean, 'too'?"

She laughed. "Hey, don't get offended. Like it or not you're part of the upper class. There's an aura about people like you, whether or not you intend it. Not with you so much, but your brother Ike? Definitely. And that woman he was with? She could party in Rhode Island and fit right in."

"I'll admit Audrey is a trip, especially around another beautiful woman. She's frustrated because after dating Ike off and on for a decade, my brother still hasn't proposed."

"Warren and Charlie? They were nice. And your twin, Teresa, and her husband…what's his name?"

"Atka."

"Yeah, him. They're high-end. He was quiet, but your twin went out of her way to include me in the conversation. I appreciated that."

"Aliyah."

"Yes, Terrell."

"My last name is Drake, not Westcott. Yes, my family

is wealthy but we're not stuck up. They will adore you as much as I do and will never, ever make you feel less than the beautiful woman you are. Are you listening?"

"Yes, I hear you."

"Good. So drop the cape and lose the heart shield. You don't have to be tough with me."

She reached up and kissed his cheek, then settled against his shoulder. "Thank you. But I'm keeping my cape."

"I guess that's okay. Might need your help in beating the women off me."

"Whatever, you cocky dude."

"I thought that's what you loved about me."

This earned him another swat, on the arm this time.

"I've heard about your jerk of an ex's family. Now, tell me about yours."

"What do you want to know?"

"Whatever you want to tell me—siblings, parents, growing up in New York."

"When people hear New York, they think of Manhattan. I grew up in Brooklyn. There's a difference. Each borough has its own personality."

"I look forward to a personal tour."

"That could be arranged."

"So tell me about it."

"I loved growing up there. Sure, it was hard. Times were tough. My parents didn't always get along. We siblings fought like…siblings. But love was there, always, and unconditional acceptance. The whole block was like one big family. There was a unique, palpable energy created by all the cultures and classes and languages, dialects, foods, traditions…all blending together. When I was little, the block was one big playground. We'd hopscotch, double-dutch and play games in the middle of the street, to an international soundtrack. From hip-hop to R and B, reggae to calypso, the straight-ahead jazz from our neighbor, Mr. Johnny, to the gospel every Sunday by Miss Francine. It was the best life, fun and carefree.

"By the time I turned twelve the area had started to change. Gangs, drugs and illegal activities that used to be on the periphery made their way to our neighborhood, and our block. When the neighborhood changed, some of the neighbors changed. Some of my friends changed. Mama tightened the reins and I lost my innocent outlook. I'm the oldest of five, three brothers and another sister, and felt I had to protect them. I still do."

"The dark side can come off looking quite attractive. How'd you keep from getting caught up?"

"My parents. Mama is a nurse, with a strong work ethic. My father is a jack of all trades—construction, handyman, repairman, moving man, whatever you need. He used to drive the train—the subway—until he got injured and had to go on disability. He received a small settlement that they set aside as a college fund for us. The odd jobs keep him busy and contributing to the household.

"They both taught education as the holy grail, the ticket to a better life. I had observant teachers who encouraged me and when they saw that their lessons were too easy, they pushed me higher, farther, faster. I developed a love for learning so while my friends were into boys, I was into books."

"Really."

"Uh-huh."

They talked well into the night. She was impressed at Terrell's genuine interest in her, asking questions and listening intently. It hadn't been this way with the others. Most conversations had been all about them. By the time they spooned into peaceful slumber, there was something else Aliyah was really into. The man beside her.

* * *

"Mommy?"

"Yes, Kyle."

"I had a dream last night."

"Sit down and eat your cereal, Kyle." She poured almond milk into her bowl and joined him at the table. "What did you dream about?"

"Mr. Drake."

Aliyah almost choked on granola. "Oh, uh, really?" she sputtered, taking a sip of water to clear her throat.

Kyle nodded. "I heard his voice. He called you baby!"

"Hmm. That was some dream." What had this child been doing awake at three in the morning?

"I woke up because I thought it was real!"

How'd he hear us? Then she remembered. Terrell had called out to her as she left to get water. Now, because of his slip-up, she was on a slippery slope. The very reason why she had rules in the first place. "Dreams can often seem real, honey, even though they're make-believe."

"Hey, maybe we can invite Mr. Drake over!"

Lord, this child! "Why would we do that, honey?"

"So we can play together!"

Been there. Done that. That's why she was dragging right now.

"Mr. Drake is a grown man, Kyle. You'll have to play with boys your own age."

"But he played with me on Halloween.."

"That was different. Lots of kids from your class were there."

"Then I could show him my puzzles and stuff because he teaches math!"

"What about Mr. Adams? Don't you get to work with him and show him stuff in class?"

"Yes. But I like Mr. Drake. He's fun."

Aliyah wasn't sure how to feel about how much her son

liked Terrell. That he now had role models like Terrell and Luther was good. But she didn't want him becoming too attached. Herself, either, for that matter.

"Did you make your bed?" Another nod. "Then hurry and finish your sandwich. Miss Lauren will be here soon to pick you up."

Chapter 12

On Wednesday, Terrell wasn't scheduled to be at the center but he stopped by anyway.

"What's up, Big Lou!"

Luther walked over and offered a fist bump. "What are you doing here today?"

"Just stopped through real quick—checking on things. How's it going?"

"It's good, Tee. Great time with the family on the weekend. That thing y'all had at Drake Lake and the ranch? That was cool, man. My kids, the wife, everyone loved it."

"I can't take credit for any of that. There was a committee that put all of that together, the rides, everything. Wasn't even my land. That ranch belongs to Warren."

Luther waved off the comment. "Please, if it belongs to one Drake it belongs to all."

"True that." Terrell walked around the room. "You're doing a good job with these kids, man. I never could have imagined it, but daddyhood looks good on you."

"There's nothing like it, Tee. You should give it a try."

Terrell raised his hands in surrender. "That's all right. I'm good."

Luther laughed. "Hey, I'm glad you stopped by. Check this out." He walked over to a bookshelf filled with colorful books, puzzles and stuffed animals, and reached for a piece of paper on top of it.

"Look at this."

Terrell took the paper. It was filled with mathematical equations. Aside from the fact that it looked to have been written by one of Luther's charges, it looked like good old addition and subtraction to him. He shrugged. "What about it?"

"Kyle did that."

"Did what? Copied this out of a workbook?"

"No. He did the math."

Terrell looked at the paper again. These weren't a string of "two plus two" or "five plus five." The first problem involved three figures. The second, four. By the end of the page, the problems were in the hundreds of thousands to either be added or subtracted.

Terrell looked at Luther. "Impressive. But I guess not too terribly surprising considering his mother is a doctor. He's probably been playing with her calculator since he could crawl."

"You misunderstand, my brother. The kid did this without a calculator, without using his fingers and without taking much time to give the answer. I was the one who used a calculator to see if what he wrote down was correct!"

"Are you kidding me?"

"Man, I swear. Blew my mind. I said to myself, we've got a little genius in the class."

"You mind if I take this with me? I want to make sure his mother knows about it."

"Well, actually, I was going to tell her myself. Give me an excuse to, you know, have a conversation with her fine behind."

Terrell folded the paper and placed it in his shirt pocket, talking over his shoulder as he walked to the door. "Go home and converse with your lady. I'll make sure Ms. Robinson gets the news about her son."

After a quick visit with Marva and an impromptu meeting with the center's director, Terrell headed back to Drake Realty. On the way, he called Aliyah.

"Hey."

"Hello, beautiful. How are you?" he asked.

"Busy. What's up?"

"Called to tell you about your son."

"What, did something happen?"

"No. He's fine."

"Oh, okay. Then what?"

"Your son might be a little genius. Have you had him tested?"

"No."

"You should. Luther showed me some math problems he did. I was blown away."

"He has a thing for numbers."

"I'll say. Some of my teenagers couldn't handle the problems he solved."

"Look, I gotta go."

"But you know about this, right? His ability to calculate in his head and stuff?"

"Not really. Tell me later. 'Bye."

Later that evening, his call went to voice mail. She didn't return it.

The next day he arrived early at the center, before it was time to tutor his students. He wanted to see Kyle's ability for himself. He peeked into the room. It was empty. He walked outside to the playground behind the center. Luther sat on a low wall watching the students periodically, and checking his cell phone.

"Good afternoon, Luther."

"Hey, Terrell. What's up, man?"

"Not a lot—waiting for my guys to get here."

"How's it going with them?"

"Hits and misses. Improvement overall, and a few who've grown significantly. But there are a couple who just aren't interested in learning. I'll be fortunate to talk them out of not quitting school altogether."

"That's the way it is sometimes. We do what we can where we can."

"It's crazy how a kid as young as Kyle can run mathematical rings around kids more than twice his age."

"Yeah, I told the wife about what I saw him do yesterday. She found it hard to believe he'd done it on his own."

"I do, too, to be honest with you."

"You should check it out. Hey, Kyle!"

Kyle was sitting at the edge of the asphalt, playing with rocks. When Luther called, he jumped up and ran over.

"Hi, Mr. Drake!"

"Hey there, Kyle. How are you, buddy?"

"Good."

"So I hear. Yesterday, Mr. Adams showed me the math problems you solved. All of the answers were correct. That was very good, Kyle."

"Thank you."

"Mr. Drake would like to see you work. Do you think you could solve a few problems for him?" Luther asked. Kyle nodded.

"Good." Luther looked at Terrell. "You want to do it as soon as this break is over?"

"I'd rather do it now, without the other kids. Hold on." Terrell reached for his phone and called the center's office. "Miss Marva, can you ask one of the interns to come to the playground? I need someone to watch Luther's class for a bit." He paused to listen. "Good, thanks."

A few minutes later, one of the interns came outside. Terrell, Luther and Kyle went back to Luther's classroom. Terrell wrote a six-figure mathematical problem on a whiteboard and asked Kyle to solve it. After a few seconds, Kyle walked over and wrote down the answer.

Terrell looked at Luther, who shrugged. "Told you."

He felt a bit embarrassed, but Terrell pulled out his phone, tapped the calculator app and checked Kyle's answer.

"That's correct, Kyle," he said.

"I know." Said without a shred of doubt or ego.

"How'd you figure it out so fast?"

"I don't know, Mr. Drake. I just do it."

"Here, let me give you another one." Terrell placed another problem on the board. Kyle solved it just as quickly. He looked at Luther. "To actually see him do it is even more amazing."

"He's not counting on his fingers or taking a lot of time to think about it."

Terrell pulled out his phone. "I'm going to put three problems on the board this time, okay, little man?"

"Okay." Said in a tone that implied he was totally bored. "Then can I go back outside?"

Luther looked at his watch. "It's time for them to come back in. I'll go get them."

Terrell finished the problems, handed Kyle the marker, then pulled out his phone and took a video of Kyle as he quickly solved the problems. After confirming that once again, the answers were accurate, he gave Kyle a high five.

"No wonder you were so interested in the flash cards I had a few weeks ago. You might be ready to study with the big boys after all!"

"The teenagers?" Kyle's eyes widened.

"Yes. Would you like that?"

"I don't know."

Terrell noted the boy's discomfort and belatedly realized the prospect of being called out in a room full of teens may sound intimidating. "No worries. We'll leave you here for now, okay?"

"Yes, that's better. Thank you, Mr. Drake."

"Thank you for showing me your skills."

Luther returned with the rest of the kids and Terrell left to tutor his teens. On the way he attached the video of Kyle's performance to a text for Aliyah. The question was simple: Like mother, like son?

Chapter 13

Aliyah stifled a yawn as she stepped into the break room. Her cranky exhaustion was all Terrell's fault. That walking caramel lollipop had strolled into her world and turned it upside down. Booty call. Yeah, right. That's what she called him but they both knew he was becoming more than that. Much more. But she wasn't ready to admit it. Nor was she willing to stop it from happening.

After finding an empty table and sitting down with salad and caffeine-laced soda in hand, she pulled out her cell phone and took it out of silent mode. Seeing Terrell's name reminded her of their quick conversation earlier today. She opened his text message and smiled at his question. Until she read it again. Then it became a reminder. Like mother, like son. Though it is a statistic she'd never wanted to be a part of, she was a single mother raising a son. Even now, at the age of five, her son was very aware that unlike his friend Conner, Kyle's daddy was not in the home. Thankfully, aside from his number fascination, Kyle's attention span was short. The few times he'd asked about his father, her honest yet brief answers had been enough.

"Where is my daddy?"

"Your father lives in Rhode Island."

"Where is that?"

"It is near where Nana lives in New York."

"Why doesn't he live with us?"

"Because he is married to someone else."

An image of Terrell popped into her head. She shut down the train of thought before it could catch hold. She was not one to fantasize about what could never be. She had no doubt that someday Terrell would make a great father. But it wouldn't be to Kyle.

She opened the attachment and watched the video. Confused, she played it again, watched as her son walked over to the board, glanced at the numbers, then quickly wrote down the answer. He did the same thing with the next problem, and the next. It was clear he'd either memorized the answer or was copying it from what she couldn't see. She called Terrell.

"How'd you do it?"

"You watched the video."

"Yes."

"I didn't do anything. It was all Kyle."

"Look, Terrell. I know my son. He's been hooked on math games and puzzles since he was three, but he didn't solve those problems. Did you have him memorize the numbers or were they written somewhere out of camera range?"

"Neither. I came up with the problems in my head and wrote them down. He solved them."

"That quickly?"

"Yep."

"I don't believe you."

"I didn't believe Luther when he told me, either. Told him I had to see it to believe it. I saw. I believe."

"But how? It's like he just glanced at the numbers and then wrote down the answer."

"That's exactly what happened. That's why I called you all excited, woman! But you blew me off. You were busy."

"I didn't and I was. Wow. He stands there for just a second, then walks up to the board and writes the answer left to right. How is he adding those numbers?"

"I pretty much asked him the same question, asked how he knew the answers. He said he just did."

"Maybe Lauren's been teaching him. Or Conner's oldest brother, Conrad. He's around fifteen or so. Maybe he's been working with him."

Her voice trailed off as she watched the short video once again.

"I think it's him taking after his brilliant mommy." No answer. "Aliyah."

"Sorry. I'm sending the video to Lauren, and asking if she or Conrad have been working with him." She also sent it to her family. "Now, what did you say?"

Terrell repeated his statement.

"Thank you, but Mommy wasn't solving problems like that at five years old. Darn it."

"What?"

"Mama has a dinosaur phone. It says the file is too big to send her."

"Upload it to YouTube. That way you can just send the link."

"Good idea." She looked at her watch. Break time was over. She walked toward the nurses' station. "I'll do it when I get home."

"Cool. Send me the link, too."

"Okay."

"Are you rushing me off the phone again?"

"Pretty much."

"Ha! You're a trip."

"No, I'm east coast. We keep it real. Your workday is over but I'm still on the clock."

"What do you say I meet you when you get off the clock?"

"Negative. When I finally get to bed, the only thing I want to do is sleep."

"That's unfortunate."

"I'll let you make it up to me."

"When?"

"Friday night. We can go somewhere and be naughty for a couple hours."

"Negative. Friday's too far away."

"It's tomorrow, Terrell."

"Exactly. And I haven't seen you since—"

"Two nights ago."

"That long?"

"Goodbye, Terrell."

"Call me later."

"Okay."

Later, when a surgery had to be rescheduled, Aliyah found herself with an hour of downtime. She updated a couple of patient files and then tackled the process of uploading her son's video to YouTube. A few minutes later, she had a link. She resent the text to her family, sent the link to Lauren and Terrell and finished her shift.

On her way to the car, she pulled out her phone.

Four missed calls. Eight missed text messages. Her heart leaped into her throat. What had happened to Kyle?

Then she remembered. The video. She reached her car, got in and tapped the first message. It was from her twenty-two-year-old brother, Kieran, who'd recently graduated from NYU.

Wow, sis. That was pretty cool. Now tell me how you got Kyle to remember all those answers, cause no five-year-old can do all that.

Next text. Her twenty-year-old brother, Joseph, who was attending a college in Iowa on a full, four-year basketball scholarship.

Look at little shorty, taking after his uncle! This is impressive. If it's not fake.

Text number three, from a cousin in Atlanta. The video had already reached extended family. Her mother, Aliyah reckoned. But still, that was fast.

Is this my cuzzo??? Wow!!! He's so smart, but then again, look at his mama. Xoxo

The last text was from Terrell.

Hope you don't mind that I sent your son's video link to a few people. No one can believe it. At least half of them have responded back to ask me how I got him to memorize those numbers! LOL. Your son is really gifted, A. You should probably have him tested. He's probably a genius. Like you...

His words warmed her heart, and other places. Handsome, successful, unassuming and genuinely a nice guy. She'd noticed it at the Halloween festivities. A smile here, a compliment there, everyone happy to see him because he made people feel good. No wonder he was a chick magnet. Good thing their relationship was casual and she didn't care about what monkeys were in his circus. Let someone else be the ringleader. Yes. That sounded good. She tapped the missed-calls icon and saw that most were from family, though Terrell had called as well. After activating her car's hands-free system, she pulled out of the parking lot and returned his call.

"Good evening."

Two common words. But the way he said them, slow and easy, in that deep, slightly raspy voice, with her imagining how his lips moved and his tongue rolled, caused her to almost bypass the next corner, where she was to make a left and continue to the highway, and Paradise Cove.

"Hello."

"Baby, I'm concerned. You sound exhausted."

"By Thursday night, I'm pretty beat. But having Friday morning off gives me time to get rejuvenated."

"Your hard work is going to pay off."

"Let us pray."

"You're headed home?"

"Yes, and no."

"What does that mean?"

"Yes I'm headed home and no, you can't come over."

"Did I ask to come over?"

"You did earlier. I made an exception to my rule the other night but don't want you to get used to coming to my house. As the video you shot plainly shows, Kyle is a very bright kid. He heard you the other night and thought it was a dream. If he saw you, we'd have a whole bunch of explaining to do."

"He said that?" She nodded. "I'm sorry. Teresa wants to talk to you about how smart Kyle is."

"Who?"

"Really? My twin?"

"Excuse me but I only met her once. And on a day where I met about a dozen other people."

"You're excused."

"I don't know what I'd tell her. The games and apps I've downloaded for him are nowhere near as complicated as the problems he solved. Lauren said she's never taught him anything like that and doesn't think her son has, either." The last few words were mumbled through a yawn.

"How far are you from your house?"

"Not far, why?"

"Because you're yawning, and I don't want to worry about you falling asleep at the wheel."

"I won't. I'm almost at Lauren's to pick up Kyle. In twenty minutes, I'll be in bed."

"Hey, I've got an idea."

"What?"

"Do you think Lauren could watch Kyle for a little while longer?"

"She could, but she won't because I'm here to pick him up."

"Babe, I can't explain now but can you trust me? Can you ask her to watch him, and then be ready to leave your house in an hour?"

"Leave my house in an hour?!"

"Okay, thirty minutes?"

"No, Terrell."

Terrell groaned. "Man, that same stubborn drive that makes you so successful is driving me crazy right now."

"Then I'll solve that by letting you go."

"That's fine. But I'm stubborn, too. So ask Lauren to watch Kyle, please, and be ready in half an hour."

"Wait, Terrell, don't—"

But he had. The line was dead.

Aaliyah pulled into the Hensley driveway, but kept her car idling. It had been a long time since a man told her what to do. Aside from her father, it had never happened, come to think of it. So why start now? She turned off the car and opened the door. But curiosity stopped her. What was Terrell up to? Where did he want her to go? The last time she'd trusted him, they'd ended up spending a magical night in San Francisco. Hmm. She closed the door and called Lauren. A die-hard romantic, Lauren had sided with Terrell and practically threatened her with bodily harm if she came in to get her son. So she didn't. She drove home.

Thirty minutes went by. Nothing happened.

Forty minutes. She texted Terrell. What's up? No answer.

An hour. Aliyah took off her clothes and got into bed.

Fifteen minutes later, she heard her indicator chirp. Terrell.

You ready?

The nerve of this guy! She yanked up her phone. No. I'm in bed. Asleep. She placed the phone on the nightstand and pulled up the covers. *Chirp.* She tried to ignore it. Couldn't. Grabbed the phone again.

Go look out your living room window.

She resent her last message, and hoped this time that not only would his phone get it, but that he would, too. *Chirp.*

It was now obvious to Aliyah that he was not getting her message. But he would. She turned off her ringer.

Five minutes went by...before someone rang her doorbell.

"What the heck?" She sprang out of bed, ready to give Terrell a piece of her mind. *So this is why he wanted Kyle gone? So he could come over here against my wishes?*

She reached the door, yanked it open and...looked into the face of a startled, uniformed stranger. Really should have checked that peephole. But she was thankful for the screen door, which she promptly locked.

"Why are you at my door?"

"Forgive me, Ms. Robinson. I didn't mean to startle you. I am here at the request of Mr. Drake. He says he could not reach you by phone, and asked that I let you know your limo is waiting."

"My limo?" The stranger stepped back, allowing her to see a big, black, shiny limousine fairly glistening under the streetlight. Her jaw dropped.

She heard her cell phone ring. Her attention went from

the man to the sound of the phone and back. Her mind was too fuzzy with fatigue to think. "Just a minute," she told the driver and then rushed to get the phone.

"Hello?"

"Good, you answered. Is Ed there, with the limo?"

"You mean the stranger who scared me half to death ringing my doorbell?"

"Sorry, baby. Couldn't be helped. You didn't answer your phone so I told him to get you. Are you ready?"

Aliyah had never been so flummoxed in her life. Didn't she text this man that she was in bed and asleep? Twice? That she was neither right now was inconsequential.

Terrell continued, as if reading her mind. "I know you're tired. This will make you feel better. I promise. Will you trust me, throw something on and be nice to Ed as he brings you to your destination?"

"Which is?"

"A surprise. Are you coming?"

"Yes," she finally huffed.

"Good. I'll see you soon."

She hung up and all but stomped back into her bedroom and over to the closet. "I can't believe he's pulled this," she mumbled, pulling on jeans and replacing her night-shirt with a simple T-shirt. *I shouldn't go. I should just go out there, tell Mr. Ed that's there's been a mistake and send the limo on its merry way.* She thought this, even as she slipped on sandals, reached for her purse and headed toward the door.

Half of her was exasperated at the gall this man had. But the other half, the lower half specifically, was getting excited.

Chapter 14

Terrell had surfed the internet, looking for sites of local companies that could provide the service he wanted. No luck. So he resorted to the familiar and called up his go-to girl.

She answered immediately. "Tee, what's up?"

"Hey, Tee. You still in town?"

"No. Atka had a business meeting first thing this morning so we left last night. I thought I told you."

"You may have. There's a lot going on."

"Tell me about it."

"From what I saw, you're handling it well—marriage, motherhood, the blog and how fast it's growing. Sometimes I still can't believe I'm an uncle. Not once, but twice!"

"Yes, my son, Logan David, and Warren's daughter, Sage."

"Speaking of babies and baby making, where can I find a mobile spa company, someone who does manicures, pedicures, facials, et cetera, as a home visit?"

"Really, brother? All of that for a segue?"

"No," he said, laughing. "You know I'm always about family but my question is why I called."

"Is this for Aliyah?"

"Yes."

"Hmm. She's got you working, thinking outside the box. Normally it's your women doing all the work. Interesting.

Though I can see why. Not only is she gorgeous, but she's smart. And her son is the cutest. I like her."

"Good. Now can you help me?"

"Sure. When do you want to do it?"

"In about thirty minutes."

For anyone else such a request would have been impossible. But Teresa was one of the most connected women in all of PC, and the right amount of money could always get an appointment. So by the time he'd sent the limo and then texted Aliyah, everyone he'd summoned to take care of his lady was either setting up or on the way.

When she arrived, Terrell was waiting at the side door, the direct entrance to his wing of the Drake estate.

"Hello, beautiful." He gave her a hug.

Stepping back, she said, "This can't be your house."

"It belongs to my parents. This is just my wing. Come with me."

She took Terrell's outstretched hand and followed him down the hallway. "This is the largest private home I've ever seen," she whispered.

"It's pretty big," he said with a chuckle as they neared his suite. "Which is why you don't have to whisper. My parents are all the way on the other side and, trust me, you can holler even and they won't hear a thing."

"And we know this because... Never mind, don't answer that question." She took a moment to survey the pictures lining the hallway. "This is nice, Terrell. Really nice."

"Thank you."

"Did you grow up here?"

"Pretty much. My parents had this home built twenty years ago, when Golden Gates was established as the town's gated community. I had just turned eight when we moved in. My parents did a major renovation seven or eight years ago."

They reached his suite. The doors opened to a room that

had been transformed from a bedroom to a spa. Dim lighting combined with fragrant white candles to create an ambiance of fantasy. Aliyah was floored. "Did you do this?"

"I helped. Go on in."

She did, and was immediately drawn to his massive custom bed. "Wow, very nice. This room is fit for a king."

"And that—" he raised his arm in the other direction "—is for you, my queen."

She turned, and had to pick her jaw off the floor.

Amid the sea of flickering tea candles were two massage tables. A short distance from them, a spa pedicure chair. A delicious scent of jasmine mixed with something fruity tickled her nostrils. Soft music played in the background. Across the room, in the living area's fireplace, red embers glowed. Aliyah took in the fantastical scene and felt like Cinderella when invited to the ball.

Terrell came up behind her and placed his hands on her shoulders. She turned into his embrace. "This is all so amazing, Terrell. I don't know what to say."

"Then say nothing." He gave her a quick kiss on the lips. "Just enjoy."

She walked over to the massage table nearest her. "I was thinking about how badly I needed one of these just the other day! And this, with the music and the aromatherapy, is an even better atmosphere than I imagined. That's jasmine I smell, right?"

"Yes."

Aliyah turned, startled by the strange voice, even more surprised that there wasn't one person who'd quietly entered the room, but two.

"I'm sorry, dear friend. I did not mean to scare you."

"Aliyah, this is Sanje and Heaven, owners of Heavenly Spa Treatment, a mobile service that, as you can see, brings the spa to you."

"To further answer your question," the woman, Heaven,

said to Aliyah, "in the infuser is our product called Surrender, a combination of jasmine, ylang-ylang, bergamot and a couple secret ingredients, all designed to help you de-stress, relax and be at peace."

"For me to achieve all of that may take more than just one sitting."

Terrell's voice turned sexy. "That can be arranged."

"We will travel wherever needed," Sanje said.

"Sounds great." Aliyah placed her hand on the table, felt the soft, cotton spread. "I'm ready."

Heaven stepped forward. "Then let's get started."

Thirty minutes in and Aliyah felt like putty in Heaven's capable hands. If his satisfied grunts were any indication, Sanje's work on Terrell was excellent as well. Aliyah luxuriated in the feeling. She could get used to this. She could also get used to Terrell in her life. As quickly as the thought came, Aliyah worked to dispel it. She didn't know if she could trust someone like Terrell with her heart. But when it came to making that decision, she realized, it might be too late already.

Chapter 15

Terrell sauntered into the boardroom, more than ready for the Monday morning meeting at his family's firm. Since finding out that he was being considered for the position of VP of sales and marketing, he'd doubled his sales efforts, often working eighty-hour weeks. Last night he'd received an email that proved his efforts were paying off. A professional organization whose membership represented several companies planning expansion had chosen Drake Realty as their sole realtor and consulting firm.

"Good morning, all!" He continued to where the drinks were located.

"Morning, son." Ike, Sr. turned from pouring a cup of coffee to greet him.

The other ones present—Ike, Jr., Warren and the company directors—chimed in as well.

"Who's that kid everybody's talking about?" Ike, Jr. asked. "The math whiz who goes to our center."

"Where'd you see it?"

"Teresa's blog."

"She put it on her blog? Cool."

"I saw it last night. The little tyke is pretty popular. The video has already gotten over five thousand hits."

"Seriously?" Terrell pulled out his phone and clicked the YouTube icon. "Dang, that's crazy. The video's been up less than seventy-two hours."

The director of property management asked for the link, and checked it out. "Wow, that's really something. Are you sure you didn't coach this kid?"

Terrell shook his head. "Not at all. In fact, I should make another one where people give him arbitrary numbers off the top of their heads so people know we're not cheating."

"I say unless this young man is ready to sell some residential and commercial property, we table this discussion and get on to the Drake matters at hand."

"This is a Drake matter, Dad." Everyone looked at Terrell. "Whatever positive buzz is generated through this video is great for the Drake Community Center—its programs, activities, et cetera. It could bring national attention to not only the center, but also our town. Yes, the child is very bright. But it doesn't hurt us that he is being taught our center. Whether or not he'll opt for a career in real estate is a decision that is decades away. But that his video could benefit our center in the short term is a very real possibility."

"Good point, Terrell. So now that I have a more complete picture of this kid and the relevance of his video to various Drake holdings, can someone send me the link?"

Aliyah stared at the number in disbelief. An hour ago, Terrell had texted a message for her to pull up Kyle's video to see how many views it had gotten. A week ago, she was surprised to see that over five thousand people had watched her son solve math problems. When Terrell mentioned that his sister had posted the link on her blog, Aliyah believed it was her subscribers and the blog's growing popularity that had caused the spike in numbers. When texts from her brother said his video had gone viral, this number was what she thought he was talking about. But no. He'd seen what she was now looking at. A video with over a million views.

She called Lauren. "Hey, girl. Did you know that Kyle's video has gone viral?"

"No!" Aaliyah could tell Lauren was at her computer; could hear her clicking keys. "Oh, my goodness, Aaliyah, this is amazing! Your son makes being smart and doing math look fun!"

"Terrell suggested I have his IQ tested. I agree, and plan to look into it."

"Speaking of Terrell, how's it going?"

"How's what going?"

"Oh, right. It's just casual sex. Doesn't mean anything."

"Exactly."

"Though seeing the two of you together, that's not the vibe I got. You make a good couple. Even Calvin said so."

"We enjoy each other's company. I'm not thinking of anything beyond that."

"You know what? That's probably best. But getting back to Kyle, there's a test for his age group called—" there was a pause and Aliyah heard more key clicking "—it's called an intellectual assessment scale. Oh, and here's another one. The Wechsler test. Both look to be specifically for his age group."

"Thanks, Lauren. Later tonight, I'll check those out."

That was the plan. But the night got busy and so did the days ahead. The video continued to draw attention. When a flurry of comments suggested the video had been staged and Kyle had been given the answers to memorize, Aliyah was contacted by a local TV reporter and asked if his team could provide their own set of problems for Kyle to solve and film the results. She agreed.

Two days later, Aliyah managed to get two hours of her shift covered so that she could take Kyle to the television station. There, Kyle was treated like a mini-celebrity as they prepared a series of complicated addition and subtraction problems on a whiteboard. The producers confirmed, on camera, that no one outside of those filming the project had seen the numbers. As he'd done on the previous video, Kyle studied each set of numbers for a few seconds and then simply wrote down the answer. From left to right. Without any visible calculation, no finger counting, no carrying numbers over, nothing. It was the first time Aliyah had witnessed it. The moment brought tears to her eyes.

"That's amazing, Kyle," the popular reporter said, after he'd fact-checked the answers using the calculator app on his cell phone. "How do you do it?"

Overwhelmed by the lights, cameras and extra attention, Kyle shrugged. "I don't know."

"If adding by longhand, most of us do it this way." The reporter walked over to the board, wrote 250 + 250 on it and then tabulated the way the average person did, by carrying the one from the second column's five plus five to show that two plus two plus one equals five, for the sum of 500. "But you don't do it that way, Kyle. You write the answer from left to write. How do you figure it out so fast?"

"I…" He fidgeted, looked at Aliyah.

"Don't be nervous, son. Just explain as best you can."

"I just see the numbers and I know the combinations, the answers. So I just add the first number to the number on this side—" he pointed to the left "—and then I write it down."

The reporter looked into the eye of the camera. "Did you get that, folks? Yeah, right. I didn't, either. And that's what makes this kid so special. We're going to keep our eye on you, Kyle. You're going places. And if you're going places, you'll want to stay tuned for the traffic report, after this."

After taking pictures with Kyle and the production team, the reporter approached Aliyah. "I must tell you, ma'am. I didn't believe that video for one minute. But your son proved me wrong. I really meant what I said to the viewers. You have a very special kid there."

"Thank you. I think so, too."

He pulled a card from his side pocket and handed it to her. "If I can be of any assistance in helping his star rise… I will definitely do my part."

The segment aired locally, on the MBC evening news. The next day, it was repeated on the network's national morning news show, *This Morning*. After that, it seemed that everyone Aliyah encountered, from the campus to the medical center to the grocery store, knew about Kyle. His peers at the community center thought he was a celebrity since he'd been on TV. Aliyah worried that all the attention might be too much for him to deal with. Goodness knew that with her already busy schedule, the increased phone calls she'd received had been a bit daunting. But so far, Kyle pretty much remained the kid he'd always been. Aside from the increased exposure, the TV interview had reminded Aliyah to look into intelligence testing for Kyle. He was in kindergarten now but who knew? Perhaps her son belonged in first grade. It was time to speak with a counselor who could help her chart his educational path and lay a foundation that guaranteed success.

On Saturday morning, mother and son did the usual— headed out for pancakes, Kyle's favorite. They entered the restaurant and were assailed.

"There he is!" The young woman who had frequently waited on them was beaming. "I saw your video, Kyle. Didn't know you were so smart!"

"What do you say, Kyle?"

"Thank you."

The other server joined them. "Well, look at this. We have someone famous joining us today!"

Various employees came over to speak with Kyle, even the cook and several customers came over. When their orders were taken, the server informed them it was on the house.

"Remember this lesson," Aliyah told Kyle when everyone left their table. "Being smart can take you far in life, and sometimes get you free pancakes!"

They continued to chat during breakfast. Aliyah was continually amazed at Kyle's view on various situations and circumstances he observed. He was able to articulate his position and even debate certain points. Her little boy was becoming a little man. She really enjoyed their conversation.

"Are you ready, Kyle?"

"Yes."

"What should we do next? A movie, or maybe a bookstore at the mall?"

"The bookstore!"

"Okay." Her phone rang. "Let me get this first. Hello?"

A brief pause and then… "Hello, Aliyah."

Hearing his voice made her stomach drop.

"Aliyah? Can you hear me? This is Ernest."

She took a quick sip of water, and prayed the egg white frittata she'd eaten didn't make a reappearance. "Hello."

"I'm sure you're surprised to hear from me. It has been some time since we've spoken."

"Yes." A simple answer, but while absorbing a spontaneous combustion of shock, awe and anger, it was the best she could do.

"How are you?"

"I'm fine."

"And school?"

"Good."

"Excellent. What do you have, two or three years left before you're Dr. Robinson?"

Seriously? The father of my child, whom I've not spoken to in almost three years is going to call out of the blue and expect me to happily join him in a casual chitchat?

"Why are you calling?"

"Mommy, let's go."

"One moment, son, okay?" She returned her attention to the phone call. "I'm in the middle of a few things. Is there a quick question or reason for your call?"

"Was that Kyle I heard? Is he there?"

Where else would he be? The moon? "Of course."

"He is the reason I'm calling, Aliyah. While I've supported him financially, I've come to the realization that money alone is not enough. He needs me. It is time for me to correct an error and reconnect with my son."

Chapter 16

"The mall is the other way, Mommy."

"I know, Kyle. Mommy has to go home and take care of something. I'm going to pick up Conner so the two of you can play together. Okay?"

"Okay."

Aliyah breathed a sigh of relief that the news about Conner satisfied Kyle's curiosity and shut down any more questions. She was still reeling from Ernest's unexpected phone call. The effort it had taken to remain calm had brought on a headache. She wouldn't be surprised if her blood pressure was sky-high. Feeling herself about to explode was why she'd ended the call and called Lauren, and was now making a beeline to her house. Five years later, and he wants to be a daddy? He'd had a realization? He qualified the monthly checks he'd send as support? Compared to the worth of both him and his family, what he'd sent Kyle over the years was a crime.

She needed to call back Ernest and get answers. Find out why all of a sudden he'd discovered a parental gene. But the conversation had to be private, without Kyle. And it would have to happen after she calmed down.

After getting the boys settled in front of a video game with snacks at the ready, Aliyah went into her bedroom and closed the door. "Breathe, Aliyah." She sat on the bench at the end of her bed, closed her eyes and worked to slow her heartbeat. Had she been able to sit still long enough, that might have happened. But she couldn't. Too much anger-fueled energy and boiling blood. She paced the length of the room, cursing out Ernest in her head, appalled at his nerve. She jumped when her phone rang, not yet ready to speak with Ernest, but determined to try anyway. She needed answers.

Good thing for her it wasn't him.

"Terrell. It's you."

"Who were you expecting? You almost sound relieved."

"I am. I thought it was Ernest, calling me back."

"Kyle's father?"

"Yes. After almost five years, he called and started chatting as though it was a perfectly normal thing to do." The memory alone made her livid. The pacing began again. "And then almost as casually informs me that through some recent revelation he now has clarity that his son needs him, go figure, and that it's time they connect."

"What did you say?"

"Fortunately, not what I was thinking. Kyle and I were having breakfast. I told him I'd call him. But I need a minute to get over the shock of hearing from him, and the anger at the presumptive, entitled attitude I heard when he talked about Kyle." She stopped pacing and took a breath. "Why is he calling? That, I did have time to ask. His answer? For my son! Really. What could have possibly happened to bring this on? Did he fall down, hit his head and suddenly remember he was a parent?"

"No. He probably saw him on TV, on the national morning show."

His answer hit her like a cold glass of water in the face. Of course.

"His calling caught me so off guard, I totally spaced. That's absolutely why he thought of us—the intelligent, charismatic, well-mannered son he's never met being on national TV. Now the timing of his calling makes sense. He didn't hit his head. He watched the morning news. So was the call about Kyle, or about the positive notoriety that is swirling around him right now? Is it because his son is being called a genius that he suddenly wants to claim parentage?"

"There's only one way to find out, Aliyah. You need to call him back, not to argue but to have a conversation and get an answer to all of these questions. You need to know what's on his mind."

The thought that some selfish motive and not love was what might have driven her ex to reconnect was too gut-wrenching to contemplate. It zapped her energy. She plopped down on the bed.

"I don't know if I can even deal with this right now."

"Do you think putting it off will make it any easier?"

"Not really."

"Then maybe you shouldn't. Who knows, it may not go as badly as you imagine." Aaliyah didn't know, and didn't answer. "Would you like me to come over for support?"

"No. But you're right. The sooner I have the conversation, the more information I'll have to make decisions. Your calling me was perfect timing. It helped to talk it out. Thank you."

"No worries. I've got your back. Call and let me know happened."

"I will." She ended the call, went out for a glass of water and to check on the boys. When she returned to the room there was no hesitation. She opened the incoming-call screen and tapped the number.

"This is Ernest."

"Ernest, it's Aliyah."

"Hello, Aliyah. I'm sorry to have caught you at a bad time earlier. Is everything all right?"

"Hmm...not exactly, to be honest."

"What's wrong?"

"You have no idea?"

"I'd rather not speculate, Aliyah, when you can just tell me."

"Okay." *Breathe, Aliyah. Discuss, don't argue.* "Your calling out of the blue is shocking to say the least, and your reason even more so. You say it is to reconnect with Kyle. For that to happen, you would have had to be connected with him in the first place. That is not the case. In fact, I can't think of anyone who tried harder to be disconnected from a child. First, through denial and then, through dismissal."

"Aliyah, it sounds as though you are still smarting over our breakup, perhaps even still wishing for something that can never be."

It was her first real laugh of the morning. After catching her breath, she adopted his proper tone. "Please rid yourself of such fantastical notions. The woman who believed herself in love with you has grown up and moved on. Kyle is who you denied, and after paternity was proven, still chose to dismiss from your life."

"It was not my choice, Aliyah. There were many factors involved in the decision. It wasn't a black-and-white issue."

"You're right. It was simply a black issue. A little black boy named Kyle issue, more specifically. That was the only factor to have been considered because it was the only one that mattered. Oh, wait, it was the only one that mattered to me. For you, money was clearly an equal consideration. That, and control. How do I know? Because what you spent on that cutthroat attorney could probably have paid for Kyle's college education. So please understand these issues, not wishful thinking, are why I may come off sounding a little perturbed."

"There's no doubt I've made mistakes in the past, but why are we rehashing that? I'm here now, and would like to move forward. I understand you've relocated to the west coast. That makes regular visitation more challenging—"

"Visitation? Did you mean to say introduction, because that's the first thing that usually happens with someone you've never met."

"You are right, Aliyah. And your anger is justified. I, too, have grown older and wiser, and in the process now acknowledge that regarding several matters better decisions could have been made. We can't go back into the past, so I've contacted you to fix the present. I want to get to know my son, Kyle. And as much as you may hate me, Kyle has a right to know his father."

She took a deep breath, and clenched her hands into fists to stop them from shaking. Belatedly, she realized that while water was good, a glass of wine may have been better.

"I'd like to ask you a question."

"Sure."

"After all these years, what made you call now?"

"It wasn't one single thing, Aliyah, but several."

"Such as?"

"Getting older, maturing, getting married."

"Right. You brought home someone your family found worthy."

"She is someone I've known since childhood. Our families have been friends for years."

At one time, the news of Ernest marrying would have been devastating. That now all she felt was sorry for his wife was proof that any romantic notion toward him was long gone.

"Have you by chance seen a recent video of Kyle?"

A hesitation, but only briefly. "As a matter of fact, I have! You remember Roosevelt, right? I believe he was about to get his doctorate when the two of you met. His wife is a PhD also, specializing in early childhood education. Someone brought the video of a so-called whiz kid to her attention, and she told Roosevelt about it. When he went online to view it, he clicked on another link that had aired on television, recognized you and contacted me. Given that I'd already planned to contact you, I felt the timing was a sign that my decision was the right one."

"Oh, so the television segment isn't why you called me. This was something you'd already planned."

"The facts are as I've stated, but nonetheless, my son's intellect is indeed impressive. Of course, given both yours and my level of intelligence, his high IQ is not surprising. My grandfather graduated high school at the age of fifteen."

Good for him. "Here's the situation, Ernest. While I agree that Kyle should know his father, the fact of the matter is he does not. I have told him about you, and showed him pictures. I am in agreement that you two should meet. But it needs to be at a pace that is comfortable for Kyle."

"Kids adapt quickly. He'll be fine. I would like to see him as soon as possible. Too much time has passed already."

The more things change, the more they stay the same. "Here's what I'm willing to do. I will consult with a child therapist trained in this area to learn the best way for us to proceed, and share those findings. I also need to know that this isn't a request predicated on a temporary desire. If you are not planning to be a part of his life for the rest of his life, then we can't go down this road."

"That choice and this journey is not up to you. Kyle is my son, legally and biologically. I will be a part of his life, and he will get to know the paternal side of his family. This can only happen through regularly scheduled visits to Rhode Island."

"That possibility is a long way from happening. Let's

start with the therapist and then something easy, like a telephone conversation. How's that sound?"

"Like a suggestion from one who's forgotten who I am, a man of means and ability to make things happen. I'm hoping we can resolve this amicably, but if necessary, legal action will be taken."

"I have full custody of Kyle, Ernest, and that is not going to change."

"We'll see about that."

"Yes, we will."

After a near-sleepless night filled with tossing and turning, Aliyah's anger had not waned. The nerve of Ernest! Calling her as if that were perfectly normal, something that happened all the time. Asking about a son that he at first denied and later abandoned. She hadn't seen him in three years, but was sure the size of his jeans had changed. It would take tailor-made ones to fit the ginormous *cojones* it took for him to call her. And his request? Regular visits? Across the country? Was he serious?

Unfortunately, Aliyah believed that he was. But when it came to her son and what was in his best interest, she would not back down.

Chapter 17

For once, Aliyah was thankful for the heavy three-day work schedule at UC Davis. She'd managed to transform anger into energy and give her patients the best care possible. Focusing on the management of their pain caused her to manage her own, and after a couple days had passed she was able to put the conversation with Ernest in better perspective. She'd also talked with a colleague who recommended a child therapist and had made an appointment. Taking this step made her feel better, too.

What didn't feel so good was not seeing Terrell. Dealing with Ernest had thrown off her entire weekend schedule. She'd canceled their Saturday night date to take Kyle and Conner to the movies. Sunday was filled with study and Terrell had had an event on Monday night. Several texts had been exchanged, but they'd talked only once in the past three days, and it was now late afternoon on Thursday. She missed him, but right now would forego Novocain and have a root canal before admitting it. Ernest's sudden reappearance in her life had brought up old memories, reopened old wounds and reminded her why she'd decided not to enter into a serious relationship right now. The most she would acknowledge was if she were to change her mind and want a commitment, it would be with a man like Terrell.

As if thinking him up, her cell phone rang. "Yes, I got your messages and was going to call."

"Good evening to you, too, Ms. Robinson."

"Hi."

"Busy?"

"Not at this very moment—am in between surgeries and was just checking my phone."

"I miss you."

She wouldn't say it back. She'd bite a hole in the side of her mouth first.

"No comment? Something like, 'I miss you, too,' or 'looking forward to seeing you'…something like that?"

"Nope."

"Dang, girl!" Terrell laughed. "Why you want to hurt me?"

"Your ego can take it. You're a big boy."

He paused, then said, "You still haven't told me about this past weekend, and how the conversation went."

"I know. It's been busy and I needed some time to think. But I will."

"I don't like how you sound, Aliyah. It's not just being tired. There's something else there. What is it?"

"I'll tell you later."

"Promise me you'll call tonight?"

"I promise."

Later, as soon as she'd put Kyle to bed and gotten comfy in her own, she did just that. "Hey, you."

"Um, the way you said that sounded so sexy, better than when we spoke earlier. How are you?"

"Better now."

"Of course. Because you miss me and now I'm here. You don't have to say it. I already know. Don't worry. The next time we're together I'll make up for this time we've spent apart."

"Gosh, you're smooth."

"And I mean every word. That's what counts. Now tell me about this knucklehead and what he wanted."

She did, the short version. "He didn't mention the video initially," she said, finishing up. "Only that he'd grown to realize the error of his ways and wanted to correct them."

"Do you believe that?"

"Not for a second. So I asked him straight out if he'd seen it."

"Has he?"

"Of course. And the fact that he didn't mention he'd seen it, that I had to bring it up, convinced me beyond all doubt that it's exactly why he called. In the past couple weeks, total strangers have come up to Kyle and me to talk about it. The waiters at the restaurant, even the cook came out to congratulate him. Our breakfast was on the house. People who've seen the video talk about it. So had the video been truly irrelevant, then saying he'd seen it would have been the first thing out of his mouth."

"Do you think he's serious about trying to get regularly scheduled visits established?"

There was silence as Aliyah pondered the question. "I think that this isn't solely his idea—that his wife and definitely his image/status/perception-conscious mother have been in his ear. When Kyle was simply the illegitimate child of a commoner, he had no value to the Westcott brand. But a child genius? Suddenly they can see themselves in him. He's become 'our child,' when before I was on my own. Now, he has the nerve to mention his grandfather, who graduated high school early, implying Kyle's intelligence is from their gene pool. His family is probably rethinking their stiff and vocal opposition to Kyle taking the Westcott name.

"If I know his mom, she wants to flaunt Kyle to her friends in a continued effort to prove their superiority. Not on my watch."

"Have you contacted your attorney?"

"Not yet."

"From what you've told me about this family, I suggest you do that ASAP. And I hope your attorney is ready for hardball because that is the type of game that's going to be played."

Terrell's words caused her another sleepless night. The Westcotts were used to winning and given his track record, the attorney she'd used before would be no match for their legal team. She'd need time and money to secure a comparable lawyer and she was short on both. There was never a good time for a custody battle, but now, in the middle of a fast-tracked residency program, was especially inconvenient. And ironic, given she'd always wanted Kyle to have a relationship with his father. But did Ernest really want to get to know his son, or was he capitalizing on being the father of viral video whiz kid? Time would tell.

She looked at the clock. Two hours until her shift at Living Medical. She went online to check her emails and search the web. But the thoughts persisted, too many to allow her to focus. Her nerves were too raw to sit still. So with Kyle having already been picked up by Lauren, she grabbed her purse and keys and headed out. Just as she reached her car and got in, her cell phone rang. It was one of her colleagues at the center. Due to a schedule mix-up, they were overstaffed. Lucky Aliyah had the day off.

More time to think. *Just what I needed.*

She called Terrell. "What are you doing?"

"Working. What about you?"

"I just found out I have the day off. This happens so rarely, I don't even know what to do with myself."

"I can think of more than a few things I could do with and to you."

"Ooh, sounds delicious. Want to play hooky?"

"I'll call you back in ten minutes."

He did it in five, and a short time later he picked her up and they went zooming down the freeway in his over-priced sports car. Top down, sun shining, hair blowing in the wind and singing hit pop songs loud and off-key. A spontaneous trip to Napa Valley was the perfect diversion.

"What's in Napa besides wine?"

"I don't know. Eating and drinking has been the extent of my experience."

She pulled out her phone and searched the web. "'Twenty things to do in Napa,'" she read. "Wineries, vine-yards, wineries in castles, vineyards on the hillside…ooh. We can take a balloon ride. Have you ever done that?"

"Can't say that I have."

"Can you say that you want to?"

"It might be fun."

"We could do a bike tour. Visit a museum." A phone call interrupted her search. Another unknown number, one of several she'd received since Kyle's video went viral. "Hello? Excuse me, who is this?" Terrell closed the con-vertible top. "Yes, this is Aliyah." She made a face, her eyes widening as she looked at Terrell.

What? he mouthed.

"That sounds excellent. I'm sorry, just a bit shocked right now." She listened, swatting at Terrell as he tried to get her attention. "Is that the only day available? Hmm. Then is there a way I can make a call or two and get back with you?" She mouthed something to Terrell. He couldn't seem to decipher the words. "I understand. I will call you back as soon as possible. Thank you! 'Bye."

As soon as she tapped the end button Terrell pounced, his expression a mixture of worry and curiosity. "What is it?"

"You are not going to believe this."

"What?"

"That was a producer from the Helen show."

"Helen DeMarco?"

"Yes! They've seen Kyle's video and want him to appear as a guest!"

"You're kidding?"

"This is crazy!"

Aliyah rarely had time to watch TV but knew that Helen was known for featuring talented kids on her show. Even she'd seen the adorable boy arguing with his mom about fixing her breakfast. He'd been invited to the show and given $10,000. He and several other of these guests had been found online.

"What's she say?"

"She said that someone had seen Kyle's video, showed it to Helen, and that was it. She told them to book him right away. There's only one problem." Her enthusiasm waned. "The show tapes in LA and they want us there Monday. I don't know if I can get the whole day off. But with all the logistics involved, I'd need it."

"If you tell them what's going on, I think they'll work with you. This is a big deal."

"I could ask Lauren."

"And miss being there for your son's debut on national TV. No, that's not going to work."

"You're right. It's not. Shoot! His assessment test is scheduled for Monday. And I'd planned to spend my day off researching lawyers. Who was the guy with the bright idea to videotape my son?"

"I tell you what, he's one smart brother. You owe him big-time. And he's definitely going to collect. Don't worry about LA, either. I'll help you get there."

"The producer said the network would buy my ticket. It's the added time of driving to and from either Oakland or San Francisco that makes this an all-day affair."

"We're not driving to either of those places."

"We're not?"

"That same smart brother I told you about has access to a private plane. He'll hook you up."

"Are you serious? And you'll come with us?"

"Of course."

She hit the call-back button. "Let me confirm with the producer and then call Mama. She's going to be so excited. This is her favorite show!"

Instead of choosing between the hot air balloon and bike tour, they did both. And Aliyah didn't think about Ernest or his visitation nonsense. Not even once.

Chapter 18

On Monday morning, Aliyah met Terrell at the regional airport.

"Good morning."

"Good morning, Ms. Robinson."

"Mr. Drake! What are you doing here?"

She got out of the car and opened the back door. "Come on, boys."

Kyle and Conner, who'd been invited along at Kyle's request, scrambled out of the backseat.

"What are you doing here, Mr. Drake?" Kyle repeated. "Are you coming with us?"

"Yes, Kyle, I am."

"Why?"

"We're flying to Los Angeles in Mr. Drake's plane, so we can get there faster."

Conner's eyes widened. "You have a plane?"

"The company I work for owns it. But I get to use it."

"Cool!"

"Where is it?" Kyle asked.

"Behind that building, on the runway. If everyone's ready, we'll go there now."

Once they were in the air and settled, with the boys being entertained by a friend of Stan's who was clocking hours toward his pilot's license, Terrell leaned over and snuck a kiss.

Aliyah gave him the side eye. "Don't. Start."

"I couldn't resist," Terrell replied, his sexy eyes still fixed on her mouth. "You look gorgeous. I like your hair loose and curly like that. You should wear it that way often."

"Thank you. It'll work for television but as a doctor, not so much. For that job, the good old ponytail is most efficient."

He reached over, grasped a tendril of her hair and rubbed it between his fingers. "Nice and soft. What I wouldn't do to…"

Pulling away, she gave him a warning between gritted teeth. "Behave!"

The petulant look he offered made her laugh out loud. "You are so silly."

"That's what you love about me."

An hour later, four excited Northern Californians landed at LAX. For the boys, the trip had been a great adventure, made extra special because of Stan, the pilot, who let each one come into the cockpit and "fly" the plane. Having Conner along proved to be a great distraction that prevented inquisitive Kyle from asking more questions about Terrell being there. There were more questions. Of this she was sure. His quick glances back to the two of them left no doubt.

The studio had arranged a car to meet them at the airport. Kyle and Conner kept up a steady chatter during the forty-five-minute ride from the Los Angeles airport to Hollywood and the studios where the Helen show was taped. They were ushered inside and led down a hallway to the greenroom, where one of the show's assistant producers joined them.

"Good morning, everyone!" Greetings abounded. "Flight okay, no problems?"

"No, it was fun!" Kyle said. "We got to fly the plane!"

A confused expression flitted across the producer's

face, but she just smiled and said, "Awesome!" She turned and kneeled. "You must be the famous Kyle Robinson!" He nodded.

"Speak up, Kyle," Aliyah said.

"Yes." His voice was just above a whisper.

"Kyle, don't be shy. Remember what Mommy said earlier? We have to speak…"

"Loud and proud."

"That's better."

"Good morning, Mommy," the producer said with hand outstretched. "My name is Jade, I'm here to take care of you, and walk you through the entire process so that everyone knows what's going on and can relax and have fun. Does that sound good?"

Everyone replied in the affirmative.

Turning to Terrell, she reached out to shake his hand. "Are you Kyle's father?"

This got Kyle's attention. Aliyah swallowed a moan.

"No. I'm Terrell Drake, assistant director for the Drake Community Center, which Kyle attends."

"And where this gift was discovered," Aliyah added.

"Well, we can't wait to hear all about that, but we'll save the details for in front of the camera. Right now, what I'd like to do is get both of you—" she looked at Aliyah and Kyle "—down to makeup and wardrobe—"

"Eww. I'm not wearing makeup!" Kyle's declaration was clearly not up for discussion.

"Are you sure?" Jade asked, clearly amused as Kyle vehemently shook his head. "You don't have to, young man. But the studio lights can get a bit warm. So they'll just take steps to make sure that you're not shiny and that your pretty mommy looks her best. That's a great color by the way," she said to Aliyah. "That your dress is maroon and not a loud red will read very well on camera.

Once they're finished in makeup, we'll come back here and wait for your cue."

"When will we meet Helen?" Aliyah asked.

"Not until you're introduced. She prefers to meet you just as the audience does, after you're introduced. That way the conversation is very organic and natural, as if she were meeting you for the first time...because she is! Any other questions?" She looked down. "Oh, I'm sorry, little one. I didn't introduce myself to you. What's your name?"

"Conner."

"He's my best friend!"

"Aww, that's nice. You came here to show support as Kyle makes his debut?"

"Yes."

"Well, that's a good friend. We'll make sure you have a front row seat in the audience. How about that?"

"It's good."

"Okay. As you can see, Terrell and Conner, there are snacks, drinks and, let's see, yes the *LA Times* is on the table. Feel free to help yourself to anything. Other than that, just relax and we'll be back in a half hour or less."

A short time later, Aliyah, Kyle and Jade stood just behind the curtain that opened to the soundstage for the Helen Show. Aliyah was struck by how ordinary and plain everything looked. To her, television was a world of glitz and glamour. She was expecting luxury, everything high-end. But backstage, at least, looked like any office, USA. She found it fascinating.

"You're on after this commercial break," Jade whispered.

Kyle looked at Aliyah. She reached for his hand and kneeled down. "You're going to do fine, baby. Just answer the questions like the little man you are. Okay?"

"Yes, Mommy."

As she listened to Helen make the introduction, a

woman she'd seen on TV and in magazines, the moment felt unreal.

"This kid," Helen continues, "makes me wish I'd studied harder in school and not played hooky during my math class. He does in his head what most of us can only do with a calculator. And I can't wait to find out how. Please join me in giving a warm welcome to the math magician… Kyle Robinson!"

They stepped from behind the curtain to thunderous applause. Aliyah was amazed at what she saw. All of the glitz missing backstage was on full display in every area caught by a camera lens. She felt Kyle's hand tighten on hers as they walked over to a smiling, standing Helen, who when they reached her, kneeled down and gave Kyle a hug.

"Have a seat, you two. It's great to have you on the show."

"It's great to be here," Aliyah replied. "What do you say, Kyle?"

"Thank you."

"So, Kyle. I've seen the videos of you working those long math problems in your head. People my age can't even do that, at least not without a calculator. How did you learn to do it?"

"I don't know."

"Did Mommy teach you, or is this something you learned in school?"

"Mommy buys me math videos for my tablet and I play with them. And then Conner's brother, Conrad, showed me, um, his homework for school. And it was math. And I asked him what he was doing. And he showed me. Then I said I wanted to do it. And he let me. And I got the right answer."

"Who's Conner?"

"My best friend. He's right there." Kyle pointed him out.

"Hi best friend, Conner," Helen said with a wave. "So Conner's brother is how old?"

"He's like..."

"Fifteen," Aliyah answered.

"Fifteen! You helped a fifteen-year-old do his homework?" Kyle nodded. "Boy! Where were you twenty years ago?"

The audience laughed.

"When did you get interested in numbers? Mom?"

Aliyah explained, starting with Kyle's early ability to count and his using building blocks to do simple math equations, to her downloading the first numbers-oriented games and increasing their difficulty as he continued to master them.

"But I had no idea he was at the level all of you are seeing," she explained. "I'm just as surprised as you are."

"How'd you find out?"

"Through the Drake Community Center in Paradise Cove. I'd enrolled Kyle there for tutoring, mentoring and other activities they offer. His teacher, Mr. Adams, saw a paper with math problems on it that had been left in his classroom somehow and noticed that the handwriting of the answers looked very elementary. He asked his five- and six-year-old students if someone had done it. And Kyle raised his hand.

"Mr. Adams didn't believe it, came up with some more problems, watched Kyle solve them and still couldn't believe it. That's when he contacted Terrell Drake, the assistant director, who was also floored. Terrell—Mr. Drake—contacted me asking how I'd taught him to work math that way. I had no idea what he was talking about so he shot a quick video to show me. That's how this all started."

"Such an incredible story, it really is," Helen said, as the audience applauded. "Kyle, are you ready to do some problems here, for the audience?" Kyle nodded. Helen stood. "Well, let's go over to the board, buddy, and do some math!"

The audience applauded, oohed and aahed as Kyle correctly answered the math problems Helen wrote on the whiteboard. Aliyah looked on as the proud mom that she was and gave Kyle a big hug when he rejoined her on the love seat.

"I tell you what, Kyle. You're going places! And I'm not the only one who thinks so. Some pretty important people and friends of the show have also seen your video. They've come here to meet you and to offer something I think is pretty cool. Everyone, please help me welcome a staff member from one of the top-ranked college math-and-science programs in the country. From the Massachusetts Institute of Technology, it's Mark Oberman!"

A handsome, bespectacled gentleman who appeared to be in his midforties came out to the sound of applause. He shook hands with Aliyah and Kyle, and gave Helen a hug before being seated.

"Mark, what do you think about Kyle, here? Pretty amazing stuff, huh?"

"Absolutely," Mark replied. "It is exciting to see someone so young so incredibly gifted." He turned to Kyle. "Good job, young man."

"Thank you," Kyle said, shaking the hand offered to him.

"Mark's not just here to congratulate you. He has something else he wants to say, but first—" she reached behind her and brought out a box "—we thought you might like a new video player to try out on your flight home."

Kyle jumped up, more animated than he'd been all morning. "Thank you!"

"It's loaded with all sorts of fun math stuff—equations, algebra, geometry…the stuff that gave me the heebie-jeebies when I was in school, but that you'll probably enjoy."

"Thanks!"

"Thank you," Aliyah said.

"Mark has something as well. Mark?"

"Yes, Helen. As many of you know, MIT has one of the best-ranked math-and-science curriculums available. Our campus is filled with bright, energetic minds who thrive in a culture that supports their dreams and aspirations, and their intellectual gifts. We seek out these types of students, not only those in high school and ready to graduate, but those who, like Kyle, show great potential at an even younger age. When those of us in the math department viewed Kyle's video, we knew he was the type of student who'd do very well in our environment. So I'm here on behalf of the university to offer to Kyle a full, four-year scholarship to our undergraduate program."

The crowd broke out in wild applause. Aliyah sat stunned. Kyle's eyes beamed. He enthusiastically shook Mark's hand. Aliyah, batting away tears, gave Mark a hug. Helen segued into a commercial break. Kyle's official TV debut was over.

Back on the plane, with the boys totally engaged in Kyle's new game, Aliyah and Terrell sat in the back, unnoticed, holding hands.

"Thank you for what you did this morning," Terrell said.

"What did I do?"

"You gave me and our center a major shout-out on national television. That's huge."

"I had to. You and your center are the reasons I even know about my son's talent, that Helen found out about it and now, why I don't have to worry about his college education. Geez! I'm still in shock over that. Totally unexpected."

"Tell me about it."

"Wait until this show airs tomorrow. Mama will be beside herself. My phone will be ringing off the hook."

"What happened today is a very big deal."

"Yes," she said, her voice becoming lower as she looked at him with sultry eyes. "And you are a large part of why today happened. I'm very thankful for your taking interest in my son and his abilities."

"Well, you know, I kind of have a thing for his mama."

"Yes, she knows that. She kind of has a thing for you, too."

He leaned over and whispered, "I can't wait until my thing gets to hang out with your thing, so we can do some things…know what I'm saying?"

"Then we should make arrangements for that to happen as soon as possible. I'd hate to keep a good thing waiting."

Chapter 19

Terrell had been up since five and at work since six. Part of the reason was that business was booming. The other part was because for Terrell, like most Drakes, work was his passion. Ike, Sr. both encouraged and expected hard work and stellar results. And he'd led by example. Not only that, but Terrell had also agreed to act as consultant on a totally separate project not connected with Drake Realty. He was now up to his eyeballs in work, suddenly juggling both divisions of a very busy department. Good thing he was the man for the job.

"Excuse me, Terrell?"

He looked at the intercom, surprised to hear his assistant's voice this early. Then he looked at the clock and was shocked that it was already nine o'clock. He'd been crunching numbers and reviewing his former colleague's open prospect for three straight hours? No wonder his neck was stiff.

Reaching up to massage a kink, he responded. "Yes?"

"I have a Lauren Hensley on line one."

Lauren? Even with dozens of clients and hundreds of acquaintances, he could almost always put a face to a name. Right now, however, he was drawing a blank.

"Find out what company she's with, please."

"Sure, one moment."

He rolled his head from one side to the next, then stood and stretched.

"Terrell, she said she's Conner's mother, Kyle's best friend?"

"Oh, okay. Put her through." He sat, a frown creasing his brow. Why would she be calling him? Had something happened to Kyle? Or worse, Aliyah? He pushed the speaker button. "Terrell Drake."

"Good morning, Terrell. I hope I'm not bothering you too much to call you at work. I tried the center first and they gave me this number."

"No problem, Lauren. How can I help you?"

"It's about Kyle and Aliyah. You know his appearance on the Helen Show is airing soon."

"Yes, I'm aware of that."

"Well… I'm not sure if a lot of other people know about it, such as the friends he has at the center. So I thought it would be nice to put together a little celebration for Kyle, a watch party, for him and some of his friends. Aliyah is always so focused on work, so I thought a fun afternoon would be good for her, too. I'm calling you for two reasons. One, to invite you to join us. I know you and Aliyah are friends and that she'd love you to be there. And two, I'd like to invite some of his friends who attend the center and wondered how I can get an invite to them."

"First of all, Lauren, that's a great idea. Where do you plan to have this party?"

"I'm not sure. Probably Paradise Cove, because most of the kids who attend the center live in or near there. Maybe a pizza parlor or… I don't know. I need to go online and see what's available."

"Would you like to have it at the center? We've got the room and equipment to watch the video, and we'd also be willing to buy the refreshments and whatever else you need."

"Terrell, that would be perfect! Thanks so much!"

He reached for his cell phone and tapped the calendar app. "It's no problem. What date are we looking at?"

"We're talking real casual here so I thought as soon as this Saturday?"

"Okay. Tell you what. I'm going to call the person who's in charge of that age group and give him your number. His name is Luther Adams. He can help you get all of this set up and give me the details. Okay?"

"Yes, that's great. Thanks, Terrell. I'm sure Aliyah and Kyle will appreciate it."

"No problem." He disconnected the call and tapped Luther's name on his cell phone. "Hey, Luther, what's up, man?"

"Just another day at the office, bro."

"I hear that, man, and will make this quick. I'm calling to give you the number to a parent of one of your students. Her name is Lauren Hensley. Her son's name is Conner."

"Yeah, Kyle's friend."

"So you know who I'm talking about, obviously. She called because Kyle's appearance on the Helen Show airs today but she doesn't think a lot of his friends either know this or will remember to watch it."

"Kyle Robinson is going to be on Helen?"

"That's right, you don't know this. Everything happened so fast but yes, Aliyah got a call on Friday for them to fly up yesterday to tape the show. It airs today."

"He got invited because of the video?"

"Yes. Someone from her staff saw it, showed it to her and next thing you know Aliyah is getting a call."

"That's amazing."

"That's not all. Someone on the staff at MIT saw it and offered Kyle a full four-year scholarship."

"Get the heck out of here."

"I'm serious."

"How do you know all of this?"

Terrell grimaced at the question. Most of the time, he forgot that he and Aliyah seeing each other was on the down low. "Because of time restraints, I offered Aliyah use of the company plane, and then accompanied them as a Drake Center representative."

"A representative of the center, huh? Is that how you're defining your latest rap game? You forget I know you, right? When it comes to Aliyah, and that stacked body of hers, the center is not what's on your mind. Because if anyone should have been repping, it's me. I'm the one who manages that age group, and the one who told you about Kyle's math skills."

"That's true, and if another similar situation comes along, with more notice, I'll be sure to include you in the plan. But this was last-minute, late Friday afternoon. Because of her schedule, she didn't think she could make it. That's why the company plane was offered, and why I went along. That and the fact that this gives the center some excellent publicity."

"So you were with her late Friday? I see the rap skills are working. Man, Drake. I wish I could bottle and sell whatever potion it is you slip these women to make them fall for you."

"Just taking care of professional business, brother. Just doing my job. Speaking of, Conner's mother, Lauren, wants to put together a little watch party there at the center. Something casual, I'm thinking the rec room with the big-screen TV—with light refreshments, you know, pizza and drinks or something like that. She wants to do it this Saturday, so my first question is whether or not you're available this weekend, and secondly if you can be at the center because I'm not sure I can and someone from staff has to be on site."

"I don't think we have anything going on. I'll have to

check with the wife to be sure. I'm curious, though. Why did she call you?"

"Probably because she met me at the festival on Halloween and knows I'm the AD at the center. She wanted to be sure and invite his friends, who mostly go there. At any rate call her and handle it. Whatever you two decide is fine. Just tell Miss Marva I've approved the event and will have my assistant put in the proper paperwork later on."

"All right. I'll take care of it. But don't think I'm not aware of your change in attitude when it comes to the shorties. I thought you were allergic to kids."

"When I have to be around them, I take an antibiotic."

"Yeah, one called Aliyah."

"Ha! Don't hate the player, bro. Hate the game."

"When it comes to that sister, you might want to think about retiring from the game. That girl is beautiful. And studying to be a doctor? If you were smart, you'd get serious and start dating her. Real talk. You're not getting any younger. Keep on going down this playboy road and you'll end up being the old man in the club, wearing a polyester suit and a bad hairstyle, trying to talk to women who could be your daughter."

"You know what, Luther? For the very first time since I've known you, brother, you just might be right."

Chapter 20

Aliyah stood chatting with a few of the other mothers as workers at the center began the party cleanup. When she saw movement from the corner of her eye, she turned to see Luther approaching.

"Excuse me, ladies." She took a few short steps to meet him. "Luther, thanks again for your all you help in putting this together, and coming in on a Saturday to oversee it all. I really appreciate it."

"It was no problem, Aliyah. Glad I could help."

"I means a lot. I've never seen Kyle so happy, and I enjoyed myself as well. This is a wonderful program."

"I agree, and that's due in large part to Terrell and the vision the Drakes had when this center was built. They put a lot of their own money into making sure that the building and everything in it were first-rate. He was supposed to be here, matter of fact." Luther's expression was one she couldn't quite read, but one that suggested there was more to this simple statement than met the ear. "Wonder where he's at?"

She wondered, too, had been looking forward to seeing him. Probably more than she should have. This week, the tables had turned. It had been Terrell working long hours and cutting short their phone conversations. It was she who'd asked him for a late-night rendezvous and him passing with the excuse of too much work. Her disappointment and melancholy feelings at their not being together forced her to admit to herself what she'd probably deny to others. She was falling in love with Terrell, and had been since the first day they met. Not that she knew what could come of this emotion. When it came to her schedule, she was looking at another couple of years of crazy. Now, with Terrell's likely promotion, he'd be working around the clock. Would the blaze of desire burning inside them be able to withstand long absences and time apart? Would he lose interest in her, or worse, meet someone else? Not long ago, she'd dismissed the possibility of anything serious happening between them. Now, at least privately, she could admit that if he wanted to take this friendship to another level, she wouldn't refuse.

But of course, no one could know this, least of all Luther, who Aliyah knew was not just a coworker but a friend. To the outside world, Aliyah hoped her face conveyed a message that she couldn't care less.

With the room almost empty, Lauren walked over and joined them. "Excuse me, guys." Then to Aliyah she said, "I'm heading out, kiddo."

"Me, too. Luther, thanks again. Kyle will see you Monday." She turned to Lauren. "Where are the boys?"

"On the playground. They just ran out and I told them they could stay there until I came and got them."

"Okay, let's go."

They walked to the playground where a few children, including their two boys, played. "Wait." Lauren placed a hand on Aliyah's arm to stop her. "I wanted a minute before we got the boys to talk with you and make sure you're all right."

"I'm fine. Why wouldn't I be?"

"Aliyah." Lauren fixed her with a look. "I know you were expecting Terrell and looking forward to him being here. He said he was coming. I don't know what happened. Had Luther talked to him?"

"I didn't ask. It's okay, Lauren. Really."

"Hey. How long have I known you? Since you were what, fifteen or sixteen? I've been with you through every jerk who came your way. I know when you're feeling a guy, and you're in way deep with Terrell Drake. And personally, I think that's great. I like him, Aliyah. I think he's a catch. So a little advice that you didn't ask for? Don't be afraid to love him. Hey, why don't I take Kyle with me? You can call him and maybe get together?"

"Thanks, but no. This will give me time to spend with my son. He's the male who needs my attention."

Aliyah's phone rang. She checked it. Terrell. "Hello?"

Lauren walked over to get the boys.

"Hey there, sweetheart. I meant to call you earlier but I ended up in an impromptu meeting and didn't get the chance. Are you still at the center?"

"Yes, but we're getting ready to leave."

"Who's we?"

"Kyle and I, and Lauren and Conner are also here."

"Any chance she can watch Kyle so that you can come over to my place? I'm still at work, and will be here for another hour at least. But I'd sure love to know that when I get home, you'll be there waiting."

Lauren followed the boys out, a questioning look on her face. Kyle and Conner ran ahead.

"Can you hold on a minute?" Aliyah muted the call.

"Is that who I think it is?"

Aliyah thought to be deceptive, but knew there was no use. Lauren knew her as well as anyone. "Yes."

"So...want to rethink my offer and let Kyle come with us?" Her face was one big smirk.

"I hate you when you're right."

They both laughed. Lauren slowly walked away but said

over her shoulder, "If you want keep your happiness a secret, you might want to turn down that glow."

"Hey, Terrell. That was Lauren. She's taking the boys."

"Yes! I'm going to get some tonight!"

"You are silly."

"Girl, my balls are about to turn blue." She laughed. "And I think I'm going blind in one eye."

Aliyah continued chuckling as she walked to her car. His jokester side was cute, but that he'd obviously not been with anyone else was what really had her giddy. "What time should I meet you?"

"Let's have dinner first. I'll pick the place and text you."

"Sounds good."

Later that evening, Aliyah pulled into the Paradise Cove Country Club parking lot and texted Terrell her arrival, as he'd requested. Within minutes, he was opening her car door and warming her with his embrace.

"Um, you smell good."

"Thanks." A car door slammed. She abruptly pulled away and watched as shortly afterward a well-dressed couple walked by them. They greeted Terrell warmly. Behind them was another woman—young, beautiful—whose look was blatantly seductive as she also spoke. He responded, but his focus was on Aliyah. "You okay?"

"I'm not very comfortable in the country club setting, and definitely not up to watching women flirt with you all night."

"Ashley flirts with everybody. But you don't have to worry about any of that." He offered his arm. "Right this way."

They bypassed the sidewalk to the main entrance and went around the building to a side door, which Terrell unlocked with a key on his keychain. He motioned Aliyah inside and placed his hand at the small of her back as he led her down a hallway to a set of double doors, and opened it. "After you."

She stepped inside and stopped short, shocked at what appeared as a wonderland before her. The room was small, intimate, with a table set for two. The ivory-colored walls and deep burgundy-and-gold decor enveloped her in luxury. Dozens of white candles shimmered beneath large crystal chandeliers. Breathtaking.

She turned, her look questioning. "What's all this?"

"To apologize for missing your party, made private because I also remember how you don't like uppity crowds."

He reached for her hand and led them over to the table. They sat. Aliyah continued to look around, conflicting emotions blocking her words. This man was everything she'd ever dreamed of and more, yet a part of her was still guarded against becoming too close. The part that bore the scars of past pain was waiting for the real rich, successful guy to show his true, arrogant, condescending colors. The ones that Ernest and all of his friends had eventually shown her.

"Terrell, this is so thoughtful. I don't know what to say."

The door opened. A waiter carrying a champagne bottle approached.

"You can take time to think about it after the toast."

"Good evening, Mr. Drake. And you, miss."

"Cliff, this is my lady friend, Aliyah."

"It is a pleasure, ma'am."

"I've known Cliff all my life."

Aliyah smiled. "The pleasure is mine."

Cliff popped the top, poured each a frothing flute of bubbly and quietly left the room.

"Do you know every single person who lives in this town?"

"No, but I probably know over half of them." He held up his glass. She did, too. "To you, Aliyah Robinson, for being an amazing woman, an up-and-coming doctor and an outstanding mother who's raised a genius for a son."

"Aww, that was sweet." She leaned over for a kiss. "Thank you."

As they toasted, Cliff returned with a tray of fresh-baked rolls, spiced butter and paper-thin strips of veal. Each helped themselves to the appetizer.

"This is so good," Aliyah said after her first taste.

"The chef was lured away from a top-rated restaurant on the east coast and has been here about ten years. Everything he cooks is first-rate."

"Just so it doesn't bug me all night, who is Ashley?"

"The girl we saw coming in?"

"Is there more than one?" She smiled to cover the jab. Or investigation, depending on how one viewed it.

"Not in this town, that I know of. Your question came out of nowhere so I was just making sure."

"If you don't want to answer—"

"No, not at all. You can ask me about anybody we meet because more than likely I'll be able to fill in the background. Ashley pretty much grew up here. I've known her since I was around twelve, or so. She dated Niko off and on for years, until he met Monique. Shortly after that she hooked up with a guy in Los Angeles. Until tonight, I thought that's where she was."

"So she liked your brother, not you?"

"She liked all of us and to answer the question that's really on your mind, yes, I've been with her before, along with half the guys who live here. I'm not ever going to lie to you, Aliyah. I'm a grown man and I've been doing grown-man things since I was thirteen. I've been with a lot of women, most of them casually. The one time I was in a serious relationship, I didn't sleep around. And even though you refuse to use the *R* word, I'm not sleeping around, looking around or interested in any other woman right now. You've got my attention, baby. That's all I'm saying."

Aliyah exhaled and took a sip of champagne. "I've got a confession to make."

"Okay."

"I can't believe I'm making it but..." Another drink of courage. "Even though it was meant to be casual, the feelings I'm beginning to have for you aren't casual at all. They're deep and hopeful and quite frankly scare me to death."

"Because..."

"Because I've only felt this way one other time, and it ended badly. People assume otherwise but when it comes to men and dating, I don't have a lot of experience. At first it was because of college, I needed a scholarship and put all of my attention toward getting good grades. Then one of my then best friends got pregnant at sixteen and it totally changed her life, but not in a good way. That experience was my birth control throughout the rest of high school because I had no interest in going down that road and tempting fate. Which is probably why I fell so hard for Ernest and placed such value in him and his opinion. I tried so hard to make everything perfect. That's the type of person I am, I guess. When I'm involved in something, it's all the way, a hundred percent, you know? And I'm trying to hold back on how I feel, because..."

"Because, why?"

"Because now is not the time for me to attempt a relationship and even if it was, you're not interested in having one."

"How are you so sure?"

"Because that's what we both said when we met."

He reached over, took her hand and rubbed a comforting thumb across her palm. "What if I told you I'd changed my mind? What if told you that I'm feeling you just as much as you're feeling me? Would you take a chance on this being a relationship?"

"Terrell, I don't know. There's already so much going on and I don't want this to be complicated."

"It doesn't have to be hard. It can be as easy as you finally admitting what I've known for a while."

"What do you mean, that you've known?"

"Girl, I know you're in love with me. I put that Drake on you, baby. You couldn't help it."

Aliyah huffed. "Wow, really? What an arrogant thing to say!"

Terrell smiled and kissed her hand. "I thought that's what you loved about me."

Chapter 21

Amazing what honesty could do. Terrell's pride soared at being one she could trust. She'd not only faced her fears, but also allowed herself to be vulnerable by voicing them. In that moment, the dynamics shifted. The walls came down. And feelings deepened. It took some convincing, but he talked her into returning to the Drake estate, and spending the night. Now however, in the clear light of morning, Aliyah's initial reservations of spending the night in his parents' home came back full-force. Terrell's inviting her to stay for Sunday brunch brought on a full debate.

"It's not like you haven't been here before."

"That was different!"

"How so?"

"Because first of all, I didn't know before I came over that it was your parents' house. And secondly, I left in the middle of the night. They never knew I was here."

"Are you sure?"

Aliyah looked grief-stricken. "You told them?"

Her reaction made Terrell laugh loud, and earned him a punch on the arm.

"That's not funny!" It actually was, kind of. As long as it was a joke. Otherwise, she would have been mortified. Her mother was no prude, but she would have been had Aliyah brought over someone to spend the night—it would not have been okay and it definitely would have not been in her room. Ernest's family, the Westcotts, were even worse. During their three-year courtship, she'd stayed twice at their family manse. His mother, Cordelia, put her in a guestroom so far from where Ernest slept that they might have been in different zip codes. Even so, she'd had the nerve to knock on her door at midnight under the pretense of having heard a noise. That lie was as see-through as freshly cleaned glass. No doubt she was sure Aliyah had snuck into her pious son's room with a potion to taint him and take his virginity. He was nowhere near virginal, but you couldn't tell Cordelia that about her son. In fact, she spoke so harshly against being intimate one would think Immaculate Conception was how Ernest arrived.

"You didn't tell them, right?"

"No, but had I done so it wouldn't have been a problem. Just like it's not going to be a problem today."

"I can't do it. I cannot waltz down those stairs after being intimate with their son under the same roof, and meet your parents for the first time! That's just too embarrassing."

"My parents won't judge you. They're not like that. Last night, you did acknowledge this was a relationship, right?"

"That is correct."

"Then it's time to meet my folks." Aliyah scrunched down and covered her head with the sheet. "Okay, I've got an idea. Instead of taking the stairs we can exit through the side door and enter through their front door. It will be as though you just arrived."

She slowly pulled the sheet away. "I appreciate the invitation, Terrell. Really, I do. Being with you and what I've experienced when meeting those in your family that I have so far is as different as night is from day to my time with the Westcotts. It's helped to further heal that part of me that was so destroyed by their callous behavior. It means a lot and I want you to know I'm grateful."

"Why do I feel a *but* coming? And not the one I always enjoy when it comes my way?" He reached for her backside.

She scooted away from him and sat up. "I want to meet your family. But not today. And not like this, sneaking around and being deceptive. Acting as though I've just arrived when I'm probably wearing a JHS face."

He frowned. "What's that?"

"A just-had-sex face."

"Girl!" He reached for her again. She dodged him, laughing, and jumped out of bed.

"Come back here!"

She tried to shut the bathroom door but he was quicker. "Out! I've got to use it."

"Not until you promise me something."

"I mean it, Terrell. Give me some privacy. I've got to use the bathroom!"

"Not without your word."

"Okay, what?" Aliyah squirmed as she tried without success to push him out the door. Like trying to move a stone statue bolted in concrete. "What?!"

"That you'll join us for Thanksgiving."

"Okay. Now get out."

"Both you and Kyle."

"Okay, fine." The squirming had turned to hopping. Not cute.

"No. Promise me."

"Terrell!"

"Do it."

"Okay, Silky, I promise. Thanksgiving. Now move before I pee on your floor!"

She tried to get out of it. In the week and a half since Aliyah promised to spend Thanksgiving with Terrell's family she'd come up with every reason possible to renege on her vow. He was having none of it. He'd even called her later that night and confirmed, made sure that she was not scheduled for work that day, both jobs, and school, so that later she couldn't use those excuses. Like now. When she seriously wanted to act like a woman and change her mind. Silly, she knew, to feel trepidation about spending the holiday with the Drakes. Especially after Terrell had explained that the day would be less formal than at other times and held outside, at Warren's ranch, and called for casual attire. They'd even invited another family with kids Kyle's age, just to make sure her son was comfortable. Terrell really had thought of everything. If she wasn't so sure about this not being the time for a relationship, and him not being the type of man to have a relationship with, she could see herself up and falling in love with him. Yep, hook, line and sinker. If she weren't so sure that she wouldn't.

With a last look in the mirror, and final self-approval that the flowing peach-colored maxi with fall-colored leaves paired with wedged brown ankle boots and a belt of the same leather was just the right amount of casual and chic, she stepped out of her bedroom and into the living room, where Kyle sat watching TV.

"Are you ready, Kyle?"

"Yes."

"You look quite handsome today." She turned off the television and lights, and set the alarm.

"Thank you."

"Grab your jacket. It might get cold later." She reached for a gift bag, and the shawl beside it. "We're going to meet Mr. Drake's family. I want you to be on your best behavior, okay?"

"I always behave, Mommy."

She smiled. "You're right, son. Mostly, you do."

A short time later she pulled into the wide expanse of concrete and gravel that served as Warren Drake's driveway. Several other cars, SUVs and a Jeep were already parked there. Music and the sound of voices floated from behind the house out to greet them, stirring up Aliyah's belly of butterflies. She pressed her hand against her stomach and with a last look in the rearview mirror exited the car, grabbed Kyle's hand and headed down the path toward the sounds.

As soon as they'd reached the end of the path and turned the corner, Aliyah saw a familiar face.

"Aliyah, hello! Welcome back."

"Hi, Charlie." The two women shared a warm embrace. "I hope we're not late."

"Not at all. They all came early," she said, tossing her head in the direction of four tables of six, and a bit farther away a kiddie table for four. "You know how family can be. No manners at all." She looked at Kyle. "Hello, little fella."

"I'm not—"

"Kyle." Her stern voice and slight hand squeeze squelched the oncoming argument. "Miss Charlie knows you're five. She meant that as someone not as tall as her."

"Absolutely," Charlie agreed, with a quick wink to Aliyah. "You're on a ranch, son. Around here you're not big until you're at least three hands. To a horse, know what I mean?"

He shook his head. "You have horses? Mommy, can I ride the horse?"

"What makes you think you can ride a horse?"

Both Aliyah and Kyle turned around.

"Mr. Drake!"

"Hey, buddy. Hello, Aliyah." He gave Kyle a high five and Aliyah a slight hug.

"Are you just getting here?" Aliyah asked.

"No. I went over to Teresa's real quick. She and Atka just arrived this morning. They'll be over in a bit. Come on, let's go meet everybody. Starting with Becky!" A young, petite woman with twins in tow stopped in front of them. "Becky, this is my friend Aliyah and her son, Kyle. Kyle, these are Becky's children, Matt and Melinda. They're five years old, too. And big, like you."

"Hi, Kyle." Becky turned to her children. "Say hi, guys." They did. "Kyle, would you like to come with us? We were just heading down to the barn to feed the pony."

"Ooh, can I, Mommy?"

"Of course. Don't run! Stay with Miss Becky!" She watched him run off, chattering away with Matt. "And here I thought it might take him a while to warm up to new kids."

"It did. About five seconds after the word *pony* was spoken." He reached for her hand. They walked over to a table of chatting adults, whose conversation stilled as they approached.

"Everyone, I'd like you to meet Aliyah Robinson. She's here along with her son, Kyle, who's already gone cowboy and went to ride a horse."

Aliyah turned to him with a worried look. "They're not going to actually ride it. Are they?"

"Don't listen to Terrell. He's always teasing." Aliyah smiled at the attractive woman with a flawless complexion, sparkling teeth and eyes, and a hand outstretched. "I'm Terrell's mother, Jennifer. Pleased to meet you."

"And you, Mrs. Drake."

"No need to be so formal, dear. Jennifer is fine. This is my husband, Ike, our dear friends and neighbors, Chet and Bonnie Donnelly, and Charlie's family who are also her and Warren's neighbors, Alice and Griff."

"It's nice meeting everyone, though I doubt I'll remember all of your names for more than five minutes. But please, don't hold it against me."

"Terrell tells me you're in your residency to become an anesthesiologist?"

"Yes, Mrs. Drake, um, Jennifer. I am."

"Then it's a wonder you remember your own name sometimes. We will forgive you."

Aliyah gave a quick nod, and a smile she hoped belied her nervousness.

It did not.

"No need to be nervous around us, Aliyah. We can be a rowdy bunch at times but it's all bark. No bite—" she lowered her voice conspiratorially "—unless we're backed into a corner and then we'll snap off your head!"

Aliyah exhaled on a wave of laughter. Less than a minute in and she knew Terrell was right. The Drakes were nothing like the Westcotts. By the time they'd made it around the yard, meeting the rest of Terrell's family and other guests, Atka and Teresa had arrived along with Aliyah's appetite, which had been overtaken by butterflies.

The catered affair was happening buffet-style. After fixing their plates, Aliyah and Terrell joined Charlie, Warren, Teresa and Atka at one of the tables. After a few general questions to and about Aliyah, Charlie turned their attention to Kyle.

"Have you guys seen her son on YouTube?"

"Yes, and it's phenomenal," Teresa replied.

"He's a mathematical genius," Charlie went on. "Was on the Helen show and got a scholarship to MIT!"

Jennifer, seated at the table next to them, overheard. "MIT?"

"Yes," Charlie answered.

"How'd that happen? Sorry, but I didn't start eavesdropping until midway through the story."

They laughed. Aliyah turned her chair slightly to make eye contact with Jennifer. By the time she was finishing up with the quick version of the story, everyone was listening.

"I wish I could take credit," Aliyah said. "I did notice Kyle's fascination with numbers and encouraged it with puzzles and later video games. But what you guys are seeing on video and television was as much a surprise to me as it was to you."

Niko's wife, Monique, wiped her hands on one of the monogrammed linen napkins, which even though they were in a backyard, seemed quite appropriate. "But who taught him how to add and subtract such huge numbers? Surely that didn't come from the games alone."

"No, the video games and the creative math exercises were only the beginning. It was a teenager named Conrad, the older brother of Kyle's best friend, who worked with him on solving larger problems. But even he had no idea Kyle had taken it as far as we all now see that he has."

"As far as an exceptional education," Jennifer exclaimed. She held up her glass. "I believe that great opportunity deserves a toast." Everyone raised their glasses. "To Kyle, a smart young man with a very bright future being raised by an obviously very smart mom."

"Hear! Hear!" The cheers rang out as glasses clinked.

"I appreciate that, Jennifer," Aliyah said, once the voices had quieted. "But I also have to give some of the credit to Terrell. After all, he's the one who videoed him and suggested I put it online. Had that not happened, we wouldn't be having this conversation."

"Interesting," Jennifer replied, eyeing her son over a glass of sparkling wine. "I've never known Terrell to take much of an interest in young children. That he's involved at all is quite noteworthy."

"Mom, if you're going to try and fish for information right in front of me, the least you could do is hide the pole."

"Son, I am merely stating an observation. And whatever secrets you think you have... I already know them."

"Whoa!" Niko said. "Man, you know you can't pull anything over on Jennifer Drake." Then to Aliyah he asked, "Do you work at the center?"

"No, I'm in residency at UC Davis."

"Ah, a doctor?" Ike, Jr., who'd spent most of the conversation observing, chimed in for the first time.

"Yes, an anesthesiologist."

"Now that's a woman who can hang with Terrell," Ike, Jr. said. "If he gets out of line, she can just put his ass to sleep!"

The yard erupted with laughter and teasing. Terrell gave just as good as he got and Aliyah wasn't spared from the ribbing. By the time dinner was over she felt like part of the family. And to think her paranoia almost made her miss this good time and great family? Perish the thought!

After a day of food, fun and more laughter than her sides could handle, she pulled Terrell aside. "Babe, I should go. Kyle's getting sleepy and I owe my folks a phone call."

"You haven't called them today?"

"Yes, earlier, before I came here. But my mom called again this afternoon and I need to call her back."

They said their goodbyes. Jennifer insisted on walking with them to the driveway.

"Jennifer, your family is wonderful and the food was delicious. Thank you for making me feel so welcome in your home."

Jennifer gave her a light hug. "It was my pleasure, dear. You're welcome anytime, with or without my son." She watched as Terrell stopped to say something to his twin. "We've just met, but still, you are quite impressive."

"Thank you," Aliyah replied. "But anyone who studies diligently and works hard can become a doctor."

"Perhaps, but I'm not talking your being a doctor. I'm talking about your accompanying Terrell to a major holiday meal. Trust me, it doesn't happen often. And never has he chosen to invite a lady who's spent the night in our home."

Aliyah could have dropped dead right then.

Jennifer chuckled. "Oh, don't be embarrassed, dear. Very little happens in my coop and with my chickies that this mother hen doesn't know about. Just wait, you'll be the same with Kyle. I think spending quality time together is essential to getting to know each other. I look forward to knowing you more."

After making plans for the weekend with Terrell, Aliyah left with Kyle for the quick drive home, made even faster by his nonstop chatter. That he was impressed with ranch living was an understatement. Next year, he informed her, there would be no Avenger. Kyle was dressing up as a cowboy! Once home, the chatter stopped, and for her son sleep came quickly. With Aliyah, not so fast. But she didn't mind. She spent time on the phone with the family back east, enjoyed a quick chat with Lauren and even caught the last of *The Best Man*, her favorite movie. Through all of this, however, Aliyah's mind replayed the past several hours and the difference a day made. The switch had happened so quickly and subtly that she just now admitted it was true. When thinking of Terrell, she thought of the *R* word. And for the first time since she'd met him, she didn't run from the truth. She was in a relationship with a man she adored from a family that was simply amazing. Her heart was nearly bursting with joy and she couldn't stop smiling.

Until just before going to bed, when her cell phone rang and she checked her ID. Ernest. She let it go to voice mail.

Chapter 22

"Aliyah."

She turned around, looking up from the chart of her next patient. "Yes, Doctor?"

"Is it true that the whiz-kid video is your son?"

"You've seen it?"

"I think just about everyone in the hospital and on campus has seen it."

"Oh, my."

Aliyah was genuinely surprised. Juggling Ernest and Terrell, handling the eventual reentry of his father into Kyle's life and a booty call-turned-relationship on top of a work schedule on overload had taken all of her attention. But now, considering that the video had gone viral and her son had appeared on Helen, she shouldn't have been surprised.

She reached her next patient's room and stopped. So did the doctor. "My son is eleven years old and can't figure out those types of equations in his head. Everyone in his class uses calculators. Heck, I'm forty-five and can't figure them out that way. How does he do it?"

"I have no idea and quite frankly, neither does he. It's a gift."

Her phone vibrated. Unknown caller. An image of Ernest came to mind. She looked at her watch and let it go to voice mail. "Sorry, Doctor, but I've got to—"

"Me, too, but hey. Good work with Mr. Smith. He's an old codger and your bedside manner is exceptional."

"Thanks, Doc."

Three hours passed before Aliyah was able to take a break. Because she was gaining expertise in both pain management and cardiothoracic anesthesiology, cases often overlapped and left her little if any downtime between patients and procedures. Mostly she didn't mind it. Focusing on patients kept her mind off less pleasant thoughts. Like Ernest and what her mother had said when they'd talked last night. Her mother was right. Ernest had a right to know his son and vice versa. Aliyah agreed. His knowing Ernest wasn't the problem. It was the other Westcotts and their uppity thinking that she wanted to keep away from her impressionable son.

Still, right was right, so instead of going to the break room she headed to the exit and her car. On the way, she told herself that speaking with Ernest didn't have to be difficult. That if both were civil, polite and reasonable, appropriate arrangements could be worked out, including a cordial relationship to maintain for the sake of their child.

She reached her car, got inside and dialed his number.

"Thanks for finally deciding to return my call."

Not the best start, but she kept to her plan. "Hello, Ernest. I apologize for not calling earlier. It was a busy weekend, and I wasn't available."

"You work overnight now?"

Ignore, don't argue, she thought. "I'm sure you're calling about Kyle and visitation rights. While my reaction to your request hasn't been overly enthusiastic, I do want you and Kyle to know each other. It is in his best interest to know both sides of his family and I will do everything I can to insure his mental and emotional health."

"I'm glad we're finally on the same page. I can fly down this weekend."

"You coming here is probably best but this weekend is too soon. We still need to meet with the therapist."

"For what? What's wrong with him?"

"Nothing is wrong with anyone, Ernest. I just know that an experience like this can be very confusing, even upsetting for a child his age. I'm sure we both want to proceed in a way that is least likely to cause any unnecessary angst in his life."

"He's meeting his father, Aliyah, not a serial killer."

"He wouldn't know the difference." An immediate reaction that she'd have liked to have back. "I didn't mean that the way it sounded, Ernest. It's just—"

"Look, Aliyah. You've had five years to do with Kyle as you please. Those days are over. It is time for me to step in and place him on the path that as a Westcott, he must follow. And by the looks of things, I'm not taking action a moment too soon."

Civility flew out the window with politeness on its tail. "By the look of things? Are you serious right now? First of all, Kyle is a Robinson, not a Westcott, by your design."

"That will be rectified as well."

"Secondly, the only path Kyle must follow is where his heart takes him. His will not be a life dictated by an archaic and asinine set of societal rules. This is the page you and I will be on before Kyle is allowed out of my sight to be left alone with you or your family."

"And we should leave it up to you? Someone who thinks it's okay to parade a child on television like some trained animal?"

The comment knocked Aliyah back in her seat. "I must have heard incorrectly just now. You can't be talking about Kyle's appearance on Helen, the one that led to his having a full college scholarship."

"Yes, one that will disappear as soon as they figure out the trick you've used to make that possible."

"It's no trick, Ernest. Kyle is formulating those answers. Had you watched the show yourself instead of relying on secondhand information, as you've obviously done, you'd know this."

"No five-year-old can solve those types of math problems."

"At least one can."

"I don't believe you, and I will not have my son become a mockery. What happens with him is no longer up to you alone. I will have equal say in my Kyle's life."

"Eventually, perhaps. But right now, in this critical period of the two of you meeting, we're doing things my way."

"You think so?"

"I know so."

"We'll see."

"Ernest, I don't want to… Hello?" She looked at her phone. He'd hung up. The call had definitely not gone as she'd planned. Was she being unreasonable in wanting advice from a counselor? What if Ernest met Kyle this weekend and everything went fine? Question after question bubbled up in her head, driving her crazy. She placed another call.

"Good afternoon, Ms. Robinson."

"According to whom?"

"Hey, wait. I'm not looking at your booty!"

"Ha!" Terrell's remembering this as their very first exchange made her laugh out loud, something which under the circumstances was very hard to do. "Thanks. I needed that laugh."

"Why? Is something wrong?"

"Yes, but you're at work and undoubtedly busy. We can talk later."

"If there's a problem, we can talk now."

"Okay. I talked to Ernest."

"I take it the call didn't go very well."

"Not as I'd hoped. I wanted he and I to calmly, rationally discuss a plan of action for introducing him into Kyle's life, which, for me, begins with his seeing a therapist."

"Ernest?"

She laughed again. "No, silly. Kyle. Although on second thought the both of them being seen is not a bad idea. Maybe even the three of us in some type of family counseling. I just know that these types of situations can go really good or really bad depending on how they're handled. So rather than just jumping in with no forethought, I want us to have rules and a game plan, and having been the steady parent in his life until now, I believe I have the right to decide how this happens. Am I wrong?"

"I wouldn't say that you're wrong, however, I wouldn't be surprised if you aren't being overprotective, maybe more than is necessary. I also know that women sometimes use the kid to get back at the father. This isn't something I think you'd do consciously but…it happens."

"I want Kyle to know his father. With all the craziness associated with how he and I ended, the three years we were together weren't all bad."

"What was it about him that you found attractive? Because from everything you've told me so far, I don't see how he even got your number, let alone a date."

"This guy I'm dealing with now isn't the Ernest who approached me on campus. That guy was polite, intelligent and sure of himself in a way that a then nineteen-year-old girl hadn't seen before. He was my first real boyfriend—heck, my first real date. The boys in my neighborhood were focused on sex, hip-hop and easy money. Nice enough guys, but they could have cared less about calculus or the political climate or weightier topics that I thought about. Ernest and I could talk about anything and he wouldn't just listen. He'd actually have an opinion. I was so enamored that it took a while to realize that his became the only opinion that mattered even in relationship-oriented conversations where both viewpoints should have mattered. I didn't have anyone to measure him against and was too focused on school to give it much thought. Until that last year, when I met his parents. Their abject displeasure at his dating choice changed our dynamic immediately and completely. Once I got pregnant, and his inheritance was threatened, I saw a side of him that I didn't know existed. Or maybe it's just that I took off the rose-colored glasses."

"What are you going to do?"

"Apologize, for one thing. No progress can be made if this becomes war. I'll also schedule the therapy session as soon as possible. I'm really not trying to keep Ernest away from his son. The sooner the therapist gives the green light, the sooner their meeting can happen." She looked at her watch. "Thanks for listening. I feel better just having talked all of this out."

"I'm glad to hear it. I always want to make you feel good."

She smiled, opened her car door and headed back to the hospital. "Stop it with the sexy talk. You know what that does to me."

"Exactly why I'm doing it, babe. See you after work tonight?"

"You are so bad."

"I thought that's what you loved about me."

"I'll show you what I love about you, a little later on."

Chapter 23

Both Terrell and Aliyah had busy weeks so they had to settle for face time on Friday at the center. It would be brief. Terrell would only be there to sign a few documents and she'd be on her lunch hour, which by the time she arrived would be forty-five minutes because she was running late.

Her cell phone rang. Terrell, no doubt, who was as punctual as a Rolex. She pressed the car's answering device. "I know! I'm on my way."

"Where are we going?"

"Oh, uh, Ernest. Sorry about that. I'm on my way to a meeting and running late."

"Something for school?"

"No, it's a community center that Kyle attends."

"A community center?"

Determined this time to stay upbeat and on the high road, she ignored the slight sound of derision in his voice. "Yes. It's a wonderful, state-of-the-art facility in Paradise Cove, not far from Davis. They offer a variety of programs and activities along with tutoring, mentoring and just having fun. As an only child, it's been a great place for Kyle to learn interactive skills as well. He loves it there."

"What's the name of this place?"

"The Drake Community Center. Check out their website." Said because she knew that's exactly what he'd do.

"I think you'll be impressed. So, you got my messages—the apology, about Kyle's progress in kindergarten and the appointment for counseling being scheduled?"

"Yes, I did. But I'm afraid your schedule isn't going to work for me and my family."

Aliyah tensed immediately, her hands gripping the wheel. She took a deep breath and relaxed her fingers. Getting upset again was not an option. "I totally understand, Ernest, and when making the appointment asked for the very earliest date. She came highly recommended and is one of the top child therapists in the country, which I'm sure is why she's booked three to four weeks out."

"I'm not going to wait that long to meet Kyle, or introduce him to this side of his family. We're going to Martha's for Christmas and plan for him to join us."

She pulled into the center's parking lot and turned off the car. "I'm sure Kyle will love spending time at the Vineyard with your family, but there is no way that can happen in three weeks. Ernest, please know that I am not trying to be difficult nor keep you from your son. The two of you will spend lots of time together. But that's after he gets to know you, and feels comfortable enough for me to leave him alone in your care. Yes, you're his biological father. Yes, I am pleased that Kyle will get the chance to know his dad. But the truth of the matter is right now, in his eyes, you're a stranger. Can you understand that from his point of view?"

"Did you take him to see a counselor before leaving him at the center? Huh? Did you drag out the process and set up a bunch of roadblocks before those strangers took care of your kid?"

She exited the car and walked to the entrance. "My best friend's son, Conner, goes to this center. That's how I found out about it. Conner and Kyle are best friends and I knew that with someone familiar around him, he'd be fine. Even so, I did due diligence regarding their programs and faculty before he joined."

She reached Terrell's office, tapped his open door and entered.

"Good afternoon, Ms. Robinson. You're looking lovely today."

"Good afternoon!" She motioned for Terrell to hold a moment. "Ernest, I'm at my appointment. Can I call you later this evening?"

"You're at the Paradise Cove center?"

"The Drake Community Center in Paradise Cove, yes."

"Okay, then. No problem, sweets. We'll talk later."

She scrunched her brow as she ended the call. "That was odd."

"Talking to a knucklehead usually is. Have a seat." He reached behind him, took a carryout bag from the credenza and began removing its contents.

She sat. "Actually, believe it or not, that conversation with Ernest was relatively civil."

"Now, from what you've told me about him, that is odd."

She laughed. "I know, right. But more than getting along, he called me a pet name I haven't heard since before we broke up."

Terrell's hands stilled. "What did he call you?"

"Down, tiger," she joked, noting his change in demeanor. "Nothing bad. In college, I was known for always having some type of candy in my purse, book bag, pocket, wherever. He started calling me sweets."

"I knew it," Terrell said with a feigned sigh. "I'm going to have to beat a brother down for trying to step to my woman because she's the baby mama of his child."

"Ernest and I reconnecting romantically is the absolute last thing you'll ever have to worry about."

"For his sake, that's a good thing." He handed her a wrapped package. "Your gourmet lunch is served."

After wiping her hands with a sanitized cloth, she pulled the tape securing the paper. "Roasted turkey? With mayo and mustard?" Terrell nodded. "You remembered my pickles, too?"

"Just as you requested."

"Thank you."

"I bought us sodas from the cafeteria. Is cola okay?"

"Sure."

He handed her a covered, plastic cup filled with ice and soda. "Thanks, babe."

After a couple of bites, Terrell reached for a napkin. "I've been meaning to ask you something."

"What?"

"In our family, Christmas is a big deal. We don't choose names. Everybody gets something for everybody."

"That's nice."

"So what do you want?"

"Me? You don't' have to get me anything."

"I know I don't have to. But what do you want? Or let me word it a different way. When out shopping, what types of stores are you drawn to?"

"Usually the kind that allow me to go in, get what I want and get out in as little time as possible." She took a sip of cola. "I appreciate you asking but really, finding out what's really on Ernest's mind and then getting him to leave my life as quickly as he came will be gift enough."

They continued chatting casually, enjoying their lunch. She was just about to leave when a young man dressed in a navy blue suit knocked on Terrell's door.

"Yes?"

"Excuse me, sir. Are you Terrell Drake?"

"Yes. Come on in."

The man entered, his attention going from Terrell to Aliyah.

"How may I help you?" Terrell asked.

"Actually, I think she's who I'm looking for. Aliyah Robinson?" he asked with a smile.

Aliyah turned to him in surprise. "Yes, I'm Aliyah Robinson."

"Okay, great. Then this is for you." He handed her a white envelope.

Taking it, she asked him, "What is this?"

The smile left the stranger's face as he answered, "You've been served."

Before she could think to ask a question, he turned and left. She looked at Terrell, at the envelope, and back at him.

He held out a letter opener. "Only one way to find out what's inside."

"I can't imagine…" she began, before an image of Ernest's face came to mind. Her hands stilled, briefly, before she gave the opener a forceful pull and cleanly slit the top. Displaying a calmness she did not feel, she pulled out the envelope's contents and began to read. A few lines in, she got up and closed Terrell's office door.

The look on her face made Terrell sit up straight. "What is it, babe?"

"It's the answer to Ernest's earlier behavior, and questions about the center." She sat, shoulders squared, looking at Terrell. "He wanted to know where I'd be so he could serve me this motion seeking full custody of my son."

"Damn." Terrell sat back in his seat. "Well, at least now you know what's on his mind."

Chapter 24

A stunned Aliyah returned to work but left shortly afterward. She was too upset to focus on grams and milliliters, and such focus was too important when lives were at stake. Lauren had offered the distraction of a night at the theater. She'd passed on the show, knowing nothing short of a resolution would take her mind off of Ernest's special delivery. The invitation for Kyle to spend the night with Conner was gratefully accepted. Terrell had called twice. No, she didn't want company or to go out. Yes, she was doing okay. No, she hadn't been able to reach Ernest. Yes, she would call back later, and loved him, too.

She sat, in the afternoon quiet of her living room, turning over the day's events in her mind. Before the national exposure highlighting his intelligence, she couldn't have paid Ernest to visit Kyle and now he wanted full custody? He'd have a better chance of turning water to wine.

The ringing phone startled her out of her musings. After reading the ID, she snatched up her phone and tapped the speaker button. "Mom!"

"What's the matter, Aliyah? When listening to the message, you sounded upset."

"Upset is putting it mildly." For the first time since opening the envelope, tears flowed. In between sobs and expletives, she told her mom what had been going on. "Two months ago is when I heard from him, out of the blue. And because I want to handle this in a way best for Kyle, he's going to grow impatient and demand full custody? His son has waited five years to meet him. What should Kyle demand? That's what I want to ask him if he'll ever return my call."

"It doesn't surprise me that since he's famous and being touted as a little genius that they now want to claim him."

"Go ahead and say I told you so."

"Girl, I don't have to state the obvious. Nor is there any joy in being right all along. I've been around people like that before. When push comes to shove, they cling to their own kind. Now he wants to bring his son into the fold, and leave you with nothing."

"It'll never happen," Aliyah spat. "I'll do anything to keep my son with me. Anything."

"Well, I guess you need to start with a good lawyer. Do you know somebody who handles cases like this?"

"I'm going to call the same attorney who handled the case for child support. If he can't do it, hopefully he can recommend someone. Whatever happens, it has to be fast. The hearing is set for next month."

"So soon?"

"I know, shocked me, too. Knowing how they operate, strings were pulled to make it happen quickly, probably hoping that I won't have time to prepare a proper defense. But I'll be there, lawyer or no. Even if I have to walk in there armed with nothing but the power of my conviction, the truth of his absence and the strength of a mother's love, I'll fight. And I'll win."

"I believe you, baby. And your family will be supporting you every step of the way."

"I'm worried about you."

Three days had passed since Aliyah received the summons demanding that she appear in court regarding her son's custody. Terrell had tried to be supportive, and patient, but felt he was failing in both categories. Today, no matter what excuse she came up with to not come out, he wouldn't take no for an answer.

"I'm okay, Terrell. It's just taken a minute for the shock of Ernest's actions to wear off, and for me to mentally regroup and prepare for what's next."

"Which is?"

"Securing an attorney for the trial, which is happening this month."

"Whoa! How was the case able to get on a docket so quickly?"

"Westcott money, no doubt. I contacted the one who handled my paternity case, but he's not available. He's given my information to a colleague, but I have yet to hear from him. When I do, the first thing I'm going to suggest to the attorney is that we request a continuance for time to adequately prepare."

"Perhaps you should request his contact information and put in a call first thing Monday morning. Unless the judge grants the motion for a continuance, you have very little time to lose."

"I can't believe he's pulling this crap! Making it worse is the fact that this is not about Kyle. It's about prestige and control and image-building, and not having the world know that he has a son who forget about besides a small child support check has never take care of, but that he's never even met!"

"Baby, I can't imagine how upsetting this is for you, but try and calm down. The stress isn't productive."

"I know. I'm just so angry."

"And rightfully so. But you're doing everything that you're supposed to be doing. You've got to trust the process, and believe that justice will prevail."

"If justice doesn't, you can bet I will. I'll disappear,

take my son and leave the country. Change my identity and start a new life. Anything to make sure my son isn't taken away and subjected to a life with the Westcotts."

"Let's hope it doesn't come to that."

"Let's hope not. But if it does, I'll do it. I mean it. Protecting Kyle is all that's on my mind."

"I believe that, which is actually why I'm calling. Mom and Dad have made reservations at the club. Some type of announcement. I want you to come."

"Thanks, Terrell, but I'm not up to that kind of crowd right now."

"It's not going to be whatever type of crowd you're thinking. This is a private affair, like the dinner we had. Only family and a few close friends will be there."

"Oh, I still can't. Just remembered that Lauren and her family went out of town. Camping trip, I think."

"I considered that angle, which is why Betsy will be at our house taking care of the little ones. Kyle will get to have a play date with the twins. Next."

"Oh, don't sound so smug. I still don't want to go."

"I know you don't. But being consumed by this situation with Kyle's father isn't good for you. It's just a couple hours, babe. A chance to be distracted, if only for a little bit. Then later, I have some ideas for relieving the stress and tension from your body."

"Now that I can definitely use."

"I'm glad you're coming around. This isn't formal, but it is the club. Just put on something cute and sexy and be ready by six. I'm sending a car."

"That's not necessary."

"I know. But it's what's going to happen. I'll see you soon."

Aliyah was a woman of her word, but Terrell still breathed a sigh of relief when just after six his driver texted that he'd just picked her up and was on his way to the Paradise Cove Country Club. When she entered the private room thirty minutes later, his heart stirred. Not just because she looked stunning, which she did, in a deep red sheath-style dress with silver pumps and jewelry, but because just beyond the simple makeup, upswept do and polite smile Terrell detected the tenseness around her ruby-red mouth and the newly formed worry lines at the sides of her eyes. Worry lines that Kyle's father's callous actions had caused. In this moment Terrell realized two things. One, that he'd do anything in his power to take those signs of worry away. And two…he didn't like Kyle's father. Not at all.

He walked over to meet her. "You look beautiful, baby." They shared a hug. "How are you feeling?" His hands dropped to her shoulders. He lightly kneaded the tension.

"Better now."

He lowered his mouth to her ear. "Better still, later. I promise."

The sound of tinkling crystal got their attention. It was Jennifer, standing beside Ike, at the head of a long, rectangular table for twenty. Taking Aliyah's hand, Terrell led them to empty chairs near the front. Aliyah nodded hello when eye contact was made, and gave a subtle wave to Charlie and Warren, as she and Terrell sat across from them.

"Good evening, family. I'm sure you're wondering why we asked you here tonight for dinner. First of all I can allay any fears or concerns by saying that Jennifer and I are happier than we've ever been so there is no divorce on the horizon."

This caused a few titters. Everyone in the room knew that the Drakes had one of the strongest marriages on the west coast.

"And while this may be disappointing to some, I must also inform you that Jen is not pregnant."

A slight gasp and sharp punch to the arm was proof that even Jennifer was surprised at this comment. She joined everyone in laughter, though, and shook her head as she took a seat.

"Everyone here knows that although this is a family-owned business, no family members get a pass. In order to be a part of this company and most certainly to progress to higher levels within it, one must have the proper education, work ethic, natural ability and drive to go above and beyond the call of duty in their endeavors. Such is the case with the person whom I'd like to discuss tonight."

Terrell's brow creased. He looked at Ike, Jr., who shrugged. Others in the room showed similar confusion. Obviously very few if any besides Ike, Sr. knew the announcement that was about to come.

"Recently, something has been brought to the attention of one of our executives, which is leading to his unexpected and immediate departure from the firm. It's unfortunate, but necessary. This person has done exceptional work for many years. I consider him not only a valued employee, but a trusted friend. I'm speaking of Hugh Parker."

Terrell's confusion deepened. As VP of Sales, Hugh was his boss. And he was leaving? What had happened that would cause him to leave the company? And why hadn't Terrell been told about it?

Ike, Sr. smiled at Terrell. "I can see by the look on my son's face that he is as stunned as I was when Hugh came to me with the news that a family situation was causing him to have to relocate. In a moment, I'll let him share as little or much as he wants to about this personal issue but right now, I'd like to ask everyone to grab hold of your wine or champagne or shot glass, whatever you're imbibing, and help me congratulate and welcome Drake Realty's newest executive and Vice President of Sales, Terrell Drake."

Stunned didn't begin to convey how totally unexpected this news was to Terrell. For several seconds, he didn't move, waited for the cloud of confusion to lift. Only when he felt Aliyah's hand on his shoulder, and turned to see her smile and extend her glass, did he react to his father's announcement and the subsequent applause. He slowly rose from his seat and walked to where his dad stood. They shook hands and embraced. Proud father. Humbled son.

Aliyah took it all in, genuinely happy for Terrell's success. And glad she'd accepted his invitation. He'd been right. The break was needed. Tonight, she'd bask in the shadow of his happiness and the strength of his arms. Tomorrow would be enough time to renew her worries about Kyle, and the future.

Chapter 25

Sunday morning, after their standard pancake breakfast, Aliyah drove herself and Kyle to Sacramento and the movie theater where she and Terrell had agreed to meet. When she pulled into the parking lot, he was there waiting.

Aliyah got out. "Hey, Terrell."

"Hello."

She walked around to where Kyle was strapped into his booster seat and opened his door.

"Mr. Drake is here!"

"I see him, Kyle. Now unbuckle yourself and get out."

"Why is Mr. Drake here?" Terrell walked up next to Aliyah. "Mr. Drake, why are you here?"

"Let's go, boy."

"But, Mommy, I—"

"Do you want to see the movie or not?"

"Okay." Kyle blew out a breath as he unfastened the seat belt.

Aliyah looked at Terrell. "Did this child just huff at me?"

"No, not a huff. We teach them yoga at the center. I think he was practicing deep breathing."

"I can tell already. You're going to be no disciplinary help at all!"

Kyle's kiddie sneakers had barely met pavement before starting up again. "Mr. Drake. What are you doing here?"

"Well, I heard that a certain young man did very well

on a test recently. So I asked his mother, Aliyah, if I could come and help that young man celebrate."

"You're talking about me!"

"Oh, am I? Was it you who passed the test?"

"Yes," Kyle said, amid laughter. "You knew that."

They purchased tickets and after a stop by the concession stand for the obligatory box of popcorn, sweet treats and soda, the trio were happy to find seats together in the crowded theater. Aliyah sat between Terrell and Kyle. She got her son situated with his popcorn and candy, then turned to take the soda Terrell had been holding and placed it in the holder.

"I didn't expect an afternoon movie to be this crowded."

"That's because you don't have kids. This show will probably break box office records this weekend."

The movie was clearly aimed at the younger crowd, but while walking out, Terrell and Aliyah admitted they'd both liked it, too.

"What are we doing now?" Kyle asked Aliyah.

"If you're not too stuffed with popcorn, I thought we'd grab a bite to eat."

"Mr. Drake, will you come?"

Terrell looked at Aliyah. "If your mother doesn't mind."

"No, I don't mind."

"All right. Tell me where we're going and I'll meet you there."

The trip to Arden Fair Mall turned into a full afternoon and evening together. The decision to work off an all-American late lunch turned into a mini-shopping spree that included the Disney and Apple stores and one of Aliyah's favorites for Kyle, Abercrombie Kids. It also included her preventing Terrell from buying whatever she said she liked as a Christmas present. She'd never been overly materialistic and when dating Ernest, costly gifts usually ended up costing something extra. When she told Terrell she didn't want him to buy her anything, especially something extravagant, she meant it. By the time they headed to the parking garage, weariness had slowed Kyle's chatter to a minimum. A rare thing.

They stopped just inside the garage. "Where are you parked?" Terrell asked.

"Level two. What about you?"

"I'm down here. But I'll walk you to your car."

"Thanks but that's really not necessary. The elevators are right over here and our car is directly across from them."

"Are you sure?"

"Positive." Terrell followed as Aliyah headed to the bank of elevators.

"Call me when you head out. Let me know you're safe."

"Will do. Thanks for everything. Kyle, did you thank Mr. Drake for the gifts he bought you?"

"Yes, but I'll do it again. Thanks, Mr. Drake!"

"You're welcome, little man."

"I'm not little!"

Terrell took a step forward, towering over Kyle who though big for his age was no match for six-two. "You're littler than me."

Kyle looked respectfully sheepish and begrudgingly acknowledged this truth. "Okay."

On this funny note the three parted company. As promised, once on the freeway, Aliyah called Terrell.

"Just wanted to let you know we are on the freeway and headed home."

"How'd you beat me to the freeway and I was on the first floor?"

"I guess it comes with knowing how to drive."

"Whoa!"

"You forget I'm east coast. When it comes to knowing how to navigate we can teach you westerners a thing or two."

"Is that right?" Said as his voice dropped an octave.

"What do you think, Kyle?" Asked so that Terrell would know their call was not private.

"I can't drive so I don't know."

"Ha. Good answer. Terrell, we'll talk later, okay. Thanks again."

She disconnected the call and was about to turn up the stereo when Kyle spoke.

"Mom, can I ask you a question."

"Sure, babe."

"Do you like Mr. Drake?"

"Of course, Kyle. I try to like everybody."

"No, I mean *like him* like him. Like a boyfriend."

At this question, Aliyah was shocked but not surprised. She'd known this conversation was going to have to happen sooner or later. Tonight was as good a night as any. Still, she wasn't going to say more than necessary.

"I like him like a good friend. Mommy doesn't have a boyfriend."

"Do you want a boyfriend?"

"Maybe someday."

"I think Mr. Drake would make a good boyfriend."

"You do?" Kyle nodded. "Why is that?"

"Because he's nice. And smart. And rich, too!"

That last one was unexpected. "How do you know that?"

"'Cause I heard one of the teachers say that."

"Kyle, were you eavesdropping?"

"No, they were talking loud."

"Ha!"

"Mommy, if Mr. Drake was your boyfriend, would that make him my dad?"

Aliyah hesitated at Kyle's jump to this unexplored terrain, which was not only foreign, but stickier than the cinnamon bun Kyle had had for dessert.

"No. If Mommy were to date someone, that person does not become your father. If I were to ever get married, then that person may take on the role of your father. But you already have a daddy, Kyle, even though you've not met."

"Why not?"

"Because he lives far away, on the other side of the country, closer to Grandma."

"So."

Indeed. "So it's a long way to visit."

"But we visit Grandma. And Uncle Kieran came here."

"Yes, that is true." She took the opportunity while exiting the freeway to glance over at her son, gauge his expression. It was one of simple curiosity. About something that, in this moment, Aliyah understood he had every right to know.

"Would you like to meet your father?"

Kyle nodded. "I guess so."

"So if that were to happen, say in the next month or so, you'd feel okay about it?" Another nod. "I think it would be good for you to know your dad, so I'll see what I can do about that happening, okay?"

"Okay. But can I tell you something?"

"Sure?"

"If I could choose my own daddy, I'd choose Mr. Drake."

There was no comeback after a statement like that. So Aliyah didn't even try. She turned up the radio and joined Kyle in getting happy with singer Pharrell.

Chapter 26

"Are you ready for bright lights, big city, babe?"

"I'm more than ready!"

With December had come shorter days, cooler temps and just last night a dusting of snow. Aliyah had barely noticed, so focused had she been on the upcoming trial. Since their time in Sacramento, that and work had been her life. It had taken encouragement, begging and finally threats to pry her away from the computer and researching cases. She'd had several conversations with Mr. Simmons, the man her paternity attorney had recommended, the one who was preparing her custody case. They'd even had a "face-to-face" meeting via the internet. He'd told her not to worry, that the argument for her to maintain full custody was a strong one and that if for any reason the judge forced a joint arrangement, it should be gradual and at her convenience. Those words sounded nice but for all intents and purposes, Mr. Simmons was a stranger who, aside from his professional conviction, had zero attachment to the outcome of this case. This made Aliyah wary. She also met with Terrell's attorney friend, who'd been reassuring, but for Aliyah that wasn't enough. By the time they walked into that Rhode Island courthouse, she planned to be almost as well-versed in child custody law as he was. Meanwhile, this one-on-one adult time Terrell had planned was much needed.

They headed into the hangar. A familiar face was there to greet them. "Hello, Terrell. Aliyah."

"You remembered my name. Hi, Stan."

"I always remember a pretty lady," he said with a wink. "What's going on, big guy?"

"You got it, man," Terrell replied. They shook hands.

"So is it San Francisco again?"

"You didn't get my message?"

Stan pulled out his phone. "I guess not."

"I sent you some pertinent information. Check it out."

Terrell gave Stan a pat on the back as the three headed to the plane. Within minutes, they were airborne and headed east.

Once they got settled, Aliyah turned to Terrell. "What are we doing this time?"

"I didn't make plans for this trip. Thought we'd be spontaneous, just go with the flow."

"It must be nice to take off anytime you want, and do whatever it is you want to do."

"I don't look at my situation like that. I have responsibilities and obligations that don't allow for a leisurely lifestyle."

"I didn't mean to imply that yours was a life of leisure, but that when you do have the time, you also have the means to go where you want and do what you want. It's a lifestyle that most people don't even think about, let alone dream about."

"I guess you're right. When it's all you've ever known, you don't even think about it."

"That you had a privileged upbringing yet still treat the average person with decency is a testament to Jennifer and Ike and the way you were raised."

"My parents never let us think we were better, only blessed. As for decency," he said, pulling her closer to him and placing his hand on her inner thigh. "I want to change your mind about that by spending every moment in Sin City being as indecent as possible."

"Sin City?"

"Yes, we're headed to Vegas."

"How exciting!" She gave him a hug. "I've only been there once before. A weekend with a few of my classmates, to celebrate our graduation."

"It will only be for a weekend again. But we're going pack it full of fun."

He did exactly that. Packed not only with fun, but also with a sense of fantasy, too. Starting with their hotel suite, if one could call it that. Though it was at the top of the Palms Casino, to Aliyah, condo or apartment seemed more appropriate. One of seven luxury penthouses in this popular strip hotel, the suite was over three thousand square feet of pure luxury. From the floor-to-ceiling windows that offered some of the most amazing views in all of Vegas, to the gourmet kitchen, complete with on-call chef, to the 24-hour concierge and car service, everything was designed to make one feel special. Like royalty. Pampered. Loved.

After enjoying the stainless-steel pool table while playing with a special set of balls, Aliyah and Terrell showered and dressed for 7:00 p.m. dinner reservations at Ceasars Palace followed by front row seat at Mariah's show. It was a party crowd in the mood for a good time. Terrell and Aliyah joined right in, making friends with the couple next to them and once Mariah took the stage singing along with all of their favorites, and swaying to visions of love. The next day brought a helicopter ride to the Grand Canyon, dinner on a bluff and a night of making love in front of the two-way fireplace with the neon lights of the Vegas strip twinkling in the background. It was enough to make a woman lose her mind, fall in love and forget about any problem she'd ever had. Almost.

Sunday came and all too soon it was time to return to

California and reality. They arrived at McCarran International Airport and the terminal for private plane customers within minutes of the time Terrell had given Stan that they wanted to take off. One of several advantages Aliyah observed in taking a charter. No security line. No X-ray machine, removal of shoes or jackets. Just a smile, warm greeting from the pilot and on the plane you go.

When it came to the romance of their relationship, Terrell often made the first move. Not today. As soon as the plane had leveled, Aliyah unbuckled her belt and snuggled into his arms.

"This weekend was incredible. I needed it more than I realized."

Terrell placed an arm around her shoulders, gave one a light squeeze. "You're way more relaxed than when we left, that's for sure."

"Hard not to be, with a man who wanted to make love to me seven ways from Sunday."

"I didn't hear you complaining."

"Not at all."

"Good, because I'm not finished."

"Maybe not, but I have to go home as soon as we land. The situation with Ernest has had me distracted. I have a ton of studying to do and need to stay focused from now until we break for the Christmas holiday."

"That's cool." Without warning, Terrell lifted her out of the seat.

She yelped. "What are you doing?"

He situated her on his lap, with a leg on each side of him, then reached for his belt. "I'm getting ready to stroke that kitty," he murmured, underscoring the point by placing a hand beneath her dress and flicking her nub through her thong.

"Can we do that?" She looked behind her. "What if Stan comes out?"

"I guess we'll give him a show. Sit up for me, for a minute."

She did. He rose up enough to pull down his jeans and boxers. His ever-ready appendage bobbed a greeting. She looked first at his powerful manhood and then into his dreamy eyes. Once again he reached beneath the mini dress he'd seen at Ceasars Palace the night of the concert and returned to buy for her the next day.

"Did I tell you how much I like this dress?"

"Ooh." A gasp escaped from her mouth as he slipped a strong forefinger beneath the lace and ran it down the length of her folds—up, down, once, twice, a slide inside, wetness. And then…

Rip.

Aliyah's eyes, half-closed, flew open. "Terrell, you tore my panties."

"I did," he said, replacing his finger with his now rock-hard dick, sliding back and forth, becoming wet with her dew.

"Those were Victoria's Secret."

"I'll buy you some more."

Finding home, he lifted his hips. She lowered hers. He palmed her cheeks, softly squeezing as he slowly, completely filled her. Love-making, raw and hot, as if they hadn't done it once already before leaving the suite. Their passion grew as the plane descended, their mutual orgasm heightened by the surroundings, getting thoroughly sexed from forty thousand feet all the way down until the tops of houses came into view.

After catching their breath, Terrell kissed her quickly. "Come on, baby. Now that I've made you a member of the mile-high club, let's clean up real quick."

She scooted off his lap and stood. "Is that what that term means?"

"For some it is."

"Yes, those with private planes and private bathrooms." Said as they both hurried through a spin-cycle shower.

"You'd be surprised. I know people who got initiated in a regular plane, some while flying coach even."

"Eww. Please don't tell me that. It's hard enough for me to sit in those seats as it is."

"Hey, to be forewarned is to be forearmed."

"That's disgusting."

"Yeah but sometimes nasty can be so nice."

Chapter 27

Over the next week or so, Terrell spent more time with Aliyah and Kyle. Family-oriented activities, even those involving little people, could actually be quite fun. Who knew? With as much time as he'd spent between PC and Davis, he'd seen very little this past week of his mom and dad.

Seconds after walking into the library, where his dad was enjoying a spot of brandy while his mother drank tea, he found out his absence hadn't gone unnoticed.

"Look, Ike! A stranger in our home?"

"See, I told you to start taking ginkgo biloba," Terrell replied, walking over to kiss his mother's forehead. "They say memory is one of the first things to go!"

"Bite your tongue, son!" Jennifer laughed. "You'd better hope you're in the shape I am by the time you're fifty-something."

"You know I'm teasing, Mom. You look as beautiful now as the day I was born."

"How much do you need, Terrell?" Ike, Sr. asked. "Pouring it on that thick means you must want something."

The jovial camaraderie continued as Terrell walked over and poured himself a brandy, before joining his mother on the leather couch that had been custom-made for the room.

"I do have something to share with all of you," Terrell said.

"You're getting married?"

"No, Mom."

"She's pregnant."

"Dad, really? Come on, now. You know I handle my business better than that."

"Taught by the best, you should."

"Oh, Lord," Jennifer gasped, in a feigned voice of desperation. "How much Drake can a poor woman take?"

"I got it, honest, Mom."

"That you did." She set her teacup in its saucer on the table. "What do you have to share?"

"I think it's time for your last bird to fly the coop. I'm ready to buy a home."

"Oh? What's brought this on?"

"I just think it's time." Said with a shrug. "I'm an executive now, almost thirty. Everybody else was almost out of the house by the time they were my age. Heck, Julian and London are out now."

"Because neither of your younger siblings live in the state. You have an entire wing to yourself, a private chef at your disposal, maid service and no mortgage. I know plenty of people who'd give their eyeteeth to be in your place."

"That's a mother talking, son. No matter how old you get they want to keep you tied to their apron strings. But I understand. The time comes in every man's life where they want to plant their feet on their own front porch."

"Just because I'm asking questions and offering opinions doesn't mean that I don't understand. This is about Aliyah, isn't it?"

"It's about me not wanting to be living in my parents' home when I turn thirty."

"Uh-huh. And it's about Aliyah not wanting to sleep with you in your parents' home even before then. You should have seen how embarrassed she was when I mentioned her being here."

"When'd you do that?"

"When she came out for Thanksgiving."

"Dang, Mom!"

She waved away his outburst. "Don't get all flummoxed over the matter. I wanted her to know that she was welcome here, as a grown-up. That she didn't have to sneak around or feel guilty. That, woman to woman, I understood. I think she appreciated it."

"I guess so. She didn't mention it."

"Good for her. A woman worth her salt will never tell a man everything."

Aliyah looked around her as she waited for the massive creation of gold-plated steel guarding Golden Gates to open and allow her medium-sized sedan to go through. Having been here a few times, she should have been used to the opulence of this, the most coveted section of not just Paradise Cove, but of Northern California. But she wasn't. The immaculately manicured lawns, marbled statues, colored fountains and more plant varieties than she could count never ceased to amaze her. Every time she came here was like entering wonderland.

Especially today. When Terrell called with the news that he wanted her opinion on some homes he'd be showing, she immediately played along. He'd often referred to the conversation from a month or so ago, when she called him up and flirted by pretending to be a potential buyer. She'd learned a thing or two about Mr. Terrell Drake during their whirlwind time together and figured showing her the room and decor wasn't the only thing he wanted to do during this walk-through. That's why there was nothing beneath her halter-styled maxi except sun-kissed skin.

Your destination is on the right. Upon hearing the GPS

instruction, Aliyah took one look at the understated yet undoubtedly overpriced home Terrell had selected to show her and burst out laughing. Even after she started working full-time and made six figures, she doubted she could afford any house located behind those dazzling golden gates. A doorknob, maybe.

Halfway up the walk, the door opened. Terrell stepped into the entryway. "You must be Ms. Robinson."

"I am."

He shook her hand and then pulled her into a kiss that began soft and easy, then turned ravenous.

She laughingly backed out of his embrace. "Gee, that is some way you have of greeting your clients, Mr. Drake."

"There's only one client I greet like that." He gave her lips another quick peck. "You look good. I like that dress."

"Thank you."

They went inside. The foyer was impressive, much smaller than the one in the Drake estate but made commanding by a modern-designed chandelier—wrought iron and crystal—that made for a stunning focal point. A short hallway led into the open-concept living, dining and family room with lots of windows and uninterrupted views.

"So…what do you think?"

"This. Is. Amazing."

"You like it?"

"It's one of the most beautiful homes I've ever seen." She stepped into the expansive living area, over to the fireplace and then to the windows. "I can't even imagine living in a home like this."

"Why not?"

"Have you seen the average New York apartment? One could probably fit in this living room, definitely the living and dining room combined. But there's so much space here. And the ceilings. I love that they're so tall."

"The two-story-high ceiling has been popular for a

while now. I love them also. They make the room appear even bigger than it is, and gives you a feeling of openness and freedom."

"Look at this kitchen!"

Terrell followed behind her. "Do you cook?"

"Not a lot, especially with my schedule. But with a kitchen like this I would, and definitely more often. This is beautiful. Look at these fixtures."

"Our designers are top-notch. We keep the look clean and neutral, so the owner can add their stamp."

"I don't know if I'd add anything."

"You wouldn't want to paint the walls or change the counters or back splash?"

"I don't think so. The ivory-colored walls add to the brightness, and these understated earth tones complement them perfectly."

"So if you were looking for a home, this is one you'd buy."

"With California's sky-high prices, I'd probably not see this home. My first would probably be a condo."

"Please send the technical doctor out of the room and bring in a woman who loves shopping and spending money when the sky is the limit."

"Okay. Put that way…yes. This is a home that would probably suit most women's tastes. So far, I can't think of anything I'd add or change."

"If you do, please let me know."

"Why? I'm not buying it."

"Right, but hearing your thoughts will help me pre-pare for possible buyer objections. And home designs in the future."

"Just as long as any assistance I provide is reflected in a proper commission."

"Consider it done." He reached for her hand. "Come on. There's more to see."

Chapter 28

Aliyah looked at the number and frowned. She recognized it; had seen it recently on Terrell's phone. But why was someone from the Drake estate calling her? She looked at Kyle, deep into a Disney movie, tapped the speaker button and closed her bedroom door.

"Hello?"

"Hello, Aliyah. It's Jennifer Drake."

"Mrs. Drake."

"Please, call me Jennifer. I hope you don't mind my calling. I asked Terrell for your number."

"No, not at all. I just can't imagine…is Terrell okay?"

"Terrell is fine, dear. I'm actually calling to speak with you."

"What about?"

"It sounded like a good idea in my head, but now, in the moment, I may be stepping way out of line."

Aliyah didn't like the sound of that at all. Had she heard about Terrell's intentions and was calling with a "steer clear" warning regarding her son. "If so, it wouldn't be the first time."

"Oh, my."

"No, not for you stepping out of line. I meant it wouldn't be the first time someone interfered in my…not interfered but—"

"Dear, interfering is exactly what I'm about to do and

if it makes you at all uncomfortable or you are not interested, just let me know and we'll both forget this call ever
happened."

"Okay." But not really.

"It's about your upcoming court date. I hope you don't
mind that Terrell shared just a bit of what's happening with
your son, his father and his father's family. We Drakes are
a very close-knit family. There is little if anything happening in our lives that isn't eventually known by all of us. So
please don't be angry at him for discussing this with me.
After our brief conversation concerning it, I pried him for
details. I'm a very good prier."

Aliyah's laugh was genuine. She finally relaxed. A little. "I believe it."

"He told me about the status of your son's father's family, and the airs you endured while dating their son."

"That's a nice word to use for how I was treated."

"I'm sure there are others, but focusing on those is counterproductive and not why I called. I've heard of the Westcotts in Rhode Island."

"You have?"

"Yes, very indirectly. A dear friend of mine grew up
on the east coast and is very connected to society there.
Her family knows their family and, well, the circle tends
to be one where most of us at least know of each other.
What I'm saying is I can just about imagine what you've
had to deal with, being considered common in their eyes.
Not true of course. You're the polar opposite of that. But
to those with superficial standards for judging. Because I
know what you're up against, I'd like to offer a...consul-
tation of sorts. You are headed into battle. I'd like to help
ensure you're properly armored, starting with a tailored
suit from my personal designer."

"Oh, Mrs. Drake, I couldn't—"

"You can, and you should. This fight is for something

most valuable. Your son. You should employ every available resource to make sure it's a fight you win."

A few days later, as Aliyah rode to family court in Providence, Rhode Island, along with her parents, her brother, Kieran, and Lauren to serve as a character witness, she was dressed in the tailor-made way Mrs. Drake had suggested, a conservative charcoal-colored pantsuit that fit perfectly and felt great. Paired with a matching designer handbag and pumps, along with a strand of classic pearls and matching post earrings, Aliyah knew the look was the type of classic, understated elegance that people like Mrs. Westcott would find properly impressive. At this moment, however, clothing was the last thing on Aliyah's mind. It was going to take more than designer clothes to win this battle. After what had transpired in the past forty-eight hours, it would take a miracle. She settled back in her seat, looking out at the overcast day as gray as her mood, the recent developments and the conversation about them she'd had last night with Terrell. Right before hanging up on him.

"Baby, calm down."

"Calm down? Don't tell me to calm down! Did you not hear what I just said? My attorney's got pneumonia, the judge has failed to grant a continuance and I've been assigned some court-appointed lawyer who knows me even less than Mr. Simmons who didn't know me at all!"

"I'm not saying you don't have every right to be upset. I want to help you, and that can happen more quickly if we're both rational and focused solely on winning. No matter who is representing you, no matter who is the judge, the only thing that matters is you having full custody of Kyle."

"Don't you think I know that? I'm more aware of that than anyone. What you're not aware of, what you don't know, is the Westcotts, and the type of power they wield in this state. And the judge is probably in the family's back pocket as well. It has made my chances of winning very unlikely, Terrell. So being calm, rational, any of that is just not going to happen right now. And if they try and take away my son, I'll act the kind of crazy that will make them think I invented the word."

They arrived at the courthouse. The court-appointed attorney met her in the lobby. Her family continued to the family division and the room where her case would be heard. For the next thirty minutes she conferred with the attorney. When she entered the courtroom she felt a little better about what was happening. But not much.

The room was smaller than she expected, looked nothing like those courtrooms seen on TV. Her eyes went straight to the Westcotts, sitting on the right side of the room, her family on the left. As if feeling her eyes on him, Ernest turned around. Seconds later, so did his mom. Aliyah took in Ernest's smug expression and his mother's judgmental face without flinching. But inside, she was a bundle of nerves wrapped in a blanket of trepidation.

Ernest whispered something to his mother, then stood and walked over. Aliyah straightened her shoulders, adopted a look of confidence she didn't feel and braced herself for what she hoped wouldn't become an ugly confrontation.

"Hello, Aliyah."

"Hi, Ernest."

"You look well. It's clear the California sun agrees with you."

I wish I could say the same about the Rhode Island winter. The thought popped up immediately. Fortunately, she squelched it before it escaped from her mouth.

"Thanks."

The right response even though she preferred the first one.

"Aliyah, I hope that after we've settled this matter, we can establish a civil relationship. For the sake of our son."

Said without actually choking on the phrase. If not for the nausea this comment caused, she might have been impressed. With Kyle in mind, however, she put her feelings about Ernest aside.

"I agree, and provided the judge acts with reason and I maintain sole custody, I'm prepared to act as civilly as I'm treated. I've talked to a therapist about our situation and she believes that if handled correctly, integrating your meeting Kyle and becoming a part of his life can happen with minimal disruption, either physically or mentally."

"I could have told you that, and thought I did. However, I'm glad that talking to a professional made you feel better."

"Ms. Robinson," her attorney called out. He motioned her to join him at the front table. Without another word, she left Ernest standing in the aisle.

"Ms. Robinson, I've just conferred with the Westcotts' attorney and they've presented a reasonable alternative to sole custody they'd like you to consider."

"The only consideration that is reasonable is for sole custody of my son to remain with me. Period. End of story."

"Look, I don't have to tell you about the Westcotts' influence. To have the case heard here when the child lives elsewhere is already a huge exception. The attorney they've hired is the best on the eastern seaboard. What they're willing to do is change the request to shared custody, fifty-fifty, between the two of you, provided you move here, to Rhode Island."

"You can't be serious."

"As the child's father I think it's reasonable—"

"Have you forgotten—" Remembering the size of the room and the stakes, Aliyah paused, took a breath and lowered her voice. "Have you forgotten that I'm in residency, in California? My suggestion is that Mr. Westcott consider a relocation. Why don't you share that and then tell me how he likes it."

He left to do her bidding, but Aliyah was done talking. Right now she figured her time would be better spent thinking about what countries didn't extradite and what could be her new last name. Because if the judge granted the Westcotts either joint or sole custody, Aliyah would take Kyle and go on the run. To get him, they'd have to find her first.

The door to the judge's chamber opened. He looked quite "judgely," Aliyah decided, like someone fair, with common sense. Then she saw him nod and smile at Mr. Westcott. Perhaps he was a fool.

Before she could decide, the door behind her opened. Whoever it was held no interest for her, until she took in the judge's scowl. She turned around. Her heart almost stopped.

Taking seats behind her family were Terrell, Julian and Jennifer. Another man, a bit older, attractive, dressed in a suit, said something to Jennifer before continuing forward. He smiled. She nodded and watched as the Westcott attorney and her court-appointed chap scurried forward to join the stranger as he approached the judge.

"Good afternoon, Judge."

"Afternoon, Counselor. Surprised to see you here. Your case is scheduled for next week."

"I'm ready for it, too, Judge. Which I can't say for the one I'm handling right now, that of Ms. Robinson and her son, Kyle. Having just been hired moments ago, I am going to need a bit of time, not much, to confer with my client. I request an immediate recess to do so."

She could tell the judge didn't like it. Or him. Aliyah couldn't be sure.

"This case is fairly straightforward. I'll grant you one hour."

"Thank you, Judge. Based on what I've learned so far, one hour is all I'll need."

The stranger walked over to a stunned Aliyah. "Ms. Robinson, if you'll come with me, please."

She did as requested, glancing at the Drakes as she passed by.

"Nice suit," Jennifer said.

Aliyah managed a smile, but didn't answer. Instead she spoke under her breath to the man beside her. "Who are you?"

"My name is Dave Butler. I've been hired by the Drakes to ensure you win your case. Which is good news for you. Because I don't lose."

Chapter 29

"I know I was there to witness it, but what just happened?"

Aliyah's father, Joe, who was staring out the window, turned and answered. "The Westcotts finally ran in to somebody with more money than them." His eyes then slid from the daughter he loved to the impressive young man now sitting beside her, the one who'd rarely left her side since court was adjourned not an hour ago.

They were all in Jennifer's suite at the Omni Hotel, where she'd suggested they meet to talk and regroup following the abrupt turn of events at the courthouse. Aliyah, whose relief from the stress of it all had caused a near swoon, sat at the end of a long couch, knees pulled to her chest, a pillow at her back and Terrell by her side. Joe, Aliyah's mother, Delores, and oldest brother, Kieran, sat at the dining room table. Terrell's brother, Julian, sat in one of two club-styled chairs, busily texting away on his phone. Jennifer, poised and totally unruffled, sat in the other. The attorney, Dave Butler, had just left.

Aliyah sat up. Placed her feet on the floor.

"Feeling better, Lee?"

Aliyah smiled at her mother. "A little."

"Do you need something to eat? Joe, go downstairs and see if they have a sandwich, or soup or something."

"Don't bother," Jennifer said, rising quickly. "I'll have room service bring something up."

"I'm not hungry," Aliyah said.

"I'll still place an order. At some point, we'll need to eat." Jennifer continued on into the bedroom.

Aliyah placed her chin in her hand, eyeing Terrell intently.

"What?"

"You never mentioned knowing an attorney here."

"That's because I didn't."

"How'd you find Attorney Butler?"

Terrence sat back, placed his right ankle over his left knee. "After talking to you yesterday, I was too distracted to work. Hearing you that upset really bothered me."

"I'm sorry. I didn't mean to—"

"Don't apologize. It's how you felt. I called Niko, told him what was happening over here."

"Who's Niko?" Delores asked.

"Terrell's brother," Aliyah answered. "And an attorney, also." She turned back to Terrell. "What did he say?"

"Nothing that could have helped you legally, of course, since his background is corporate law. But he remembered a former colleague who went to Brown. Got in touch with him, explained the situation. Then that friend knew somebody who knew somebody and the next thing I knew Niko was calling me with Dave Butler's phone number.

"Apparently Dave also grew up in Rhode Island, is very familiar with the Westcotts and also with the goings-on that happen during certain judicial processes. Most importantly, I hear that a few years ago he handled a case that involved a family of siblings in foster care being abused. Authorities had information about it but nothing was being done. At least not fast enough for Dave's liking. So he went to the media. You see how charismatic he is and how eloquent of a speaker. The cameras love him and I guess the media did, too. He beat a pretty loud drum and every time he did, it got coverage. Things happened quickly after that and those children were saved from a very dire future. Looks like he's been somewhat of a media darling ever since.

"There's probably more to the story than any of us will ever know, but the about-face that the judge did in granting a continuance leads me to believe that something shady was happening in that courtroom and if he hadn't gotten his way, Dave Butler was about to go to the press and turn on a big old spotlight."

"What you've just told us is story enough. For the Westcotts, appearances, status and perception are everything. The very last thing in life they'd want is negative publicity." A slow smile spread across Aliyah's face. "That's it! Why didn't I think of this before?"

"What?" It was the first word Kieran, who adored his sister and hated to see her sad, had spoken since they arrived.

"The next time I talk to Ernest, I'll let him know that if he continues to seek full custody of Kyle, I'll go straight to *TMZ*."

Kieran shook his head. "That fool probably won't know what that is."

"You're right, and as angry as I am, and as much as he deserves it, I would never stoop so low as to do something like that."

"All's fair in love and child custody cases. Except my choice would be the *Providence Journal*." This suggestion from Julian, with eyes still glued to his phone.

"The local newspaper?" Terrell asked.

"Yes. Not too long ago, they did a story on Dave."

"My attorney?"

Julian nodded.

"That's what you've been doing, reconnaissance on Dave Butler?"

"Gathering information is what the internet's for."

Jennifer walked out of the bedroom. "Soup, salad and sandwiches are on the way. I hope someone's hungry."

"I'm glad you went ahead and ordered, Jennifer." Aliyah released a sigh as she stretched. "I'm feeling a little hungry after all."

Aliyah's optimistic mood lasted for another hour. Until she received a text from Ernest, requesting a meeting. She agreed to meet him, knew that as little as she looked forward to this conversation it was one that had to happen. At Terrell's insistence, she suggested they meet in lobby. "In case you need backup," he explained.

Turns out, neither back up nor threats was needed. When Ernest met her, it was to let her know that in re-thinking the situation regarding the development of his relationship with Kyle, he now felt it best to proceed at a more conservative pace. That once they'd known each other a while, and Kyle was a little older, the custody arrangement could be revisited.

Aliyah listened and agreed. No need to expound on her definition of "a little older," even though Kyle would be eighteen and grown before she relinquished custody. But the meeting had gone so much better than she had expected, she figured this tidbit counterproductive. Ernest and the rest of his family would find out soon enough.

A week before Christmas, Ernest flew to Sacramento to spend time with the son he'd not seen. The interaction was initially awkward—Ernest obviously not used to being around children, Kyle overwhelmed and shy in the company of "Dad." Kyle got a mountain of early Christmas gifts and Ernest took pictures, no doubt to use in his new claim to fame. Aliyah didn't too much begrudge this. Who wouldn't want to be known as her son's father? Kyle was amazing! Still, when they stood to part ways at the restaurant, she could have sworn that the look on Ernest's face was one of relief.

On the way home, Aliyah quizzed Kyle. "Did you enjoy the visit, Kyle, spending time with your father?"

"It was okay, I guess. He talks kind of funny. But I liked his watch. It was like a computer! But he doesn't know how to play video games. Mr. Drake can play way better than him. Ernest is my father, but I think Mr. Drake is way cooler."

Aliyah looked at her son and smiled. "You know what, buddy? I think so, too."

Chapter 30

Filled with work and Ernest's visit to meet Kyle, the days passed in a blur. It was Christmas Eve, and neither Terrell nor Aliyah had to work until after the New Year. Both were grateful for the break. The excitement in the air came not only from the opportunity to relax and enjoy each other, but also because Aliyah would be enjoying her family as well. The drama in Rhode Island had brought the families closer. Julian and Kieran were becoming fast friends. Her family initially balked at the generous invitation, but after much cajoling and a little bribery, the Robinsons had accepted the Drakes' invitation to spend the holiday in Paradise Cove.

Terrell arranged a limo to be sent to the airport but in the end, Aliyah was too excited to wait the forty-five minutes to an hour it would take for them to get from San Francisco. She and Terrell ended up riding along.

They met them at baggage claim, then walked to the car. When she reached the limo, her father stopped in his tracks. "Is this for us?"

"Yes, Dad. It was either this or a van to get all of us in one vehicle."

"You picked us up in style," he murmured, shaking his head as he climbed inside the designer stretch. "The last time I rode in one of these it was for a funeral. I was about to ask you who died."

It took a minute and some maneuvering but soon all of the luggage and all of the Robinsons were in the limo and headed to Paradise Cove. It was the first time on the west coast for all except Aliyah's father, who'd visited LA in his twenties, and Kieran, who'd helped his sister move. Delores was unusually animated as she remarked on the wide-open space and coastal beauty. Having spent most of her life surrounded by brownstones and skyscrapers, her mother said she felt like traipsing through the fields they passed like Julie Andrews did in *The Sound of Music*. The miles flew by quickly as Terrell answered questions and provided a running commentary of the area he'd lived in his entire life.

They reached Paradise Cove. "This town is so pretty," Delores exclaimed. "And so clean!"

Joe whistled. "We're not in Prospect Heights, that's for sure."

As they neared Golden Gates, Aliyah turned so that she could surreptitiously watch her parents' reaction. When the limo stopped and the gates began to open, their expressions did not disappoint.

"You live here?" Her sister Danaya asked, eyes filled with wonder as she looked around.

Aliyah laughed. "I wish. The Drakes are in real estate. There is a vacant property that has yet to sell. So instead of putting you up in a hotel, he offered to let you guys stay there."

Minutes later, the limo pulled into the driveway of a Tuscany-styled home. Its tan exterior, rich mahogany-colored roofing and deep red shutters and front door stood out among the other homes with subtler features.

"This is it?" wide-eyed Danaya asked Aliyah.

"Yes, this is home sweet home."

"Wow." Danaya pulled out her cell phone and began to take pictures. "I'm in Hollywood!"

"How big is this place?" Joe asked. The question was asked casually, but knowing her dad she figured he was counting Drake money.

"Huge," Aliyah answered. "You'll see."

They entered the fully furnished home. "I thought you said nobody lived here," Delores said, looking around at the elegant furnishings.

"No one does. All of this—" she began with a wide sweep of her hand "—is called staging. The homes are furnished to give potential buyers a homey feel, and make it easy to imagine themselves in it."

"I can't imagine living in a home as nice is this," Delores admitted.

"Me, either," Aliyah replied.

"I can," Danaya sang, dancing to music that only she heard. "Lee, which room do I get?"

"There are five bedrooms so you have choices. Let's go pick one out."

"I want the master suite!"

"Keep wanting!" Delores called out. "I might not see myself living here, but I'm sure going to enjoy spending the night."

After getting everyone settled into the show home, the limo took them all over to the Drake estate. The Robinsons had thought Terrell's home impressive but upon seeing where his parents lived, their jaws dropped. Aliyah watched her parents grow pensive as they walked to the entryway. However, any discomfort they may have felt disappeared with the sincerity of Jennifer's warm embrace, and Ike Sr.'s inviting Joe for a spot of brandy.

After introducing her parents to Ike, Sr., she continued with her siblings. "This is the next oldest, my brother, Kieran, my brother Joseph, Jr., who we all call JoJo, my brother Myles, and my youngest sister, Danaya. Guys, this is Mr. Drake."

"Please," Jennifer said while reaching to embrace Kieran in a light hug. "Just Jennifer and Ike is fine. My family is out back, waiting to meet all of you. Right this way, please."

Gathered around the pool in the backyard were Niko, Monique, Ike Jr., Warren, Charlie, Teresa, Atka, Julian and London. The only one of Ike and Jennifer's children not present was Reginald who, after spending Christmas with his wife's family, would fly out for New Year's Eve. On a nearby table was a casual spread of barbecued meats, root veggies and salad that would be washed down with ice-cold lemonade or chilled wine. When the Drake men found out Kieran was a basketball star in Iowa, trash talking abounded. They'd barely wiped the last bit of sauce from their fingers before heading to the courts for some basketball bonding. Those who stayed behind enjoyed a glass of vintage wine from the Drake cousin's vineyard, and a mildly chilly evening conversing around the outdoor fireplace. By the time the men returned from the basketball court Aliyah's parents were tipsy, she and Terrell were tired and everyone was ready for bed and looking forward to the next day.

Christmas morning arrived warm and sunny. Used to cooking a large meal for both hers and the extended family, Delores hardly knew how to simply relax and wait for a catered meal. But when Jennifer suggested they all get manicures, pedicures and facials from an in-home spa company that worked on holidays, Delores happily agreed. She later told Aliyah that Jennifer's lifestyle was one she could get used to. Aliyah's heart warmed. Nothing would make her happier than for her family to move out west. With her dad a die-hard New Yorker, that would indeed be a miracle move.

They took separate cars—Aliyah's parents with Ike, Sr. and Jennifer; Kieran with Niko and Monique, JoJo, Myles, Danaya and Kyle with Terrell and Aliyah—and the rest in cars of their own. For the Robinsons the surprises continued when the sophistication of the homes in Golden Gates gave way to the casual yet chic comfort of Warren's ranch. The families enjoyed a veritable feast of turkey, ham and freshwater salmon from the Drake Lake project, with all of the usual holiday trimmings rounding out the menu. Several friends and extended family members joined them, including Lauren and her crew, Luther and his family and others from the realty company, the ranch and the center, who'd found themselves away from their own families on this special day.

Shortly after dinner was over, as most were relaxing in and around the pool in Warren's backyard, their conversation was interrupted by the loud sound of a low-flying plane heading in their direction.

Teresa shielded her eyes from the sun and leaned toward her husband. "That plane is quite low, honey, don't you think?"

Atka nodded. "Yes, unless it's landing somewhere nearby."

"Has a landing strip been built out here?" Ike, Jr. inquired.

"Not that I know of," Warren replied.

"Looks like there's a sign or something trailing behind it." At Julian's observation, everyone looked up.

"Oh, one of those message planes," Jennifer said.

"I wonder who it's for."

Terrell, who was standing directly behind Aliyah, wrapped his arms around her and answered, "I have no idea."

Everyone was quiet, waiting for the message to come into view. As it did, Aliyah read it out loud:

"Will...you...marry...me..." As the plane reached them, a banner dropped from the window, completing the question. "Aliyah?"

For a beat, nobody moved. Then everyone reacted at once.

"Oh, my God!"

"That's cool!"

"It says Aliyah!"

"Mommy! That's your name!"

Aliyah turned to Terrell, who wore a smug, satisfied grin. "Terrell, what is this?" Her eyes glittered with unshed tears.

"Part of your Christmas present. Since you'd never tell me what you wanted, I had to improvise." He pulled out a blue box and got on one knee. "Will you do me the pleasure of becoming Mrs. Drake?"

"Yes!" Aliyah threw her arms around him as everyone cheered.

"Where are we going?"

After being surrounded by thirty people for a weekend, and with Kyle at his second home, the Hensleys, Aliyah was looking forward to spending a quiet New Year's Eve at her humble abode.

"I need to go check on a property real quick."

"Now? Tonight?"

"Yes, where your family stayed. It will only take a minute. I'll be showing it next week and just want to make sure the cleaning company did their job."

"Oh, okay." They reached the home that Aliyah's family had fallen in love with. "Make it quick."

"For that to happen, you'd better come with me."

"Terrell, just hurry up."

"Come on! This client I'm working with is as finicky

as they come. I need a woman's eye to make sure everything is in the right place."

Her compliance was preceded by a harrumph and a sigh,
but Aliyah got out of the car and followed Terrell up the
stairs. He opened the door, then stood back to let her enter.

"You had this done so quickly, Tee. The family just
left today." All except Kieran, who'd decided to hang out
with Julian, who'd encouraged him to move here. "That
was quick."

She continued into the living room, noticed the fireplace
mantel and stopped short. "What are my family's pictures
doing here?" Slowly, she moved forward, stopping in front
of one of her favorite pictures of her parents. It had been
taken when they were her age.

"And here's me! Where'd you get...when did you do
this?"

Terrell feigned ignorance. "Those weren't there before?"
She swatted his arm. "Maybe your mother put them to,
you know, make the place more comfortable, to feel more
like home."

"You may be right. And in the rush to get to the airport, probably forgot them." She went back to the pictures.
"Well, too bad, because she won't get them back now. I'm
taking them home with..."

Her words slowly faded away as she reached for the
card propped up behind the pictures:

Ms. Robinson: Thank you for helping me close the
deal. The house is yours. Welcome home.

"This isn't."
He nodded. "It is."
"All that time you told me about a finicky buyer?"
"You can be kind of finicky."
That statement produced a jaw drop. "I am not finicky."

"And a bit stubborn, too."

"I can't believe you tricked me. Or are you tricking me now?"

"No trickery," he replied, closing the distance between them. "Later, you can ask your mom. She helped me with the pictures."

"Mom knew, too?!"

"Not until a couple days ago. I swore her to secrecy."

"Look at you. Barely in the family and plotting against me."

"I've got it like that, babe. I thought that's why you loved me."

Later, Terrell walked from the kitchen with two drinks and joined Aliyah, who was lounging in in a faux mink, upscale, oversized beanbag by the burning fireplace. He'd teased her when she'd seen it in a vintage shop and fell in love. Now it was one of their favorite places to cuddle.

"This holiday was crazy fun!" He handed her the glass.

"Thank you, babe." She took a sip. "It's hands down the best Christmas season I've ever had. I've never seen my family so happy. Mama is ready to move out here and even Daddy had to admit that the idea of never having to shovel snow again was appealing. I still can't believe JoJo at your parents' house, teaching Kyle how to slide down the banister."

"You forget that at one time that place housed six knuckleheads, a tomboy sister and an irksome diva. There isn't a thing your brothers could have done that we haven't done or at least tried."

"Thank you for that."

"For what?"

"Treating my family so kindly; making them feel welcome. All of your family was wonderful."

"You're welcome, but it was my parents who issued the invitation. Specifically, my mom."

"I know and I thanked her, too. But I saw how you went out of your way to include them, especially my dad. He's a simple guy, used to the ordinary and at times felt uncomfortable, almost overwhelmed. You saw that and made sure he wasn't left out of whatever was happening. I saw Warren doing that, too."

"Anyone who's important to you is important to me. And anyone who's important to me, is important to my family. That's Drake, baby. That's how we roll."

She nestled deeper into his arms. They shared a quick kiss. "This holiday season was so wonderful it felt unreal. A part of me is like, wow, did that really happen?"

"It certainly did. In fact, I think somebody got engaged."

"Someone most certainly did." She held out her hand, watched the fire and the subdued lighting make the three-carat diamond sparkle and flash. "I keep thinking someone will pinch me and I'll find out I'm dreaming. Ouch!"

He chuckled. "I couldn't resist it, baby. You've got so much goodness back there to pinch."

"There are no words to describe how beautiful this ring is, babe. I won't be able to wear it often, but when I do, it will be with such pride."

"What do you mean? You can't take off your wedding ring."

"Of course I can."

"Why?"

"During cleaning, for one, or washing dishes. Would you like it to accidently slip down the drain while I'm rinsing a glass or flatware? And then there's work. I think it's too flashy for a hospital setting."

"Married male doctors don't wear wedding bands?"

"Not with large diamonds that can double as an assault weapon."

Terrell laughed. "I guess I see your point."

"I'll wear the band," she said, running her hand beneath his sweater to run her nails down his chest. "Even if wearing nothing at all, I'll be your wife regardless."

"Good to know, since that will be your state of dress most of the time."

"That might prove a bit traumatic for Kyle."

"Ha! Correction, in the master suite."

"That could possibly be arranged. And speaking of arrangements, we need to talk about your desire for me and Kyle to move in with you ASAP."

"What, are you going to tell me we have to be married first?"

"No, though that would be nice. But there's more to consider."

"Like what?"

"Like Kyle transferring schools in the middle of the year, and my no longer having Lauren and her family right around the corner to help me take care of him, and they help me a lot. Not to mention my residency at UC Davis and interning at Living Medical, that continues for at least another year and a half. I know it's not a long commute but moving here there are a variety of logistics that would have to be worked out."

"None of that is a big deal," Terrell replied, dismissing her concerns with a wave of his hand. "That's what help and assistants and nannies are for. So first of all, if you think it will be too disruptive, then Kyle can stay where he is until summer. You'd still do the residency at UC, of course, but construction is almost complete on the PC's urgent care center. Not sure what kind of staff it takes to run it. But maybe you could do your interning there."

"Possibly, but that still doesn't solve the problem of Kyle being cared for or my commute."

"A live-in nanny, someone he knows, like Miss Marva, who sometimes watched me when I was young. We can also hire a driver so that you can study or read or do whatever you need to make your commute time beneficial, or sleep at the end of those long, hard shifts. Next excuse, I mean, problem, Ms. Robinson?"

"You know what? Your brother's nicknamed you correctly, Silky."

"No! Not you, too!" Terrell said, while jokingly pushing her away. "They used to drive me crazy with that nonsense, all because of my skills when it came to the ladies."

"Oh, really? What skills are those?"

He slid his eyes over her with a look of supreme confidence. "All of the ones that have you about to become Mrs. Drake. Uh-huh, now. Those skills, baby."

She swatted him. "Shut up, you're so cocky. Mr. Silky, smooth-as-silk," she added, mimicking his brothers. "And before you can say it, yes, Terrell Drake, that's what I love about you."

* * * * *

LET'S TALK
Romance

For exclusive extracts, competitions and special offers, find us online:

f MillsandBoon

🐦 @MillsandBoon

📷 @MillsandBoonUK

♪ @MillsandBoonUK

Get in touch on 01413 063 232

MILLS & BOON

THE HEART OF ROMANCE

A ROMANCE FOR EVERY READER

MODERN

Prepare to be swept off your feet by sophisticated, sexy and seductive heroes, in some of the world's most glamourous and romantic locations, where power and passion collide.

HISTORICAL

Escape with historical heroes from time gone by. Whether your passion is for wicked Regency Rakes, muscled Vikings or rugged Highlanders, awaken the romance of the past.

MEDICAL

Set your pulse racing with dedicated, delectable doctors in the high-pressure world of medicine, where emotions run high and passion, comfort and love are the best medicine.

True Love

Celebrate true love with tender stories of heartfelt romance, from the rush of falling in love to the joy a new baby can bring, and a focus on the emotional heart of a relationship.

Desire

Indulge in secrets and scandal, intense drama and sizzling hot action with heroes who have it all: wealth, status, good looks…everything but the right woman.

HEROES

The excitement of a gripping thriller, with intense romance at its heart. Resourceful, true-to-life women and strong, fearless men face danger and desire - a killer combination!

To see which titles are coming soon, please visit

millsandboon.co.uk/nextmonth

GET YOUR ROMANCE FIX!

Get the latest romance news,
exclusive author interviews, story
extracts and much more!